THE MOON AND THE OTHER

JOHN KESSEL

THE MOON AND THE OTHER

SAGA PRESS

LONDON · SYDNEY · NEW YORK · TORONTO · NEW DELHI

SAGA PRESS

AN IMPRINT OF SIMON & SCHUSTER, INC.

1230 AVENUE OF THE AMERICAS, NEW YORK, NEW YORK 10020

SAGA PRESS and colophon are trademarks of Simon & Schuster, Inc.

For information about special discounts for bulk purchases, please contact Simon & Schuster Special Sales at 1-866-506-1949 or business@simonandschuster.com.

The Simon & Schuster Speakers Bureau can bring authors to your live event. For more information or to book an event, contact the Simon & Schuster Speakers Bureau at 1-866-248-3049 or visit our website at www.simonspeakers.com.

Also available in a Saga Press hardcover edition

Interior design by Brad Mead

The text for this book was set in Bulmer MT.

Manufactured in the United States of America

First Saga Press paperback edition December 2017

2 4 6 8 10 9 7 5 3

The Library of Congress has cataloged the hardcover edition as follows:

Names: Kessel, John, author.

Title: The moon and the other / John Kessel.

Description: First Edition. | New York : Saga Press, 2017.

Identifiers: LCCN 2016036740 (print) | ISBN 9781481481441 (hardback) | ISBN 9781481481458 (trade paper) | ISBN 9781481481465 (eBook)

Subjects: BISAC: FICTION / Science Fiction / General. | FICTION / Science Fiction / Adventure. | GSAFD: Science fiction. | Fantasy fiction.

Classification: LCC PS3561.E6675 M66 2017 (print) | DDC 813/.54—dc23

LC record available at https://lccn.loc.gov/2016036740

FOR THERESE

THAT'S WHAT HISTORY IS:
THE STORY OF EVERYTHING THAT NEEDN'T
HAVE BEEN LIKE THAT.

—CLIVE JAMES, *Cultural Amnesia*

THE MOON AND THE OTHER

CHAPTER ONE

As Erno worked, his Aide whispered Persian phrases into his ear.

Can you direct me to the immigration center?

He would repeat the words after the cultured voice, intent on his accent, while he did the mindless labor that, back in the Society of Cousins, would be managed by an AI. He'd been studying doggedly since he'd come to Persepolis. Each shift enlarged his hoard of workplace idioms, of terms necessary to carry on a political conversation, of pickup lines—even of ways to express his feelings.

His body lay elsewhere, strapped to a frame in a control cubicle, but he perceived himself to be deep in the cold of Faustini crater, linked to a Remote Operating Device that gave him the strength and reach of a giant. There, in perpetual night, he loaded carriers with heaps of billion-year-old ice. There he cut and scooped and carried, under the glare of the lights, in service of Persepolis Water and Cyrus Eskander, the Shah of Ice.

Would you speak more slowly, please? I can't understand you.

He watched the other RODs spread across the floor of the crater. The flare of a plasma cutter dazzled his plugged-in eyes. When the ice-laden regolith calved and avalanched, tremors made him shift on his plugged-in legs. If he looked up and adjusted the gain on his eyes, he could see a brilliant star-strewn sky. He didn't look up very often.

Sometimes he would take a break from language lessons and ask his Aide to read him Persian poetry. He still had that—he still, sometimes, could be swept away by words. When he was high, like the seventeen-year-old he had once been, he even fantasized writing some *ghazals*. Such verse was hard to master, hiding knotty psychology beneath a zigzag surface. The Persians were all about wit, ingenuity in concealing motives, and complex status games. He liked the old poems best, the works of Sa'di and Hafêz.

> *If that Shirazi Turk would take my heart in her hand*
> *For the mole on her cheek I'd give Bukhara and Samarkand.*

This metaphorical Turkish lover with a mole: Was Hafêz proclaiming the depth of his love for her, or his self-disgust at feeling desire for someone so low on the social ladder? Both at once? The story went that when Hafêz was hauled before the Emperor Tamerlane for failing to pay his taxes, Tamerlane upbraided him for saying he would give these great cities, the jewels of the empire, for the blemish on his lover's cheek. Hafêz replied that such poor judgment was the reason he was indigent.

Erno knew something of indigence, and poor judgment. The back of his head still throbbed from last night's brawl, and he had trouble focusing. They were working a notch in the depths of the basin. The RODs operated by Taher Neeley and Devi Singh were down the line from him. The cart that followed Erno was almost full, shy only a few hundred kilos of capacity. Here the percentage of frozen water was the highest in the basin, blocks and sheets, at depth, which was why they had followed this notch so far. Dark walls towered over them, a canyon where the only light came from the blue arcs and the cutters. When he touched the beam of his cutter to the rock and ice, steam rose immediately. Dark blue glints among the powder and stone. He had to widen the beam to a millimeter so the vapor would not refreeze as soon as he cut it.

The external temperatures here were among the coldest in the solar system, as low as forty degrees Kelvin. If you weren't careful you could create a pocket of vapor and cause an explosion. Machines regularly malfunctioned in such cold. Metal crumbled, ceramics became conductors, and even the most hardened processors were prone to soft upsets: Some stray cosmic ray sets off a circuit in a CPU and there you are with a flaring jet, a dead communicator. In the days when people instead of RODs did this work, the fatality rate among ice miners was the highest on the moon.

That is lovely, but it costs too much. Do you have a less expensive one?

It was hard to concentrate. Lately Erno's thoughts had been drifting back to his home in the Society. He wondered what his sister Celeste was doing. Or Alicia—the last time they had slept together, they had fought. He could hardly remember the details. More than ten years had gone by, and it seemed like it had happened to another person. He imagined himself sitting on the soccer field below the Men's House, looking down on the floor of the domed crater. Now he worked in a society where men held the highest status, yet he had never felt more powerless.

In the years of his exile Erno had learned a lot about what his mother had called "the patriarchal world." Places that Tyler had described as utopias. And Tyler was right: This outside world manufactured utopia, but it was only available if you could pay for it. There were many ingenious, lovely things to be found in Persepolis. Most of these things Erno would never have.

May I escort you home? Are you doing anything tomorrow?

Erno was twenty meters deep in the notch. The glare of his cutter threw broken reflections through the surface, flares of light that shot back at odd angles when it struck fracture planes deep within the walls. He moved the cutter a meter to his right.

A flash and concussion.

Slowly, the entire wall of ice-laden regolith towering above him collapsed. He heard Devi's cry, doubled, in both his phones and from somewhere in the background of the control center where his body lay. He backed his ROD off a step, but already the ice was sliding around it in a slurry of black chunks, glinting with reflected light. It was at the ROD's ankles, its knees. He struggled to wade through. Ahead of him, Devi's ROD was riding the cart; Taher's hesitated and came back for Erno. The avalanche knocked Erno down. Taher was ten meters away, three meters; he was standing over Erno, trying to pull aside the heaps of rubble. It was useless; in seconds Erno was buried completely, and his eyes went dark.

Then pearl gray nothingness as the system pulled him back. He blinked hard once, twice, and reoriented himself to the sweat and disinfectant stink of the operators' cubicle. He released his wrist restraints, reached up and rolled the thinking cap to the back of his scalp. He started to disentangle himself from the rack.

Beside him, Taher was peeling off his own cap. *"Avazi ashghale bishoore kesafat!"* he said, and Erno knew exactly what he meant.

• • • • •

The population of the moon came to about 3.2 million people, most on the nearside, in twenty-seven self-contained colonies scattered over thirty-seven million square kilometers. The largest was Persepolis, at five hundred thousand people, and the smallest Linne, in the Mare Serentatis, at fifteen hundred. In addition there were scientific stations, industrial facilities, and exploratory outposts. There were even hermits, extended families of antisocial loners dug into holes in the sides of rilles, or living in metal huts buried under three meters of regolith on desolate maria. The colonies were constructed in lava tubes, in networks of manmade structures buried in canyons, in multilevel underground cities carved out of billion-year-old rock, in vaults and corridors, in ancient volcanic bubbles, and in a few domed craters like the one that housed the Society of Cousins.

The earliest colonies were scientific research outposts established by nation states from Earth. Later came industrial and military facilities, investment opportunities, and get-rich-quick schemes. Then came the political and social experiments. Separatist groups, ethnic minorities. Political refugees. Religious factions seeking private utopias. Mixes of all of these.

Erno's first stop after exile from the Society was Mayer colony in the Lunar Carpathians, dominated by hard money libertarian capitalists of the Austrian School. At eighteen he'd been fatally naive about the world outside of the Society. He'd made many mistakes, including taking a job with a fraudulent company that collapsed, leaving him on the street.

In the ten hard years that had taken Erno from Mayer to Persepolis, he had lived in eleven different colonies. His first stop after Mayer was Rupes Cauchy and eight months as a gardener. Then Aristarchus, where he wore out his days and his back as an aquaculture worker monitoring fish tanks, with a break now and then to shovel chicken shit. In Sabine, near the Apollo 11 landing site, he actually got to use a little of his biotech training, as an over-the-counter virus cook (*Change your skin in three weeks!*). That lasted nineteen months. In Tycho he worked in an environment plant. In Huygens he was a low level drone for a drug dealer.

Everywhere, everyone talked about Persepolis, the richest colony on the moon.

It was all about water. In Persepolis, they said, water was as cheap as titanium. In Persepolis, you could *bathe* in water. People in Persepolis learned to *swim*. One of the drug mules told Erno he knew of someone in Persepolis who had actually *drowned* at Tehran Beach.

Erno had never considered seeking his fortune there. Something about the prospect—maybe the fact that his mother had spoken of the colony as if it were the essence of patriarchal madness—kept him away. But when the network got busted and Erno had to flee with only the clothes on his back and a few possessions thrown into a satchel—ten years, ten years and he left Huygens no better off than when he'd left Mayer—the first cable train out of the colony was southbound, and the decision was made for him.

The evening before the accident, on his way to a night of heavy drinking, Erno had paused at the water sculpture in Anahita Square. The square rose, open, through the city's many levels, a mammoth atrium with gleaming white balconies. High above, the faux sky of the clearest blue was now turning violet. Twilight fed shadows beneath the colonnade of the Zoroastrian temple, inside which the fire continually burned, and darkened the entry of the mosque where the muezzin would soon call the evening prayer. A hundred meters across the square stood the Majlis, the People's Assembly.

The sculpture, a complex network of pools and waterfalls, filled the air with mist and white noise. Lights gleamed in the balconies above. Ticket scalpers hovered near the entrance of the Kazedi Concert Hall. Cafés were transitioning from afternoon tea drinkers to evening diners. At one of them, two waiters went among the tables shaking out wine-red tablecloths that billowed in the fragrant air and slowly settled over the tabletops. The men set places with white linen serviettes. Erno watched the beautiful women coming from the shopping district, a few lines of Yeats running through his head.

> *When my arms wrap you round I press*
> *My heart upon the loveliness*
> *That has long faded from the world . . .*

Persepolis was a tribute to the human aspiration to bring the world under graceful rule. If you wanted to dress in style in Tycho or Aristarchus, then you dressed the way the rich in Anahita Square dressed. If you wanted to be an artist, you moved to Persepolis, drank coffee in the café of the New Museum, and sought to get your work hung in the Sikander Gallery. A young pop musician in Rima Asiadaeus aching to make it big knew that he had somehow to play the clubs in the Ahura-Mazda district. An actor seeking a career of any import schemed to appear on the stage of the Ajoudanieh Theater. Restaurants, museums, football clubs, and universities: Those of Persepolis might find rivals in other colonies, but never superiors.

None of these pursuits interested Erno. Erno lived in Pamenar, a neighborhood of immigrants and guest workers that lay just below the lunar surface in a city where status rose the deeper you went underground. He shared a room with Zdeno Bartoš from Rima Marius, who repaired construction bots, and Fabrizio Longo from Linne, who dreamed of becoming a great chef but meanwhile worked in the kitchen of the Hotel Manuchehr. Fabrizio was an ebullient dreamer, Zdeno a taciturn Christian Socialist who, between benders, volunteered at the shelter at the Orthodox church. Erno did little more in the apartment than sleep. Every night he prowled the restless concourses, listened to music in clubs, ate chelow kebab in cheap restaurants, dabbled in immigrant politics, and wondered when boredom or desperation would finally make him do something that he could not escape.

He was supposed to meet Taher and the others, but the tea shops were not open until eight in the evening. He left the fountain and crossed to the Majlis. Over the entrance the Persian inscription read, "Were it not for Iran, I myself could not exist."

This late in the day, the assembly had adjourned, and the wide and high rotunda held only a few tourists and a couple of security officers, uplifted apes. In the center, on a pedestal inside a crystal case, rested the Cyrus Cylinder—the genuine, millennia-old relic. The twenty-two-centimeter-long clay antiquity covered with Akkadian cuneiform, repatriated from the British Museum a century earlier, symbolized the colony's devotion to the liberal policies that the legendary Cyrus had proclaimed for his subject states.

A young mother and two children were examining the exhibit. The boy read the description from the display.

"Is it real?" the little girl asked.

"Yes," the mother said. "It is over two thousand five hundred years old."

"It's just clay," said the boy. "Anybody could break it."

Founded by Iranian utopians tired of decades of theocracy and centuries of incursions from East and West, seeking a Persian future equal to its past, Persepolis was one of three colonies begun by different groups at the lunar south pole. With access to continuous solar power in the highlands and stores of ice in the Aitkin basin, it had grown and absorbed its neighbors.

The colony's founders brought with them a desire to recapture the glories of ancient cosmopolitan Persia. Though committed to the religious wellsprings of Iranian culture, they established a secular government. Muslims made up forty percent of the population, with the rest divided among Zoroastrians, Sufis, Christians, Jews, Sikhs, and Hindus, and a significant percentage professing no religion. Sunnis were welcomed; even Baha'i were welcomed, as long as all acknowledged the sovereignty of the civil state.

Iranians on Earth called Persepolis a fatally westernized faux-Persia, apostate from the living Iran. The founders countered that they harkened back to the true Iran that existed before the imposition of Islam. In Persepolis Shi'ia fundamentalists yet sought to establish the Twelver school as the state religion, but the memory of the troubles suffered by the Islamic Republic kept them in check. At the other end of the political spectrum, anticapitalists wished to break the power of the great families and broaden social equality, but the wealth of the ruling class, and the general prosperity built on a foundation of ice, militated against change.

There were internal conflicts. Policies toward uplifted dogs, for instance, were a matter of contention between Muslims, who considered them unclean, and Zoroastrians, who believed a dog's gaze drove away evil spirits and employed them in their *sagdid* funerary rite.

Among all of this, the status of guest workers like Erno was not something the Majlis spent much time debating.

Erno stepped back out of the building just as the muezzin began his evening call to prayer. Men streamed toward the mosque. Erno waited until the voice died, then walked out of the square and down a concourse until he came to Mosaddeq Way, spiraling up from the base to the top of the city.

Three levels up he came to Dorud, the city's oldest and roughest neighborhood. Shiraz Concourse had once been a showplace, sadly fallen in the past thirty years. An elevated tramway shadowed a long colonnade of shops and clubs. Men young and old idled in the street, playing Nard on a small table near the tram station, talking politics near a genetic surgery, drinking tea in the cafés.

Competing music spilled out of clubs: a woman singing a song in Persian, the throb of Chinese dance music. A tram hummed by overhead as Erno stepped under the archway of The Spirit of Wisdom, a tavern catering to expats, into a room of small metal tables and the smell of tobacco. Serious Muslims and believing Sikhs might decry such taverns, but the place was crowded.

On the pixwall played the public affairs program *Here's the Point!* Its host, the canine investigative reporter Sirius, shared the screen with a human colleague. People were consigned to the freezers here for lack of work, yet they gave media jobs to dogs. The Society of Cousins considered it cruel to uplift animals and imposed strict limits on manipulating the human genome, but the rest of the solar system did not observe such niceties, and *Here's the Point!* was very popular. Sirius was an outspoken advocate for the rights of uplifted animals. His personal assistant, Gracie, was a capuchin monkey.

The volume was low, but Erno caught a reference to an "upcoming election in the notorious Society of Cousins." He stopped to watch, but at that moment Taher called, "Erno! Over here."

Fabrizio, Zdeno, and Taher occupied a table in a corner. "Good evening," Erno said.

"Greetings, Cousin," said Zdeno, a big man with an impressive blond mustache.

"Wine!" Fabrizio said. He signaled toward the tavern owner, who came over with a glass. Erno thanked him.

They had a bottle in front of them, an inhaler, and the standard hookah that sat on every table. Smoking, so rare as to be remarkable back home, was common in the taverns. So they smoked, they inhaled, they drank mood teas. They slipped from Persian into their native languages. Fabrizio spoke English, and Taher's parents had been refugees from England. Zdeno knew English well enough to carry on a conversation.

Fabrizio told about his working with a new chef who was so short that he could not reach the top shelves of the pantry. Taher eyed the next table over, where two young men sat watching, heads wreathed in smoke. "Watch your language," he said. "Those guys are *basiji*."

"They have no authority," said Erno. "If they try anything we'll get them arrested."

Fabrizio studied them. "We're guest workers. We take jobs meant for good Muslims, then spend our earnings on wine."

"Yet here they are," Erno said, "missing evening prayer. Fuck them."

One of the men said a few words to his companion.

Zdeno, drunker than anyone, seized on the subject. "The purpose of society is to enable all of God's people to prosper. But multiethnic societies are trouble."

When Zdeno got going, the mix of high-flown political theory and personal resentment reminded Erno of the earnest debate among the masculinists back in the Society.

Taher took a hit from the inhaler, then passed it to Zdeno. "Difference means persecution. Always true, anywhere you go."

"Some places are worse than others," said Erno.

"You don't like it here?" Zdeno said.

Erno already had a buzz on. "I'm tired of being on the bottom."

Fabrizio said, "We could learn a lot from you Cousins."

At one time Erno would have laughed at that. "Maybe," he said grudgingly. "Fowler is no paradise."

"You're just pissed because they threw you out," said Zdeno. "But trying to defuse violence through social practices suited to male and female biology—not police or drugs or neural engineering—it's admirable."

"Plus, I hear the sex is good," Taher said.

"Are the women forced to say yes?" Fabrizio laughed. "Maybe Zdeno might stop talking."

Erno needed to piss. He got up, knocking over his chair. Overcompensating, he tried to catch it and hit the knee of one of the two men at the nearby table. "My sincere apology," he said.

"You are a drunkard," the man said in English.

"You are correct," Erno said, raising his index finger. "But I am a drunkard student of your great poets," he added, practicing his Persian. The man looked at him stonily.

When he returned from the men's room, Taher was telling Zdeno and Fabrizio, "The whole point of the *hegira* was not to escape our culture, but to recover it."

"Cousins are the opposite," Erno said. "The reason the Society moved to the moon was to create a new culture. New songs, new stories, new myths." He took another hit on the inhaler.

"I have nothing against the Society of Cousins," Zdeno said. "Except the idea of them causes trouble with women everywhere."

Fabrizio groomed his mustache with his forefinger. "There's that," he said. "Plus, men there can't vote."

"Yes, I couldn't vote there," Erno said. He set down the inhaler.

"And I can't vote here. Most nearside men are just low-grade neural nets for rent. If they ever make an AI with common sense, they'll turn people like us into fertilizer."

Taher said, "I'm a citizen—"

Taher's citizenship, which he never ceased talking about, was a joke. Taher's real given name was George; his parents had escaped to the moon when the British Isles fought the Caliphate. He was no more Persian than Erno.

"Which shows what citizenship gets you," Erno said. "Look over there." At another table five men were smoking hashish. "They probably don't make any more money than we do. That guy in the middle, doesn't he work at the mine?"

Taher looked over, squinting. "That's Kemal. He's in the distillery. He makes twice what we make."

"The thing is," Fabrizio said, "is that we are all brothers and sisters. Everywhere. No matter what genetics, cultures, politics."

Zdeno laughed. "When Fabrizio takes over the kitchen, everyone will eat for free."

Erno bumped the table, rattling their cups, and the inhaler started to fall. Fabrizio caught it. "We're the oppressed," Erno said. "We're like criminals. Half the people in the freezers are migrants like us."

"They're in the freezers because they broke the law."

"Everyone breaks the law," Erno said, "when they need to."

"You too, Erno?"

They didn't know that he'd gotten his mother killed; he wasn't about to tell them. "In Mayer, ten years ago, I robbed a man that lived next door to me. I needed money, so I broke into his rooms. And I stole his hand."

"You stole his *hand*?"

"It was artificial. It was stupid—I took it with me when I fled the colony. I still have it. Someday I will give it back." Erno's mood only got blacker. For all he knew, Alois was as dead as his mother.

"We all do bad things," Fabrizio said. "Nobody is blaming you."

Erno gestured at the next table. "You think those men wouldn't like to put us out the nearest airlock?"

One of the men looked up.

"Keep your voice down," Taher said.

Erno broke away from the man's glare. "At least in the Society a man can do whatever he wants, and the polity supports him. He wants to be a poet, then he writes poetry. And people listen. They *care* about poetry. Not like here."

"You hate it so much here," Taher said, "then go back."

Erno's anger had run to its habitual dead end. He never spoke of home without longing—until faced with the prospect of return.

"I'll never go back," he said.

"Let me buy you something to eat," said Fabrizio, touching Erno's forearm. "The *chelow-khoresh* here is pretty good. And coffee—you have to admit Persepolis has the best coffee. Meanwhile, why don't you recite us one of these poems you're always talking about."

"Yes," Zdeno said. "Something in Persian. Make it sing."

Erno looked at them bleary-eyed. Why not? He stood. "I'm sure our neighbors won't mind. They're no doubt poets themselves." Turning his back on the other table, he declaimed, "Here is the wisdom of the great king Hushang, grandson of the very first king of all time, Kayumars—Persians do love their kings—and Hushang was a good one.

> *"In his time he struggled mightily*
> *Planning and inventing innumerable schemes*
> *But when his days were at an end,*
> *For all his sagacity and dignity, he departed.*
> *The world will not keep faith with you*
> *Nor will she show you her true face."*

Erno found himself swept up in melancholy. Poetry was all he had.

"Shut up!" came a voice from behind him.

He turned. The man who had locked eyes with him was scowling.

"That's right, I said quit your fool's bumbling, you pallid eunuch. You have no right to those words. Go back to whatever godforsaken hole you came from."

Erno touched his hand to his forehead, then to his breast, and made an elaborate bow. "I beg your pardon, brother. May I be your sacrifice?" The elegance of his gesture was marred when he had to catch his hand on the edge of the table to keep from falling.

He turned to Zdeno and Fabrizio and leaned in, shielding his mouth with the back of his hand. "There's no music in that man's soul."

"Calm down, Erno," Zdeno said.

He heard the men stir. "What did he say?"

"I *am* perfectly calm," Erno told Zdeno, "because I *do* come from a godforsaken hole. Which reminds me of another poem"—he switched to English now—"by the great Celtic poet William Butler Yeats, spokesman for another abused minority. He said:

> *"The night can sweat with terror as before*
> *We pieced out thoughts into philosophy,*
> *And planned to bring the world under a rule,*
> *Who are but weasels fighting in a hole—"*

He had gotten only this far when they hit him in the back of the head with a chair.

• • • • •

Devi was the last out of the rack in the ROD control cubicle. She came over to Erno. "What happened out there?"

Erno rubbed the back of his head where the neural fibers on the inside of his cap had not wanted to let loose. He could still feel the knot where the guy had hit him with the chair, and when he looked at his fingertips, despite the dim light from the telltales, he saw a gleam of blood. "I got buried, Devi. I think that's obvious."

"You shouldn't have been so deep in the crease! And you"—she turned to Taher—"should have known better than to try to pull him out. Now we've lost two RODs instead of one."

Taher towered over them, so tall that when strapped to the rack, his feet hung over the end. "I thought I could pull him out. Then we wouldn't have lost any."

"Explain that to Mr. Buyid."

Erno couldn't let that happen. If he lost this job, he would be expelled from Persepolis. He couldn't take another flight, or worse, ten years in a freezer. "Buyid would have to shut down the operation for a shift in order to use the other RODs to dig ours out," he said. "We'd be fired. Please, Devi. You keep things quiet here, while Taher and I suit up and go retrieve the RODs."

"Exo? In person? You can't do that."

"I'm not going out there," Taher said.

"I've logged extensive hours on the surface," Erno said. "We did it all the time back in the Society."

"At forty degrees Kelvin?"

"Do you want to get fired?" Erno asked.

Devi's brow furrowed. She glanced around the other alcoves, where other three-person teams lay in their racks, still plugged into their RODs, oblivious to what had happened. "The shift will be over in three hours. I can't keep Buyid from finding out for long."

"He doesn't care what goes on here," Erno said, "as long as the quotas are filled."

"Maybe. But if Eskander ever hears about it, we'll all be in trouble."

"We're already in trouble. Give us two hours. If we're not done by then, you turn us in."

"I must be crazy," Devi said. She reached for her cap. "Just get back quick, and don't get hurt."

"Come on," Erno said to Taher, and they headed out of control and down the corridors to the airlock complex. Taher started cursing the minute they were away from the center. "I haven't been exo in three years. Do you know how cold it is out there?"

Erno didn't know what he was supposed to do about it. "Yes."

The seldom-used personnel airlock was down an ancient industrial tube whose walls had been sealed with cement thirty years ago and not cleaned since. The concrete path that ran down the center of the tube was crusty with the grit of decades; if you kicked up a pebble it would racket off the wall and bounce for meters before coming to rest. The air tasted of ozone from the cutters and electric carts.

Taher opened the chamber that held the heavy-duty surface suits. He powered one up and walked it out of the closet. Unlike the light, flexible skinsuits Erno was used to from back at Fowler, this was a massive lozenge with two pillarlike legs that ended in triangular intelligent feet like some ungainly waterfowl, and massively insulated power-assist sleeves with articulated artificial hands for delicate work. Erno opened the suit at the waist and climbed in, fitted his legs into the suit's servo legs, then leaned forward and dove arms first into the top. The suit's top swung up and sealed him inside. Erno took a tentative step. He had trained on such a suit when he came to work at the ice works, but had logged only the minimum time, and never out in Faustini. His boasted surface experience had come in completely different circumstances.

Taher sealed himself into his own suit. His voice sounded in Erno's helmet. "So, let's get this over with."

They walked the awkward suits through the archway at the end of the chamber to the secondary personnel airlock. The corridor was empty. Had Devi somehow managed to clear the place of witnesses?

The secondary airlock was full of trash. The ice works had been one of the first industries built at Persepolis, and the least modernized over the years. As long as profits could be made selling water, there was little immediate market incentive to improve efficiency or prevent waste. In practice this meant that machinery got neglected unless it broke down. The secondary airlock had not been used for a long time, and workers had come to take breaks in it. The floor was covered with food wrappers. Fines from the lunar surface were everywhere, caked on walls, switches, and valves.

Taher pressed the exit sequence and the old valves began cycling air out of the lock. When the pressure fell below thirty-six millibars they opened the outer hatch and walked out into the maze. Some of the lights were out, which made the corners darker than sleep. Erno switched on his helmet and shoulder lights. The floor rose as they reached the end of the baffles and came out onto the surface.

For three months he had been working out here by remote, but this was the first time he had seen the surface in physical presence. The basin fell a thousand meters below the lunar surface and never saw sunlight. The rail system for the carts exited from the processing facility and ran across the surface, beneath area lights, to the mining sites a kilometer distant. Taher and Erno moved over to the track and mounted a small car. Erno hit the controls in his suit and the car started up; through the seat he felt the low rumble. He drew his hands up out of the gloves to keep his fingers warm.

They rode out to the mining cleft. As they approached, the size of the deposits was impressed on Erno in a way he had never experienced by remote presence. The ice, which had been gathering here for billions of years, rose in a dark mass from the rugged floor of the crater. Faint starlight revealed heaped and humped shoulders and blocks and cliffs, starting small but, ahead of them, rising thirty meters or more. The mining that had gone on for sixty years had eaten away maybe ten percent of the estimated mass, but the rate of use had accelerated in the last decade. Some estimated that, at the current rate, the basin's deposits would be exhausted in thirty years.

"I'm already cold," Taher said. "What are we doing out here?"

Erno had enough with his whining. "Shut up, Taher," he said. "Nobody made you come."

"You asked me."

"And you said yes. Take some responsibility for yourself."

"Excellent talk from a guest worker."

"Yeah, I'm a guest worker, and you were raised here. And both of us are working in this frozen shithole. What does that tell you about yourself?"

"I should have let those men dismantle you last night," Taher said.

Devi's voice came over the comm. "I can hear all this."

"Shut up, both of you," Erno said.

It came to Erno then how angry he was, angrier than he had ever been since he had left Fowler. Enraged, out here in an antiquated suit trying to cover up an accident that wasn't his fault, in a job he hated, in a place where he was and always would be a stranger. Furious at the way everything inevitably went, at his loneliness and powerlessness and at the dumb brutishness of reality.

But there was more to it than that. He'd been furious the night before, too. With those other drunken men he'd acted out of dick measuring, trying to win a stupid contest of intimidation. It wasn't him, losing his sense of proportion like this—or at least not what he used to be. He had changed, been coarsened by living among men always looking down on him, asserting mastery, pushing him under so they could be up. He used to let this go, taking the properly detached Cousins' attitude—most of his childhood had been about learning to avoid these testosterone-fueled games. But now it had come to matter to him. He was becoming the man that Tyler had wanted him to be. It had taken a decade.

So now I'm truly ruined, Erno thought. I'm one of them.

The cart ran down the long decline into the notch where they had been working. The sky retreated into the gap above them; the lights on their suits, and the area lights ahead, were the only illumination. He had to get out of here. He couldn't live like this anymore. He hoped Taher would spread the story of his rage. He would rather be what Anadem had called him back in Mayer—The Deadly Señor P—than what he was: a refugee with no prospects, dependent on a culture he didn't understand.

When they arrived at the notch, they spent the next hour cutting though the icy rubble to reach the RODs. Devi's ROD was there with them, and she helped move what they cleared. They worked sloppily now, not worrying about wasting water through overheating and sublimation. When they cleared Taher's ROD they found it functional and told it to return to the shed under its own power. But they couldn't find Erno's. Erno thought he knew where it should be, but the shape of the notch had been completely altered by the collapse. They wasted thirty minutes uncovering nothing.

It was ten minutes shy of the two hours Devi had granted them, and Taher was hinting they should go back and face Mr. Buyid, when Erno, balancing on a heap of jumbled avalanche ice, spotted a metal foot five meters below him. He clambered carefully down into the pit.

"Erno, we need to get back," Taher insisted.

Devi's voice chimed in. "There's no time, Erno. The rest of the crews are coming out of link and already know something is up. Buyid is going to know regardless of whether you save the ROD."

Erno ignored them. He tried to steady himself on the slurry of crushed fragments at the bottom, beside the partially exposed ROD. Eager to be done with it, he turned his plasma cutter on full and directed it at the surrounding ice.

A blast of steam flew into his faceplate, obscuring his vision. He lost his balance. The mountain of broken ice that towered above him began to slide, then fall, slowly, inevitably. Pieces drummed on the helmet, shoulders, and back of his clumsy suit. He dropped the cutter and tried to move but it was useless. For the second time that shift Erno was buried in ice.

But this time he would not wake up back in the control room. He tried to move. Even with the magnified strength of the suit's servos, he could not budge. Everything was black. His left arm was twisted at an odd angle, and a shooting pain lanced his hand. He felt the cold creep up his arms. He withdrew his right one from the sleeve, but his left was trapped. His hand was going numb.

What was that verse he had read just the other day? Something about the thousand ill turns of fate. Hafêz had that one right.

CHAPTER

TWO

NIGHTLIFE WAS NOT A SPECIALTY OF THE SOCIETY of Cousins. The free enterprise zone closed down after midnight, so Mira was surprised when she heard voices as she and Carey moved along the row of closed shopfronts.

"Hide," Mira whispered.

She ducked into the alcove. Carey slipped behind the statue of Tiresias in the center of the concourse. Three women and a man came around the bend. The man stumbled a bit on the low steps that circled the trees. One woman giggled and the other two caught him, arms around his waist.

"Wake up, Stevie!" the laughing one said. "We need you tonight!" The others laughed, too.

Stevie shrugged off their help. With his dark hair in his eyes, he reminded Mira of Marco. "I'm ready—always ready."

The heliotrope sun tunnels in the concourse roof were folded closed, and the partiers missed Mira in the shadows. Once they were past, Carey came out from behind the statue. "Stevie's got his work cut out for him," he said.

"Augment," Mira told her Aide, and it superimposed details from the last colony architectural survey over her vision. At the back of the alcove, instead of a blank wall she saw a door. She felt around for the frame, but found nothing.

She backed away. "There's a door under there."

Carey pulled the crowbar from beneath his long coat. He set the pointed end against the corner of the wall and drew it back to strike.

"Wait," Mira said. "A tram."

Along the tramway suspended from the roof of the tunnel a double car approached and slid by, almost empty, windows glowing.

Mira said, "Okay."

Carey rammed the thin edge of the bar into the wall with a crunch. Bits of stucco flew away and drifted to the pavement. He kept at it, quick and remarkably quiet, until he hit the door. He took off his coat, then took up the bar again. She admired the way his shoulders worked beneath his shirt. The rubble gathered around their feet. In a few minutes he had the doorframe completely exposed.

Mira put on her spex. "I'm recording," she said.

Carey unlocked the door with a code breaker he had gotten from some lover of his who was a constable. They slipped through a vestibule into a big room.

The place had once been a club called the Oxygen Warehouse, closed down a decade ago after the riot that Thomas Marysson had provoked with one of his standup routines. Mira had been fifteen back then, newly adult and wrapped up in her own problems, but her younger brother, Marco, had followed Marysson obsessively. When Marysson caused a fatal vacuum blowout, the Matrons closed the club and hoped it would be forgotten.

Mira tried the lights, and one of the small spots lit a low stage. The rest of the room was a dark jumble of overturned tables and chairs. Behind the bar stood the remnants of a dismantled tea synthesizer.

Carey stood on the stage, facing out. Mira kept him in the shot: She would edit all this out later. He addressed an invisible audience, "Let me tell you what it means to be an untreated sociopath."

"No one's laughing," Mira said.

"Tough crowd."

"Hold this," she said, unclipping a lamp from her belt. "Move to the bar, then sweep across the tables and end on the stage," she told him. "Don't get too far ahead of me."

"Who are you ordering about?" His voice was a little slurred; he had drunk a bulb of Perceive before they'd left her place.

"You," she said. She turned the spex directly on him.

He reached into his breast pocket. "I brought you something." He withdrew a small box and held it out to her.

Puzzled, she opened it. It contained a little horse made of black glass. A tiny white blaze gleamed on its face. "I had Val make it for you," Carey said. "He's getting good, isn't he?"

He clearly intended it to mean something, but given how free Carey was with gifts, there was no way to know what. Just as quickly as her heart rose, she pushed it down. "It's lovely." She kissed him on the cheek. "Thank you." She set the little box on a table. "Let's do this."

"All right."

They ran through a tour of the wreckage, then did it again for good measure. Mira shot some inserts. A shard of broken glass glinting in the dust. A spray of dried blood on the edge of an overturned table. A constable's baton in the shadows by the stage.

Carey grew bored long before Mira was ready to quit. He wasn't really a member of the Discussion Group. Just a man a lot of members had slept with, or wished they had.

He rubbed two fingers across the floor and smeared grime across his nose. "Hey, Mira—help me out. Do I have dirt on my nose?"

She came over and peered into his face. "I can't see anything worth paying attention to."

"You need to look more closely." He took the spex from her face and placed them on a table. He put his hands on her waist and pulled her to him. The kiss went on for a while, his tongue flicking lightly over hers, delicate, not forcing.

She never ceased to be astonished that he wanted her. Still, it was no fun if it was too easy. So when his hand slipped into the back of her pants, Mira pushed him away. He lost his balance, but graceful as always landed on his hands and bounced back up. She snatched a chair and held it between them. "Get back!"

Faster than she could react, Carey seized a chair leg and twisted it out of her hands. She turned; he caught her shoulders. As they fell he flipped around so that she landed on top of him. Mira grabbed his hair with both hands and pulled his face to hers, wrapping her legs around him. Their teeth bumped and she cut her lip. She laughed. She pulled off her shirt and he suspended her in the air, kissing her breasts, her belly. When they had her pants off, he nipped the inside of her thigh with his teeth, a sharp little stab of lovely pain, and then his warm mouth was on her, and she leaned back on the gritty stage with her fingers in his hair, pressing his head down into her.

After Mira had come, they lay beside each other. She leaned over him and bit his nipple. Now he did not wait—he was on her, sliding into her, at first rough and insistent but then slowing. He put his hand, fingers splayed, onto her belly and pushed down on it as they moved together, gradually rolling into a rhythm. Carey became more insistent, she could hear his breaths, and it built and built until he shuddered and came, and she did again, both of them spontaneously bursting into laughter.

She rested her head on his shoulder, in the circle of his right arm. He was warm and he smelled good. She placed the fingertips of her right hand against those of his left. Her hands were so much smaller than his, and darker. They might have been different species.

Her mother would have told her how risky it was to get attached to a man like Carey Evasson. Mira had suffered listening to her mother's complaints about the things various feckless boyfriends had done to her. It was so weak, thinking about boyfriends, especially at her mother's age. It was embarrassing, to the point where Mira vowed to make neither that mistake nor any of the legion of mistakes her mother had made. Yet here she was lying next to Carey, running her finger down his taut belly. Teenaged girls loaded images of him into their pixwalls.

The longer they lingered, the more chance someone might notice the break-in. Mira pulled on her pants and padded across the room. She switched on augmentation and found a door around a corner at the end of the bar. It opened on a much larger space, the cavelike warehouse into which the club had been built. Rock walls here, and a high roof; some of the old bioluminescent fixtures still glowed faintly. She passed a rack of old oxygen cylinders. As she walked, a little tentative, around the chilly warehouse, her Aide told her, *Call from Roz Baldwin.*

"I'll take it," she said. "No video."

"Mira?" Roz's voice in her ear.

"Yes," she said.

"Can you put me in touch with Carey? He's not answering."

"I haven't seen him."

Roz let a silence stretch. Mira did not attempt to fill it. "Well, if you see him, tell him I need to speak with him."

"If I run into him I'll do that, Roz."

"Okay. See you tomorrow."

"Bye."

When Mira slipped back into the club, Carey was pulling on his clothes. "Did you get a call from Roz?" she asked.

"I didn't answer."

"She just called me."

Carey pulled his thick blond hair back and tied it behind his head.

"Are you and Roz fighting?" she asked.

"Not really."

"What's it about?"

He looked at her ruefully. "Val."

Carey seldom mentioned him, but here it was, the second time tonight. "What about Val?"

"Roz doesn't want him hanging around with any masculinists. She says Hypatia is just using me to get at my mother. Not very flattering, is it?"

Not flattering, probably true. Mira laughed. "Your mother was Matrons chair. Do you think everybody wants you just because you're good in bed?"

Immediately she regretted it. Carey looked hard at her. He pulled on his boot. So beautiful in the stark shadows, his brows drawn together. He stood, stomped to settle the boot, floated off the floor, and came down lightly.

She picked up the box with his gift and put it into her pocket. In the vestibule, as they were about to leave, he said, "I don't think I'll come back with you tonight."

"Carey, you know—I'm sorry. I know there's more to you than that." She heard the need in her voice and despised herself for it.

He shrugged into the long coat and picked up the crowbar.

"In two days I'll be posting the videos," she said. "I could use your help. Meet me in the garden near the Men's House at oh-two-thirty?"

After a moment: "Okay."

Mira slipped her spex into her pocket. She poked her head out into the street; it was deserted. She stretched up to kiss Carey; he kissed her back, barely.

"Thanks for helping," she said.

"Solidarity." He shook his head, low-lidded eyes on her, and swiftly disappeared down the concourse.

Love is just a feeling, she told herself.

• • • • •

FROM *The Odd Side of the Moon: Lunar Utopias and Social Experiments*
#5: THE SOCIETY OF COUSINS

. . . to the mating and social structures of bonobos, its accompanying practices are not exactly like anything seen on Earth.

The locus of power in the Society of Cousins is the family. Typical Cousins families are large, extending to

mothers, sisters, daughters under the age of fourteen,
brothers, lovers, husbands, and sons. One way to
understand Cousins social structures is to realize that
everything is designed to foster co-operation in young
women while encouraging the isolation of young men
from one another.

At age fourteen, girls reach their majority and must
leave the family to make their way in the world. At this
point, though still in school and under the influence
of mentors and friends, they lose any legal tie to their
mothers.

A Cousins girl grows up knowing that her success
in life is going to be dependent on her ability to make
alliances with other girls and older women. Young
women live together. They gossip, they compare
feelings and opinions, they gang up on one another and
watch one another's backs. They do each other's hair.
They sleep together. They fall in love. They tell jokes
and complain and listen to one another complain. They
start enterprises and run for public office. They argue
about what they will do with their lives and calculate
who among the older women they might cultivate.

Certain charismatic and accomplished women gather
to themselves circles of younger ones as lovers, protégés,
sister-wives. Two or more Cousins women may go to the

government center and register, select a middle name or have one given to them, and establish a new family, but more commonly young women will marry into an existing family headed by one or more of these matriarchs. The affectional nature of the family is undeniable, but as political power in the Society arises from the family, some families function as political organizations.

Because each generation of females must separate from its parent generation, there is less opportunity for nepotism. Leadership of a family always passes outside of genealogy, to someone who has "married in." A matriarch may convey her authority to a sister, but ultimately, it must go to someone who is not a blood relative.

It is possible for a Cousins woman to live alone, but it is rare. Such cases seem to be as often a matter of temperament as of political statement.

• • • • •

Opposite the university café, plastered onto the wall of the next terrace up, was Mira's most recent graffito, a two-meter-wide video retelling the myth of Actaeon. A stag flees through a stylized forest, pursued by a baying pack of hounds. The dogs corner the stag and leap upon it. Close-up of the stag's frightened eyes; it lifts its head, mouth open as if trying to speak, but all that comes from its throat is an animal cry. The dogs tear the stag to pieces.

Mira nibbled at a warm biscuit and eavesdropped on the three women at the next table.

"What is she trying to prove?" the pale woman of about Mira's age said. "This 'Looker,' whoever it is, can't be a woman."

"Looker isn't a woman," the second said. She was older, with gray hair and very dark skin. Mira had seen her before; she was part of the Amarillo family, a professor of engineering.

The third, wearing a red, low-cut top, took a sip of tea and said laconically, "It says, 'Made by a Woman.'"

"She makes Actaeon into a hapless victim of the insane bitch Diana," the pale woman said.

"It's not a new reading," the third said. "Ovid's version ends with a debate about whether the goddess was fair to him. After all, he was just attracted to Diana, that's natural. But she turns him into a stag. A beautiful potent male animal, unable to speak."

"He lowered himself to that. He violated her privacy, objectified her. He could have turned away as soon as he realized where he was. Looker makes that part plain. Instead he ogled her."

"You look at the naked goddess, you pay the price," the one in red said.

"So it's wrong for him to feel lust?" the fair woman asked. "You never feel lust?"

"Of course I do, darling—when it's appropriate."

"What about the dogs? They're his dogs, and they're all male, and they tear him to pieces."

The woman in red smirked. "Man's best friend."

"Looker isn't teaching mythology," said the engineering prof. "It's a provocation."

Mira wished she could keep eavesdropping, but she had to get all the way to Materials at the end of the West Concourse. She left the café for the metro.

The university café was on the northeast terraced slopes, overlooking the heart of the colony, the largest domed crater on the moon. One of the architectural wonders of the solar system, the Fowler dome testified to all that the Society of Cousins had accomplished through an ethic of co-operation. Every Cousins child had drilled into her that it wasn't engineering that had built the dome, but a culture that surrounded and constrained the demonism that had almost destroyed the Earth and that still ruled the other lunar colonies, Mars, and the Jovian satellites.

Most of the crater's floor was given over to farming, but a wedge from the center to the southeast crater slopes made up Sobieski Park, with its pond, amphitheater, and sixty-year-old oaks. From the center of the crater's floor rose the kilometer-tall Diana Tower that supported the dome. Rim to rim, the dome stretched more than four kilometers. Its exterior was covered with several meters of lunar regolith, shielding the inhabitants from radiation, but its opaque inner surface was a screen. Today it glowed clear blue with high cirrus clouds. A repair crew, tiny at this distance, hung suspended on a scaffold from that sky.

A flyer wearing a bright blue-and-white skinsuit and wings like some human jaybird soared low over the terrace, then banked, beating her mechanical feathers as she climbed upward again. Others lifted themselves on the thermals hundreds of meters above the perimeter road, or swooped down over residential complexes or fields of soybeans before rising on updrafts. Though she had not flown in seven years, Mira remembered that feeling of freedom.

She descended to the metro and caught the next train for West. She found a seat. "News," she told her Aide, and settled back to read her preferred print reports projected onto her right eye's visual field.

A story from Earth about a strike by uplifted racehorses: video of the thoroughbreds picketing Churchill Downs. A review of the latest Leila Eskander musical epic from Persepolis. A hair's-on-fire editorial on the threat presented by male gangs should the initiative to expand the franchise fail.

People on the train were talking about trouble in the Kamal Hestersson district: protests by the helium miners, who claimed that the low status of their jobs should qualify them to vote. More of these protests all the time. Across the aisle from Mira, a little woman with brown hair told her friend the patriarchies were supporting the troublemakers.

As it passed from the crater into a concourse, the train rose from underground and became an elevated tram. This concourse was commercial and fairly busy at this hour, numbers of Cousins like her passing through on their way to the airlocks, others opening shops and diners, some men working the *mita* cleaning the streets. Here and there Mira saw a woman wearing a red armband to show her sympathy with the Reform movement. The heliotropes were full open now, and sunshine, broken by the leaves of the trees planted down the nave of the lava tube, flooded the north side of the concourse, falling on shop-fronts, ivy-cloaked walls, and the flags of the walkways. When the tram passed the Tiresias statue, Mira saw sealer sprayed around the seam of the door they had broken into, light against the dark stucco.

After the night with Carey, she'd been unable to sleep. She'd loaded the footage they'd shot, but she hadn't gotten any further than his image on the video editor. Carey on the stage at the Oxygen Warehouse. "Let me tell you what it means to be an untreated socio-path." Raffish, self-assured, willing to try anything, his intellect hidden like a banked fire.

His legend as attractive trouble had started when he was fourteen. On the first night of Founders' Week he'd arranged to meet some friends out on the lunar surface. He never showed up. At that time his mother was the chair of the Board of Matrons. The entire colony was mobilized in a week-long search, without success. Carey was presumed dead.

When, three months later, he turned up at the North Airlock, consternation turned to outrage. He had been living at an abandoned construction bunker in Esnault-Pelterie crater, where he had drugged himself silly and, amazingly, written a memoir, *Lune et l'autre*. As punishment he was made Invisible for six months, but his little book about the anxieties and pleasures of being an adolescent male in the Society became the rage among the young. The instant his internal exile expired, he emerged as the most popular boyfriend in the colony. It didn't hurt that he was a rising star in martial arts, bound for the Lunar Olympics.

He drove Mira crazy. At times he acted so fecklessly she had to try hard not to look down on him. The fact that he had written the memoir, and was so openly and unselfconsciously critical of the Society, proved that there was more to him than fame or family or bedroom skills. But it didn't look like anything would ever tap that quality, the heart of her desire.

The tram turned a sharp angle to arrive at the terminus. Bruises on her back from the hard stage of the club protested as she shifted in her seat. Right now Carey was probably at home with his nieces and nephews, or at the gym. She could call him.

Better that he should call her.

"West Airlock Complex," the tram announced. Workers for the morning shift at the fusion plant, the solar collection fields, and the nanotech and biotech labs descended from the platform, where they would suit up to make the bus trip across the surface. Mira and a dozen others headed on foot down the spur toward the Materials Lab.

Mira had just reached her workstation when Roz Baldwin came by. She embraced Mira and kissed her on the cheek.

Preemptively Mira asked, "Did you ever reach Carey?"

"Not yet."

So he hadn't gone to her last night.

Roz had recently cut her red hair in a short bob that, despite the fact that she was a big woman, made her look girlish. She managed the Materials physical plant, and though she was not a difficult person, her humorlessness got on Mira's nerves. "We're moving you to a new station," Roz said. "Come with me."

To Mira's surprise, Roz led her to a station in the workroom that housed Eva's research team. It was a move up. Eva was the greatest physicist ever to come out of the Society. Her papers of twenty years earlier on Planck-Wheeler time and space were still widely cited. Mira's skills in theoretical physics were pedestrian; she could find her way around a statistical report and she was good at running simulations, but Eva had never expressed much interest in her before. She wondered what was behind this sudden change in her status.

"Eva's asking all the project groups to prepare progress reports for the Board. She'd like you to organize all the lab's notes on fullerene scrubbers."

"What's going on?"

"The election," Roz said. "If Reform takes control, expect some policy changes."

Mira didn't get her implication. "How soon does she need it?"

"Not immediately. Two, three weeks."

"All right, then."

"Okay. Oh, and if Val comes by later, send him to me."

"Sure."

"Thanks."

Mira watched Roz move across the workroom. Everyone in the lab knew her history. The same age as Carey, as a teenager she had emigrated to the Society with her father, the plant geneticist, Jack Baldwin, who became Eva's lover. A year after arriving, Baldwin killed himself, and orphaned Roz was taken in by the Greens. She and Carey became lovers, had a son. The fact that she was not Eva's biological daughter had resulted in the peculiar situation that Roz, Carey, and Val were all members of the Green family.

Mira wondered how much Roz knew about Carey and her.

When Mira ferried her things to the new station, she managed to knock a stylus off the back of the desk. She got down on her hands and knees and felt for it between the desk and the wall, and her fingers fell upon some small thing. She pulled it out—it was a ring. Dark silver metal—titanium?—with an inlaid pattern of two green vines twisted around each other, circling the band to join up with themselves. Mira slid it onto one finger. It was too large for her fingers, but fit snugly on her thumb. A man's ring.

She put it into the drawer. When she broke for lunch, she grabbed an apple and a protein bulb from the lab refrigerator and sat in the break room. Two other grad students, Tanya and Peter, had the colony video feed on the wall.

On the screen Hypatia Camillesdaughter was talking with Mandy Moirasdaughter, whose blab show was a guilty pleasure for half the colony. "This is a dangerous moment in the history of the Society," Hypatia said. "But with danger comes opportunity. Elimination of the two-tiered suffrage system will transform us."

It was Mira's day to encounter all of Carey's other women. Hypatia taught History of Gender at the university. Her infamous essay about the Thomas Marysson revolt, "*Stories for Men* and the Bloody Y Chromosome," came close to justifying the sabotage that had gotten Marysson and Erno Pamelasson exiled.

Mira admired Hypatia's biting wit; Hypatia did not suffer fools gladly, and she thought the Society of Cousins was rife with fools.

Mandy said, "Some people charge that you are just a narcissist and your movement is about personal aggrandizement."

Hypatia laughed. "Aren't you a narcissist, Mandy? I don't trust people who don't love themselves."

"You've been married and divorced twice, from the Weavers and the Scarlets. You have male lovers and you don't seem to have close women friends. And you're the head of a movement aimed, among other things, at giving men the vote. Why should women support the Reform Party?"

"Women are active at every level in the Reform movement."

"I didn't say you lacked acolytes. But several former associates of yours are, to say the least, not fans."

"It's sad that supporters of the status quo resort to attacking my personal life instead of engaging with the issues." Hypatia seemed deeply amused. "Every day men and boys go ignored in our families, and you ask me about my marriages."

"That's a new one—the idea that we ignore men and boys," Mandy said. "All right, then. What's to keep men, if they all have the vote, from trying to establish a patriarchy?"

Hypatia laughed. "You're not serious."

"On the contrary," Mandy said. "Majority rule by males invariably leads to suppression of women and minorities. Look at Earth history."

"Disenfranchising half the population to quiet your anxiety is a high price to pay," Hypatia said. "We pay it every day—and what does it buy us?"

Tanya was watching with Mira, but Peter had his head down over a submolecular simulation he was running on his tabletop. He munched a sandwich and brushed crumbs off the image.

"Do you think she's going to win?" Tanya asked.

Peter didn't bother to look up. "I don't care about voting."

"Forget voting. Think of the opportunities in the patriarchal universities. Wouldn't you like to study in Persepolis?" Tanya turned to Mira. "What do you think? Open information could make our future."

"Science is already open," Mira said. "We publish our papers for everyone in the solar system. We read the papers from everybody in the solar system."

Peter finally looked up. "There you go."

On the wall, Mandy said, "The idea that gender is entirely a construction was demolished a century ago. No matter how it expresses, it's in our genes. To deny the reality of the billions who devoted their lives to being 'male' or 'female' is inhumane. Are men and women myths?"

Hypatia examined her fingernails. "Gender determinism is a fog that keeps us from securing justice for everyone."

Mandy smiled. "It's that kind of statement, Professor

Camillesdaughter, that convinces so many in the Society that you are Looker. Are you?"

"I wish I knew who Looker is, so I could give her a big, sloppy kiss."

Mira's face flushed. Tanya asked Mira, "You think she'll take over the Board?"

Startled, Mira mumbled, "I'm not very good at politics."

"I thought you were in the Discussion Group at the university."

"Not lately. Their rules on what I'm supposed to believe change faster than I can keep up with."

Tanya grinned. "Truth. Some friends and I are meeting at the temple tonight. Want to join us?"

"Sorry. I'm busy."

Peter turned off the simulation and got up. "Hey, female hegemon," he said to Tanya, "are we going to do any work today?"

Mira went back to her new desk and tried to focus on assembling her notes. She'd been working with two others on adapting bottom-up nanodevices to rebuild tissue damaged by contamination with fullerenes. The technology worked well in the lab, and it had large practical applications in environments that had been sloppy with their use of the hazardous materials.

But her head wasn't in it. How could Mira compete with someone like Hypatia Camillesdaughter? She was everything Mira wanted to be. She saw the hypocrisy in the Society and did not let some phony notion of sisterhood keep her from telling the truth. She was funny and sarcastic and nobody treated her like an outcast.

The Reform Party had a slate of candidates pledged to her two-pronged program: open the Society to outsiders, and extend the franchise. If the franchise was extended, Hypatia would surely be able to win a colonywide election. She'd be head of the Board of Matrons, by some measures the most powerful woman in the Society.

Mira tried to call Carey, but only got his Aide. She told it to pass along that she had called, then regretted calling at all.

Midway through the afternoon Valentin Rozsson sauntered into the workroom. "Mira," he said, "new workstation?"

"Hello," Mira said. They embraced. He was taller than her and his red hair brushed her cheek. "Carey gave me your horse. It's beautiful."

Val brushed his hair back behind his ear. He had his father's grace and his mother's freckles. There was some quality about him—everyone saw it—an amusement at the world unlike the temper of a typical fifteen-year-old. His mind was quick, his smile disarming. "Is Roz here?"

"She's in the back with your grandmother. She wants to speak with you."

"I'm here to pick up a stock of glass for the workshop. Should be an order in the system."

As low intern on the Materials totem pole, Mira took care of filling requests. She called up the Fowler Glass Institute account. Several varieties of colored frit and three grades of cullet: soda glass, combustion glass, lead glass.

"I'll go down with you," she said.

They left the administrative level and descended to the vast warehouse. Mira coded in the order and the system sent a bot down the cavernous room between twenty-meter-high ranks of storage bins. The bot found the designated slot, rose on hydraulics, forked a bin out of the array, brought it down, and trundled it off to distribution. A couple of *mita* workers scooped out each variety of three-centimeter glass disks, packaged them for transport, and loaded them onto a cart. Mira got into the driver's seat, Val climbed into the passenger's, and Mira drove them out the big doors at the end of the warehouse.

"Carey told me to say hello," Val said.

"You've seen him?"

"At school. He was doing a mountain climbing tutorial in virtuality. He's friends with the instructor."

"He has a lot of friends," Mira said, fixing her eyes ahead. She pulled the truck up in front of the lab housing the old stacked-pinch fusion reactor.

Mira got out; Val came around to the driver's side. He leaned against it, his arms crossed. "He likes you."

"He likes everybody."

"That's a problem?"

"I guess it depends on your frame of reference."

"I don't know about that," Val said. He watched her for a moment. He had his father's eyes: level brows, beautiful lashes. Just a boy, yet he acted with such self-possession.

"If Roz asks after you," she said, "how much should I lie?"

Val kissed her cheek and climbed into the truck. "Tell her I've thrown over all propriety. Solidarity!" He grinned wickedly and drove away.

• • • • •

FROM *The Odd Side of The Moon: Lunar Utopias and Social Experiments*

#5: THE SOCIETY OF COUSINS

. . . the theory that human violence is fundamentally a male phenomenon, based on male reproductive strategies. All Cousins practices related to the treatment of boys and men are designed to channel "male demonism" into nondestructive enterprises, and to prevent those men with the patriarchal temperament from combining into the powerful, status-driven coalitions that the Society sees as the foundation of nationalism, war, colonialism, imperialism, unfettered capitalism, rape, infanticide, genocide, and the sad history of human tyranny.

Unlike girls, Cousins boys never reach their majority. Instead they are pampered and petted, indulged in their pastimes and challenged in their education. A boy may choose a career in any area of art, science, sport, or social service, or may choose not to work at all. Whatever path men pursue, their career choices are supported to the limits of the Society's resources. This difference in treatment begins early. In a typical extended family, for instance, the daughters must share rooms while the sons are given their own.

This indulgence is paid for by the sacrifice of political power. A man obtains the right to vote and hold office only by giving up "male privilege" and becoming a permanent *mita* worker. Every citizen, through the *mita*, performs six hours per week of the mundane and unchallenging work that keeps the Society running. For a man to become a permanent *mita* worker carries no status—except to earn the franchise. Few men feel this is worth it.

The status of a man is determined, first, by the status of his mother, to a lesser degree by the status of his family, and finally, by his own accomplishments.

Sex is the common coin of Cousins society. There are few restrictions on sexuality, except for the protection of children under fourteen. Adolescence for boys is a sexual playground that goes on into adulthood. Men are valued for their sexuality, praised for their potency, competed for by women. In any family or group of women living together, male friends stop by one evening or another. They come and go; the women entertain them and assess their performance.

From puberty on, men are schooled by older men and women on how to give and take pleasure. A man who can give such pleasure is recognized and respected throughout the Society. Welcome in any bed. Admired and envied by other men. Every Cousins girl has vids on her wall of famous lovers: star athletes, dancers and acrobats, writers, musicians, singers, even scientists.

Though men may marry, they still live in the family of their mothers. Cousins marriage has nothing to do with the marriage of blood relatives, as is commonly misunderstood outside the Society. Similar to the concept of "walking marriage" among the Musuo on Earth, men may have sex with any consenting woman— and consent is given with a freedom that is unheard of in patriarchal societies. Fidelity is not demanded or encouraged. Under these circumstances, formal marriage between women and men is rare.

Homosexuality is encouraged, and men may marry other men, but the concept of a large family made up solely of men raises alarms among the Cousins. To reduce this possibility, when men marry they still must live together within either of their families. If they divorce, they automatically return to their birth families.

The key to understanding sex and gender among the Society of Cousins is this: Though the performance of gender may be fluid, for legal purposes the Society ties the assignment of "male" or "female" strictly to biology. A person genetically female (by birth or chromosomal modification) is female, and a male is male. This leads to the curious practice that, with biological change of sex, transsexuals gain and lose responsibility, power, and legal rights. The many varieties of gender and nongender evident in other human societies may be present among Cousins, but their legal rights and cultural authority are nonetheless linked to their biology, not the gender they present.

There is an active transgender community in the Society, but to the Cousins legal system, transgender females are males, with no more rights than men. This is, in some ways, as much a source of political conflict as the treatment of cis-males.

Any children resulting from sexual congress belong to the mother. In practice it is often a matter of indifference who the father of a child may be. At home, men may be deeply involved in the lives of nieces and nephews, and beloved within their families. But they gain no authority from this, own no children, inherit no property.

• • • • •

Carey helped Jesse up from the mat. "Go again?"

"You're kidding, right?" Jesse said. He put his hands together and bowed; Carey returned the gesture.

"My turn," Thabo said.

"Jesse's right. Let's take five," said Carey. He went over to the bench where Dante sat, took up a bulb, and squirted some water into his mouth. Jesse lifted his shirt to look at his ribs. "Ouch," he said.

"Sorry," said Carey. Carey *was* sorry, but he had liked hitting Jesse. It felt good to get the better of another man in the ring.

Ruǎn tā was a martial arts style developed for lunar conditions, where gravity was less than on Earth but force and mass were the same. While it had realized, to a degree, the fantasies of flying portrayed in countless kung fu films of the twenty-first century, the practice proved more complex than the dream. The human body did not move in slow motion. The genetic manipulation that increased bone density in low-G ensured that bodies could take the stresses of combat, but *wushu* practice had to be greatly modified.

Still, as on Earth the goal was to improvise, think under pressure, and control one's emotions. Carey had earned the silver in *Ruǎn tā* in the Lunar Olympics, the first Cousin ever to medal in the sport. The New Guangzhou masters said he might have won gold but for an inability to match his external skills with the inward mindfulness that bespoke true balance. The pure pleasure Carey took in winning was, he knew, a sign of his imbalance.

Two women took over the ring. Light on their feet, they circled each other.

Carey's Thursday sessions with his friends were as much a chance to talk as anything else. He had known Thabo twenty years: He was the man Carey could talk to when he needed advice or just a sympathetic ear. Jesse and Dante were more recent additions.

Though Jesse hated talking about women, this was Thabo's week to guide the conversation and they were up to their gills in woman talk.

"You can do better," Thabo told Carey.

"You don't know Mira," Carey said.

"That's because she alienates everybody who tries to know her."

"Who are you talking about?" Jesse asked.

"One of Carey's women. Mira Hannasdaughter."

"Don't know that one."

One of the women fighters swept the feet out from under the other, taller one, who caught herself on her hands and flipped upright again. Her long brown braid whipped through the air. Dante, who had been watching closely, snapped his fingers in appreciation.

"Mira's trouble," Thabo said. "Always angry."

"She has things to be angry about," said Carey.

"She might get somewhere if she wasn't so sarcastic," said Dante. "She's smart."

"You know her?" Carey asked.

"Not carnally," Dante said. "I was in seminar with her in materials science."

Carey had a hard time explaining to them what was special about Mira. When she mocked him he had trouble explaining it to himself. She didn't patronize. She respected his intelligence enough to criticize him the way she might a woman. She kept after him about *Lune et l'autre*: If he'd written something that critical of the Matrons as an adolescent, how could he as an adult fit himself so comfortably into the slot the Society had prepared for him?

Depends on how you define comfortable, he'd told her.

Yes, she was angry, but Carey did not feel that her anger, when it was aimed at him, was any different from the anger she directed at anyone else in the world who fell short of her peculiar standards.

The question of whether he loved her was one that he had only lately spent any time on. That, too, depended on your definition. He liked the sex, but sex for Carey had always been easy. He liked sleeping with Hypatia, too, and with lots of other women. But as his athletic career approached its inevitable decline, he wondered what he would choose to do for the next phase of his life. The fact that Mira expected him in some way to challenge the Society made her different enough to command his attention.

"So why do you like her?" Thabo asked.

"Well, for one, she doesn't ever ask me about *Ruǎn tā*."

"Who's her mother?" Jesse asked.

"She doesn't have a mother. Her mother left the Society."

"And Roz doesn't have a mother. You got a thing about women without mothers?"

"That explains why she's interested in you," Thabo said. "She wants an alliance with *your* mother."

"She already works for my mother. And Roz."

"The plot thickens," Jesse said. "The antisocial woman after the hottest man and the most powerful Matron in the Society."

"How *is* Roz?" Thabo asked. Thabo had known both Carey and Roz since they were all playing hockey at age fifteen. Carey suspected Thabo was half in love with her.

"She's fine. Val is apprenticing at the Glass Institute." Carey watched the women spar. The brown-haired fighter was good. Flexible, strong, self-contained.

Dante didn't seem to be able to take his eyes off her. "Who's Val?" he asked.

"My son."

"You have a son?"

"Yes," Carey said.

"I have two," Jesse said. He swiveled on his bench, absently fingering the scar on his neck. He had almost died during a hockey game when, in a scramble for the puck in front of the net, the blade of a skate got under his mask and severed his carotid. He came close to bleeding out right there on the ice. "I see Eric when I visit his mother. I'm glad I don't have to deal with him. Don't see much of Charlie since his mother and I drifted apart. You never talk about any kids."

Carey had known Jesse for three years now, and the subject of children had not come up. "Val's fifteen," Carey said. "Smart, funny. He makes me laugh." He paused. "I told him something today I shouldn't have."

The conversation moved to post-athletic careers. They discussed Thabo's plans to become a coach. Could he be a good enough one to warrant colony support, or would he end up in the aquaculture farm? Jesse was already resigned to taking up a job in the helium-3 mines. He'd been doing his *mita* there since he was a teenager; his mother was a manager at the fusion plant. She could get him a good job, something without too much drudgery. He liked getting out on the surface, seeing the real sky. He did not seem too concerned about losing whatever small attention came from sports.

"You'll end up doing colony work," Dante said. "Then you can entertain yourself voting." The tall woman ducked a roundhouse kick by executing a neat side roll. "Nice!" Dante said.

"The Society is supposed to valorize the worker. Instead it wants us to be effete drones," Jesse said. "Of course, I think even you drones deserve the vote. I know, it's inexplicable, but that's just the kind of man I am."

Carey tolerated Jesse's rants, though of late he had been getting more strident. Jesse considered Carey a lightweight. Carey imagined telling him that Mira was Looker, and he was helping her.

They were right about her abrasiveness. She had no politesse at all. There was some great hurt inside her. It made Carey want to protect her, though if he ever told her that she would laugh.

The two women ended their session. They bowed to each other and stepped out of the ring. The one with the braid glanced over at Carey and the others. A slight smile.

Carey asked Dante, "Who is that?"

"Don't you know her?" Dante said. "That's Abidemi Bethsdaughter. She's a constable. Supposed to be a revelation in the saunas."

"Never noticed her," Carey said.

"You could do me a favor," Dante said. "Hang around after we're done tonight."

"I've got a date," Carey said.

"This could be your date," Dante said. "Come on. You owe me this, Carey."

"I don't know," Carey said.

Thabo got to his feet. "Our turn," he said to Carey.

Carey and Thabo sparred a couple of five-minute *dui da* sets. Not real combat, more a dance with improvisation—real combat would have been over in a minute or less. The women who had just finished stayed to watch, and another woman and man came over. Between rounds Carey observed Dante chatting with the brown-haired woman. She was quite attractive.

That distracted Carey, and Thabo caught him in a leg hook and got him off balance. For the rest of the session Carey felt out of synch. "Got you this time, son," Thabo said. Carey nodded ruefully and they joined Dante and the women.

"Say, aren't you Abidemi Bethsdaughter?" Carey said.

"I am." She embraced him, kissed his cheek. He brushed his lips over her ear. She smelled of flowers and sweat.

Dante raised an eyebrow. Abidemi introduced him to her partner and friends. They chatted a bit about the practice. Carey toweled his face and hair, and offered her his most winning smile. "You've met my friend Thabo? And this is Jesse."

Abidemi smiled back at Carey. "You gentlemen need a sauna," she said.

Well, it was hours before he was due to meet Mira.

· · · · ·

Mira had devoted two nights to getting her video into shape. She spent her off-work hours at her cluttered desk, sucking on the carb and protein mixes she lived on. On the shelf beside her stood her collection of horses, from ancient plastic models to fully animated miniatures. Among them the new one Val had made. Beside them a still photo of her and her brother Marco, ages thirteen and ten.

Love is just a feeling.

Her idea for this graffito was to intercut images she'd shot at the deserted club with video of men at work and play in the colony. A big man in a skinsuit, face invisible behind his black faceplate, holding a huge solar panel in place while another bolted it to the rack. A gray bearded man pruning trees on the inside slope of the crater. Three little boys playing in the Sobieski Park fountain. Erno Pamelasson on trial, stone faced as someone described how he had caused his mother's death. Two middle-aged men in coveralls tending a room full of chickens. Just a couple of minutes, all irony, no statements. A simple title: *Stories of Men*.

She printed out a dozen copies. While the printer worked she changed into the stealthsuit and climbing shoes she wore when posting her videos. She stuck the hood, grip gloves, and a can of spray mastic into her belt. She went back to her tediously slow printer, still working on the last few copies, rolled up the one-by-two-meter sheets, slid them into a black, nonreflective quiver, and slipped it on. The tightly rolled videos stuck up over her shoulder, and she could easily reach them with her right hand. It was almost 0200. She drank a bulb of electrolyte and slipped out of the apartment.

The facade of the modular apartments was silent, most of the lights out, though she heard music coming from the end unit shared by two women who worked in agriculture and their male partner, a worthless poet.

Mira moved swiftly through the quiet concourses, her heart full of anticipation and something approaching glee. Why spend time with Tanya and her crew at the Diana Temple, women so alike they might have been produced by an object printer? Mira was Looker, outlaw social critic, radical artist, the one who told the truth. She avoided neighborhoods that were still active this late and emerged from her underground district into the crater, beneath the projected night sky.

From the rim road she descended the slope through a forest of aspen, bristlecone pine, and alder by way of one of the many winding pathways that descended toward the crater floor. It was 0220 when she reached the Men's House. This late at night it was closed and the playing fields of the plateau were deserted. The Men's House had been one of the early creations of the Society, a place where men could gather, free from the intrusion of women. In the wake of the Durden revolt and the vacuum blowout, it had been closed for two years, but social pressure and its almost institutionalized status had opened it again.

A slight breeze rustled the leaves of the aspens. Mira sat on a bench in a bower just off the path, where she could see who might be coming but they could not see her. She didn't know why she cared so much that Carey should help her. It wasn't right, she knew—not right by the standards of a mature Cousins woman, and definitely not right by the standards of her own heart. Yet here she was, at—she checked the time—0247, not ready to start without him, though the videos, and the idea of posting them, and the aspirations they represented, were entirely her creation. Hers, not his. She couldn't tell what Carey's aspirations were, except to have sex as often as possible with as many women as possible.

It was 0255, and her self-questioning was reaching its apogee, when a figure in black came quietly down the path. A vast relief flooded through her, washing all her anger away. She moved out of the shadows.

He stopped when he saw her. "Mira?"

It wasn't Carey—it was Val. "What are you doing here?" she asked.

"I want to help you."

"Where's Carey?"

"I don't know. He told me about your plans. I can't believe that you're Looker!"

Mira shook her head. "I can't believe he told you."

"Don't be mad. I'm glad he did. It's demented."

She tried to collect her thoughts. Val's hair was pulled back and he was dressed in nonreflective tights and shirt. He had on climbing shoes. He was just the age Marco had been when he died.

"All right," she said. "But you have to be quiet, and you have to do just what I say."

His smile was stunning. "Of course."

She drew one of the rolled-up videos from her quiver. "Let's start simple—on the side of the Men's House."

They found a good spot, visible not just from the path but to anybody down slope looking up, and pasted the video onto the wall. Unactivated, it was transparent, nonreflective, hardly visible. When they had posted all of them and were safely away, she would turn them on remotely.

They spent the next two hours posting Mira's videos in a dozen places around the colony. Mira was surprised how much she enjoyed working with Val. He was so clearly delighted to be taken into her confidence. It turned out he was one of her biggest fans. "I loved the one with the Founders arguing about whether it was okay to punish the man who wanted to be punished," he said. "The expression on the man's face when she said no! We were all laughing so hard."

"That was just a joke." She tried to explain what she was trying to do. "The best part, Val, will be when you are in a crowd of people tomorrow, and they are talking about the video—it doesn't even matter if they hate it—and you know that you did it, and they don't."

The last place Mira chose to post was the most difficult: twenty meters up on the reinforced concrete rim wall that formed the base of the dome, overlooking the road that circled the crater. She found a spot above a broad esplanade in Gilman, where an avalanche of apartments, refectories, and public buildings tumbled down the slope to the crater floor. Val swore so fervently that he was an experienced climber that she let him join her. The wall's surface had grooves, each about ten centimeters wide, the facing pebbled with regolith. It was a decent surface for bouldering, and they climbed up to just below where one of the great cermet ribs that formed the substructure of the dome arched out of the wall. She planned to fix the video to the smooth inside surface of the support. Canted forward over the plaza, it would look down on every citizen who passed below, impossible to ignore.

She'd hoped to find a place with enough purchase for her feet that she could use both hands to affix the video, but there was nothing. Without ropes or pitons, they would have to work one-handed. She was glad to have Val with her. They clung to the wall, breathing hard; in the faint light from the stars and the road below, Val's face was split in a grin.

"You spray the mastic," she said, handing him the can.

But she let it go before he had grasped it; Val fumbled and it fell away. He attempted to grab it in midair, but instead batted it to the side. His foot slipped. She heard his gasp, saw for a second the dismay in his eyes as he began to fall, before she snagged his arm with her free hand. She almost came off the wall herself, but he scrabbled against the masonry, his foot found purchase, and he was steady again. Her heart slammed in her chest. She felt the rough face of the concrete on her cheek.

"Thanks," Val said.

Some seconds later, the tumbling can hit the tiles of the plaza with a metallic crack, then rolled. Mira looked down. Two women crossing the plaza had stopped; one was looking at the can at her feet, the other leaned back to look up at them.

"Climb," Mira said.

They scaled the last few meters to the top of the rim wall. There was a ledge a meter or two wide between the face of the wall and the inside of the dome. "This way," Mira said, and they hurried along the top of the wall. When they came to the next structural rib, they had to carefully slip down off the edge and crab-climb to the opposite side before they could again gain the top of the wall.

"I'm sorry, Mira," Val said as they ran.

All Mira could think of was Marco falling, falling.

"My fault," she said.

• • • • •

They found a place above the empty rim road and climbed down. If the people who had seen them had called the constables, so far no one had showed. Mira thanked Val for his help, made him promise to keep her secret, and told him to get home as inconspicuously as possible.

When she entered her apartment she found Carey sitting on her bed, which he had folded down from the wall. "Where have you been?" he asked.

She slung her gear into the corner. "Don't be stupid; I'm not in the mood." She got a bulb of water and squirted it into her parched mouth.

"I'm sorry. The Salon went long. I was there at the Men's House, but you were already gone."

She turned and just stared at him. "Val showed up instead."

Carey looked surprised. "I should never have told him about it."

"You think so?" Mira recalled the moment when Val's foot had slipped—saw the spray can tumble as he swatted it, heard his sudden intake of breath. "Val's not like other boys. You have to take better care of him." She said the words calmly, no trace of sarcasm.

Carey looked down at his hands. "That's his mother's department," he said, equally calm. "It's not what I do."

Mira slumped into her desk chair. Sometimes his fusion of privilege and passivity infuriated her, but she could see that under his ability to charm his friends, he discounted anything he had ever accomplished. "Why not? I know you love him. I think maybe he's the only person you truly love."

He looked up. "I know him better than Roz does. Better than any woman ever could. I *was* him."

"So live with them. If any man could, you could. You're all Greens."

"And be ignored? Any new woman joins the family, she already has more authority than I have. Even the men who live with their kids don't do the real work of a father."

"The real work of a father? I don't think anyone is looking for a patriarch around here."

"I don't want to be a patriarch. But a nice start would be if the Society acknowledged the connection between me and Val. I want the rights of a parent, and the responsibilities. I don't know exactly what a father is supposed to be, but I want to be one. Give me the chance, I could redefine the term."

Mira felt her anger drain away. "So why don't you?"

"Why don't I what?"

"Redefine fatherhood. Own your son. Take everything you are and have experienced and make a statement."

"You're kidding, right? I can't do that."

"Do you know how weak that sounds? You act like you have no choice."

"You don't know what it's like to be a Green. My mother, my aunts, Roz—the dynamic there has no place for the kind of father I could be."

"Then take Val away from that place."

Carey looked at her skeptically. Watching him think about it, it occurred to her that, without intending to, she had said something that was going to change their lives.

CHAPTER

THREE

AS A GIRL AMESTRIS WAS FASCINATED BY THE STORY of Tahmineh, daughter of King Samangan. When the hero Rostam visited her father's palace, Tahmineh, having heard tales of Rostam's valor, was so consumed by desire that she would have no other man. After all were asleep she snuck into Rostam's room and offered herself to him. They spent one exquisite, fateful night together, after which Rostam departed.

There was a lot more to this tale: a son unknown to his father, treacherous kings, a tragic ending. That was what everyone else saw in it. But that was not what captivated Amestris.

No woman Amestris knew growing up—her mother, her aunts, her sisters, other schoolgirls—seemed likely ever to behave like Tahmineh, to see what she desired and take it. It was not what Persepolis taught its women. Yet Tahmineh was praised, not condemned, for her boldness. Her mind and body, the *Shahnameh* said, were pure, and she seemed not to partake of earthly existence at all. Wasn't she as heroic as Rostam, in her way? A woman possessed only by herself, who wanted only the best, and who when the opportunity presented itself would rather be immolated than take the safe path.

> *If you desire me, I am yours, and none*
> *Shall see or hear of me from this day on;*
> *Desire destroys my mind . . .*

It had been three weeks since she had last gone clubbing, and desire was destroying Amestris's mind, and so she found herself one evening in the corridors of Dorud. The crowds in Shiraz Concourse were sprinkled with foreign businessmen, tourists, and guest workers. Men vastly outnumbered women, and those women not accompanied by husband or brother were with women friends. Amestris was alone. Her beautifully tailored *jilbab* was form-fitting, with an elaborately embroidered neckline over a plain black bodice. Though her clothing could not in any technical way be said to be immodest, that would not be much defense if she ran into some self-appointed morality police. She might rely on its fine tailoring and obvious expense as evidence that she was not a person to be trifled with, but whenever things got particularly sticky she could always fall back on her last name.

Normally she would have confined herself to the clubs in the finest hotels; it was evidence of how nothing else would do that she was in this rough neighborhood. Rudabeh's Garden catered to university students, political radicals, expats from other colonies and Mars, and the small multigendered community. At the door an augmented orang, in a child's Persian, asked for her membership. Amestris held her wrist beneath the scanner and, satisfied, the doorman let her in.

As soon as she entered, she flipped the wimple back to her shoulders, showing its violet lining, and unclipped her jet-black hair. Among the patrons she recognized Katayoun, who handled civil water contracts for the colony. Ali Reza, who came from one of the oldest families in Persepolis and could not be said to have any job other than entertaining himself. A few others, friends and former lovers.

Amestris found a booth, among women dressed in tight saris, pants suits, skirts, and blouses. Both men and women gave evidence of every sort of cosmetic manipulation: Persepolis was the body mod capital of the moon.

She ordered a tea called Feral. The edges of her vision vibrated. In an alcove she shared the hookah with two women who chatted about vacationing on Earth, and a man who told of climbing Olympus Mons during his last trip to Mars. The man, Arsalan, claimed to be an engineer for an energy corporation.

After a while the women left, and Amestris and Arsalan settled into a more intimate conversation. He had high cheekbones and dark skin, very dark eyes. He said he was thirty-three years old, ten years her junior. He touched his finger to the back of her hand, traced a line there from her wrist to her index finger. The brush of his dry skin made her tingle. He leaned close. He reeked of cologne.

"I spent the last three days on the surface, calibrating a new solar collector on the basin wall. My eyes are tired of squinting, and looking at you is a balm."

"If you had to squint, your suit must have lacked a sun shield."

He paused to appraise her. "You're right. That was not strictly true. But can you say you don't like me looking at you?"

"I'd like better your being honest with me."

"Honesty is essential to seduction. Once you can fake that, anything is possible."

"We've yet to discover what is possible."

"Something must be possible. At the very least, you want to be distracted."

"That doesn't sound very romantic."

"I am very romantic. Will you marry me?"

Amestris laughed. "I don't do sham marriages."

"It's as real as any marriage. More honest than most."

She would shine him on. "And you'll give me how much in dowry?"

"Let's say we set a *mahriyeh* of one hundred rials."

"Suppose, instead, I give you—three hundred."

He drew back. "I am no gigolo."

"And I am no whore. So perhaps we can find an arrangement that does not involve money. Give me something you genuinely value. I will give something I value to you. What do you have to give?"

Arsalan studied her. "I give you my genuine attention."

Amestris rolled the mouthpiece of the hookah on the table. "That's good. But can you make the world disappear? Can you give me that?"

"Not permanently. The world will come back again, inevitably."

He looked momentarily sad, and that convinced her. He really was quite handsome, and after all, the tired version of manhood he had tried to present was only what most men in Persepolis thought they were supposed to offer. Some women even liked it.

"There is a hotel—" he began.

"I'll select the place. Come with me."

Outside, the sound of competing music still drifted from the clubs. An emaciated man in an exo suit begged for alms. Amestris gave him a rial. Arsalan's fingers twined with hers.

As they passed the door of a tavern, shouts came from within and two men were thrown into the street. One, with long, fair hair, stumbled and fell, then bounced up, muttering something in English. When he started back inside, his companion grabbed him by the arm.

Arsalan put himself between them and Amestris. She steered Arsalan out of Dorud to the Hotel Gorbanifar. It was a residential hotel, not one of the ones, little more than brothels, that lined the bazaar in Dorud. In the spotless glare of the lobby, they made their arrangements with the clerk, Gabba, a man of middle years with an impressive black beard.

Amestris asked for a suite. When Arsalan tried to pay, she put her hand on his arm. She did not know whether he was wealthy or whether he had saved up for three months in the effort to impress, but she did not want him to pay for anything.

Their suite, lit by recessed amber lights, featured a divan, a low glass-topped table, a heated tub of scented water, a window with a view of earthrise over the Lunar Carpathians, and a very large bed. The carpet over the warmed stone floor was elaborately figured in flowers and trees.

As soon as the door closed behind them, they were in each other's arms. Amestris kicked off her shoes and fell onto the divan. Arsalan kissed her lips, neck, ear. He pulled her to him. She pushed him back and lay on his chest, staring down into his face, but after a moment he rolled her onto her side, undid her belt and tugged the *jilbab* over her head. He kissed her breasts and belly. He talked to her, called her names. She tried to guide him, to little effect: He was impatient. But he was strong, and he was eager for her, and Amestris was able to lose herself for a few moments before he climaxed, gave a little moan, and lay heavily on her.

After some time he pulled himself up and poured them each a cup of wine. They lay together on the divan, the light from the crescent Earth painting their bodies. "Did I hurt you?" he asked.

"No," she said. "You didn't hurt me."

"You are so lovely."

She put down her cup and kissed him, slowly, brushing her lips against his. He seemed to think that was a signal. He lifted her up, carried her to the pool, and stepped in with her still in his arms.

Rose petals floated on the surface. The warm water undulated thickly, slowly, throwing off large drops as they moved. Arsalan was more patient this time. Trying to feel something, she wrapped her legs around him, felt his slick chest against her breasts. The water carried away most of the scent of his cologne. Her hand on his back, his breath on her forehead, her ear. As he moved against her, the water splashed into her face, and she closed her eyes. He took her wet hair in his hand and pulled her head back below the surface. She went with it—but he would not let her up. She struggled, and still he held her down. She kicked at him, used her fingernails on his back, found his face with her hand. Finally he released her. She sputtered, gasping for breath. He gave a low laugh and moved to kiss her neck.

She pushed him away. "Stop!"

He pulled back. "What?"

Amestris climbed out of the tub. The water streamed slowly from her, and then clung to her body, held by surface tension. It was a distinctly uncomfortable feeling, to be encased in a film of water. Gradually it slid down from her head, shoulders, chest. She felt sick. She took up a towel and covered herself. "You can't use me that way."

"You liked it." He looked up at her, chest-deep in the water, and relaxed back against the wall of the tub, arms resting on the ledge.

He didn't think anything had happened. She wrapped herself in the towel, picked up his jacket, and threw it at him. "Get dressed!"

He surged up to snatch the jacket as it floated through the air, holding it high to keep it from the water. "What is wrong with you?"

"Leave. I want you out of here."

Slowly, Arsalan climbed out of the tub. She threw him a towel, then got onto the bed, pulling the duvet up around her. Earthlight cast his biceps in relief, showed his sloping, muscular shoulder, delicately painted his slender hips and legs. Whether he was born with it or engineered into it, he had a beautiful body. Sullenly, he took up his clothes and in short, violent motions, pulled them on.

At the door he turned. "Whore," he spat, and walked out.

She lay on the bed, breathing deeply to calm her raging heart. Tears gathered in her eyes. For a long time she lay there. Why did she do this? So a night of sex might flood her brain with dopamine? She could find that at much less cost in a cup of tea.

She supposed she needed the physicality: Nothing else would do. Some command of her genes at the prospect of producing a child. Yet she had no desire for children. Was she so much an animal that nothing—her intellect, her culture—could overrule that impulse?

Or maybe it was the culture that made her this way, damaged her so that she gave herself to men who tried only to take her, not understanding that she could not be taken, only given? Idiot dream.

Another sordid connection with some dangerous clown bearing a heroic name.

He was right: The world had not disappeared.

• • • • •

She was awakened by a woman who came to clean the room. Small, dark, a tight cap covering her hair, the woman turned the dawn light up on the pixwall. Silently she plucked a container from the caddy she carried and shook a cloud of nanobots into the tub. The bots drifted like dust to the water's surface, then activated and disappeared, devouring organics. The woman took out a small net and began skimming sodden rose petals off the water.

Amestris's pillow was damp from her wet hair. Her clothing lay scattered about, one shoe standing, the other lying in its side under the table. Her head throbbed. She tugged the duvet up to her neck. "What time is it?" she asked.

Her Aide whispered in her ear, *Five twenty-two.* Simultaneously the woman, not turning to her, said, "It's five twenty-two, madam."

"So early?"

"You may stay if you like. I need to clean the room."

Amestris could object to being disturbed so early—had Arsalan spoken to Gabba on the way out? Maybe Gabba had sent the maid specifically to discomfit her—but Amestris did not have the spirit for it. She gathered up her clothing. On her hands and knees she fished the shoe out from under the table. The woman ignored her. Amestris dressed, left three coins for her on the bedside, and fled.

The concourses were empty now. In the main ways, people with early shifts were going to work, waiting for the train, opening shops and restaurants.

Wash the wine stain from your dervish cloak with tears,
For it is the season of piety, and the time for abstinence.

The few other passengers on the tram were servants on their way to work in her neighborhood. She recognized several, and had no doubt that they knew her. Across from her an interactive poster bore the alert face of Sirius, the investigative canine: "Dog Star!" it proclaimed. Amestris closed her eyes to keep it from talking to her, and rested her head against the back of her seat.

The tram ran along one of the primary concourses, then entered the tunnel that took them outside the city. Eventually it emerged into Nabiyev, the satellite community where her family had their primary residence. A few people got off with her. The neat little station was quiet. Amestris passed through the sliding door into her neighborhood.

Originally constructed by North American investors, Nabiyev began as four roofed artificial canyons that formed a square, into the sides of which had been carved dormitories, warehouses, and workshops. After being taken over by Persepolis fifty years ago, it had been reconstructed into an exclusive residential enclave. The central square of lunar rock had been blasted away and the area thereby opened turned into an elaborate park, with trees, flowers, intricate pathways, and reflecting pools. Pomegranates, figs, dwarf cherries, eucalyptus. The bees that hovered over the flocks of lavender produced some of the best honey in the colony. Water had been invested extravagantly. The roof shield could be set from complete transparency to any number of projected false skies, from earthlike blue to the traditional patterns of a Persian mosaic. From her childhood on, Amestris had daily escaped from her family to this park with her friends, giving the slip to Mrs. Barnhardt, her indulgent and unreliable governess.

On the canyon walls, the utilitarian dormitories had been expanded into private residences fronted by a colonnade of pointed arches. Amestris hoped to sneak in through the servants' entrance to her room without arousing her parents' attention. Forty-three, yet she crept around like an adolescent. To quiet her step she removed her shoes. When she turned the corner near the alley to the servants' entrance, she found herself face to face with their neighbor, Mr. Kalbasi.

"Ms. Eskander?" he said. He saw the shoes in her hand and looked down at her feet.

"Good morning, Mr. Kalbasi." Kalbasi was a pious rug merchant, very proud of his fundraising for the Twelver mosque. Glad for the wimple that hid her shamefully tangled hair, Amestris bowed her head and slipped past him to the back door.

The cook, Farah, was in the kitchen, but she could be trusted not to say anything. Amestris crept to her room and took several hundred milligrams of a noötropic, drank a bulb of electrolyte, stripped, and took a shower. She untangled and braided her hair. The mirror showed dark circles under her eyes. She poked another two hundred milligrams of stimulants, dressed for work, and went down to breakfast. Her mother, her sister Fatima, and brother-in-law Kayvon were already there, seated on cushions around the low table. The room opened onto the courtyard with its eucalyptus and pool. Three sunning turtles were lined up on a log.

Her mother, stone silent, did not meet Amestris's eyes. She poured tea for Fatima and Kayvon.

"Good morning, sister," Kayvon said. Kayvon fancied himself a man of subtle wit, heir to the great Persian courtiers. Through his marriage to Fatima he hoped to whisper into the ear of their father and control the financial destiny of Persepolis. In reality, he was a sarcastic boor. Had he not produced a pair of sons by Fatima, Cyrus Eskander would not have tolerated his presence.

Amestris took orange juice and a slice of passion fruit. Her stomach could not tolerate anything more.

"We trust you slept well," Kayvon said. He spread jam on a piece of lavash, his eyes not meeting hers.

"Very well, thank you, brother," Amestris said.

Leila and her husband, Dariush, entered, holding hands. Dariush was a former bicycle racer, two-time winner of the Lunar Tour de Apennines. Stunning Leila, the youngest of the three sisters, was an actress; she and Dariush were the focus of much media gossip. Was she pregnant? Would she end her career in order to raise a family? Was Dariush considering unretiring to enter the 2149 race? Was he jealous of Leila's association with leading man Zal Bayzai? Yet despite the fact that her career made her a focus for the desire of myriad strangers, Leila was never criticized for her public profile, her work, her income.

At twenty-three, Amestris had been on the path to becoming famous herself, an accomplished concert pianist. She had drawn the attention of every man, and enjoyed that attention. But at that time her father had needed an heir to the business more than he needed a celebrity. He explained to Amestris how if she should enter the water corporation and let herself be schooled to take over once he was gone, she could become the most influential woman in the history of Persepolis. Always the dutiful daughter, instead of pursuing a musical career, she consented. By doing so, she told herself, she would escape the trap of marriage and its stifling restrictions.

Amestris had enjoyed wielding power, but she soon came to realize that any she had was only on loan from her father. She was an Eskander. Perhaps her beauty had gained her some influence independent of family, but beauty was transitory.

Recently she had overheard one of her subordinates at the office talking with a visiting businessman from Tycho. The visitor had remarked on Amestris's beauty. The man said, "Ah, you should have seen her when she was twenty!"

Her father entered the breakfast room and greeted all of them. He leaned over and kissed Amestris on the top of her head. "My dutiful Amestris."

"Good morning, Father."

Cyrus was impeccably dressed in a pearl gray suit that exactly matched his hair. His fingernails were manicured, the long, slender fingers of a man who had never done manual labor. The cuffs of his blinding white shirt protruded a centimeter past the sleeve of his jacket. "How lucky I am still to have one virgin among my daughters. Do not ever marry, my dear."

"Where could I find a man to compare with my father?"

Cyrus sat and unfolded his serviette. "My dear, today I must meet with some scientists visiting from Earth. In my absence I need you to take charge of the operation in the Aitkin basin. The ice retrieved there in the last months has increased in the percentage of heavy metals."

"Yes."

"There has been more wear and tear on the remote devices. I would like you to open a new seam in the western quarter of de Gerlache. We will still, of course, pursue the current operation."

"Yes, Father." The fact that he would bring this up at breakfast was intended only to humiliate her in the presence of her sisters. He could as easily have mentioned it on the way to work, or in the office. He was commenting on her absence last night.

Amestris could do nothing about it. "I shall have to go into the office immediately then, to make the preparations," she said. She bowed her head, kissed her mother, and left the table.

The station was now busy with people chatting with each other or muttering to their Aides. Among the businessmen and the well-dressed wives heading to the colony center for shopping, she saw a turbaned Sikh with his daughter. The girl, scarfless, her shiny black hair braided into an intricate coil atop her head, wore an athletic tunic over pants. She carried an orange football. Amestris had loved to play football. Cyrus had come to all of her games, had praised and encouraged her.

"Remember, always, Ajooni," the father, on one knee beside the girl, said, "you must keep your head up, yes? See the whole field, not look down at the ball. Yes, my infinite one?"

Thirty minutes ahead of her regular schedule, Amestris arrived at the company's offices off Anahita Square. Her work day started badly. In her box was a note from Saman Kazedi asking if she would join him for the midday meal on Wednesday. She hadn't spoken with Saman in a month, and the emotional baggage that came with seeing him was not something she needed right now. She put off answering. She met with the purchasing agent for the Sabine Water Authority, who had come halfway across the moon to discuss the renewal of the colony contract. It did not help that he was a dark, urbane Frenchman who resembled Arsalan, and that as they talked water prices for six-month delivery he treated her as if she were a child.

The negotiations were not helped when the lunar commodities market opened at 0930 and water futures fell thirty-two points. Prices for June through August delivery declined steadily throughout the morning, on rumors that Eskander was about to open a new deposit in the de Gerlache crater. Had her father known this information was out when he spoke with her? Amestris did not know how it had leaked, but she knew her father would hold her responsible. As soon as she could escape the Sabine representative, Amestris ordered her traders to hedge their positions on the August delivery contracts, and she spoke with several managers about delaying the mining of the new ice deposit. But even if that led to an eventual turnaround, the damage was already done in the prices they were seeing right now, and there was no hoping for a favorable deal on the Sabine contract.

She met for the midday meal with Sima Mozaffari. Sima was one of Amestris's inspirations and confidants. Of her generation, Sima was one of the few who had blazed a trail into business, following a career rather than a family. She was active in the Persepolis Professional Women's Organization and had served two terms in the legislature. Although she was seventy-five years old, through careful anti-aging treatments her skin was supple and her eyes clear.

They embraced and kissed. After some small talk, Amestris found herself unable to uphold her end of the conversation.

"You look tired," Sima said, breaking a piece of nan to go with her eggplant.

"I was out late last night."

"So I surmised."

Amestris did not want to recount her experience. In the light of day it seemed not dangerous but pathetic. "Do you ever wish you had left Persepolis when you were young?" she asked Sima.

Sima regarded her with her large brown eyes. She had not indulged in any extreme cosmetic alterations; she wore the face that Allah had given her. "If I had left, it would not have been for some other lunar colony. Mars, maybe. We make choices, and live with them."

"I don't think I've had an unencumbered choice in my life," Amestris said.

"Unencumbered choices do not exist." Sima touched Amestris's wrist. "What's wrong, my dear?"

"I don't—you know what's wrong. I've told it all to you a hundred times. My father, my mother, my work. I should never have given up performing."

"I did not know you then, but you've complained since of how constrained your life was at that time."

Amestris picked at her adas polow. "Sam Kazedi asked me out again."

"Does he still want to marry you?"

"Yes." Amestris laughed. "You see, nothing changes, no matter what choice I make."

"Send him around and I'll marry him. I would make him a good wife."

"Sam doesn't want what he can have. Only what he can't."

"In that respect you are well matched."

"Don't tease me, Sima."

"I don't mean to. What you say is true. Maybe we should emigrate to the Society of Cousins, you and I."

"Yes, we'll be Matrons, with many boy lovers. We'll cut our hair and wear terrible clothes."

They ate in silence for a moment.

"Sometimes I feel like such a failure, Sima."

"You know what I think. You should stop working for your father. Live alone, do nothing for a while. Travel. Figure out what you can do that will give you some satisfaction."

Amestris had heard this before, and it was good advice. Not that she had ever managed to act on it. She looked at Sima and asked herself if that was who she wanted to be in thirty years—and then felt bad for judging her friend.

After lunch she returned to the office, where Ali from the production staff wished to speak with her.

"I must pray," she told him. She ignored his faint look of surprise and retired to her office. In her bathroom she washed her face, hands, feet, and mouth. She wet her head and took the seldom-used prayer rug and turbah from the cabinet opposite her desk. She knelt toward the pixwall, on which she called up an image of the Ka'bah—the closest approximation, given the position of the Earth in the lunar sky from the south pole, of Mecca—and performed the afternoon prayer.

"In the name of Allah most merciful and mercy giving. Celebrate the praise of you, Lord, and seek His pardon. He is ever disposed to mercy," she said aloud. She tried to find peace in pressing her forehead against the turbah, in abasing herself before God. She felt some seconds of clarity, but her mind could not be still, slipping to images of Arsalan, her father, the Sikh man and daughter on the train.

"Peace and the mercy of Allah be on you," she concluded, on her knees, facing to the right and to the left. She rolled up her rug and put it away, feeling no more centered than she had before she had begun.

She summoned Ali. "What is it you wished to tell me?"

"There's been an accident in the south cutting."

• • • • •

A mining team had lost two Remote Operating Devices in an avalanche, and two of the team had gone out in hard suits to try to retrieve them. They had caused a second avalanche. One of the two had severe frostbite. The other, a guest worker, had lost his hand and almost died.

The officious shift manager Buyid sent the worker who had instigated this foolishness directly from the clinic to Amestris's office. To her surprise, his records revealed that he had been raised in the Society of Cousins, from which he had been exiled over ten years earlier. Amestris had met only a handful of Cousins before, none of them male, and certainly none who had been exiled.

Ali ushered the man into her office, then withdrew. His file said he was only twenty-eight, but he looked older. Dirty blond hair too long, his cheeks chapped from freezing. He stood in the doorway wearing a fresh corporate jumpsuit. His left arm, by his side, ended in a bandaged stump.

"May I be your sacrifice?" the man said. She was a little surprised he knew the archaic greeting. Under the circumstances it was only too appropriate.

"I don't know," she said. "May you?"

He stood looking square in her eyes, unblinking. His own were very blue. "I don't think I have much choice in the matter."

"Your accent is good, Mr."—she glanced at his records on her screen—"Pamelasson."

"I go by Pamson."

"Mr. Pamson, then. How long have you known Persian?"

"Not long. I have been taking language drugs and studying."

That could explain the accident. The same drugs that lengthened attention span and increased auditory sensitivity reduced awareness of other sensory inputs. His reflexes had probably been compromised.

"Have a seat," Amestris said.

There was something familiar about him. He sat in one of the two steel and fabric chairs opposite her desk. She took the other. If he was intimidated by being brought to her office, he did not show it. He let the bandaged stump of his left wrist rest on the arm of the chair.

She made him describe the sequence of events from his shift. "Your hand was frozen beyond repair while you were trapped in the ice," she said.

"Yes."

"I'm sorry that your contract does not cover such injuries. You'll need to have another hand grown and grafted. If you don't have the money, perhaps the Red Crescent will take you on as a charity case."

"I have resources," Pamson said.

That should be it, then. Fire him and send him on his way. She was about to dismiss him when she realized where she had seen him before. "You were in Dorud last night. I saw you thrown out of some tavern."

For the first time the man seemed nonplussed, as if he were more embarrassed at being caught drunk than to have wrecked valuable equipment, lost his hand, be on the point of losing his job, and likely evicted from the colony.

He said, "What were you doing in Dorud?"

That was it: Out the door with him. Instead, Amestris found herself curious.

"How long have you been working here, Pamson?"

"Call me Erno. You must already know that I've been here seven months."

"And how have you been treated?"

"What do you mean?"

"I mean, we don't have many people of your—background here. Your cultural background." Her father, on the few occasions they had done business with the Society, had warned her not to think of Cousins as "a people," since they did not originate from a single ethnicity.

"I'm not a Cousin anymore."

"That's one of the things I'm interested in. Why did you leave the Society of Cousins?"

"I was exiled. You should have that in my records, too. It's no secret."

"But the circumstances? One cannot make a judgment without knowing the circumstances."

"What kind of judgment? The authorities here knew my background when they gave me a guest worker visa."

"And your visa, though it might be revoked at any moment, is not in jeopardy from me," Amestris said. "You shouldn't worry yourself about that."

She waited.

"I killed my mother."

Was he trying to unnerve her? She was not in the mood to be toyed with. "My understanding is that the Cousins are nonviolent. I thought you spent all your time making love."

"No. We take time out for murder."

Exile from a pariah colony, guest worker, violator of company rules, street brawler, murderer—he was the poster child for a restrictive immigration policy. He seemed to want her to fire him. Well, he would get his wish soon enough. Still, this was not the behavior she had expected. She looked into his pale face, his blue eyes. It was worth one more question before the door. "I don't think you murdered anyone. So why do you tell me that you did?"

He looked at her without speaking, then shifted his eyes away. He muttered something, but Amestris caught it: "Fate has a thousand turns of ill, and never a tremor of good will."

Now she was genuinely astonished. "You know Hafêz?"

He met her gaze again. "I write poetry."

"You have felt that your fate is ill?" She sat back in her chair and contemplated him. He was a well enough made young man who had seen some hard use. The guarded look on his face was a veil over—over what? Anger? Despair? Critical intelligence?

"I've had bad luck."

"That's no wonder, if you take risks like you did today."

"I have to take risks. My skills are unrecognized here, my education useless."

"Skills? What skills have you?"

"Back home I was a biotechnologist, working with Lemmy Odillesson."

"Who's Lemmy Odillesson?"

"He's the most renowned ecological designer in the Society," Erno said. "That makes him the best designer in the solar system. Lemmy repaired the ecology when the system collapsed at Clavius. He designed the environment for the Chinese Mars colony. I worked with him for four years. I know more than most of the e-designers on the moon."

Amestris considered. "You're not a citizen. We didn't let you into Persepolis to take good jobs away from our people."

He held up his bandaged arm. "I suppose I could take up embroidery."

Despite the fact that nothing that had happened to him was her problem, she was taken aback. She got up from her chair and went to the window that overlooked the city square. Cool light poured down on the vast space, crowded with men, women, and children. Across the way the minarets of the grand mosque stretched up three levels of the atrium.

Without turning to see him, she asked, "Does it hurt much? Your hand?"

"They gave me a pain blocker."

She kept her back to him. "It's a waste having somebody like you—Cousins trained—mining ice."

"I'm honored to hear you say that, *khanom*."

Khanom. An honorable matron. She turned to him. She walked over to his chair, leaned down, and kissed him on the lips.

He kissed her back, reaching up to put his good hand on the back of her neck, pulling her gently down toward him. He was not rough. With his bandaged arm he coaxed her over the side of the chair into his lap. His lips parted from hers for a breath, then came back, slightly open. He smelled a little of some disinfectant the clinic had used. She felt his chest rise and fall.

Amestris drew back, opening her eyes. His own, centimeters away, looked into hers. The blue of his irises, she saw, was mixed with green around his pupils. She saw the slightest tension of the lines at the corners of his eyes. She did not believe that he felt no pain.

"What do you want?" he whispered. "Tell me what you want."

Could he make the world disappear? This drifter, this exile? She doubted it, and besides, she was tired of oblivion. What she wanted was to take the world into her hands and bend it to her will. She studied him.

"Are you going to fire me now?" he asked.

"Yes, I am. And if you really are the environmental engineer you claim to be, I will marry you. Then, you and I will start a business."

CHAPTER FOUR

A LARGE, SUNLIT CLASSROOM IN THE FOWLER GLASS Institute. Along one wall stood three pot furnaces, one with its door open blasting heat into the room. In the neatly organized workspace stood a steel-topped table, another with a series of hand tools— diamond shears, jacks, scoring knives—and within arm's reach of this, a bench. A bucket of water and several block molds rested on the floor. Valentin Green Rozsson, fifteen, was about to take his test to become a master glassblower.

The bank of theater seats was occupied by Val's grandmother, Eva Maggiesdaughter, his mother, Roz Baldwin, several aunts and political friends of Eva, and Carey Evasson. Mira sat quietly in the back row.

Val's instructor, Olivia Rosesdaughter, a tiny woman whose muscular brown arms were marked by little burn scars, worked as his assistant.

Val's master's test was to create a goblet. A long pipe rested with one end in the furnace. Inside, molten glass glowed bright yellow. Val, his long red hair tied back, settled his goggles over his eyes, took up the pipe, rotated it, and drew it out with a glowing gather of glass on its end.

Swiftly, turning the pipe in his hands, he carried it to the steel table and rolled the glass on its surface until he had formed it into a truncated cone. He pulled the pipe back, shifted the end to his mouth, and blew steadily into it, still turning it as he blew. Rosesdaughter set a metal cylinder on the floor. When Val had a bubble started he lowered it into the cylinder and blew until the glass expanded to take the shape of the mold. Rosesdaughter split the cylinder and Val removed the bubble, the surface now marked with a pattern.

His face flushed, Val sat down on the bench and rested the pipe across the horizontal rails at either end. He rolled the pipe to keep the incipient goblet from sagging and took up one of the jacks from the table. The lower gravity of the moon was a boon to glassblowers, who did not have to worry so much about the glass deforming as they shaped it. Lunar blown glass pieces could be made to a size not possible on Earth.

Rosesdaughter lit a handtorch and adjusted its blue flame to a few centimeters, then set it beside the bench where Val could reach it. She used another rod, the punty, to pull a second gather, which Val fused to his original bubble and pulled to form a braided stem. Val's gaze remained intent on the work, lips pursed, sober. He fused another gather to the stem and, using pliers, pulled it into a circular base.

With the handtorch he reheated the glass. His face took on a sheen of sweat. Rolling the pipe with the palm of his hand, he flattened the base of the evolving goblet with a wooden paddle, which began to smoke when touched to the near-molten glass. One of the great expenses of glassblowing was replacing these paddles after some period of use. Designers had created paddles from any number of synthetic materials, but the master glassblowers all insisted on cherrywood, no matter the expense.

Mira leaned forward. Val was deft, intense, steady. Heartbreakingly beautiful. His fabrication of the goblet was a dance. Extraordinarily sexy.

She glanced over at Carey. Since their conversation about fatherhood, Carey had been taking more interest in Val. Often, after they had made love, Carey would talk to Mira about how he had felt about Val after he was born, before he and Roz broke up. He told stories about Val, how he had this thing about animals, how he seemed happy all the time. Carey's voice held an affection that she did not recall hearing when he talked about anything else.

Rosesdaughter pulled another small gather of glass. She held the punty with this new glass level while Val, using the diamond shears, fused it to the base of the goblet that was still attached to his blow pipe.

He used large mashers, which he wet in the bucket of water, to cool the end of the bubble attached to his pipe, then, delicately, snapped it off. He traded Rosesdaughter the pipe for the punty with the attached goblet, and now, using jacks and the handtorch, got to work cutting and shaping the lip of the bell at its top.

Forty minutes into the test, as Val was performing the delicate final step of detaching the goblet from the punty, someone approached from behind Mira and sat next to her. Hypatia Camillesdaughter.

"Good afternoon, Mira."

Mira could not have been more surprised. She had not ever spoken with Hypatia outside of the Discussion Group. "Hello."

Hypatia might be there to see Carey, but she had come to sit with Mira, not Carey. Maybe Hypatia wanted to scope out Mira as a rival for his attention. Or maybe it had something to do with Eva and the upcoming election. But still, she had come to sit with Mira.

There was a smattering of applause. Mira turned back to see Val, wearing heat-resistant gloves, raising the goblet. Rosesdaughter, smiling, carried it off to the annealing oven.

Val turned off the handtorch, took off his goggles, wiped his brow, and came forward. Everyone got up to congratulate him. Roz embraced him, as did Eva. Warm voices and laughter. Carey hung back. Val looked over, broke away, and went to him. Carey bear-hugged him. He whispered something into Val's ear, then sent him back to his mother.

"A talented boy," Hypatia said.

Mira turned to her. "What are you doing here?"

"Always so blunt."

One of the women, one of Eva's Matron friends, looked over at them. She frowned.

"Some people complain about it," said Mira. "Professor Camillesdaughter."

"Call me Hypatia, please."

Today Hypatia wore what amounted to a costume: a pale orange short-sleeved dress printed with a pattern of large roses, gathered tightly to show off her waist. A double string of faux pearls around her slender neck. Her blond hair was swept back from her forehead, and she wore the archaic makeup of a European woman of two hundred years ago: powdered cheeks, eyeliner, orange lipstick that matched her dress. The effect of this parody of patriarchal era femininity, on her athletic frame, was pure aggression. That she assumed such flamboyant contradictions annoyed her opponents and attracted her acolytes. She would piss in anybody's water bulb.

Mira didn't think of herself as one of Hypatia's acolytes. She would have given anything for her approval, yet the professor's sudden appearance intimidated her. "You're here to see Carey?"

"I'm here to see you."

"Why?"

"Well, for one thing, I am impressed with what you have achieved as Looker."

Mira tried to maintain her poise. She glanced down at the others on the work floor. The furnace door was closed. While Val and

Rosesdaughter put the workspace back in order, Roz and Carey were talking. He held her left hand as they spoke.

Roz, Mira, Hypatia, all Carey's lovers at one time or another, in one room. It must happen pretty often to Carey, but of course everyone acted, in the good Cousins way, as if any awkwardness would be the height of bad taste. Eva glanced up at Mira and Hypatia, then turned back to her family.

Hypatia calling Mira "Looker" in the presence of Matrons who despised Looker was intended to make her nervous. All right, then. No retreat.

"It's about time somebody figured that out," Mira said. "I'm surprised you didn't get it before now—Hypatia."

Hypatia smiled. "Nicely played."

"Can we avoid the status games and just talk?"

"You know that we can never avoid the status games."

"Right. But it might be easier if we didn't play them here."

"You may not realize it, Mira, but I've had my eye on you for a while," Hypatia said. "Let's leave Looker aside for now. I want to speak to you about something else—the trial of Marysson and Pamelasson. I've wondered since you first came to the Discussion Group what your attitude was about testifying against them."

Mira bit her lip. "They made me testify."

"You could have refused."

"I would have paid for it. I don't have many friends."

"Neither do I. Most people don't have more than one or two real ones." Hypatia leaned toward Mira, touching a finely manicured finger to her leg. "You remind me of myself at your age. I'm being sincere here, Mira."

"Thanks for the alert."

Hypatia smiled.

Val, Roz, Eva, and the others were leaving. Carey came up to their row. "I hope I'm not interrupting," he said. He leaned over and kissed Hypatia. Mira watched his hand slip inside her arm to touch her waist.

He kissed Mira's cheek as well. She felt the warmth of his face.

"I'm surprised to see you here," he said to Hypatia.

"It does you credit to come support your son," Hypatia said. "Not enough men do such things."

"You know about Val?"

"You mentioned him once. But I'm really here to see Mira."

"Oh," Carey said. He shifted from one foot to the other. "Actually, I need to speak with you sometime. Something you might be able to help me with."

"You know I'm always happy to see you."

Carey seemed unusually subdued. "Listen, Mira," he said, "I won't be able to get together with you tonight. Can we talk later?"

"All right," said Mira. She watched the two of them.

"Well, I'll say good-bye, then." Carey nodded to them both and left.

Mira could not follow the currents going on between Hypatia, Carey, Roz, Val, and herself. Was this a political interaction or some interpersonal spider's web? She prided herself on spying political motives, but she wasn't so good at the interpersonal stuff. It was the topic for an hour-long conversation with some intimate girlfriend. Mira didn't have one.

She watched Carey go. She decided to run right at it. She looked Hypatia in the eye. "What is it you want from me?"

"I want you to meet Daquani Jeffersdaughter and Juliette Mariesdaughter."

"Why? What do you need me for?"

"Because you are not like all the other earnest young Reform Party supporters. You're not dazzled by my reputation or afraid of anyone's intellect. What you've accomplished as Looker shows a daring that I don't see in one out of fifty."

It was a heavy load of flattery, the kind Mira had never received from any woman in a position of influence. The fact that she loved hearing it so much made her doubt herself.

"If it comes out that Looker is in the Reform Party," Mira said, "that's not going to help your cause."

"People already think we *are* Looker. In fact, I want Looker to do more, leading up to the vote."

The room had emptied. The light from beyond the big windows was fading. Only Rosesdaughter was still there. She called up to them, "I'm going to close this classroom now. You'll need to leave."

Mira stood. "Thanks."

She turned back to Hypatia. "All right," she said, "I'm in."

It was only later, thinking of the look Eva had given them, that Mira realized Hypatia had chosen the glassblowing as the place to put this proposition so that Eva could see her with Mira. And with Carey. And that the most likely way for her to have found out that Mira was Looker was if Carey had told her.

• • • • •

On the wall of Eva's apartment hung an oil painting by that greatest of the Impressionists, Mary Cassatt, *Jules Being Dried by his Mother*. Fresh from his bath, the long-haired androgynous boy, perhaps six or seven, stands, arms hanging limply by his sides, while his mother embraces him. His right hand touches his mother's left where it holds the towel that strategically covers his groin. The mother's cheeks are round, her Cupid's bow lips bright red. Hair done up, exposing her matronly neck, she is wearing an elaborate gown of white and yellow with a plunging neckline.

This painting had been an unconsidered presence in his life for as long as Carey could remember. In recent years he had very gradually come to hate it. He studied it from where he sat at the table on the terrace. It was a tribute to how respected his mother was that they had such a terrace, overlooking the juniper woods planted by Roz's father twenty years before. Above them the dome reproduced a brilliant night sky. Down the arc of the crater's rim gleamed the lights of the train station. Breezes brushed Carey's face as he leaned back in the comfortable chair.

The family's weekly dinner was a brilliant business. Eva knew everybody, and even those who did not love her respected her, so there was seldom a meal that did not include at least one or two friends, old lovers, artists, political allies and rivals, brilliant scientists, and hangers-on.

These were not formal affairs. Eva accommodated the moods of her guests and steered the conversation their way. His mother might be a genius but she never forced herself into the limelight. She was a remarkable person, and Carey loved her more than he could say. But living in the heart of the Green family was driving him crazy.

Tonight's guests were another former chair of the Board of Matrons, Debra Debrasdaughter, the musician Shari Klarasdaughter, and a professor from the university, Lemmy Odillesson. Shari was so famous that her music was played even in the patriarchies. Debrasdaughter was a sprightly ninety-eight; she'd been born in the first years of the Society on Earth, had served three times as chair, and was respected by all factions in the colony. Calm and funny and a little scatterbrained, she had been Carey's football teacher when he was a boy. Carey had never heard of Odillesson, an awkward genobotanist whose specialty was environmental design.

Then there were the Greens, Eva's sister Patricia and her wife Sylvia, Carey's cousin Zöe, and Zöe's current husband Ngamo. Their seven-year-old twins, Chimalum and Obafemi, whom everyone fussed over, and Zöe's new walk-in boyfriend whose name Carey didn't remember but who wanted to talk about the disappointing showing of the martial arts team in the last Lunar Olympics.

After the salmon soufflé and a dessert of fresh strawberries, the children had been put to bed. Eva opened several bottles of colony wine and served them in a set of glasses that Val had blown himself. Carey finished one glass while the others talked, then had another. He twirled the stem of the glass shaped by his son's breath. Val was expecting Carey that night and still the dinner dragged on. Eva told one of her terrible jokes, something about a young physicist and the indeterminacy principle, and everyone laughed.

"Carey," Debrasdaughter said, "Eva tells me that you're considering taking a job on the *mita*. Congratulations."

His cousins looked at Carey sideways. Zöe's *Ruǎn tā* fan boyfriend seemed surprised. "What? Does that mean you won't be competing anymore? You're going to *work*?"

"I've worked hard all my life," Carey said.

No one responded to that.

"There's going to be some disappointed fans," the man—Stefan, that was his name—said.

"Some disappointed girlfriends, too" said Zöe.

Sylvia said, "Oh, I expect our Carey will find time for them."

"Carey has been seeing Mira Hannasdaughter from the lab," Eva said. "You remember her, Patricia? She's a little shy."

"She's not shy," said Zöe. "She's one of the most difficult women I've ever met. She criticizes everybody she meets. There's not a woman in her graduate class she hasn't alienated."

"Well," Eva said, "there are reasons. As soon as she reached majority her mother dumped her brother onto her, left her to raise him without any help. She was fourteen, trying to take care of a ten-year-old, and she wasn't any good at it."

"Then she should have gotten help. There's more help available for child rearing than for anything else in the Society."

"She didn't do anything wrong," Carey said. "She just had bad luck."

"Did I hear about this?" asked Debrasdaughter. "It was seven or eight years ago. Her brother died in an accident?"

"Yes," said Carey. "She's never really gotten over it."

For a while they discussed the irresponsibility of Mira's mother. Some women were just not meant to have children. It was unfortunate that any so unsuited to it felt they had to, and embarrassing that the system sometimes failed to step in when such situations arose.

"What I'd like to know is what Mira was doing at Val's mastership exam last week," Patricia said.

"More to the point," said Sylvia, "what was Hypatia Camillesdaughter doing there?"

"Talking to Mira, apparently," Eva said.

"Two lovers at once, Carey," Ngamo said. "Uncomfortable?"

"I doubt she had anything to say to that young woman," Patricia said to Eva. "She's testing *you*. This election."

"I'm not sure Hypatia isn't right," Eva said. "I understand why the Founders set up our electoral system, but it only leads to unrest among men—and the women who take their part."

"The average man in the Society has as much freedom as any man in human history. They don't realize how bad it is out in the patriarchies."

"Next thing you know, male gangs," said Stefan darkly. "These Spartans."

"Men have real grievances," Klarasdaughter said. "And if we don't solve them ourselves, we just give the patriarchs a pretext to condemn us."

"They don't care about the condition of their own people," Ngamo said. "Don't you agree, Professor Odillesson?"

Until now Odillesson had been content to listen in birdlike silence. Startled, he looked around the table, and finally said, "I don't know anything about politics. I guess there are many unhappy young men? There's so much that they could spend their time and energy on."

Odillesson was about as far from an alpha male as one could get and still carry the XY chromosomes. Yet Carey felt a surge of envy for the man. He had work that mattered to him, a purpose to his life. Carey said, "I think, if you don't take Hypatia seriously, on election day you are going to be very surprised."

"Maybe you can tell me why anybody would trust her," Zöe said. "She's such a phony. On Monday she's a transgressive radical, on Tuesday she valorizes the patriarchy. She feints to the left, she steps right. She's a rarefied intellectual spouting jargon-laden theories; she's a woman of the people chanting slogans only a halfwit would credit. The only constant is that she's right and the rest of us are hypocrites and fools."

"She seems to have gotten you pretty excited," Carey said.

That brought the conversation to a halt.

His aunt Patricia said, "Come to think of it, Carey, I was almost as surprised to see you at the exam as I was to see them. You've never taken much interest in Val's education. You didn't say a word when we talked about him serving this apprenticeship."

"I don't recall being consulted about that," Carey said.

"No one asked you because you never cared," said Zöe. She didn't add, but he could hear her thinking, *You were probably too busy fucking Hypatia*. They never thought of him in relation to Val, and never would, because the degree to which Carey did or did not interact with him had no legal consequences.

"*Ruăn tā* takes a lot of Carey's time," Ngomo said.

"Apparently not anymore," said Stefan, with a short laugh.

How lovely it would be to get fifteen seconds alone with Stefan in the ring. "No, not so much anymore," Carey said.

"You're going to be a voter," said Patricia. "So what was it you were talking to Hypatia and that young woman about?"

Carey flipped his napkin onto the table. "We were planning our overthrow of the Society of Cousins." He got up and left the terrace.

"Carey?" his mother called after him.

"Let him go," he heard Patricia say.

"Too much wine," said Sylvia.

Carey retreated to his room, mad at them, mad at himself. He stood at the open window looking out over the woods, then began stuffing clothes into his backpack. Other than his mother, he was the only person in the apartment with a private room. Imprisonment by privilege, the Spartans called it. Well, soon he would have to get by on the resources that he could earn for himself.

He lay on his bed and stared at the ceiling, waiting for the guests to leave. From outside, Hector, Eva's cat, leapt onto the windowsill, then launched himself across the room to the bed. A large black-and-white tom, Hector terrorized the birds in the woods, but despite his lunar-gravity leaping ability never seemed to catch any. He butted his head up against Carey's chin until Carey scratched him behind the ears. His purr was very loud.

At one time the conversation at the dinner table would have floated past Carey without incident. Now there were trapdoors in every exchange. All his life people had praised him for his sunny disposition, how deftly he dealt with conflict and wryly sidestepped problems that tied others into knots. They loved the insouciance of *Lune et l'autre*. He was getting to the point where he considered that younger self some sort of dunce. It was as if his skin were raw from being flayed, and the slightest touch made him flinch. But who had flayed him? He had to admit that, with a lone exception, his life had been without difficulty. He had suffered hardly a single thwarted desire.

Hector settled down at the end of the bed and went to sleep. Carey listened as the guests finally left, and then he went out to help clean up. He didn't speak to anyone as he busied himself clearing the table. After the rest of the family had turned in, Eva came out to him on the terrace.

"Are you all right?" she asked. "Is something wrong?"

He avoided her eyes. "Nothing worth talking about now."

"Well, when you're ready," she said.

She retired to her room. When the apartment was silent he got his backpack and slipped out.

Most of the Greens lived in this same neighborhood, but a year after Val had been born Roz had moved away. Carey understood that he, and his series of girlfriends, were the reason. His aunt was right—it was only lately that Carey had renewed his interest in Val. He should have been more engaged. He could tell Val things about being a man that Val would never get from Roz or Eva or the congress of women who surrounded them. As an uncle Carey might attempt that role with nephews. But with his son? Not so easy.

Roz's apartment was underground, in a semicircular residential concourse with a café on the corner and a playground in the center of the loop. Some Ag workers bound for the late shift idled in the café. A robot street polisher moved slowly over the pavement, whirring steadily.

Beyond the café, the roof of the neighborhood rose to twenty meters over the playground, the lights currently turned low over a play structure, swings, a pit full of colored building blocks, and a climbing wall with auto-belaying ropes. Two teens, too old for this place, sat on the benches near a circular trampoline where a third bounced, doing slow somersaults. It was Val.

Carey sat on a bench away from the boys. He watched Val twirl and twist in low-G while still maintaining their conversation. The boys were talking about mountain climbing; they planned, when they were older, to do Mons Huygens in the Lunar Apennines, the tallest mountain on the moon.

"Forget Mons Huygens," Val said. "We should climb Mons Veneris."

"Been there," one of the others said. "Overrated."

The talk devolved into a series of sex jokes. Carey had heard them all; Jesse had told one of the same ones at the last Salon.

On one of his bounces, Val's eyes locked with Carey's, and he grinned but did not stop his twisting aerial ballet. After a few more minutes he flexed his legs when he hit the trampoline and came to rest. "Gotta go," he told the others. "See you tomorrow."

Val picked up his pack and came over to Carey.

"Sorry I'm late," Carey said. It would help if they got settled before Roz realized Val was not coming home. "When does your mother expect you?"

"Not until twenty-three hundred."

Twenty minutes from now. "Let's go, then."

They descended a level to the tramway and rode it to the second major corridor south. Carey felt a wave of affection for Val. Trouble would come of this, but he would deal with Roz, he would deal with Eva. He had his son with him, and they were going to live together, no woman in their home, just the two of them.

On the tram, Carey watched their reflections in the glass of the opposite window. Val was more slender, more gangly, but he could see himself in his son's face. Val looked pensive.

"Do you know your father?" Val asked.

"I never met him," Carey said. "I asked your grandmother about him. She said she was with him for only a few months, when he did some materials engineering. He never took an interest in me. Later I learned he left the Society, moved to Mars."

"Do you ever wish he'd been around?"

"I didn't think of him. I lived in the middle of the Green family. Eva was in the lab a lot, and then she was in politics. But at the end of every day she would always sit down with me and ask me how my day was. She listened to whatever I had to say. Then she'd tell me some terrible joke."

"They are terrible. I like them."

"When I was six I told her, 'Stop trying to be funny. You can't make a joke.' 'I made you,' she said."

They got off the tram and climbed a level to the apartment of Donald and Devlin Irisson. Carey expected the place to be dark, but the lights were on and the beat of music sounded through the walls. When he hit the door chime it was a full minute before Donald answered, face sweaty, a sloppy grin on his face. "Carey!" He hugged Carey and kissed his cheek. "Come in, Cousin!"

Carey held back. "You were going to be gone by now. I've got Val with me."

"Bring him in! Jada is here, and Llana, and a couple of the Solon sisters."

Val peered past Carey. "Looks like fun."

"We're not here to party, Donald. This is serious."

Donald's grin became cynical. "It's a serious party."

"You promised us the use of the place."

"Use it all you want. We'll be out tomorrow. Couple of days at the latest."

Carey drew a deep breath. "You know what this is about. I'm not playing games."

"I guess there's a first time for everything." Donald closed the door in their faces.

Carey sighed. He'd had to think hard to come up with two men living on their own not under the close observation of their mothers and sisters. Donald and Devlin were as close to useless layabouts as the Society produced. He felt humiliated to have them treat him like this.

"What now?" Val asked.

To take Val back to Roz would be even more humiliating. He should have involved Mira, but he'd wanted to do all this alone. He'd told himself that keeping Mira out of it would save her trouble when it came out, since she worked with Roz, and for Eva, but it was more pride than strategy. Too much pride was foolish: Men got themselves into trouble when they mixed up making the smart decision with impressing people by the size of their dicks.

"Come on," he said. They rode to the concourse where Mira lived. The little park with dwarf maples opposite her apartment was quiet. Carey hit Mira's door chime.

Mira answered, wearing shorts and a loose shirt. She looked at Carey, at Val, then back at Carey. "Is this what I think it is?"

The surprise in her voice was not encouraging. "May we come in?"

Mira opened the door wider and stepped aside. Her apartment was larger than she ought to have commanded—three full rooms and a private bath. By rights when her brother died she should have been made to move out, but she had managed, by finding a woman to move in and then chasing her out a few months later, to slip past the housing authority.

She folded down two chairs and a small table from the wall, then pulled the tabs on three bulbs of tea. While they heated she drew over her workstation chair and sat.

Her silence made Carey nervous. "Can Val stay here for a couple of nights?"

"You didn't arrange an apartment before taking Val," Mira said flatly.

"He didn't take me," Val said. "I came on my own."

"I had a promise of an apartment," Carey said. "But Donald and Devlin Irisson are still in it. They'll be out in a couple of days."

"And you couldn't wait."

"Val didn't want to wait, and I didn't want to make him wait."

Mira sipped tea from her bulb. "Yes, you can stay," she said to Val.

"Thanks. Where?"

She pointed to the only closed door, and when Val hesitated, got up and went into the room with him. Carey listened to them talking through the open door. "My horse!" Val said. "Wow, you've got a whole herd."

"My brother used to play with them when he was little. This one's named Comet."

Carey sipped his tea, a bad Earl Grey. That was Mira: nothing psychoactive.

"Has Carey told your mother?" he heard Mira say.

"Not yet," Val said.

"Put your things in this drawer," Mira said, and came out, closing the door behind her.

She said, "Call Roz."

Carey put down the bulb. "Please don't treat me like this."

"Like what?"

"Like a child."

"Look, I don't know how you got him, but unless she is okay with it, Roz will be looking for him already. If this comes across as abduction, you'll be a criminal. So you need to call Roz and tell her Val is here. Let her talk to him."

He struggled to keep calm. "You've been pushing me to take this step for months. Now you act like I've done something outrageous."

"Because you've done it stupidly. Why didn't you at least tell me?"

"You should respect my choices, even if you disagree with them."

"Roz will have the constables on you if you don't call."

"I know Roz, you don't."

"What do you think is going to happen when she can't locate him?"

He ran a hand through his hair. Mira, gearing up. Why had he ever spent any time with this woman? He had the beginnings of a headache. "Give me some credit, Mira. I'm not a fool."

"No, you're not," she conceded. "But Carey, you need to tell her as soon as possible. Not only that"—her voice got lower—"you need to go public. Talk to Hypatia. We need to get the Reform Party in on this."

"This isn't political."

"What could be more political than a man claiming parental rights?"

"Fathers *have* rights."

"Not if there's a mother in the picture."

The door to the bedroom opened and Val stood there. "I'm not going back."

Carey and Mira looked at him. Carey said, "You're not going back. No matter what anyone says."

"Right," said Val. "So maybe you two ought to kiss and make up."

Carey said, "I'm going to call your mother. I want you to log into school tomorrow as if nothing has changed. It's vital."

Mira came up behind Carey and surreptitiously knuckled him in the ribs. "All right, Val," she said. "Let's fold down your bed."

Val kissed Carey. "Good night."

"Good night, Spike." Carey had to swallow. Mira took Val's arm and led him back into Marco's room, closed the door most of the way, but left a gap.

Carey opened a small window on Mira's pixwall and called Roz. Her face appeared instantly. "Carey. Do you know where Val is?"

"He's with me. We're at Mira's."

She crossed her arms. "He can't keep disappearing without telling me. He disabled his chip again."

"I blocked it."

"Why would you do that?" She sounded genuinely surprised.

"I didn't want you to interfere. In a day or so we'll be living in our own apartment. I'm telling you so you won't worry—" The look on Roz's face reminded him of the uncertain girl she'd been when she'd first immigrated to the Society.

"Why are you doing this? When have I ever kept him from you?"

"I love Val as much as your father loved you. Your father took care of you."

"Until he killed himself," she said. Her shadowed face moved close to the camera. A faint glint in her eyes. "I'm not disputing your love for Val."

"Please. Sleep on this, Roz, and we can talk tomorrow."

"You bet we'll talk."

"Good night, then."

"Nothing better happen to him, Carey."

Yet another woman who didn't trust him. "Good night," he said. He closed the window.

He stood, stretched, and rubbed his temples. He was going to have to share Mira's bed. She had not come out of the room yet.

Carey went to the door and peeked in. In the faint light he saw Val was already asleep in Marco's drop-down bed. Mira sat on the edge, face turned three-quarters away. Mira seldom spoke of Marco, but Carey had seen a video—a dark boy, strikingly like a younger Mira. You could not sleep with a woman as much as Carey had with Mira without learning something of the grief she contained.

As Carey watched, she reached out and brushed Val's hair gently away from his cheek.

• • • • •

During her midday break at Materials, Mira sucked down a protein mix at her workstation while paging through the colony forums. Though he'd tried to keep their situation private, news of Carey taking his son has gotten out and debate over him and Val was getting heated. Lots of Discussion Group agitprop, well written but marred by cant, competed with gospel-spouting Matrons talking about the Terrible and Enlightening History of Women's (*and Men's!*) Struggles to Establish a New Society Free of Violence. Then there were those for whom the politics of child custody was a snooze, but who relished the spectacle of the Green family being discomfited in public.

Mira was about to go back to her work on the fullerene project when her Aide told her Carey was calling.

"I'll take it," she said. She threw the call onto her workstation screen but kept the audio private.

Carey looked grim. "I can't believe you did this without asking me."

"Did what?" The betrayal in his eyes made her feel sick.

"You know what. The new Looker video. Ten minutes ago it went live all over the colony."

She hadn't seen him much lately; they were both too busy. A few days after Carey and Val had shown up on her doorstep, they moved out again, not to the Irissons' place, but to an apartment Hypatia had obtained. Carey took a job in the aquaculture plant. Val went to school. Mira visited them, but the dynamic between her and Carey was completely different with Val there. The sex was different. It was all different.

Carey was not eager to have his cause taken up by the Reform Party. "The more public we make this," he had told Mira, "the less Roz is going to like it."

"Of course she won't like it. But like Hypatia says, you need to get the public on your side."

"It's not Hypatia's decision to make."

As Mira had expected, Hypatia had leapt at the opportunity for propaganda that Carey and Val offered. Their story became the talk of the colony. Mandy Moirasdaughter wanted them on her talk show; to Hypatia's disappointment, Carey refused. Recognizing Mira's role in all this, Hypatia drew her into her circle of academics, politicians, activists, and artists. It was like nothing Mira had ever experienced. They thought she was funny. They sought her opinion. They openly wondered how she had wormed her way into Eva's lab and assumed it must be part of some political move. Juliette Mariesdaughter, Hypatia's

friend and university colleague, quizzed Mira about Carey's commitment to the cause.

When she didn't simply wave such psychodramas aside, Hypatia
relished them. It took a topologist to keep track of the ever-changing
romantic geometry of her inner circle. As far as Mira knew, Carey's off-
and-on thing with Hypatia was not renewed, but it still bothered her.
She wished it didn't.

Hypatia asked Mira to create new Looker videos, and Mira went to
work on *Fathers and Sons*, eight minutes on parenting as a subversive act.
A week ago she had brought her rough cut over to Hypatia's apartment to
show to her privately. Hypatia brewed tea and they sat in the living room,
side by side on the sofa like friends, like equals, while the video ran on the
wall. Mira tried to gauge her reaction. Hypatia leaned back, relaxed, her
chin slightly lifted. The line of her jaw was beautiful.

The video ended with an image of Val and Carey on the flying
stage of the Diana Tower, strapped into their wings, the wind tossing
their hair, looking like heroes of some Constructivist film of the 1920s.

"Well?" Mira asked.

Hypatia put down her teacup, turned to Mira, and kissed her on
the lips.

Her breath warmed Mira's cheek. "You like it?"

"How could I not like it?" Hypatia said. "It's exactly what we
need. The sooner we post this the better."

Mira couldn't tell whether the high she felt was the tea or something else. "There's one thing," she said. "Carey hasn't seen it yet. He

doesn't know that I've used footage of him and Val. He may not like that."

Hypatia drew her legs onto the sofa so she faced Mira. "Will he make you change it?"

"I couldn't say."

"It's great work, but we'll do it however you want."

What did Mira want? Well, she didn't want to have to cut Val and Carey out of the video—it would lose half its force. Given the reticence he'd shown lately, it was quite possible he would insist. It was frustrating. Carey stood to benefit from the Reform movement as much as anyone, yet he put this narrow vision of his interests first.

Hypatia's question was a test. Did Mira have the commitment to make a tough decision? Would she let the fact that she was sleeping with Carey, that they had both been sleeping with him, affect her judgment? She wanted to act the way Hypatia did. Who they were sleeping with was not central. They had things to accomplish. The future of the Society depended on it, and in the end Carey would recognize that.

"No, I don't think we should tell him," she said.

"Let me take it from here, then." Hypatia smiled. "More tea?"

Hypatia enlisted a select cadre of Discussion Group members to get the graffito posted in three times the number of places that Mira had been able to reach. Hypatia clearly enjoyed letting them wonder where and how she'd gotten the video.

"This is going to raise more suspicions about you," said Juliette. "Half the colony already thinks you are Looker."

"*Epater les Matrones* may be my hobby, Juliette, but you know I'm not Looker."

"If it gets out that we're helping Looker, that won't matter. A lot of the public consider Looker a criminal. We're trying to persuade people."

"We're trying to win an election. The ones who object to this video can't be persuaded; they have to be replaced."

So now it was out there, suddenly appearing in forty places around the colony, and Carey was furious. Mira had never seen him this angry—it was not his nature to take offense when he could as easily laugh something off. She tried to convince him he was too well known to keep the struggle between him and Roz private. "Please calm down," she told him. "The publicity will be a benefit, if Roz chooses to contest the issue."

"*If* she chooses to contest?" Carey said. "The only reason she hasn't asserted her maternal rights is that she doesn't want to take Val back against his will. Everybody in the Green family wants her to. Now everybody in the colony will."

"Don't be so sure of that," Mira said. "There are a lot of people, men and women, on your side of this."

"And how many of those men are Spartans? I don't want anything to do with them, and I don't want Val to have anything to do with them. You can bet Roz will be aware of that possibility."

He hung up.

The colony forum reappeared on her screen. The first comment up was someone reacting to her new video.

Behind her Mira heard the normal sound of the workplace. So far she'd managed to keep her extracurricular life from affecting her work at Materials, but Mira had already felt the eyes of her co-workers on her and Roz, heard the whispers in the lunchroom. Mira spending her break at her station checking out debate forums was not doing much to keep her new status as a confidant of Hypatia Camillesdaughter a secret. She wondered if Tanya at the next station had heard Mira's half of the conversation.

Before she could get very far back into her work, a summons appeared on Mira's screen.

> **PRIORITY:** All lab personnel are requested to meet in the conference room at 1400.

No agenda was attached. There had been nothing on the lab calendar about a meeting.

Tanya called over to her. "Did you get this meeting summons?"

"Yes," Mira said.

Parvati came by and leaned on her desk. "What is this about?"

"I have no idea." Given the drama she'd already gone through today, Mira did not fancy seeing Roz at the meeting. She kept her head down and worked until 1350, then grabbed her notebook and headed with the others to the conference room.

The lab's three principal investigators sat evenly spaced around the long table, and the grad students, interns, and support staff found places between them or perched on benches and stools, chatting. Roz sat beside Eva, her eyes on Mira. Mira raised her eyebrows at her. Roz broke eye contact.

Eva tapped a knuckle on the table for attention.

"Thank you all for coming. Let me get right to the reason for this meeting: I'm going to ask that you suspend your regular work to take on a task that we need completed as quickly as possible. There's been a policy change by the Board of Matrons. Roz and Daniel will assign each of you a portion of the research database. In most cases it will be related to your area of specialization. We need you to scrub from the public record all of the research that has come out of any Society of Cousins scientific laboratory in the last twenty-five years."

Mira looked around. The room was full of puzzled faces.

Eva continued. "This includes abstracts, scientific papers, drafts of those papers, correspondence, raw data, budgets related to any research, records of personnel attached to any projects, purchase orders, manifests, news reports, videos, and at least a half dozen other sorts of data.

"We also need to delete any papers by non-Cousins investigators to which we have had reference.

"We will not confine ourselves to physics, chemistry, or materials research, but also delete all work in biotech, environmental science, genobotany, energy research, engineering—it all has to go.

"In addition, we ask you to go onto non-Society data sites and locate copies of Cousins research. You will pass along any links you find to a team that has been set up at Information Resources, and they will take over from there.

"We are going to store all of this work, of course. We will transfer copies to an independent server with no connection to the SSS&E DataNet or any other solar system information network. Our job, simply put, is to embargo all scientific research that has been done in the SoC over the last twenty-five years.

"I am sure you must have questions. Now is a good time to ask them, and I'll do my best to answer."

The room was silent. Then Alex Sofiasdaughter said, "Why?"

"This is about the election," Tanya said. "The Board's afraid the Reform Party is going to take over and promote a policy of complete openness. It's a pre-emptive move."

Eva calmly said, "The Board has decided that scientific engagement with the outside world has not served the Society well. The patriarchal colonies persist in characterizing our work as a threat. We've tried transparency, and it has not muted their paranoia. Instead, they seek in our publications the slenderest evidence that we present some danger, deliberately misinterpreting our work, distorting our results. They look for things they can use to justify sanctions, or worse. The OLS Science Committee queries our research, we answer, they go back and concoct some new imaginary threat, then query again. The cycle repeats itself.

"The Board wants to cut off such speculations once and for all. Isolation worked well for sixty years."

Parvati said, "This is insane. Closing off access will only increase their suspicions. They'll take it as proof that we have something to hide."

"That's not the view of the Board of Matrons," Eva replied.

"*Do* we have something to hide?" Mira asked.

"We have no weapons," Eva said. "We don't do weapons research."

One of the postdocs, Patrick Caitlinsson, noted for his obsession with his reputation, jumped into the silence. "We're scientists. The free flow of information is essential to our work. If we can't publish we might as well give up."

"I don't think you really believe that," said Eva. "The Board has no intention of discontinuing research. They just don't want us to publish."

"But to be isolated from the scientific community will hinder our work," Parvati said.

Patrick added, "And anything we do discover, we won't be able to claim priority."

"Can we still access the work of non-Cousins scientists?" Peter asked.

"Yes, of course," Eva said.

"But this will have a chilling effect," said Tanya. "Outsiders will wonder what's going on. They won't be as forthcoming as in the past."

"This is going to draw much more attention than if we just proceeded as we have been," said Parvati.

"All I can tell you," Eva said, "is that the Board has considered that and has made this decision. Transparency has not stilled patriarchal suspicions. The Board believes that we should return to the minimal contact policies of earlier years."

"Minimal contact!" Patrick shook his head. "This is a complete isolation!"

And so the discussion went, for an hour or more. Mira kept her mouth shut. They were sent away, grumbling.

Daniel Karensson came by Mira's station with a list of twenty-year-old work she should begin on. She spent the next two hours dredging up lab reports, equipment invoices, personnel budgets, and attendance records regarding research that was done when she was five years old. It was a tedious chore. From her desk Mira retrieved the ring she had found months ago and played with it as she worked. She spun it until it glided across the surface, a spherical metallic blur, taking a minute or more before it lost enough angular momentum to begin to wobble and fall. The reasons Eva had given did not make sense. The others were right when they said closing off access to their research would only increase outsiders' suspicions.

Late in the day, Eva stopped by Mira's workstation. "Mira, do you have a minute for me in my office?"

"Is something wrong?"

"I just want to talk, if that's okay."

Mira followed her to the modest office. It was sparsely furnished: a desk with workstation, four titanium mesh chairs around a low table.

Beside the station were pictures of Carey and Roz as teens, and one of a younger, smiling Eva with a good-looking red-haired man, his arm around her waist. The pixwall was tuned to an image of the colony exterior from high above. The dome, covered in regolith, looked almost like a natural surface feature, a crater filled with dust smoothed over to form a convex lid. Lights glared at the airlock complexes and in lines along the surface roads to outlying labs and the helium strip mines.

Mira took a seat. On the wall opposite hung a plaque.

Nurture life.

Walk in love and beauty.

Trust the knowledge that comes through the body.

Speak the truth about conflict, pain, and suffering.

Take only what you need.

Think about the consequences of your actions for seven generations.

Approach the taking of life with great restraint.

Practice great generosity.

Repair the web.

The same creed graced the walls of half the Goddess-worshippers in the colony. Marco and Mira had made vicious fun of these pieties, inventing parodies until they rolled on the floor in laughter. *Walk in a straight line. Take only what you can get away with. Repair the spider!*

"Can I get you something to drink?" Eva said.

"No, thank you. What is this about?"

Eva sat. She was sixty or so, a decade or more older than Hypatia, but though she did not invest in rejuvenation treatments, she was a striking woman. It was her poise that drew people, and her clarity. "It seemed to me that you were as upset as anyone at the research embargo, but you kept quiet."

"Everybody else said what needed to be said."

"The one question you did ask, I evaded. We don't have any weapons research. But we do have things that we'd rather the patriarchies didn't know about."

"Like what?'

"I'd rather not say right now."

Mira couldn't help laughing. "Why call me in if you're not going to tell? Unless you're trying to get credit for honesty without actually telling me anything."

"Because you are intelligent and resourceful. You don't accept things without a reason. I'm asking that you not pursue this, for now."

"This embargo isn't going to work. Like the others said, it will only inspire more paranoia."

"I agree. But we have to abide by the Board's decision. If they're right, then the situation will quiet; if you're right, the situation will change and we'll have to make new decisions. If I were to bet, I would bet on the latter."

Eva kept her eyes on Mira's. Mira tried not to squirm. "There's another reason I wanted to speak with you," Eva said. "I hope you won't mind my saying some things I've observed about you. I mean them only in kindness."

"All right," Mira said warily.

"Pushing girls out of the family at an early age doesn't work for everyone. I hated leaving my mother. You didn't care for yours, I gather, but being on your own hasn't been good for you. You're a loner. I was, too. I trusted others and was taken advantage of. It took me a long time to get past that, but I needed to. To live in a defensive crouch is deadening.

"Your wariness is understandable. Your tough-mindedness is absolutely necessary to the future of the Society. I hope that the losses you've suffered will not kill your open-heartedness." Eva looked down at her hands. "It's hard to lose someone you love."

This was about as far from anything she could have imagined Eva wanting to talk about as Mira could conceive. "What are you getting at?"

"I'm offering you a permanent job in Materials. Being engaged in the work has given me a place, and from that I built outward to create my life. There's a chance for you here if you want it. Think it over."

Mira recalled the look Eva had given her and Hypatia at the glass-blowing demonstration. "Thank you," she said.

"You earned it. Here's another thing: Why don't you come to the

Green family picnic? You know Val, you know Carey, you know Roz, and even me, a little. Come and meet the rest of us."

This was too much. "Why are you doing this?"

"One reason is that you take a legitimate interest in Val. Roz thinks you're behind Carey's taking Val. I don't agree with her."

"Are you going to side with Carey against Roz?"

"I would do just about anything for Carey, but I'm interested in what's best for Val."

"So is Carey."

"I see that. Maybe this conflict between Carey and Roz can help work that out. Carey could use more responsibility." Eva absently tapped her fingers on her desktop, then suddenly stopped. She smiled at Mira. "Any questions?"

Mira had a score of questions. "No," she said.

"Well, then, give my offer some thought and let me know in a week or two." Eva rose, and hugged Mira, and opened the door. "The picnic is in Sobieski Park on the fifteenth."

"Thank you," Mira said.

Later, as Mira rode the tram among others going off-shift, watching the concourse glide by, her thoughts spun between wonder and doubt. Open-hearted? A permanent job in Materials? The Green family picnic?

A connection with the Greens would make Mira the envy of every scheming young woman in the colony. But Eva's matronly confidences triggered Mira's every suspicion. Her sincerity was either a sign of naiveté, which seemed impossible in somebody who had held as many political offices as Eva, or a stratagem. There was something willed about it. Mira expected wheels-within-wheels mental games from Hypatia; she did not know what to make of Eva.

That two of the most powerful women in the colony were vying for Mira's loyalty was some crazy opportunity. It left her extremely edgy. Her entire life Mira had wanted to believe that at some level she was extraordinary, yet she had been convinced that any strengths she had would never be recognized. Nothing could make her question if she was worth anyone's notice more than this attention.

Just as the tram reached her station, Mira's Aide whispered a message from Carey into her ear: *Roz has filed for the return of Val. There's going to be a hearing.*

• • • • •

From the SoC Forum

DeepThinker

Carey Evasson is at the apex of the masculinity that expresses itself in physicality, men who use their bodies as honed tools. They submit themselves to extreme discipline, push themselves to their limits and beyond. Athletes, dancers, acrobats, actors. Such men are romanticized in our Society, their lives honored and stories told. Though in theory such skills can be transferred to certain utilitarian jobs classified as work, there are few such jobs.

One big disadvantage for men who define themselves by this masculinity is that they have less access to that masculinity that defines itself in terms of technical knowledge, science, the professions. The founders of the Society did not place these different masculinities in a hierarchy, and encouraged men to express their maleness in any or all of them, but in practice these symbolic constructs—and others—are frequently in conflict.

Few men can identify with and perform equally in all, and the fact that the masculinity of professionalism has much more practical utility means that physical masculinity, though it might make for fame and sexual desirability, is slighted in the world of work. Carey is great in bed. Carey can't get a good job.

He might have hoped to be a political leader, but given the unhappy history of the patriarchies, the masculinity that defines itself in terms of domination is not allowed to express itself politically in the SoC. Though he has some of the makings of one, there are no places here for corporate CEOs or generals.

Descartes Before the Horse
Stop talking about him as if he's a case study. He's a human being.

DeepThinker

@Descartes: Of course he's a human being. I'm trying to
define what sort of man he is.

JPK

You've only got the one life, and you better do something
worthwhile with it. Can a man find that in the Society
the way he can in one of the other colonies? That's the
existential question.

Acrobat

It's Hypatia Camillesdaughter who's behind this. If the
proposition to extend the franchise passes, she will
run the Society. Is this the person you want making
fundamental decisions for all of us? She's the female
Thomas Marysson.

DeepThinker

Carey is an example of what Hypatia is fighting for. The
Reform Party's opponents might plausibly warn against
the male warrior, but it's harder to raise the alarm about
a man who seeks to express himself as a nurturer. He is
simultaneously a throwback to the male founders and
a harbinger of the new man. Opponents mutter sourly
that the radicals are using fatherhood; they say, what is

fatherhood but patriarchy? But the image of Carey and Val flying together in Looker's latest is hard to argue against.

Descartes Before the Horse

@Acrobat: We have a constitutional system. There are features built into it to prevent any one person from gaining too much authority. They've been in place and working for more than eighty years. Removing artificial restrictions on the franchise won't change that.

OldGuy

Carey's mother, Valentin's grandmother, is one of the most influential women in the Society. Carey Evasson has been a significant person since he was a teenager—remember *Lune et l'autre*? Val's grandfather on his mother's side was Jack Baldwin, whose forest you can go sit in. You should do that sometime, and look out at the place that people like them made. This is just another act in a long story.

NewGirl

@OldGuy: Is there a point to your aimless rambling?

Entropy's Child

The point isn't fatherhood or custody or voting. It's male

demonism. The history of the human race is one of mindless slaughter by men or groups of men motivated by issues of masculinity that have more to do with evolutionary psychology than culture. They'll say they are killing for freedom, or for God, or for the welfare of their children, or for love. But that's just a veneer. Not all men are equally whipsawed by these impulses—or else we couldn't exist—but check out the rhetoric of the Spartans and get back to me. Biology can be moderated but it can't be ignored, any more than you can ignore a black hole at the center of your solar system. I'm afraid the Society is being sucked back into that black hole.

AnotherMother

All this talk about Evasson obscures the fact that the basic issue is what is best for his son. Evasson has been the beneficiary of every privilege our polity has to offer. Stop talking about him.

The problem here is Roz Baldwin. She came from Earth, and she was raised by her father, and so even though she's lived among us for twenty years she doesn't understand the Society. She let this situation get out of hand, and now the welfare of her son should be taken out of hers. The Board should take Val back and put him in the custody of his grandmother. Let his mother, and Carey—if he really cares at all, and is not just using Val to increase his celebrity—see him on some strictly controlled basis. Too many people's welfare, beyond their own, is at stake.

RealGuy

@DeepThinker: stop trying to understand Carey—you can't.

Men know what Carey's going through in a way no woman ever can. Every day we navigate the world of female hegemony. The woman walking down the concourse beside us lives in a different reality.

Cousins women simply can't accept the limitations of their epistemology. The Society's history of persecution by patriarchy makes it easy for them to believe there's nothing that goes beyond the properly schooled female's understanding. But the way men survive is by constructing an oppositional consciousness that functions in their every interaction. This way of seeing is inaccessible to the female.

It's hard for our sisters to see that, and painful for those who accept it. It may seem exclusionary for us to claim the inviolate nature of male consciousness. But there it is.

DeepThinker

@RealGuy: why do you assume that I am female?

Tiresias

I'm sick of all this bipolar thinking. "Male" and "female" are categories that apply completely to no one. To the degree that the Society insists on forcing everyone into those crude pigeonholes, it is doomed.

NewGirl

I hope that people are prepared for the trouble that will come if the Reform Party loses the election. The patriarchies are watching us. What will they, through the OLS, do if the Reform movement is crushed? I think violence is coming to the SoC.

Norasdaughter

Hypatia Camillesdaughter and Carey Evasson are agents of Persepolis.

• • • • •

Mira, Carey, and Val met Hypatia, Juliette, and the rally organizers in the refectory near the square. Mira had trouble liking Juliette. Her voice—pitched low, full of drama—made Mira's skin crawl, so she asked Val if he wanted to take a walk. But Val was excited to be in on the planning, and said no.

Feeling useless, Mira got up to go outside.

"Wait," Hypatia said.

Today Hypatia was dressed like the most conservative of Matrons in a simple buff tunic, her hair in a very short cut she had adopted as the election approached. She drew Mira over to another table.

"I want you on the stage with me today," she said. "You know Carey, you know Val. On that first night they came to see you before anyone else."

"I don't make speeches."

"No speech. Just tell your story. You're a young woman, not political, on the side of change."

"Hypatia, I'm Looker."

"Nobody knows that." It was true. By now everybody in and out of the Reform Party was convinced Hypatia was Looker. Even though Mira had wanted her identity kept secret, she was annoyed.

"I can't do it," Mira said.

"You're not used to public appearances, but you will be. I see it in you. Public attention is power. You can change things."

"Not this way."

Hypatia sighed. "All right. But do me one favor: At the custody hearing I want you to speak for Carey. Will you do that for me, and Carey, and Val?"

"All right. Can I go now?"

"Go."

Mira left the refectory.

Kamal Vashtisson Square was a small underground plaza. Vashtisson, a noted architect, had designed the apartment clusters that spread along the west interior of the crater; if you turned on the public information app in your Aide you could see an image of him sitting on a bench in the square. Surrounding the square were the refectory, a gym, and a nursery school. In its middle some red-barked Japanese crepe myrtles grew in big planters. Vashtisson would be dismayed by the dull space they had named after him.

Today a low stage fronting a five-by-eight-meter screen had been erected at one end, in preparation for the rally. Mira climbed up on the wall of a planter so she could get a better look at the square.

A crowd was gathering. Men wearing work clothes were outnumbered by better dressed non-voters living on the Men's Standard. Some wore video shirts that showed images of their children, and sliding across their shoulders the slogan "A working father." Claiming concerned fatherhood was the new fad, a statement that you cared about more than sex, which was a good way to get laid.

Transgendered women, whose grievances exceeded those of men, and whose cause was part of the Reform platform, were there in significant numbers. Two students from the Discussion Group handed out signs: "No Revolution Without Men" and "XX ≈ XY." Around the edges of the square nervous constables, male and female, spoke in one another's ears in order to be heard over the hum of the growing crowd.

Heavily rhythmic pop music suddenly blared from the plaza's speakers—Klarasdaughter's "Lost the Time to Speak." A couple of men began dancing. Mira climbed on the edge of one of the planters so she could see better. One of the dancers, tall and slender, beard stubble whitening his chin, moved with the grace of someone formally trained. His coveralls were from Agriculture—East Five was the major agricultural sector of the colony, with extensive rack farms for produce and factories turning yeast and soybeans into a hundred different products.

On the stage the big screen started cycling through images of everyday scenes from the Society: men at work, children at play, residences, classrooms, a field of wildflowers on the crater slope. Between them the screen went black save for a quotation in light blue. "Be faithful to that which exists nowhere but in yourself." Then an image of rows of solar collectors on the crater ridge, each smearing the sun into a parallel line of reflection. "Much we hold dear must be done away with." A teenage girl and boy necking on a bench in a garden. "Every idea an incitement."

The crowd numbered perhaps three hundred, two-thirds of them men. The volume of the music rose. A syncopated, nervous rhythm, very loud percussion, harmonized pipes over it, an extremely simple melody, and Klarasdaughter's slurred, androgynous voice:

> *Die in a hovel*
> *Live in a dream*
> *Depends on the script*

> *Pretend it's a novel*
> *Not what it seems*
> *Depends on the script*

Breathe in the vacuum
Burn in the sun
Fall on your knees
Know that you're done
Angels from heaven
Demons from hell
Depends on the script

As the music rose to its loudest, Hypatia stepped onto the platform and the crowd cheered. She raised her arms and a field of raised arms greeted her, cries of "Solidarity!" With her came the other three candidates for the Board: Tamara Ruthsdaughter, Pat Sarisdaughter, and Daquani Jeffersdaughter. Daquani, a trans woman, was another of Hypatia's lovers, the child of a colleague at the university. The opposition joked that if she were elected, Daquani would be both the first male member of the Board in thirty years and Hypatia's second vote.

Standing in a row, they joined hands and raised them high. More cheers. The music receded and Hypatia moved front and center, right up where the people crowded close. When she spoke, floating mikes picked up her voice and amplified it.

"I am happy to see so many men and women here," she called out. "So many fathers and sons! Friends and lovers! Women! All you strong, brave women! Women who have no fear.

"Women afraid of men could destroy this colony!" she shouted.

She waved her arm at the candidates behind her, and then out at the crowd. "But we aren't afraid!"

More cheers.

"A society where orthodoxy is never challenged stagnates. We need to take risks. What has the Society accomplished scientifically or artistically that can match the achievements of the other lunar colonies? What would you rather watch, our boring idealisms or the tragic melodramas produced in Persepolis? Whose music would you rather hear? Whose virtualities would you rather experience?"

Hypatia carried on in this vein for a while, conjuring up great works of art—music, drama, video—and explaining how in the midst of tragedy, always, humans male and female had created the deepest and most meaningful art. She stopped short of asserting that violence and social disruption were a small price to pay for a vibrant and evolving society, but it was not a reach from where she stood to that place.

"We are not here to protest! We are here to resist! Protest is when you object to an injustice. Resistance is when you, by your own actions, ensure that the injustice no longer takes place!"

As Hypatia warmed to her theme, painting her picture of a reborn Society, Mira stopped listening. She'd heard Hypatia's arguments before, spiced with humor, a dash of history, an appeal to principle, and ridicule of those who didn't understand. Mira got down from her perch and circled round to where she could see both the platform and the faces of the people watching.

The man with the beard stubble who had been dancing so well

now stood near the front, a head taller than most around him. His expression wasn't that of a believer, or even somebody who sought to believe. Mira imagined he had paid some attention to the election but not much. He had some simple job and he lived in a dorm, alone.

The Society was constructed so that men would not be tempted to unite. Every man to be embraced by his mother, bound by affection and obligation to sisters, loved by many women, able to find meaningful pastimes suited to his temperament and calling forth his best efforts, so that he might earn the praise of his fellows, make himself exceptional, be loved and petted and fucked within an inch of his life. A paradise. Yet here he was, and here were scores of others. What more did they expect the Society to give them?

She felt a desire to push through the crowd, grab the man's arm, and take him away from the rally. She would kiss him. She would tangle her hand in his hair and ask him where he had learned to dance, and who he had danced with. Did he love anyone, and did that person love him still?

"—and this is what we are fighting for," Hypatia said, quieter now, the microphones picking up every nuance. The crowd quieted with her. She held her arm out toward the back of the platform, and Val stepped from behind the screen. The people, hushed at first, began to applaud, and it swelled louder and louder.

Val came to Hypatia's side. She seized his hand and raised it high, and the cheers got louder. Behind them, Val's face was on the screen, wearing a big, embarrassed, irresistible grin.

As she watched him soak it up, Mira felt increasingly unhappy. She pictured him as he'd turned molten glass into a goblet, and remembered his beautiful self-containment, his commitment only to the work. His grace with his grandmother and great aunts and teachers. Even if this applause was what he wanted, it wasn't what he needed. He was too young to be the focus of so much unmoored love. His father had experienced something like this, but that was not in service of a political program, and still he had barely survived it.

As she watched Val up there, grinning, raise both his arms, now in fists, to the largest roar yet from the assembled men and women, Mira turned her eyes back to the screen. The camera switched to the crowd, and there was the tall man, as carried away as all the others, shouting. The image split and they were both up there now, the boy and the man, the leader and the follower, flattened to two dimensions.

CHAPTER
FIVE

IT TOOK ERNO WEEKS TO FIND A BLACK MARKET SURGEON who was both skillful and discreet. The clinic was in Shiraz, a neighborhood that had started as a roofed trench outpost, like many of the earliest colonies. Along its walls rose three ranks of apartments hollowed out of the rock. Dirt blackened the grout of the pavement in a street where men in colorful shirts sat on stools or lounged against tiled walls. A ring of children kicked a fabric ball in high arcs between them while their elders watched Erno impassively, their eyes flicking silently over the gleaming prosthesis where his left hand should have been.

Next door to the office of a dog announcing himself as a "Licensed Sagdid Practitioner," the clinic presented itself as an apothecary.

Beyond its arched doorway stood cluttered shelves of patent medicines, and behind a counter a bearded man. A couple of Aideless orangs loitered around the public data terminal. The man eyed the satchel over Erno's shoulder.

"Salaam," Erno said.

"Salaam. May I be of service?"

"I would like to speak with Dr. Jahanshah."

"I am very sorry, sir," the man said. "I do not know that person. May I fill a prescription for you?"

There followed a ta'arof dance of question and answer, compliment and self-deprecation. Erno offered increasing amounts of money to no effect: The man insisted he was mistaken in his belief that surgery was done here and so of course the shop had nothing to sell him. Erno's allusion to his marriage into the Eskander family did nothing but arouse the man's skepticism. Finally Erno took the cryobox from his bag, unsealed it, and showed the hand. The man stroked his beard. He disappeared into the back of the shop. Some minutes later he returned and without further conversation conveyed Erno back to the surgeon.

Dr. Jahanshah was a gaunt man with a precise manner. In his brightly lit surgery he studied the hand for some time, turning it over in his own, flexing each of its fingers. He placed it under an X-ray microscope. He pondered the bones of the wrist, the hand's version of radial and ulnar nerves. Dark lines ran through the heart of each metacarpal, and a spray of microscopic opaque spheres infused what passed for its flesh. "This is interesting. Not mechanical, but not quite biological. Where did it come from?"

"You tell me."

Jahanshah assessed Erno through narrowed eyes. "You are from New Guangzhou?"

"I've never been there. Why do you ask?"

"Years ago, some Chinese crime families sought to adapt certain medical devices for other uses."

"This is a medical device?"

"No, I would not say that. But see, even if I attach this to your arm, I will not be able to guarantee its function. If the prosthesis you wear now is unsatisfactory, you would do better to clone a hand from your own cells. I can grow one for you in a month."

"That's not what I want."

Jahanshah bowed his head at Erno's bluntness. "As you wish. I'll need to take a magnetic resonance scan."

"Can you do without it? I don't know if it contains ferrous materials."

"Might you at the least tell me where you obtained it?" the surgeon said, Persian manners ebbing. "Working in ignorance, I can't speak for the result."

"I don't want you to speak at all," said Erno.

• • • • •

Hung over, eighteen years old, he sat cross-legged on the edge of the gel mat and drew in a deep breath of Mayer's slightly sour air. Through the window streamed morning light from an Earth landscape: forested mountains, blue sky with streaks of pink and orange clouds, a river in the valley catching silver fire from the sun. In the distance an eagle circled. As Erno tried to focus, the eagle froze in midglide, then jumped back and repeated its swoop.

A camera midge floated into his field of vision, hovering in front of his eyes. He waved vaguely at it; it danced away and then returned to fix its microscopic lenses on him again. For six months he had lived in this two-by-three-meter flop in the Hotel Gijon: a gel mattress, a false window, and dozens of surveillance bugs. Anything he said or did might be recorded—though Erno could not imagine why anyone would care what the residents of the Hotel Gijon did.

Most likely the bugs were the remnants of an enterprise that had failed. Some jackleg entrepreneur had seeded self-replicating monitors throughout the colony, hoping to sell the spy service, or the idea of the spy service, or protection from the spy service. The plan had fallen through, and now unless you could afford to have your residence scrubbed, you dealt with the bugs.

He brushed a crawling camera from his thigh, drank the ounce of water left in the bulb by his bed, ate a leftover soycake, and pulled on his stiff work clothes. They were starting to smell. He had hocked his good suit, and his old spex, and even his mother's turquoise ring. The money they'd brought was gone. Today he had to find work.

Outside his room Erno ran into Alois Reuther, who lived in the suite next door. The hotel's claim to be more than a flophouse rested on the existence of the one suite on each floor for residents of more substance than guest workers like Erno. Alois carried himself with the casual assurance of one born to wealth. His clothes were expensive and his shoes were genuine leather. Some people said that he had laundered money for the largest crime family in New Guangzhou.

Noticing Erno, Alois raised his left hand slightly in patrician greeting. The last time Erno had seen him, instead of a hand Alois had sported a glittering metal appendage with six digits and a special manipulator.

"New?" Erno asked.

"The newest," said Alois. He held his hand out.

Beneath the pure white of his shirt cuff, the flesh of Alois' new hand was olive with fine hairs on its back. Alois turned it over to show the palm.

"Cloned from your other?" Erno asked.

"No—not flesh," said Alois. "The finest artifice."

Alois wanted Erno to shake his hand. Although shaking hands was not a custom in the Society of Cousins, he did so. Alois's grip felt warm and dry. He held Erno for a lingering moment, and a furrow appeared between his eyes. He let go and placed the hand, palm open, on Erno's chest. Erno flinched.

Alois held his hand there for a moment. "I'm sorry you are troubled," he said. "Money?"

"No," Erno said. "I'm fine." He felt his heart beat against the slight pressure of Alois's fingertips.

"You are a person of merit."

What was Erno to say to that? "I'll take your word for it."

Alois let his hand fall away. "A man's word is his bond." He fixed his eyes on Erno's for a second, then turned and touched his palm to his door. The latch clicked and Alois disappeared inside.

A person of merit? Uneasy, Erno headed for the stairs.

Alois was only one of the eccentrics who lived in the hotel. On the other side of Erno lived Coventry's Brian Zeta-Plus Gonzalez, an uplifted dog who worked as a bonded messenger. One floor down the narrow stairs lived Tessa and Therese, a pair of humans only a meter tall—a genetic mod that had been tried at Einstein, engineered at half size to reduce the load on resources. It never caught on, and Tessa and Therese were left to live in a world of giants.

Erno found Anadem Benet at the desk. "Good morning, Mr. Pamson," she said. "Your rent is due."

"Tonight, Ana," Erno said. "I promise."

"I promise, when your door is locked, I will not open it."

"I'll pay," Erno said.

"*Claro*. The Deadly Señor P."

Anadem had let the rent go for two weeks. She had the idea that Erno had been born into a male harem, genetically engineered to give sexual pleasure. "Cousins are a gender-differentiated social democracy," he insisted, "not a role-reversed sexual tyranny. The founders were women *and* men; First Chair Nora Sobieski said—"

"So why were you kicked out?"

"I—I made a mistake. Someone died."

"Ah," she said, raising an eyebrow. From then on he had become The Deadly Señor P.

Erno headed up Calle Viernes to the boulevard. The Mayer lava tube had been sealed with foamed basalt when pressurized eighty years earlier. Where Erno lived, the last paint upgrade had to have been thirty years before, and the alleys were draped in shadows. Calle Viernes, along with Calles Sabado and Domingo, constituted the seedy neighborhood called the Weekend, and Hotel Gijon stood at the far end of the street, one wall built into the face of the lava tube. Across Calle Viernes were another residential hotel, a Scientology temple, and a Remote Integrated Object Printer rental; next to it a loan shark and a gambling arcade, and on the corner the Café Seville.

The boulevard wound its way through the tube between buildings walled with stucco and decorated with red, blue, and yellow tiles, lending the place its Mediterranean look. Far above, heliotropes fed sunlight down to the hexagonal panels of the light canopy. In the evenings, when the residents climbed to the roof of the hotel to drink tea and smoke, you could see down the tube through hazy, high-CO_2 air until it twisted away, a ten-kilometer-long city stretched inside a hollow snakeskin that ancient lunar volcanism had discarded several billion years ago.

The first place Erno had gone in his exile from the Society was the scientific station at Tsander, but there was no work there for an eighteen-year-old biotech apprentice without papers. Through the Lunar Labor

Market he managed to snag a job with Dendronex Ltd. in Mayer, in the Lunar Carpathians. It was a long and arduous trip to Mayer and the nearside, over three thousand kilometers, but Erno had made it by surface bus and cable train, spending all the money he had to do so.

Little spoken of among the Cousins, Mayer had been founded by Spain in 2058, then taken over by a coalition of free marketers in 2129. Here Erno's lack of citizenship wasn't a problem: Immigrants kept labor costs down. He arrived in the middle of the "Mayer Miracle." People all over the moon were talking about the economic boom fostered by Mayer's completely unregulated markets and hard currency.

At Dendronex, Erno assisted on a project to develop genome-targeting crRNAs as a bactericidal alternative to antibiotics. It was mindless work, and he wondered how the company turned a profit: Their products were a medically questionable glut on the market. Three months into his job it came out that Dendronex was a speculative front for three AI trading systems that, functioning according to ever-changing algorithms that even their owners could not follow, had inflated the Mayer Stock Exchange into the biggest bubble lunar finance had ever seen. When it burst, the waves inundated a hundred smaller corporations, fortunes evaporated, and Erno was on the street.

In the ensuing depression, Erno no longer had the cash to link his Aide to any employment brokers, so every morning he walked down to the labor pool and sat with dozens of others seeking day work. Those times when he found a posting he earned one ducat a day, which he took in coins, and subsisted on protein chili from the shop at the end of Calle Sabado. In return for ludicrous stories Erno would make up about sex in the Society of Cousins, the owner, Christophe Marble, gave him a discount.

Marble earned more by selling lottery tickets than chili. The front of his shop was a big screen promoting the glamorous lives of recent winners: Balto Santiago, Sophonsiba Bridewell, Jun Yamada. Watch him move into his new luxury condo; go shopping with her and her pop star girlfriend for clothes; see them hiking the Carpathians in gold lamé surface suits. Everyone spoke of the winners with envy. Marble called them "clowns and tramps."

At least those clowns had money. Money, it seemed, was the basis of all relationships outside of the Society. Erno had a lot of time to think about it. He was what they called "poor." Mostly, being poor was a matter of earning enough to eat and pay the rent, and then sitting around with nothing to do and not much energy to do it. Erno had spent most of his adolescence feeling ignored, but he had never felt this useless.

In the street outside the labor pool, a woman in shabby clothes peddled hot biscuits from a cart. Another sold jump blood in plastic bags. A man on the Speaker's Corner ranted about immigrants. Inside, a couple of dozen men and women sat on metal chairs; some ate biscuits they had bought outside, some mumbled to their Aides, others played cards. The *muñeco* sat in his cube with his feet up on his desk; when people tried to talk with him he would open one eye and crack a bitter joke. His white shirt and detachable collar were pristine, as if he expected to move up soon.

Erno sat with others before the pixwall replaying last night's hockey game, next to Rudi, an old man who was a regular. "Any work today?"

"Not unless you're a dog." Rudi's cracked voice bore evidence of too many years breathing agglutinate dust. "Who can compete with a dog?"

"Dogs are trustworthy," Erno said. "But people are smarter." He glanced up at the screen. "How'd the Gunners do?"

Rudi snorted, which turned into a racking cough. He leaned forward and Erno slapped his back. When the cough at last petered out, Rudi drew a shuddering breath and continued, "I can't believe they're getting paid to play that bad."

They chatted about lunar hockey for a while. Erno was trying to work up the nerve to ask Rudi if he'd lend him some cash when the voice of the *muñeco* broke in. "I need six certified RIOP handlers for Agro Construction."

Erno had spent thirty ducats getting certified on remote devices in the first month after the Dendronex collapse. The people in the waiting room sat up straight; the card games stopped. Erno closed his eyes and tried to slow his breathing.

"Sharistanian, Minh, Renker, Fernandez, Altamirano, Tajik," the *muñeco* said. "Have your prods ready."

The workers he'd named bounced out of their chairs, ran their forearms through the scanner, and were let through the bubble where they would be hustled by cart out to their posting. They left a score of the grumbling unemployed in their wake. One of the card players threw in her hand, the cards sliding across the table and tumbling slowly to the floor. "Enough," she said.

This late in the day there was little chance of any more work coming in.

"He hasn't called my name in a month," Erno grumbled.

"You need to grease him more," Rudi said.

"Grease him?"

A look of astonished amusement creased Rudi's face. "You haven't slipped him anything? Seriously?"

Erno stared at the floor tiles. Rudi's dry chuckle rasped.

"Look," Erno said, "can you lend me some cash? I wouldn't ask but I'm in a bind right now."

Rudi shook his head slowly. "Ah, boy, boy . . ." Some sympathy showed in his rheumy eyes. "It's a hard world for fools and old men."

Erno left Rudi sitting there. He couldn't imagine a worse place to be at Rudi's age than the waiting room of the Mayer labor pool—unless it was the debtor's freezers.

He wandered through the commercial district for a while, looking through the windows of the glistening shops and restaurants. He considered taking the risk of asking some passerby for a handout, but he could not work up the nerve. Plus, if he got arrested for begging he'd go straight to the freezers.

Instead he surveyed the quotations inlaid into the pavement. He stood for a while on "In the state of nature, Profit is the measure of Right." He contemplated, "Freedom (n.): To ask nothing. To expect nothing. To depend on nothing." He was loitering outside a casino on "I don't believe in a government that protects us from ourselves," when he drew the attention of one of the uplifted chimeras acting as a security guard. The chimera's ears were pointed and his pale face smooth as a baby's, ancient brown eyes impassive as polished stones. His uniform sported lighted green epaulets and a matching fluorescent belt. Attached to the belt was a stun baton. Chimeras were notorious for the dispassionate way they had with a stun baton. Erno left.

Back at the Weekend he slid into a seat on the patio of the Café Seville. The smell of empanadas made his stomach growl.

He counted his change. He had exactly seventy-two centimes. He poked the coins around the palm of his hand. His finger glided over the raised profiles of Smith on the two quarters, Hayek on the two dimes, Rand on the two pennies. What point in saving money now? He ordered a wine and watched the traffic on the boulevard: pedestrians, carts, messenger dogs. He tried to think of someone he could borrow enough from to get to the end of the week.

Three people at the next table were arguing. "On Earth they know how to run a society," said the man with orange hair.

"We're going to Earth, now?" the bigger man said.

"Why not, Luis?" said the orange-haired one. "They make big money on Earth."

"You couldn't take ten minutes on Earth," said the woman.

"Genmod," orange hair said. "Denser bones, better oxygenation."

"I would not mind visiting Earth someday," Luis said.

Erno doubted the three had the money to buy new slippers, let alone gene therapy. As he listened to their aimless blather, Alois Reuther strolled by the café. He wore his camel jacket, purple ascot, and a panama hat. A cigarette dangled languorously from his new left hand.

Erno's heart leapt at the sight of him. He should have admitted to Alois that morning that he was broke. Well, pride was foolish and it wasn't too late.

He was about to call out to him when the three who had been talking stood up and stepped into the street. "Alois, old friend," said the big one, Luis. "We've been waiting for you."

"You need to come with us," said the woman

Alois attempted to slip past them. "No, I don't."

"*Au contraire*," said the orange-haired man, putting his arm around Alois's shoulders and guiding him toward the alley beside the restaurant. "Mr. Blanc worries about you."

"Your finances," said Luis. "And your health."

"For instance, this hand," said the woman, seizing Alois's wrist. She plucked the cigarette from between Alois's fingers, flipped it away. It bounced and rolled under the table where Erno sat. "Has it been properly attached?"

They disappeared around the side of the building. In a minute came sounds of a beating. Nobody in the café even flinched. Erno got up and peered into the alley. They crouched over Alois in the shadows.

"Hey!" Erno shouted. "Stop!"

They ignored him. "Where is it?" one of them asked another, who was kicking around the trash.

"It flew over here. Why did you have to rip it off?"

"Just find it."

A cloud of security midges accumulated over their heads. Their tiny loudspeakers spoke in unison, making an odd chorus: "In all disputes, entrepreneurs must relate to one another with complete transparency. Remain here until a settlement agent arrives."

Luis reached into his blouse pocket and tugged out a card. He held it up to the midges' cameras. "I have accumulated a Social Deviance Credit," he announced.

"And your colleagues?"

The woman flashed her own card. But the orange-haired man did nothing. Luis confronted him. "What? Don't tell me you're out of SDC."

"Okay, I won't tell you."

"Fuck!" said the woman.

"Fuck," said Luis. "I don't know why I married you. Let's go." They hurried past Erno into the street.

"Why are you—" Erno started.

"Shut up," the woman said as she jogged past.

A contingent of the midges flew after them, while the main body hovered over the alley chanting, "A clash of rights has taken place! A clash of rights has taken place!"

Erno knelt over Alois. His shirt was ripped open, his leg was bent funny, and his hand had been torn off. His wrist was not bleeding, but a trickle of blood ran from his scalp. Erno ran back to the café and asked the counter man for a wet towel. He returned and held it to Alois's head. In a few minutes a bored settlement agent drove up and loaded the unconscious Alois onto his cart.

"Is he going to be all right?" Erno asked.

The agent tapped a stylus against his wristpad. "Was he all right before this?"

"Where will you take him?"

The agent ran his reader over Alois's good arm. "He's insured. I'll take him to Beneficent Dividends HMO."

"What about the men who beat him?"

The agent calmly surveyed Alois's semiconscious body. "On the violence scale, this probably isn't outside of one standard deviation. You want to make a statement?"

He didn't need to appear in the colony's legal system right now. "Uh—no."

"Good day, then." The agent climbed onto the cart and drove away, Alois's handless arm dangling off the side.

Erno took the bloody towel back to the counter man.

"They beat him up," Erno said.

The man looked harried, but took the time to say, "You don't have anyone who'd like to beat you up?"

Not yet, Erno thought. But soon.

Erno went back to his table. His glass of wine was undisturbed. He sat there and nursed it for a long time, until the waiter came by and told him he needed to order something else or leave. He stepped into the street. He walked a few paces away from the café, then stopped. Back at the hotel Anadem waited for her rent. He had nowhere to go.

The weight of the day, and of the past year, came down on Erno so heavily that he simply sat down on the curb.

Twilight came; the colony's sunlight panels were fading. Music blared from the back of the restaurant—staccato drums and pipes, a song he remembered from home, Klarasdaughter's "Sunlight or Rock." The café was crowded, talk was loud. Above the buzz of conversations came Klarasdaughter's sweet, mocking voice:

> But it seems you were mistaken
> And the truth came as a shock
> To learn which one was stronger
> Sunlight or rock.

Erno studied the pavement between his feet. Mixed from lunar regolith, the concrete was so old that it had been poured by people instead of machines. Those swirls, laden with dirt, had been brushed into its surface by some long dead hand. How many people as broke as Erno had sat here and stared at it? How many had fought with each other here, talked idiot love, concocted and abandoned plans? He needed a plan. Anadem would not have him beaten, he reckoned. He'd just be arrested and shoved into the freezers until some company thawed him out as an indentured worker.

He looked down the alley where Alois had met his own reckoning.

Something moved there. A dog was nosing around amid the trash. Erno lifted his head, got to his feet, and went over to it. It was his neighbor Brian.

"What are you doing here?" Erno asked.

The dog raised his narrow white face. "Good evening, sir," he muttered. "I smell something."

On the ground, a discarded paper twitched. There were few small animals in this colony, not even birds—not in this misbegotten place, where they didn't even have a real ecology, just people. Brian tensed, ears laid back. "Stay!" Erno said, grabbing the dog's shirt collar. He reached forward, pushed aside the paper, and there, clenched into a fist, lay Alois's artificial hand.

"May I have it?" the dog whined.

"No. It's all right—I'll take care of it." Erno reached into his pocket, pulled out his last quarter, and slipped it into Brian's breast pocket. "Buy yourself a biscuit."

The dog looked uncertain, then raised his ears and walked away, nails clicking on the pavement.

Erno poked the hand with his finger. As soon as he touched it, it fell open. In the dim light Erno could make out that the wrist was sticky with some fluid that was not blood. This was not some cheap servo. For one thing, it had independent power.

Erno picked the hand up and shoved it inside his shirt. Limp, it made a bulge that he hid by holding his arm against his side. It was warm. He could feel the fluid against his skin.

Behind the hotel desk Anadem sprawled on the chaise in her office. He was crossing the lobby as quietly as he could when she called out to him, "Your rent!"

"Back in five!" he said.

He raced up the steps. Laughter floated from Tessa and Therese's room. Outside of Alois's suite he took out the hand and held its palm against the doorplate. The latch sounded and Erno went inside. The lights came up.

He'd expected some degree of comfort, even luxury. Instead, soycake wrappers lay scattered on the floor amid the stale smell of cigarettes. A single chair, a designer piece that once must have cost a lot of money, stood in the center of the living room beside a small table and a lamp. The bedroom held a gel mat and some boxes. Searching, Erno found a tray of jewelry, some of which he recognized Alois having worn. In the bathroom were a bottle of expensive cologne and several blisters of over-the-counter anti-aging drugs. On the table beside the chair in the living room lay a journal. Erno tabbed it open to the most recent entry.

> From this is born a debate: whether it is better to be loved
> than feared, or the reverse. It may be answered that one
> should want to be both; but because it is difficult to unite
> those emotions, when you must have one of the two it
> is much safer to be feared than loved . . . because love
> is kept through a bond of obligation which men, being

corruptible, may break at the first whisper of private interest; but fear is kept by a dread of punishment, which never fails.

The closet was filled with suits, shirts, pants. When Erno pulled them out he noticed how many had patched linings and frayed cuffs. He put on one of the least worn jackets—a little large in the chest, but a decent fit. Shoes stood ranked along the floor. He rummaged through them. The ones he'd thought were leather just had a microlayer over synthetics.

In the toe of a worn slipper, Erno found sixty-three ducats in cash.

As he got off his knees, stuffing the money into an inside jacket pocket, he noticed three bugs, fixed motionless on the wall, their microcams trained on him. He had a bad moment before he assured himself no one cared enough to be watching.

He loaded Alois's jewelry into his pockets. It would be better if he did not stay in the hotel that night; Alois might return, and Erno certainly did not want to face him. Good-bye, Hotel Gijon. In the morning he would pawn Alois's jewelry and catch the next train out of Mayer.

As he surveyed the suite before leaving, he saw the artificial hand on the table where he had laid it. At the last minute, on impulse, he wrapped it in a cravat, put it inside his shirt, and buttoned his jacket over it.

When he came down the stairs, Anadem blocked his path. "Your rent, Erno. Now."

He reached into his jacket and pulled out a twenty-ducat note. "Does that cover it?"

Anadem raised an eyebrow. "Where did you—"

Over her shoulder, Erno saw two people enter the lobby: Luis and the woman. The woman had a bruise on her temple.

Anadem noticed Erno looking past her and turned.

"Does Alois Reuther live here?" Luis asked.

"Who wants to know?" Anadem said.

The man studied her calmly. "Some friends of Monsieur Blanc." He locked eyes with Erno for a moment. If he remembered Erno from the alley, his face did not reveal it. "Don't you have something else to do?"

Erno lowered his gaze and headed for the door.

"Your change?" Anadem said.

"Keep it, on account—for next week," Erno said.

They'd be in Alois's room in minutes. They'd find the rifled jewelry box, and maybe they'd put two and two together. Or the bugs—maybe they'd tap them and see that he had the hand. It was seven hours until the pawn shop opened. By then, they would surely be watching the train station.

Erno walked down to the Port Authority. The station was not busy at this hour, a few passengers waiting for the night train and the homeless preparing to catch an hour or two's sleep in dark corners. On the board were listed the biweekly cable car to Rima Sitsalis, another to Le Vernier, and the overnight maglev to the southern colonies—Hestodus,

Tycho, Clavius, all the way down to Persepolis. A second class ticket to Hestodus cost twenty ducats.

He went to the machine and bought passage for Hestodus and stuck what he had left into his pocket with the stolen jewelry. He kept the hand under his shirt, pinned between his left arm and his ribs.

At the entrance to the maglev platform, he tried to act like he knew exactly where he was going and had not the slightest worry in the world. A businessman, his carry-on trotting along behind him, passed through the portal, and Erno followed. He pressed the hand inside his shirt against his belly. As they approached the portal, its fingers twitched.

He strode down the tube to the train waiting in its airless tunnel. Most of the compartments were occupied. He slid open the door of an empty one and took a seat by the window. Against his belly he felt the warmth of the artificial hand.

He wondered what Alois was doing at that moment. He'd be dumped out of the clinic as soon as they'd patched him up. He could not know he was penniless. Back at Hotel Gijon, they would be waiting.

Ten minutes later the doors closed, the umbilicus pulled away, and the maglev began to move. It passed out of the tunnel into the bright lunar day, and as it swooped down from the Carpathians, the Earth, in its first quarter, swung into sight high above them. Erno still was not used to it; on the cable train from Tsander he had been fascinated to see the planet rise above the horizon as they came from the far side to the near.

That first sight of it had seemed heavy with promise. He was moving into a new world, one where he might take control of his life and make something of himself. It hadn't happened yet, but there was still time. The Earth hung there still, turquoise and silver, shining with organic life, as it had for several billion years. Imagine a world with air and water on the outside, where you could stand naked and the sun shining down was not an enemy but an embrace.

But the Earth's gravity would drag down a lunar-bred boy like Erno—a person of merit—flatten him, and leave him gasping for breath.

• • • • •

For ten years Erno had preserved the hand in a sealed, room-temperature cryogenic box, wondering if he should discard it. In moments of fantasy he imagined he might cross paths with Alois again and give it back. He'd been close to broke more than once and had contemplated selling it, if he could find a buyer. He never tried. He could say he was wary of the men who had come seeking it, but in the end that wasn't why he kept it, and there was certainly no reason why he could not throw it away.

No, it was something else. The hand was a marker, the physical token of a turning point in his life, the moment when he went from naive boy—though it was a mystery how he might still have considered himself naive after his mother's death and his exile—to something more. A traitor? A thief? A man?

It really would have been better for all concerned if he had never stolen it, but that choice was behind him.

And then fate had arranged it so that Erno found himself in need of a left hand. Absurd. Some people might say this proved there was an order to human events. Erno knew better. But a coincidence so colossal must have some meaning, though he could not imagine what.

After the surgery Erno felt some pain. Inflammation of his wrist, which at first made him think his body was rejecting the graft, subsided after three days. Within a week he had full function.

He was not certain about that, however, because he did not know the hand's functions. The temporary prosthesis he had worn was nothing like this. Mechanical limbs typically were poor substitutes for cloned replacements. Though this one was not exactly mechanical, it did not seem to be biological either. He wondered anew where Alois had gotten it—and what the thugs who had beaten him would do if they were ever to encounter it again.

On this particular morning Erno crossed the concourse to the office of Eskander Environmental Design & Reconstruction. Behind a brilliant white colonnade in the Iranian style, chrome and black glass and airy floating lights gleamed in the small but luxuriant foyer.

"Good morning, Mr. Pamson," said Jamshid. They had hired a young man to take calls and make appointments. He sat at a sleek black desk tucked among the bamboo, bromeliads, and laurel and did next to nothing. The waiting room held a saltwater tidal pool with miniature mangrove, surf grass, sea urchins in the shallows, and blenny swimming between the roots. Above the sofa, pix displayed various Lunar colonies in their full glory—the park at Mayer, the Tycho grassland, the juniper forest of the Society of Cousins. The scent of earth and flowers hung on the air.

"Good morning, Jamshid. I'm expecting a conference call at fourteen hundred from Mr. Richard of Aristarchus Environment Management and Mr. Lewis of Biological Instantiations. Please put them through to me as soon as they link. Don't disturb me while I am engaged with them."

"Certainly."

Erno retreated to his office. He had research to do. He called up a paper titled "Atmospheric Dynamics and Bioregenerative Technologies in Chaparral Mesosystem Type 2 Hydrologic Cycles" and tried to get up to speed.

Their first client, the Aristillus Water Authority, had come to them with a problem of increased concentrations of selenium and thallium in the water supply. The Cousins engineers Erno had studied under had a relatively simple fix: a Witt algae that ingested heavy metals that could then be filtered out of the water. Erno had engineered the algae and seeded it in the Aristillus recycling plant. Problem solved.

Their second client was Rima Huygens, where nitrous oxide levels in the air had spiked. The Huygens engineers could find no change in practices to account for it. Erno spent two weeks visiting the colony, and another month frantically running simulations before he figured out that the increase was a matter of a synergy from mutated nitrogen-fixing bacteria in the agricultural soils and a reduction in ozone production because of an olefinic bonded polymer used in construction. He prescribed abandoning the polymer and a wholesale switch to engi-neered crops that fixed nitrogen themselves.

So far, so good. The problem was that managing environments was an art—an art based in a century of research—but not a science. Even a closed microenvironment like a lunar colony, designed from scratch, was too complex to regulate solely by computer models. With the help of AIs and moment-to-moment monitoring of air, water, and soil, most colonies could be adjusted day-to-day. But AIs had no ingenuity: When things went sour it took an intuitive understanding of system com-plexity to figure out the cause. Usually there were remedies, and the Cousins had developed biological interventions more effective than the thud-and-blunder methods of the other colonies. Rather than using chemical testing and substitution, for instance, they created biosensins bacteria to monitor the elements in a biosphere and react when something began to get unbalanced, activating other bacteria to compensate.

Certain people had the knack for biosphere design. His teachers had decided Erno had this potential, and he'd apprenticed to the pre-miere ecological designer of his generation, Lemmy Odillesson. But Erno's exile had ended that training. In truth, he was flying blind half the time, scrambling to keep a step ahead of the problems Amestris's clients set him. Anxious work, buttressing his lies with actions, but he could honestly say that he had never been happier.

Amestris had something to do with that. The marriage had been accomplished easily enough, a simple civil ceremony for a ten-year contract. She resigned her position in Persepolis Water and used her savings to establish Eskander Environmental Design.

Coming from one of Persepolis's foremost families, and having spent many years working in the largest water mining firm on the moon, which had dealings with virtually every lunar colony, Amestris knew a lot of people. She was full of energy and ideas. She found an apartment for them on Sohrab Square. She took Erno to the best tailor in Persepolis and bought him a wardrobe. She made all the choices, creating for him the image of a slightly unworldly but well-dressed stranger. He was her environmental genius from the Society of Cousins, slender and sexy and weird. At parties she urged him to talk less and touch people on the arm or shoulder. "Physical contact is your trademark," she told him. "You are Cousins-trained in sex and environmental engineering."

"We don't invade each other's personal space," he protested.

"Neither do we. It's a social taboo."

"How is this going to get us contracts, if I'm alienating people?"

"You *are* an alien. That's your strength."

When it came to the work, for the first time in his life Erno possessed genuine authority. He hired two young environmental engineers from the university and set them to executing the plans he designed. He told them what to do, and they did it. Some few men back in the Society might manage a lab or colony service, but here he dealt on equal terms with people of power and influence, the majority of them men, in circumstances no Cousins man had ever encountered. He made decisions. He commanded resources, drew up plans. His mysterious background gave him cachet. When he walked into any room, it was taken for granted that he was superior to those who sought his expertise. Women deferred to him in a dozen ways. He casually wielded the personal power that Tyler had always preached was the essence of being a man.

The only problem with his new life was that just about everything he had told Amestris about his design experience was fabricated. Every day pushed him further into pretense. He spent nights on databases researching recovery techniques, sweated out presentations, acted like a project was elementary and then buried himself for weeks in desperate analyses. Fixing an environment that had gone out of balance, dealing with bizarre interconnected out-of-control feedback loops, was like dancing on the brink of a canyon.

He was loading some notes from the paper when Jamshid blinked into sight on his Aide. "Mr. Richard and Mr. Lewis ask the honor of your confidence."

"Thank you, Jamshid. Put them through. Once we are in conference, I don't want to be interrupted."

"Yes, Mr. Pamson." Jamshid disappeared from the window and the entire wall dissolved. Erno was looking into an office lounge. Two men sat in armchairs.

"Good morning, gentlemen," he said. Erno came out from behind his desk and sat down within the conference envelope.

Mr. Richard had chosen to appear as a young man in a conservative suit. Lewis was older, handsome, with graying hair. "Good morning," Richard said. "I hope you won't mind if we get right down to business."

Aristarchus had invested its agricultural resources in a system of high-CO_2 greenhouses in order to increase crop yields. The sealed greenhouses ran at a lower overall atmospheric pressure but higher partial pressure of CO_2; cultivators who worked in these environments wore respirators. Erno was familiar with such greenhouses—the only time Erno had met his biological father, he was working in one—but they were a crude way to boost agricultural production.

Over the last year the atmosphere in Aristarchus had seen an increase in carbon dioxide. Normally this was one of the simplest feedback loops to track down and remedy, but the engineers had not been able to find the cause and the colony had to resort to carbon scrubbers to keep the atmosphere stable.

"Let me tell you the good news first," Erno said. "I have found the source of the CO_2 imbalance. We may correct that relatively simply."

"Excellent. What's the bad news?"

"The bad news is that your ecology is obsolete. You are running a system that was state-of-the-art thirty years ago, but it is a cookbook environment, oversimplified for the size and complexity of your colony. It is terribly out of date."

Lewis crossed his arms. "Are you going to lecture us on basic science?"

"I beg your pardon. The fact remains that your ecology would be fine if you had a population of five hundred or even five thousand people. Instead you have fifty thousand. You have made repeated poor decisions in its expansion, and though I can solve the current carbon dioxide crisis, in six months or a year your system will produce some other problem."

In the middle of this speech, the door to Erno's office opened and Amestris came in.

"Tell us what you can do about the CO_2," Richard said.

Amestris approached the conference area. But rather than enter the envelope, she stood just outside and blew him a kiss.

Erno tried to focus on the conference. Lewis's eyes flicked in Amestris's direction, but he could not see her. "You have made widespread use of a concrete in construction whose exposed surfaces sublimate carbon dioxide," Erno said.

"We've corrected that."

"I don't think you have. You failed to mention this, but ten years ago someone there had the idea of importing the European ant *Temnothorax crassispinus* to aid in seed dispersal. You have been fighting infestations ever since, using methods so crude that you are lucky you haven't totally crashed the ecology."

"What does that have to do with the atmosphere issue?" Richard said.

"Several of your methods for interdicting this pest have led to a further imbalance in the CO_2 cycle."

At his desk, Amestris switched the conference imager to synthesize. She could now enter the envelope while the software kept her invisible to the viewers. Erno switched his own image over to synth so he could continue to speak through his avatar, presenting as him, while he dealt with Amestris. Why was she doing this? It was extremely distracting. Given the fact that he was trying to sell the Aristarchans on a radical change, one that they had not signed up for, he needed his wits about him.

"That can't be the source of the problem," said Lewis. "We've investigated all loops relating to the *Temnothorax*."

"It isn't the source of the problem per se. The problem is that your biosphere is small. Biodiversity is too limited. The ecology is not adapted to the many variables that arise in a population of your size—"

Amestris stepped within the envelope. She ran her fingers through Erno's hair, then kissed him on the top of his head.

Erno struggled to keep his voice under control. His avatar could handle the visuals, but he had to run the audio. "What I propose is a colonywide redesign and reboot. I suggest, given your resource profile, the creation of a high chaparral ecology. I can build into this system a number of bioregenerative safeguards that should stand you in good stead over the next forty years, established with the intention of producing sustainable add-ons as your population expands."

Amestris bent over him, stuck her tongue into his ear, and slid her hand inside his shirt.

"We didn't come to you for an ecological overhaul," said Richard. "We just need to fix this problem."

"I can"—Erno grabbed Amestris's wrist and pulled her hand away. She struggled, and it was all he could do not to burst out laughing—"I can give you a fix for your CO_2 problem alone. But that would be penny wise and pound foolish."

"Let me speak with my colleagues," Richard said. He called up the image of several engineers who must have been listening in on the conversation. He kept the audio on, so that Erno got to hear as one of them heatedly reminded Richard that the Society of Cousins was not a party to the OLS Standard Atmosphere Convention. Erno tried to listen, but Amestris was kissing him on the lips.

"The OLS specifies a range of atmospheric pressures from 1.01 kpa to 0.65 kpa," somebody was saying.

Erno had half an erection and Amestris was about to slide into his lap. He pushed her away. She bit his ear.

He glanced across the room. Lewis looked unhappy. "What is this going to cost?" he asked.

Amestris stood, still very close to Erno's chair. Erno pulled himself together. "Allow me and my associates a month to work through the parameters, and I will be glad to present you with the details. But I would say we are talking about a figure in the neighborhood of four hundred million Persepolis rials. Our commission would, of course, be a small fraction of this amount—one percent."

"That's not something we can agree to out of hand," said Lewis.

"Of course. This is merely a consultation. You aren't obligated to accept my analysis or take my advice."

Amestris whispered into his ear, "I am going to fuck your brains out. You are not obliged to accept my analysis or take my advice."

"If we might wrap this up," Erno said, "I have another meeting. I'll have my staff forward to you the complete report, with supporting analysis and recommendations. Think it over."

He was tugging Amestris's blouse out of her pants even before the wall went opaque. He threw her down on the ornate carpet, tore open her shirt, and kissed her lips, her neck, her breasts, her navel. She was breathing hard, her belly trembling.

If physical contact was his trademark, he would take care to reinforce that for her. Erno held her by her throat—gently, but leaving no doubt that she was under his control. She put up a struggle, clawing at his wrist with one hand, the other reaching for his face. With his free hand he seized her arm and pinned it to the floor. He turned her face to him, staring into her eyes, then kissed her. Her fingernails went from his wrist to his back, she threw her leg around his hip, and the pretense that he was taking her against her will evaporated.

Much later they lay on the rug in their scattered clothes, he on his side, she on her back. He brushed the index finger of his left hand, as lightly as possible, along her collar bone. Amestris's eyes were closed, and her chest rose and fell calmly. Her hand rested on the inside of his thigh. How good it was to feel her next to him.

In Persepolis, where male dominance was a reality, did sexual dominance games mean the same things they meant in the Society? Sex with Amestris felt a little like sex with a man back home—but that was not right; it was totally different.

Erno would watch her sometimes in their office, acutely aware of her separate, unique self. When she spoke with Jamshid or any other person of lower status her voice was calm and authoritative. Not that she ever talked down to them—in this she reminded him of his old teacher Debrasdaughter. With their clients, some of whom were people of great power and wealth, she spoke with equal assurance but a difficult-to-identify difference in tone. And occasionally, with disarming humor. Though sex was not on the table, the fact of her femininity was there, unspoken. There were moments when, to his surprise, Erno felt jealous of the attentions she paid their clients. Sexual possessiveness had never been one of his weaknesses.

Whenever things went wrong, or promised to do so, Amestris took it all in stride. She was much more optimistic than he. She seemed to know, at some cellular level, that she could make things come out right, or if not, deal with the result.

Even when it wasn't true. She had a terrible sense of direction. In the New Tabriz bazaar, beneath the beautiful, intricately figured ceiling, a place where she had been a hundred times, she'd gotten them lost. Erno was a better judge of the best way to get anywhere in the city. His teasing her about it did not faze her for a second.

Amestris took his hand, spread his fingers, turned it over, and examined his fingernails.

"Do you know the hand is an important symbol among the Shi'a? The fingers"—she counted them out as she spoke—"are Muhammad, Fatimah, Ali, and Fatimah and Ali's sons, Husayn and Hassain."

She kissed his thumb, bit the tip lightly. "I know you don't want to be dependent on me, but you should have consulted me about this hand. You don't want to make a mistake with your own body. Who did the cloning? I hope he was reputable."

"You should be pleased," Erno said. He looked past her to the window, a view of the sun rising over the central peaks on Copernicus, a study in dramatic gray, black, and white.

"I *am* pleased," Amestris said. She held his hand to her breast. Looking into her dark eyes, measuring the warmth of her skin, Erno knew she was telling the truth. He ran the hand down to her waist.

She pulled away and sat up, "I wish we could do this all day, but we have a dinner tonight."

"A dinner?"

She began to dress. "A possible client. Saman Kazedi, the founder and CEO of Kazedi Pianos. Do you know about him?"

"The pianos we had in the Society were Kazedis."

"He is a very creative man."

Erno pulled on his shirt. "I don't understand. What can we do for a piano manufacturer?"

"We'll let him explain that at dinner, but I am sure that he wants to talk to you about wood."

"Wood."

"Yes. And another thing, my beloved. We will be joined by my father and mother."

Though Cyrus Eskander had done nothing overt to sabotage them, he did not approve of Amestris striking out on her own, of her using the family name for her enterprise, and especially of her marrying a non-Muslim immigrant. On their only meeting, Cyrus had treated Erno like a servant.

"You promised me you'd never subject me to him again. What is this about?"

"My father has had a change of heart. He wants to know you better. He may be a jealous man, but he is also a businessman. I doubt that he'd admit it, but I think he is impressed by what we've accomplished in so short a time. Where there is money to be made, he is able to set aside his prejudices."

Erno brushed back his hair. "Where is this dinner?"

"The Heart of Forugh. We must go home and dress," Amestris said, leaning in to him.

He raised his new hand to her face, bracketing her cheeks with his thumb and fingers, tilting her head back. "You've been very bad," Erno said. "You've kept things from me. If I weren't such a kind man, I would be compelled to discipline you."

● ● ● ● ●

Amestris had the bedroom pixwall on, volume low, while she applied her makeup. She could hear the hum of the mister in the bath as Erno got ready. How much pleasure he took in his accomplishments. How she loved to see her father's discomfiture at her marriage to an exile on whom in less than a year she had built an enterprise that had billed 28.2 million rials in the last quarter.

From the beginning, their relationship had been a mixture of business and sex. The word "love" was not one Amestris was eager to hear. She supposed a marriage gave occasion for its use, but in her observation of the married the term was problematic.

Over the last twenty years Amestris had many times found herself in difficult situations with men. Her father, back when he still argued with her, told her that was why she should practice the modesty of Islam: Its seeming restrictions on women were for their protection.

Protection from whom, Amestris countered.

She wondered that she had not sought out a man from the Society of Cousins before. From the beginning, her time with Erno had been a mixture of awkwardness and passion. Surprise, sometimes delight, then moments of complete incomprehension. They had selfish reasons to be together—enough, when they were at odds, to undermine her faith in their marriage. And they both had enough sincere connection, wonder, pleasure, and laughter to make it seem, when things went well, that they were meant to be together.

He tried to be manly according to his understanding of what that meant, but was doomed to fail, for which she was thankful. His efforts to seem forceful, preemptory, and controlling regularly collapsed under him. In another man this would have been annoying or pathetic, but Erno's sideways decency was a saving grace. Amestris had never had so much fun with a man.

If they could sign Saman as a client, they would cement their legitimacy: Instead of only dealing with other colonies, they could count one of the major firms in Persepolis among their clients. Her father would have a hard time ignoring them.

The pixwall had turned to *Here's the Point!* On the screen were Sirius and Dasha Mohseni. The compactly built super-Doberman's sleek black coat showed his athletic neck to good advantage. He wore a fitted vest and shorts and sat on his specially designed chair beside his human co-host. Amestris turned up the volume.

"You're right, Dasha," Sirius said, tapping the fingers of his hand-paw on the arm of his chair. "Tonight we will give our watchers an inside view of the Society of Cousins. How best to deal with the challenge they pose? Are they a danger to the rest of the moon?"

The screen switched to the interior of a domed crater. In the distance the tower at its center supported the blue sky. Woodlands covered the slopes. The camera swooped over clusters of apartments and public buildings, across the farms of the crater's floor, over a wedge of park where flyers in colorful wings soared above a pond to land between white lines on green turf.

Erno came out of the bath, closing a shirt seam. When he saw the image on the wall he stopped.

Sirius's peculiar canine baritone continued under the video of a woman exhorting a crowd, holding up the arm of a good-looking adolescent boy. "Social unrest persists in the Society. Cousins assert that all they desire is to be left alone. Yet others maintain that their principles undermine the freedoms of every man and woman in the lunar world."

Silent, Erno sat on the edge of their bed. He fumbled with the shirt cuff, his eyes on the wall.

Dasha, a handsome woman with dark red hair, said, "They scoff at our traditions. Masters of biotech, manipulators of environments, their agents move among us quietly, seemingly deferential, keeping their agenda to themselves. And back in their sealed colony, while the male half of their humanity is repressed, what plans are brewed?"

The image on the screen switched to a video of a regiment of women in Greek battle dress carrying round shields and swords.

"Some trace the origins of the Society of Cousins back to the Amazons of legend," Dasha continued, "warrior women who cut off their right breasts in order to shoot arrows and wield swords. Herodotus called them 'Androktones,' which means 'killers of men.'"

"Not literally, Dasha" Sirius said. "But the men of the Society of Cousins have endured this radical system for more than eighty years. What is life like for the oppressed minority? We have with us tonight a man born and raised among the Cousins, who will give us a first-hand account of the conditions he lived under until he was able to escape— Mr. Tyler Durden."

Erno's lips compressed into a line.

"What is it?" Amestris said. "Do you know him?"

"He's the reason I'm here."

• • • • •

"Mr. Durden," Sirius says, leaning forward, "you were raised by the matriarchs of the Society. Yet you organized resistance to their regime and were exiled. Can you tell us about your movement?"

"My brothers and I asked only for the simple freedoms that even the poorest man here has. They refused to listen. In every way that a hope can be crushed, our hopes were crushed. It was devastating, Sirius."

"What is it like, being a man in among the Cousins?" The dog's large, batlike ears delicately poised, give it an air of remarkable alertness.

"Well, one is indoctrinated from birth. One is never let out of the sight of some woman for a moment. One of their child rearing adages is: 'Keep your son close, let your daughter go.'"

As he speaks, the image on the screen splits to a video of a colonywide meeting at the Society, taking place in an amphitheater. The image freezes and homes in, one by one, on the members of the Board of Matrons. Beneath each face stands her name: Debra Debrasdaughter, Krista Kayasdaughter, Eva Maggiesdaughter.

"Daughters are set free at age fourteen," Tyler says, "which is, in its own way, as cruel as anything they do to boys, fostering a competitiveness among the women that leads to lifetime feuds. The degree of scheming you will find in a Cousins politician is light years beyond what goes on in the lunar colonies your viewers are familiar with."

"Is that possible?" Sirius asks, cocking his head comically. The people in the studio burst out laughing.

Dasha leans in, a look of concern on her face. "But what about the boys, the young boys?"

"For boys it means complete emasculation."

"Emasculation?" the dog exclaims. "This is not the image we have here of the Cousins male. We are told that men are used for sexual favors, as if they were in the seraglio."

"Tell me, Sirius, what is more emasculating than to be treated as if you have no value other than your body, your sexuality community property? Persepolis men are proud and independent. They stand tall, free to choose their friends and spouses. A man among the Cousins is perpetually a boy."

"And yet," Sirius says, "in the upcoming Society of Cousins election, the Reform Party has candidates for one-third of the Board. We have reports of increasing numbers of men and women at election rallies."

"I would not hold out much hope for this election," Durden says. "The leaders of the Reform Party are all women."

"A referendum to expand the franchise to all men

above age twenty-one is on the ballot," Sirius says. "Isn't that a major step forward?"

"The Society allows it only because of the outside pressure from the Federation of Lunar Democracies and the OLS. I guarantee you, the proposition will fail. The election is rigged. Even if by some miracle it should succeed, control of the Board of Matrons by the old families is more important than any theoretical rights that have yet to be exercised."

"It sounds so hopeless," Dasha says. "Why do women insist on such a sick society?"

"They are secular utopians," Durden says. "The most terrible holocausts in human history have been perpetrated by secular utopians. The average woman in the Society is well aware that their social structure is riddled with weakness—which means ever more strict measures to maintain control. Of course, some women rebel, but they are considered a traitorous minority."

Sirius raises a paw to touch his ear. He looks sad as only a dog can.

"You organized a liberation movement. You sent out appeals for aid from the free lunar governments, but in the end, when your movement was being crushed, none of them came to your aid. Do you harbor any resentment toward Persepolis for refusing to act in your time of need?"

"No, Sirius. We knew the people of Persepolis, if they understood the truth, would be with us. We also knew, however, that we could not count on Persepolis's liberal regime to act. The myth of the fair sex still prevails here— as well it might, given the warm and giving nature of Persepolis women," Durden says, looking toward Dasha. "Yet Persepolis fears the possibility of retaliation. All the free governments of the nearside are naturally afraid of retaliation."

The inset in the corner expands to take over the entire screen, showing a woman in a laboratory peering into a genetic sequence on a three-dimensional display, then a team of Cousins bioengineers in green hazmat suits in some sort of factory.

"The Society of Cousins," Sirius narrates, "is famous for its expertise in biotechnology and environmental design. Other lunar colonies frequently hire Cousins teams to regulate their biospheres. The Apollo colony did so just two years ago—and in the last three months their ecology has suffered a catastrophic collapse." Images of hazy air, citizens wearing respirators, a hatchery full of dead chickens.

"Some speculate that this might have been sabotage. And what of reports that Cousins scientists have stockpiles of biological agents? Can you tell us anything about this, Tyler?"

"I don't doubt it's possible."

" —that they could wipe out human life on the moon, should they choose?"

"Sirius, believe me when I tell you there are women among the Cousins who are capable of such an act."

"Don't they realize that they would suffer a retaliation too terrible to contemplate?"

"You have to understand the depth of the hatred these women have for what they persist in calling the 'patriarchy.' To them simple masculinity—the fundamental nature of the male of our species, the result of the millions of years of evolution that have taken us from primitive apes struggling to survive on the savannahs of Africa to the point where we stand prepared to leap from the cradle of the solar system—this, to them, is the ultimate threat. They would rather die than see the human race, and the demon that is the male, spread to the rest of the galaxy."

Dasha shakes her head. "A sobering thought, Mr. Durden. Thank you for being with us today."

"It was my pleasure, Mrs. Mohseni, Sirius."

• • • • •

Only when it was done did Erno realize he was barely breathing. Amestris, sitting beside him, turned off the wall. She took his hand.

"Tell me," she said.

"His real name is Thomas Marysson," said Erno. "He was my hero. He was funny, and he mocked all the things that deserved mocking in the Society. I got caught up in his movement. He used me. I helped him pull a prank that panicked the whole colony. My mother, a constable, tried to get me away from him, but I wouldn't listen—until he asked me to create a virus that would have infected all the women in the colony and spared the men. When they tried to arrest us, we blew a door open into the vacuum, escaping; a dozen people were injured. My mother died."

"That's terrible," she said. She squeezed his hand. "But it's the past. He can't have any effect on you anymore."

"You saw it. They're trying to gin up a war."

"The news lives on feeding viewers' paranoia," Amestris said, looking him in the eyes. "You shouldn't take it too seriously."

"I have friends back there. My sisters, my aunt, even my father."

"They exiled you."

Her gaze was so calm, so confident; he could fall all the way into it if he let himself, and it would be a relief. She had already healed him in a half dozen ways, cooled his anger, restored his belief in himself.

She adjusted his collar. He could smell her perfume, and he flashed back to their afternoon in the office. His life was here, with her. He would never see the Society again.

"You're right," he said quietly. He stood. "We should go. We'll be late."

She took his arm in hers. "I am excited about this evening," she said. "I think you will like Saman."

On their way to the restaurant Erno's thoughts were drawn back to the interview. Marysson looked older and thinner. He had let his hair grow out, but he still affected the coveralls of a *mita* worker. These were tailored now, and had never seen a day's work. The more Erno thought about the sociopathic Marysson finding a new audience, the more worried he got.

Marysson could not have any effect if no one gave him a platform. The Persepolis media powers who put him on the news had their own purposes. But few of the viewers were sociopaths—what would lead them to credit such a man?

He tried to put it out of his mind.

The Heart of Forugh was named after the iconoclastic twentieth-century poet Forugh Farrokhzâd. Erno had read her rebellious verse. Taking dinner at this restaurant was another sortie by Amestris in her long war with her father.

If Cyrus Eskander was annoyed at the choice, he did not show it. Dressed in a pearl gray suit and white shirt with a Russian collar, he stood when they approached the table and greeted them in Persian. Erno replied in kind. He bowed to Afroza Eskander, who wore a long red tunic, intricately embroidered, over loose pants. Amestris introduced Erno to Saman Kazedi, short and broad-shouldered like someone from Earth. They sat around a low octagonal table on an elaborately worked carpet. Amestris was on Erno's left, and Saman on his right. Cyrus and Afroza sat opposite. They began with a prayer and washing of the hands and face before eating.

Servers brought out course after course. First an appetizer of yogurt and minced cucumbers. A stewlike lentil soup. Flatbread. A large bowl of rice prepared with red onions and grilled tomatoes—Persepolans were very proud of the common availability of rice and tomatoes, requiring vast amounts of water for their cultivation. A platter of spiced trout filets. With this came grilled vegetables. And for dessert several sticky pastries with thick, sweet, fragrant coffee.

The conversation was light. Cyrus was ebullient and witty; his elaborate puns and literary references flew past and Erno had trouble keeping up. Afroza spoke with Amestris about her sister Leila's latest film. Cyrus and Saman gossiped about a scandal in the Prime Minister's office. Erno noted the crosscurrents between Amestris and her parents. He observed Saman.

Saman was not as old as Cyrus, perhaps sixty. His intelligent eyes were set close together. Dark, unkempt hair, a blade of a nose, a small mouth. Amestris had warned Erno that Saman was undemonstrative on any subject other than his pianos. He sat quietly as the meal was served, but as soon as Erno asked him about his work he loosened up. He spoke English in a pleasing baritone.

"An acoustic grand piano, Erno—I may call you by your given name, may I? Please call me Sam—it is a great, ungainly beast. Such pianos are massive, at the same time fragile. Makes no sense to ship acoustic pianos from Earth, eh? When synthesized keyboards already one hundred years ago are so perfect, the acoustic is a relic or a personal extravagance.

"But I am a lover of music. Any music lover will tell you there is a difference between even the finest electronic and a traditional acoustic. So thirty years ago I decided to make pianos on the moon."

As he warmed to his subject, Saman used his hands to illustrate, almost as if he were playing a piano right there. His enthusiasm was magnetic. Before he'd begun, he said, there were no acoustic pianos on the moon and no demand for them. But Sam noticed that several of the requisites for constructing pianos were *more* available on the moon than on Earth. The best pianos used cast iron harp plates produced by vacuum casting into a mold of moist sand. Sam had the lunar regolith, finer than any sand on Earth. He had water from the South Lunar Pole. And he had, for free and in infinite supply, a more perfect vacuum than any manufacturer on Earth.

Low gravity was a problem—the traditional mechanism of the keys would not work in low-G. But Sam perfected an action that took account of the one-sixth gravity. He began constructing pianos for lunar use, and found a market among the increasing numbers of the wealthy on the moon. Later, he adapted his pianos for Mars gravity. Today, Kazedis were the only acoustic pianos to be found anywhere in the solar system besides Earth.

But he was not satisfied. "On Earth, they laugh at my pianos. A mockery of the great Steinways and Yamahas, you see? Ironic, since the descendants of those great companies are uninterested in craft and the instruments they manufacture are unworthy of the great names.

"The one thing I've lacked to make a piano equal to any ever produced, Erno, is wood. The pinblocks of my pianos are made of synthetics. The soundboards, the hammers, the hammer block. Some of these things are not as important as others. But anything that has to do with the sound—that's a different matter.

"I have tried using pressed bamboo. No, no good. Tried importing wood from the Earth, but the cost of lifting wood out of Earth's gravity is too high. And besides, to use Earth materials vexes me. I make *lunar* pianos. No, you see, what I need is a large and steady source of hardwood grown on the moon. What I need, Erno, is for you to grow me a forest."

Erno took a sip of coffee. "We do environmental design, Mr. Kazedi—Sam. Creating a forest is an entirely different enterprise. I'm not saying it's impossible, but—"

Sam said, "Amestris tells me you are a brilliant practical biotechnician, better than any on the nearside. And I am prepared to pay a large sum."

Cyrus watched them. Erno said, "This can't be done in a rack farm in some warehouse. We would need to create a large biosphere. Is that much space available?"

"I have already purchased a vacant lava tube. We will modify it to provide up to sixteen hectares. Depending on your needs, I could perhaps expand further. I would need you to produce more than one variety—for instance maple, hornbeam, basswood, beech, spruce—all these would be useful, some absolutely necessary."

"That's a tall order. A forest, even if I can create one, will not produce wood for many years."

"Might biotechnology shorten that time?"

"Perhaps we should let the young man think about this for a while, Saman," Cyrus said. "It may be something that is at present beyond the reach of his firm."

Eskander was the picture of composure. Erno turned back to Sam. "In fact, I have particular expertise in genetically modified trees," he said. "The Baldwin juniper is an invention of the Society. My mentor, Dr. Odillesson, was especially interested in forced-growth trees."

"Is he available for consultation?"

In truth, Erno's involvement in Odillesson's tree experiments consisted mostly of organizing samples of the genomes of various *Cupressaceae.* He had never tweaked the genes of a single species himself. "I should not have to consult."

"Splendid!" Saman said.

"We'll make your dream come true," Amestris said.

Sam looked at her warmly.

"It will be tricky," Erno said. "But give me the resources I need, and we should be planting by the end of the year, and you will be harvesting usable wood within five years. Perhaps as soon as three."

Under the table, Amestris touched Erno's leg. He laid his left hand over hers, his palm acutely sensitive to her warmth. He could almost feel her excitement through his fingertips, and it made his head swim.

All the way back to the apartment, she clung to his arm. She could hardly contain her pleasure. He had passed a test. He was elated.

But for one thing: When they'd left the restaurant, Saman had leaned in to embrace Amestris. It was an intimate gesture, not common even in freewheeling Persepolis. It lingered in Erno's mind.

The next day, while Amestris visited her friend Sima, Erno set about discovering what he could about Saman Kazedi in the lunar databases. Saman, born sixty-seven years ago in Tehrangeles, had emigrated to the moon at the age of nineteen. He sponsored the Persepolis Symphony Orchestra, constructed the Kazedi Concert Hall, and sat on the board of the Persepolis School of Music. And twenty years before, he had been instrumental in the performing career of Amestris Eskander.

That Amestris had such a career was news to Erno. Two decades before, she had been a promising concert pianist, and Saman had been her greatest supporter.

He replayed Saman's embrace in his mind. In the Society such contact was so common as to be invisible, the bare minimum of polite behavior. Though he'd learned a lot about Persepolis, it was hard for Erno to read how much it meant here.

Erno found and purchased a full sensory recording of one of Amestris's performances. He loaded it into the virtuality deck and pulled the cap onto his head. After a moment his senses shifted and he was seated in the front row of a darkened theater, before a spotlit piano on a low, circular stage. Around it on all sides sat a well-dressed audience. To polite applause, Amestris came down an aisle and seated herself on the piano bench. After a hushed silence, she began to play.

The piece was by an Earth composer of almost three hundred

years ago named Alkan. Erno knew little about such music, but he was stunned by Amestris's virtuosity. The audience sat rapt.

And Amestris—Amestris, in a long, simple black gown, was so lovely that it almost hurt to watch her. It was not just her physical beauty, it was the intensity and control with which she played, her absorption in the music. Her strength, her boldness. It evoked his admiration, his wonder—even envy.

It made him sad. She had never said one word to him about this hidden career. There was no piano in their apartment, hardly any music at all.

He watched the twenty-three-year-old woman play, and noticed that in the front row, a quarter way around from him, sat a younger version of Saman. Erno studied him. So clearly it might have been written on his forehead, Saman Kazedi was deeply in love with her.

After the performance concluded Erno turned off the player and paced the apartment. He got a bulb of pomegranate juice and threw himself onto the settee, the sound of the sonata echoing in his ears. It was very complex music. It made him think of Earth and the burden of its complicated history, billions of people—civilizations, wars, and nations, art forms and philosophies rising and falling, conflicting, snarling and unsnarling. The music contained that, and Amestris had mastered it. Her soul was older than his, not just in years, but in apprehension.

All of them on the moon had come from that dead history. Much as they might have sought to cut themselves off from it, it was still there, even if somebody like Erno was ignorant of it. It was there even in their misunderstandings, their myths, the things left out. The lies that Marysson told about the Society, the desire to dominate that fuelled those lies.

Erno lay down on the floor on his back, put his hands behind his head, and looked up at the ceiling, the way he'd lain in the Hotel Gijon years before. These walls were apricot, the ceiling white. Along the top of each wall ran a line of crown molding. It was not made of wood. Wood was precious.

Amestris had to know that Sam was still in love with her. Was she indifferent to the pain it would cause Sam to be in daily contact with her? Was she going to sleep with him again? Perhaps she had already. How did he feel about that? It was not like sexual jealousy didn't happen in the Society, but in his years of exile, Erno had learned that it ran down different channels here.

The door opened and Amestris came in. She saw him lying there. He tilted his head a little and met her eyes. So beautiful.

Hers flicked to the virtuality deck. On the screen were the words: "Alkan, *Grande sonate: Les quatre âges*. Amestris Eskander, 41:16."

She looked back at him. "So. How did you like it?" A little anxiety in her voice.

He got up and took her hands in his. "You are wonderful. It's as if I haven't known you until now."

She smiled warily. "You know me as well as I do you."

He thought about Saman's forest and how blithely he'd promised to create it. He pushed the worry aside.

"You didn't need to hide this from me," he said. "It's beautiful. I want to hear about it, what it was like, what it meant to you. Why you gave it up."

"Isn't there work to do?"

"Not today."

They went to a café and drank dark coffee and talked the rest of the afternoon. Amestris told him about her music and the wild life she had led. As she tried to explain what it felt like to play, her voice grew husky. He touched her hand and felt her vulnerability, as if he had a window to her heart, and swore to himself that if he did nothing else, he would keep his promises to her.

CHAPTER

SIX

A SPARTAN MANIFESTO

The Society of Women is an evolutionary dead end.

The evidence is plain to anyone willing to open their

eyes. Consider these facts:

Men are 40% of the population and do 70% of the

menial work of the Society.

Cousins men have an average life expectancy

of 111 years, vs. 120 years for the average Cousins

woman.

The suicide rate among male Cousins is twice that

of women.

Psychological violence against men occurs every day and goes unnoted.

The natural expression of male vitality is criminalized.

Under the current repressive regime, only 23% of males vote. If you live in the Society of Women, have XY chromosomes, and want to vote, your only options are to become a drone or to literally cut off your balls.

Under these circumstances:

- We demand the franchise for all men.
- We demand full and equal parental rights for all men.
- We demand an end to Effeminacy Culture. To Unmanliness. To Softness. To Delicacy. To Weakness. To Slavish Deference.

• • • • •

It's the same dream Carey has had since he was fifteen: He's crossing the dead, sun-blasted lunar surface, wearing his pressure suit, bouncing along in slow motion, no other person in sight. He does not remember why he is there. On his phones is the sound of his own breathing. He steps around a boulder and finds a body in a pressure suit. By the micrometeoroid pitting he can tell it's been out here for decades. Not wanting to, he gets down on his knees and looks through the dead person's faceplate. The desiccated face he sees there is his own.

Carey awoke, heart thudding. Hypatia stirred beside him.

He lay there for a moment, then got out of bed. In the bath he drank some water and went to check on Val. When he pushed open Val's door he found his bed empty.

"Shit." The custody hearing was coming up. No one looked over the shoulder of some woman with a child as much as they looked over Carey's.

He tried calling Val, but got only his Aide. Back in the bedroom he put on shorts, shoes, and a shirt.

Hypatia stirred. "Where are you going?" she asked. Her voice was hoarse. Too much public speaking.

"I'll be back soon." He leaned over and kissed her.

He had an idea of where Val might have gone. He'd been hanging around with some Spartans. Carey didn't like their desperate machismo and their wallowing in grievances, though on that second trait he'd be hard pressed to explain how he differed from them.

He left his apartment and climbed the north slope of the crater, bounding eight at a time up flights of stairs, startling two women hand in hand coming down. For the most part the paths were deserted. At the bike share he checked one out and took off on the nearest switchback road down to the crater floor.

When he was a kid they used to race around these same hairpins, oblivious to the chance of being blindsided by some vehicle coming up. The physical exertion made him forget his anxiety. Wind spiced with the scent of blooming yellowwood blew back his hair. The dome was a sky flooded with stars. Lights of the residences he passed winked on and off among the trees. At the bottom he sped down one of the radial roads through fields of soybeans, inhaling the smell of soil, pumping hard now, nanofiber tires gripping the pavement. The Diana Tower, growing more massive, rose impossibly high before him. A few of the offices were lit from within, but most of its surface gleamed black.

The road curved through Sobieski Park, ran among the big oaks, past the playground, the amphitheater, the fountains. Carey skidded to a halt in the plaza at the tower's entrance, abandoned the bike, and circled around the base.

The black glass of the tower reflected the distant lights spread across the crater slopes, until the glass ended where the climbing routes ran up the tower's flank. Carey found backpacks and gear stowed beneath some benches near the auto belayers. He leaned way back and scanned the side of the building.

Two figures, unbelayed, climbed steadily up the wall. As he watched, he recognized his son's particular grace, unique as a DNA print. He started to call out but thought better of it; he didn't need to attract the attention of some constable. He started climbing after them.

Carey didn't have the right shoes for it, but he had been an expert climber once and he thought he could manage it. He ascended quickly, finding the hand and footholds, taking the easiest route—no traverses, no reaches. His upper body strength was beyond theirs, so he gradually gained on them. The breezes that self-generated in the atmosphere of the dome tickled the hair on his legs and forearms. Occasionally he tilted his head back to see them above him. They had stopped now. One of them pulled something from a backpack. At first Carey thought it might be one of Mira's videos, but the shape was wrong—this was a squat, square object, not a rolled-up poster.

When Carey got within five meters one of them spotted him and froze. "Look," the person said, and gestured sharply to Val—who saw Carey now.

In a few seconds Carey was beside them. They were at least two hundred meters above the ground. When he was Val's age he had lived for this kind of risk.

Up close he saw the device, about twenty centimeters on each side; Val had already spread mastic on the wall and they were fixing it to the surface.

"Val, what's going on?"

"Nothing," the other said. He had very short hair and a smooth face.

"If it's nothing then—" Carey reached past, got his fingers under the thing's edge, and ripped it off the wall. He tossed it away and it fell, spinning, a long time until it hit the pavement at the base and shattered, splattering some kind of dark liquid in a starburst.

"What is that?"

"It *was* a smartpaint bomb," the other boy said.

"It would have gone off tomorrow morning just when the government workers were all arriving," Val said. "It would have spelled out a slogan."

"Climb down. Now."

The two of them began descending.

"One at a time," Carey said. "Be careful." He watched them slip below him, then began his own descent. Going down unbelayed was slower and riskier than climbing, but they made it safely to the bottom. The other boy jumped down the last few meters and took off as soon as he hit, bounding away, but Val waited until Carey got there. On the pavement the smartpaint squirmed, attempting to form letters, but its programming was broken.

"Come on," Carey said, stepping around the paint. They hurried away from the tower, taking one of the paths through the park.

"Who was that?" Carey asked.

"Art Friedasson. He's Dora Aikosdaughter's boyfriend."

Aikosdaughter was one of Hypatia's grad students, ten years older than Val.

"A bomb, Val? Please tell me this was his idea."

"It was my idea to put it on the tower."

"Do you know what would happen if you got caught?"

"I guess they'd probably send me back to Roz."

"How about Invisibility? You can't count on getting away with things like this."

"You did. You set off a manhunt. You hid out for months."

"And that was stupid. If you want anything to come of us being together, you have to be smarter. We're too much in the public eye."

"You've lived in the public eye your whole life!"

"And you haven't. It's not easy."

"You love it. You're part of the effeminate culture. All the Spartans know it, though they don't say it when I'm around. The only thing you stand for is whatever makes you feel good."

Val loped ahead of Carey. Shoulders hunched, taking the long strides of a surface walker, he refused to turn around all the way back to their apartment.

Carey bit back his anger. Watching Val, he remembered a time when Roz and he had taken him to a party hosted by the Russets. Val was eight or nine, and there was a flock of four- or five-year-olds there. Rather than ignore the kids, Val had taken them all in hand and organized a game. Val was amused by them and genuinely liked them. It was a sensitivity Carey had never seen from a boy that age, a sensitivity that he'd never had himself. Where had this new Val, rigid with resentment, come from?

It was easy to go flying with Val, to spar with him at the gym, and flirt with women as if Val were Carey's younger brother. But Val took Carey's restrictions as purely advisory. Reasoning didn't work. Val listened good-naturedly, but he acted as if, since they had been taken up by the Reform Party, the cause justified anything. Val had never had any interest in politics, and now he was spouting Spartan crap. Carey could order him to stay away from them, but what if he wouldn't listen? Short of physical force, how did you assert authority over someone you loved who wouldn't listen?

In other circumstances he might have gone to Eva or Roz, but that was out of the question. So was talking to anyone in social services. He really had a lack of support here. He'd asked Hypatia about it, but she told him Val was fine—his rebelliousness was simply the *joie de vivre* of any teenaged boy.

He'd just as soon not have to explain to Hypatia what Val had been up to, but he needed to talk with her about Aikosdaughter. Maybe he could leave the Diana Tower part out. Maybe Hypatia could get Aikosdaughter to leave Val alone.

When they entered the apartment, instead of Hypatia they found Mira, sitting in an armchair, her dark brows knit. Carey glanced at the bedroom door.

"She left," Mira said. "She said to tell you you're her darling, and she'll see you at the meeting."

"What are you doing here?" Val asked.

"Go to bed," Carey said. "Now."

Val stared at Carey, said nothing, and went to his room.

Carey watched Mira standing in the middle of the apartment that Hypatia had gotten for him and saw through her eyes its two bedrooms, private bath, a sitting room with a sofa and two chairs, even a kitchenette. He rubbed his face with his palm. He smelled of sweat and recent sex. He got a water bulb and sat down on the sofa. "What brings you out in the middle of the night?"

"I could ask you the same. Your parenting skills are being monitored, you know."

"I know," Carey said.

Mira said nothing.

"Mira, I'm sorry," he said. "But this isn't all my—"

"*'Mira,* I'm *sorry.'*" She got up again. "Who are you to feel sorry for me?"

He held himself in check. Why did he let her mock him like this? He tried to keep his balance. "Let's stop it, Mira. This isn't going to make either of us feel better." He stood. Her dark eyes followed him. "Just calm down. I'll make some tea."

"I don't want tea." She took two steps toward him, seized his shoulders, and pulled his face to hers, so forcefully that her feet came off the floor. She kissed him. She had her arms around his neck. He took her weight; she didn't weigh much of anything.

"The bedroom," she whispered.

His territories: the bedroom and the *Ruăn tā* ring. He'd always been able to negotiate these places, deftly managing the politics of sleeping with three women at once, keeping everyone happy, or at least occupied. But he had too much on his mind; Hypatia's and Mira's needs were too complex, the issues of Roz and Eva and Val too distracting. Mira, Hypatia, Roz, Eva—they all had their own agendas. Even Val. He should make Mira go home.

An hour later, lying beside her, Carey tried not to think about what any of this meant. It was wrong. It wasn't even good sex; too many mixed emotions—yet he had gone along with it. Mira still lay awake. He wouldn't meet her eyes.

"I have to ask you something," she said.

"Do you?" He rested on his back, his hand on his own belly, unable to put two thoughts together. He was due at the aquaculture plant in three hours.

She propped herself up and looked into his face. "Do you know about the embargo the Board has put on scientific research?"

"Of course," he said.

"Something's not right about it."

"Of course it's not right. The patriarchies are paranoid about weapons."

"What could they be after that Eva wouldn't want them to have? I mean, your mother's papers have been public for years."

"I have no idea."

"I think maybe you do. I came across records of some big project twenty years ago. A lot of resources invested. It wasn't just pure research, there was technology involved." Mira rolled her leg over his, all intimacy now, her voice low. She drew a circle on his chest with her fingertip. It irritated him.

"Why are you asking me? You said you were talking to Roz. Ask her."

"What I saw might be consistent with them building some sort of quantum scanner. Did she build a scanner?"

Carey closed his eyes and inhaled deeply, held it, and let it out slowly. "I don't know. Twenty years ago I was fifteen."

"One of these records, a security log for a so-called IQSA lab, had your name, Eva, and Roz."

"Roz did a practicum in Materials. I used to hang around."

"What's an IQSA? Why doesn't anybody know about it?"

How had he let himself get into this? "Some fabricating machine. It didn't work. The Matrons shut the project down and Eva moved on."

"So why would Eva worry about giving them a failed technology?"

"Will you leave me alone, Mira? I really don't know anything." Carey levered himself out of the bed and stumbled into the bath to piss. He closed the door behind him. In the dimness he looked at himself in the mirror. Not the face of the dead man in his dream, just the face of the man that he was. He was changing, he could feel it, but that didn't make the world easier. He couldn't really blame Mira for tonight. She had power over him only as long as he cared. Did he care?

Nothing but questions and brief pleasures. There must be some enduring life beyond this, a way of living that meant something. He might even love Mira, but that didn't mean he could stand her. He loved his mother, too, and he loved Roz.

Above everything else he loved Val, and Val was at risk of getting himself into a lot of trouble, and Carey couldn't stop him any more than his mother could stop Carey back when he was fifteen.

He had fucked up in half a dozen ways, telling Mira about the scanner only the latest. Whether he could do the things that would keep any of these people happy shouldn't be the issue. But as long as he cared, he would have to deal with it.

• • • • •

Mira climbed the stairs from the metro station into the lobby of the Diana Tower and stepped outside. A cleaning bot was attempting to remove an amoeba of smartpaint from the pavement, but whenever the bot moved to suck up the paint, the paint moved to avoid it. Two *mita* workers stood by discussing the situation.

"Maybe if we get a couple of other bots, we can surround it."

"That won't work. We need to sprinkle it with nano," the other man said. He did not look too upset.

The first worker noticed Mira watching. He smiled at her. "We've chased it halfway across the plaza."

"Looker probably did it," Mira said, and headed past them into Sobieski Park.

Mira generally avoided the park. Today the dome presented a bright blue, sunless sky, high cirrus clouds. With the thin air a visitor from Earth might think he was in some high valley in Western North America or Australia. Flyers were out in numbers. Had she bent her head back to see, Mira could have watched them launching themselves from the platform near the top of the tower, spreading their brightly colored wings to catch the air. In the distance others beat their wings slowly as they circled the perimeter. Mira tried not to pay attention to them.

She passed through well-tended woods of white oak and box elder that had been planted upon the first pressurization of the dome. Eighty years later, the trees spread their thick boughs above the turf. A mockingbird ran through an aria of birdcalls. Two squirrels chased each other around the bole of one of the oaks. A dark-haired girl in bright yellow shirt and shorts came dodging through the trees, then crouched behind one of them. In the distance Mira heard another kid counting out numbers. The hiding girl looked up at Mira and held a finger to her lips.

At the edge of the woods the park widened to include a soccer pitch, the aerofield, an ornamental flower garden, rolling hills covered with close-cropped grass running down to a pond, and the community amphitheater where colonywide meetings were held.

Just as she stepped out into the sunlight, a flyer buzzed a flock of elementary school students kicking a ball around. She swooped low over a pair of lovers lying on the grass, then banked hard—Mira imagined the stress in her arms at the maneuver—just missing one of the big cottonwoods by the pond. The idiot woman zoomed toward the aerofield, three meters above the grass, pulled up into a stall, folded her wings, and came to a jogging stop. A couple of onlookers applauded.

Two more flyers, a man and a woman, their wings and tail fins slung on their backs, passed Mira on their way to the tower and the elevator ride up to the launch platform. They were talking about thermals. Mira avoided looking into their faces.

The Green family had colonized the picnic area. The ones who had been at Val's glassblowing exam were the core of a group that must number thirty or more, ranging in age from toddlers to people in their second century. Mira knew hardly any of them. Though you could count on the Greens to faithfully do their six hours weekly of *mita* service, if it could be said that there were classes in the Society, then they were in the highest. The Greens were influential in a dozen areas: teachers, a couple of university professors, technicians, bureaucrats, scientists like Eva, engineers like Roz, athletes like Carey. They were a little light on artists, maybe, but Eva's cousin Rydell Green Marlenesson published short stories and Zöe Green Sarasdaughter had taught Mira's film production class in the university.

Two young men lay on the grass face to face, touching each other, a hand to a hip, fingers brushing hair away from the other's cheek. Nearby some girls and boys had turned off their Aides and were playing blind man's buff. The girl who was the blind man had her eyes covered with spex and stumbled around with her arms stretched out in front of her, a grin on her face.

Carey and another man were juggling three children, little ones curled tightly into balls with their arms wrapped around their knees, throwing them high into the air, catching them, tossing them up again. The children screamed and spun. When the jugglers stopped, caught the kids, and let them go, they staggered dizzily around on the grass.

"Me, me!" one of the girls said, arms out to Carey.

"Okay, but you're the last," Carey said. "You're wearing me out."

Mira nodded at him and walked past. Last night's awkwardness lingered in her mind. She was troubled by the fact that he'd felt free to tell Hypatia she was Looker. Worse, he was right that Mira would never have told Hypatia herself, and that what he'd done had given her something she'd wanted. He was right about keeping Val out of the public eye.

Mira had felt off balance from the moment Hypatia had answered the door at Carey's apartment. She wasn't exactly surprised, but she had felt wrong footed. Not Hypatia, though. Hypatia acted as if there were no emotional consequences to their romantic triangle, as if the very thought of consequences was at best an unfortunate ideological error, at worst a sign of a grave character flaw. She'd told Mira, as she dressed, that Carey had gone off somewhere to meet Val, and then glided out of the apartment as if she were passing the two of them off to Mira for the rest of the night.

And then Mira *had* acted as if Carey were passed off to her. The bad sex stuck with her, as did the feeling that it was her fault that instead of getting closer she and Carey were drifting apart.

Mira spotted Eva talking with a trim old man. She looked up, smiled, and gestured Mira over.

She kissed Mira on the cheek. "I'm glad you came," she said. "This is Hal Lizsson."

"Hello," Hal said, wrapping her in a hug. He had a big beak of a nose and a tiny mouth with parentheses of smile lines. "You're Mira."

"That's right," Mira said.

"Very pleased to meet you."

"Let me introduce you to some of the family," Eva said.

Eva took Mira around to her sister, some cousins, a couple of uncles, young women and their boyfriends. Mira tabbed her Aide to keep track of their names. Some asked her about her work in Eva's lab; they casually alluded to her relationship with Carey and Val. If the ongoing conflict over Val was a matter of dissention among the Greens, they had put it aside for the duration of the picnic. Everybody was civilized and respectful, as if there were not a court case on the horizon.

Val and Roz were helping a woman set food out on a table. The woman moved with grace, but the curve of her shoulders and the tightness of her skin gave her away as one of the very old.

"Mira, this is Liz—she's Hal's mother. Aunt Liz, this is Mira Hannasdaughter, one of the interns in Materials. We're hoping that she will take a permanent job with us after she finishes her degree."

Aunt Liz's hug was perfunctory. "Trying to join this family?" she said bluntly.

"I'm just here for the picnic," Mira said.

"You look tense. Have some tea." Aunt Liz held out a purple bulb. "I've already got a buzz on, myself. Only way I get through these things."

Mira took the bulb. "Thanks."

"Come, on Auntie, let's get these ready," Roz said, moving to one of the hampers.

Eva drew Mira away. "Aunt Liz was born in California one hundred twenty years ago. "Nora Sobieski was her elementary school teacher." Eva gestured at the bulb Mira carried. "That's her special blend. Don't drink it unless you want to spend the afternoon high."

They passed a circle of Greens sitting on the grass around two middle-aged men and a woman playing a banjo, guitar, and fiddle. Eva led Mira to a bench beneath a silver maple.

"I'm a little surprised you came," she said.

Mira was not interested in niceties. "Why did you ask me, then?"

"For one, because this is a situation I gather you seldom encounter."

"What situation?"

"A family. Alliances. Personal history, for better or worse, that people can't run away from."

"I run away?"

"I don't know you well enough to say that." Eva picked up a fallen leaf and twirled it by the stem. One side glossy green, the other whitish. "I think you could use more friends. Your work on the fullerene scrubbing is credible, but I don't see you as a physicist. I don't know how committed you are to a career in science; seems to me your heart lies elsewhere. You keep your own counsel. You're very strong—in some ways."

Mira considered taking Aunt Liz's advice and drinking the tea. "Are you trying to recruit me into the Greens or just insult me?"

"It takes a majority vote to get into the family. I couldn't get you in if I wanted to."

"If you wanted to. That's pretty blunt."

"I'm only being straight with you. If you did want into this family, you'd have to earn it."

"I don't think I would fit in."

Eva smiled. "That's one definition of a family: the place where you don't fit in. We Cousins tried to redefine it, but still it can be stifling."

"You seem to have made a lot of judgments about me already. The colony is filled with judgmental women. I don't like being judged."

"Nobody does. But I don't think people can reserve judgment, in large numbers, for very long. Regardless, the Society works."

"Not for everybody."

"It doesn't work for you?"

"It doesn't work for me," said Mira. "It didn't for my mother."

"It's my feeling that it's produced a greater degree of happiness, more evenly distributed, than any in history."

"With some individual exceptions," Mira said. The fiddle and banjo music drifted over the park. She looked at the kids climbing trees, the food laid out on the table, the lovers in every gender combination lying together, the old ones talking, the women and men teasing one another. "Besides, you're wrong—I do have friends."

"Hypatia and her crew. That's another reason I asked you. I've known her a long time. She calls me a supporter of the status quo, and I guess I am. Where we disagree, I'm happy to negotiate, but in the end it's not politics that separates us—it's what she does to people."

"She hasn't done anything to people."

"She's not interested in reducing alienation. She exploits it."

"Hypatia's not going to paper over the chasm between where we are and where we ought to be. If she's alienated—if I'm alienated, Eva—the reasons come directly out of your glorious system."

"It's easy to see the flaws in a society when it's failed you. But think about it: The patriarchies call us an 'existential' threat. It's existential, all right—it's our very existence that scares them."

"To them we're a joke," Mira said.

"Not to all of them. Some of them look at us and say, 'Well, at least the things that are destroying me here are not destroying people there.'"

"People *are* getting destroyed here."

"To what degree? In what numbers?"

Mira was sick of this. "It's all so simple. 'If it harms no one, do what you will.' How many times have I been told that?"

Eva let the maple leaf fall to the ground. "Too many, I'm sure."

"People die here every day." Mira looked down toward the big cottonwood by the pond. A breeze rippled the surface of the water, breaking and reforming the reflections of the buildings on the other side.

Eva said, "'Someone asked Vladimir Lenin once, 'In your socialist utopia, will children no longer be run over by streetcars?'"

Mira looked back at Eva. "What did he say?"

"He had no answer."

Carey was approaching them across the lawn.

"He should have paid less attention to utopia and more to streetcar management," Mira said. She set her untouched bulb of tea down on the bench and stood.

Carey's embrace was brief. He looked tired.

"Time to eat," he said. He noticed the tea. "Ah, you've met Aunt Liz. You should drink that. It will change your life."

"I don't need my life changed," Mira said.

They joined the family gathered around the picnic table. Val climbed onto a bench and helped Aunt Liz up after him. She whispered something into his ear and he stepped down. Liz lifted her hand until the family quieted.

"Well, here we are again, one more time around the sun," she started, voice strong. "Let's take a moment to remember the ones who didn't make it all the way with us this time: Peter Samanthasson, Gracen Katesdaughter."

She bowed her head, and the others followed. Mira looked at the sandals of the woman in front of her. After a few seconds, Liz said, "We give thanks to the source of all sustenance, to the people who worked hard so we might have this food, to the plants and animals who die so that we might eat. What you send, returns three times over."

"Three times over," the family replied.

"So let's eat, then," Liz said.

Val helped her down and kissed the old woman on her cheek. The family passed around bowls of fruit salad, cinnamon bread, stew, platters of cucumbers and oil, hummus, beans.

It was more than Mira could tolerate, this forced togetherness. She saw the tensions beneath the surface. Roz and Carey carefully avoided each other. The elders eyed Val's every move, while the younger women cast suspicious glances at Carey—and at Mira. She overheard one of Carey's aunts tell him, "Settle this custody foolishness without going to a hearing."

Mira took a plate and sat by herself. She had to admit, the eggplant stew was mouth-watering. Carey stayed away, but a couple of women close to her age sat with her. They asked her what she thought of the

Reform Party's chances to take over the Board of Matrons. Mira would not hold up her end of the conversation, and the talk ended in uncomfortable silence.

What had Eva hoped to accomplish by bringing her here? She knew Mira had encouraged Carey to take Val. She knew Hypatia had taken an interest in Mira. Maybe Carey had even told her that Mira had asked about the quantum scanner. Any one of these things might move her to try to get Mira on her side.

Instead Eva had given her a lecture on Cousins 101. And Carey was ignoring her, and they had tricked her into coming to Sobieski Park, and one after another flyers glided over the woods to come to a landing on the field a couple of hundred meters away.

Mira stared at the old cottonwood. It was huge, maybe twenty-five meters tall. Anyone unfamiliar with it would never spot where a limb had been snapped off a decade earlier, but Mira could see the hole that it had left.

Abandoning her plate and the Green family, she crossed the lawn to the tree. She laid her cheek against the deeply fissured, whitish bark, rough and cool. She listened to the rustling of its leaves. Love was just a feeling.

• • • • •

"I'm glad Eva asked you," Hypatia said when Mira told her about the picnic. "Keep playing her. You may learn some useful things—at the very least you'll see how she works." Hypatia enjoyed listening to

Mira's deconstruction of the Green family. She most definitely didn't seek Mira's opinion of her quoting Ulrike Meinhof as a role model.

It was election night. Mira put on tights, a loose blouse, and a wig. She found her dancing shoes, turned her bracelet pink, and moved it to her left wrist. She needed a vacation from men, and every kind of player would be at the party. She caught the metro to the university.

In the last days the debate on the public boards, in the amphitheater, in dining halls and workplaces had gotten more heated than during any election since the time when Tyler Durden had shaken the Society. Guerilla theater took over the colony's largest refectory. Three different Looker videos were posted, only one of which Mira had created. Some men and women in the fusion plant threatened to work-to-rule if the male franchise proposition failed. There were even a couple of incidents of men coming to blows with one another.

Charges that Hypatia was a sociopath crossed charges that the election was being rigged against the reformers. Rumors of agents from the patriarchies swept the boards, but whenever anyone asked those spreading these rumors to point to a single example of *agents provocateurs*, silence ensued. The closest anyone came was to say that Looker must be a plant by outsiders, or at the very least in league with them.

On the metro three loud adolescent boys swaggered up and down the car, leaning over seated women to look out the windows. The instant a constable entered from the next car they sat down and acted like the meekest sons in the colony. At the university two constables patrolled the station and several monitored the plaza.

Over the entrance to Mark Janisson Hall a glowing sign read "Reform Party Party." Young people packed the dance floor and mezzanine, even though they could get the results just as well by Aide—this sort of rally was an archaism that Hypatia had resurrected. Mira cruised the crowd. The walls sported images from the campaign. Some women with purple bracelets—trans women looking for boys—sat with another group wearing green—trans women looking for girls.

In conversation pits speculation about canvassing numbers went on, but on the floor the music blared and people danced. A tea bar offered every variety of libido enhancer, as if they were necessary. Mira danced with a woman she had seen at some of the rallies; she didn't know her name. A big girl with an expressive face and fine lips. She moved smoothly in her tight dress, her hips swaying.

"I'm Cleo," the woman said as they headed from the dance floor to the bar.

"Miranda."

Cleo stopped. "You're Mira Hannasdaughter! I knew I recognized you."

"Do I know you?"

"I was in a Philosophy of Gender class with you years ago. I used to crack up at the questions you asked, so simple, but you were sticking the knife in. The prof didn't even know he was being gored." Cleo kept her eyes on Mira as she slipped the nipple of her bulb between her lips.

"I guess I should have remembered you."

"I was male then. Cleon Small Liviasson?" Cleo's openness was guilelessly attractive.

Mira sucked on her drink. Was Cleo one of those guys who changed sex in order to pursue a political career? "After we lose this election, I may have to fuck you."

Cleo touched Mira's forearm. "And when we win, I'll fuck you."

The polls wouldn't close until midnight. In the past the results would have been available instantly, but because of rumors that the voting might be hacked there was going to be a closed analysis with representatives of all factions. Once all sides were satisfied, the results would be announced some time between midnight and morning.

Hot and sweaty, Mira and Cleo fell onto the banquette at the side of the hall. Cleo leaned in to Mira. Mira slid her hand up the inside of Cleo's leg and kissed her neck, her cheek, her lips. This went on for a while. Faint perfume and a dew of sweat.

The pixwall at one end of the room ran an image from some news show in one of the patriarchies: A black dog wearing a vest was talking to a woman, but their words were drowned out by the music. Cleo pulled Mira back onto the dance floor. Head buzzing, Mira could almost see the music surrounding the dancers like a living cloud.

She shouted into Cleo's ear. "Hypatia has a private party. Want to go?"

"You can get us in?"

Mira held up her palm. "I'm invited."

They ran out, bouncing off each other, and took an elevator down to Seven Underground, a neighborhood popular with university faculty and the politically connected. As they neared the apartment of Charlene Wandasdaughter, a lawyer and one of Hypatia's former wives, they could hear voices. On the concourse outside the apartment, people trying to crash the party jousted with anti-reformers.

Mira pulled Cleo toward the door, past a woman arguing with another: "Even on Earth, a transgendered person has more rights than here!"

"Not a great argument," the other said, "that Earth-as-an-example thing."

The first woman grabbed the collar of the other. She yelped, knocking Mira sideways.

"Use your *indoor* voice," Mira chided, imitating the most earnest of Matrons. Laughing, she held her palm up to the door and she and Cleo slipped in.

A couple of dozen people filled the apartment. Here it was not so much a party, though some people were lit and social babble punctuated the political talk. Hypatia, in black suit and brilliant smile, stood at the room's focus. She locked eyes with Mira, nodded infinitesimally, then turned back to Daquani Jeffersdaughter.

Val lounged in a pit with a very beautiful young man and woman. Nearby, Carey leaned over slightly while Juliette, her hand touching his shoulder, spoke with him, their heads centimeters apart.

"Come on," Mira said, steering Cleo into a bedroom. Three people sat on the bed. "Hypatia wants you in the other room," Mira told them. "The results are coming in."

When they left, Mira locked the door. Cleo flopped down onto the bed, arms spread, head hanging half off. "They'll be back."

"I don't care." Mira kneeled beside her, took Cleo's face in her hands, and kissed her. Her tongue played lightly with Cleo's. She pulled back and watched Cleo's pale eyes, the sheen of sweat on the faint down of her upper lip. She licked that lip. Cleo pulled her into an embrace and Mira pushed up Cleo's skirt to stroke the inside of her leg.

"Yes," Cleo said. She dragged the wig from Mira's head.

Cleo's body was exquisite; genetic replacement and hormonal therapy had transformed her into a long-legged, pale-skinned, Junoesque beauty with dark hair. But all the time they were making love, Mira could not keep her mind from slipping to Marco. The scolding voice she had used at the door was one she had invented for games with her brother.

Angry, she tried to push these thoughts aside.

It didn't work. Mira could not focus, and their sex was fumbling and unsatisfying. Cleo acted like she was having a fine time, but Mira didn't believe it. Another night it might have been funny, but instead Mira found herself with tears in her eyes.

"Please, let's stop," she said.

"What's wrong?" Cleo asked.

Mira turned her face away. "Nothing,"

"I haven't been a woman too long. I'm sorry if I—"

"It's not you."

"What is it, then?" Cleo said, some exasperation in her voice.

Mira thought of the cottonwood in the park. "My brother is dead."

"Your brother? When?"

Someone knocked on the door. "Go away!" Cleo called out.

Mira buried her head in Cleo's breast; the music throbbed from the next room. "It was a long time ago. I was seventeen. He was fourteen. His name was Marco." She kept her eyes closed.

"What happened?"

"Our mother emigrated to another colony. I don't know where she is now." Mira's voice caught in her throat. Cleo held her. "I didn't know how to take care of Marco; I was still a child myself."

"Didn't anyone step in? Your aunts. Cousins?"

"I don't *have* any. You have to listen. Marco loved flying. He took risks. It was my fault. I could have stopped him."

"Boys take risks, they—"

"Please don't say that." Mira rolled away. She opened her eyes, but she could still see it. "I'd landed on the aerofield; he was flying with one of his friends, circling each other—spin dancing. They climbed, then dove, pulling up at the last second. Marco was breaking a dozen rules. I could see him laughing. I was so mad at him; we didn't need to attract any more trouble than we had already.

"The air patroller flew in and Marco tried to get away. He swooped down toward the field—low over the trees. His wing clipped the top branches of a cottonwood." Mira stopped talking, clenching her eyes, squeezing out the tears. Cleo touched her shoulder.

"I can still hear the snap, the tree limb, his arm. He pinwheeled into the tree. The sound . . .

"I ran, people ran from the field, the air patroller landed. I got there first. One of the wings was ripped off Marco's arm. His neck was broken. His eyes were open. Seconds after I got there, he stopped breathing. I saw the light go out in his eyes, right there. I can see it now."

Mira broke into sobs. Cleo hugged her, naked flesh against Mira's. "I'm so sorry," she said softly. "It wasn't your fault."

"You don't understand," Mira said, anger overwhelming her. "We were close but then we weren't. He was harder and harder to handle, and I had other things I wanted to do. I was trying to ally with other women, and he was a drag on everything I did. I resented him. I was fed up. I wished he was gone—and then, then he was gone."

Cleo held her tightly. "It's okay. It's okay to cry."

Mira cried. Her chest heaved, emotion welling in her, and she couldn't stop. *This* was what she needed. She hadn't even known it.

Abruptly the music in the next room stopped, and there was a long silence, a faint voice in the background, followed by slowly rising talk. Mira wiped away her tears, first one eye and then the other, with the palm of her hand.

"They've got the results," she said.

"We don't have to go out," said Cleo, her low voice full of sympathy. "Stay here with me."

Mira considered lying with Cleo's warm body next to hers. But she did not want to be naked with a stranger. She got up. She reached for her blouse. In Hypatia's bathroom she washed her face.

When they came out of the bedroom the first thing Mira saw was Carey, across the room, his hand steadying the leg of Hypatia as she stood on a chair. He briefly locked eyes with her.

"This isn't the end," Hypatia said. "Daquani will represent us. Her voice is the beginning of the revolution. They know we are here and they know we are watching. Change can't be held back!"

Of the Reform Party, only Daquani had won. Among the other challengers Hypatia had garnered the lowest number of votes. And, though the margin was small, the proposition to extend the franchise to all men had failed. There was more, but Mira didn't listen.

Most of the people were deflated and some were angry. They insisted that the results were manipulated, but Mira suspected it was all because of Hypatia's terrorist quote. It wasn't fair that a few words could derail an entire movement, and she was swept by anger at both the idiot voters and at Hypatia for giving them something to be distracted by. But Hypatia did not seem upset, and Mira, to her surprise, did not care either. Fair? Only children expected fair.

"I'll get us some drinks," Cleo said. She kissed Mira on the cheek.

As soon she left Mira's side, Mira slipped toward the door.

"Mira?" Carey came toward her. She pushed away from him, past several people, and out.

The crowd outside had grown, and as Mira passed through them two constables were trying to get them to disperse. "All right," they said. "Time to go home."

Mira ran down the concourse. Corridors here and there produced knots of sullen young people. She was out of breath when she reached the university station. On the platform three boys argued with a constable, who had her baton out, twisting it nervously in her hands. Mira got on the train and went home.

In her apartment she took one of her toy horses, Comet, down from the shelf and held him tightly in her palm. She sat on her bed and turned on the pixwall. From her archive she called up a video she had not looked at in years.

She squeezed Comet in her hand and his hard little legs poked into her palm. On the screen the handheld camera looked over Mira's shoulder as she strode along ahead of it.

"Turn around, Mira!" came Marco's insistent voice.

The Mira in the video shook her head. Her black hair was long, and floated above her shoulders before coming to rest. She kept walking. They were in the West Concourse, passing some residences larger and more luxurious than the place where they lived. Ahead stood the statue of Tiresias.

"C'mon Mira! Turn around! Let's see that pop star smile!"

She whirled on him and hissed, "Turn that thing off!"

Mira was startled to see her own face, ten years younger. Round cheeks, intense dark eyes, furious brows.

On the audio came Marco's giggle. "*That's* the look I want,

230 • JOHN KESSEL

that's"—he laughed again, and zoomed in until her face filled the screen—"here it is, Cousins, exclusively, the face of the woman who's going to change the Society forever, captured by our investigative correspondent Marco Hannasson. Care to say a few words for your fans, Ms. Hannasdaughter?"

The expression on the face of the Mira on the screen cracked, the anger crumpling into what at first seemed like tears. But then she burst into laughter, and Marco's laughter, so much like hers, doubled it.

"You're crazy!" Mira, sitting in her apartment ten years later, whispered, just a second before the laughing Mira on the screen said, "You're crazy!" and put her hand over the lens.

CHAPTER SEVEN

EITHER ERNO WAS DELUDED, OR HIS NEW HAND HAD capacities he had never heard of before. For one thing, if he held it against an object for five or more seconds, he could tell its temperature within one degree Celsius.

More remarkable, if he placed his hand flat against a wall, fingers spread, he could sense the size and configuration of the room beyond.

Most disconcerting of all, if he took someone's hand, or had firm contact anywhere else with someone's skin, he could perceive their feelings and know if that person was telling the truth. He hadn't been able to put this to any rigorous test because he didn't want to reveal what he was sensing. The one person whose body he had the opportunity to touch for an extended length of time was Amestris.

• • • • •

Sometimes Erno woke in the middle of the night disoriented, expecting to find himself in the Hotel Gijon in Mayer. What was this bedroom? Who was this woman beside him? Gradually he'd calm his ragged thoughts. He would measure his breathing, roll onto his side toward Amestris and touch her thigh, feeling her warm, dreaming thought.

The night before, they'd gone to the theater and dinner with Leila and Dariush. Not much like his nights with Zdeno and Fabrizio in Dorud: Leila talked incessantly about her pregnancy, Dariush was in training and finicky about what he ate, Amestris was bright and funny but somehow distant. Erno drank too much, a bourbon from Kentucky that cost as much as he had earned his first month on the job at Persepolis Water.

In the morning, head throbbing, he retreated to his workroom and called up the models of the hornbeam genome. Scattered across his worktable were a tablet crammed with scientific papers, handwritten notes, bulbs of IQ enhancers. Across the room, under grow lights in an incubator, his most recent batch of feathery green seedlings sprouted.

He worked for an hour and a half, then saved the incomplete analysis of adjustments to low-G, accelerated growth rates, and extrapolated density. He massaged the small of his back and called a letter onto his screen. He stared at it, breathing slowly.

Amestris entered. "We've received the final payment from the Tycho Authority."

Erno blanked the screen and turned to her. "Good."

She leaned over his desk and kissed him. He got out of his chair. She yielded in his arms, and he touched his fingers to her cheek. "Lunch?" he said.

"I'm going to meet Sima," she said quietly.

He could tell she was lying. "All right. This afternoon I'll be out looking at the plantings."

"I'll meet you there later, and we can come home together," Amestris said.

"I'd like that."

She kissed him again, smiled, then left. He went back to his desk and opened the letter again.

My Dear Erno,

I am pleased to hear that you are alive and well and still doing research. You were always a good student.

It's risky for me to respond to you, but I owe it to you based on our previous association (though you must know how much I disagreed with the ill-advised actions that led to your exile). Clearly you must see the way Persepolis slanders us every day. If it were to come out that I was communicating with Erno Pamelasson, living and working in the heart of the most powerful of the lunar patriarchies, I would not be able to continue my research.

To be frank, since the election and subsequent troubles, men in the Society are suspect, even men who believe as I do in the fundamental justice of our social structure. I will not give you access to any of our work, let alone send you any samples of the species I have in development.

I still have great fondness for you, Erno, but I cannot help but question the choices you've made.

In memory of better times,

Lemmy

Months into the contract with Saman, Erno was in trouble. He had established a test planting of genetically modified maple seedlings. He had told Amestris and Sam that these seedlings would mature four times as fast as conventional maples. The truth was that signs of premature morbidity were already evident in the most advanced specimens. They would come nowhere near maturity, but he did not know why.

Unfortunately, all Society of Cousins work in that area had been wiped from the public record. In fact, all of the most advanced SoC scientific papers—not just in genobotany, but in biotechnology, physics, and materials science—had been taken down from Cousins sites. And someone had set diligent computer worms to hunt down and destroy any records persisting in other journals and databases. The scientific nets were awash in rumors, the nearside governments were talking about cyber sabotage, and there were calls for the Secretary General of the Organization of Lunar States to mount an investigation.

Half an hour after Amestris left, Erno took the tram out to the Kazedi project. The three dark red cars ran a few meters above the pedestrian concourses, turned down tunnels lined with interactive artwork, passed through neighborhoods and by warehouses. In the industrial center it stopped twice to let off workers for the fusion reactor and ice mines. He had run into Devi once on this train; when he tried to speak with her, hoping to give her a job in EED, she had turned away.

After the industrial district the tram was sparsely occupied, passing through agricultural warrens. Persepolis had the largest aquaculture complex on the moon. Great tanks of cold water held rainbow trout; warmer tanks held tilapia. Engineered bacteria and algae converted waste water into a nutrient bath that was piped into rack farms of lettuce, tomatoes, herbs, strawberries, and vegetables. The plants cleaned the water, which was aerated and returned to the fish tanks to begin the process again. Other closed systems grew lobster and shrimp, prawns, perch, salmon, and catfish. The tram passed by livestock units raising poultry and sheep, past multilevel grain and potato farms until it reached the lava tube that had been prepared for Saman's forest. Erno got off and went first to the nursery, where a half dozen employees were preparing seedlings. Gulal Barzani, his operations manager, was glad to see him.

"Another three hundred maples are ready to transplant," said Gulal, a taciturn Kurdish woman.

"And the plantings?"

"We've established another third of the first copse. But the oldest cohort does not look good."

"Let's go look at them."

They walked out of the nursery and down a wide corridor to the tube. Filtered sunlight filled the cavernous space. The air smelled rich with organics—they had produced an agricultural soil using methods that Erno had learned among the Cousins, which differed in significant ways from Persepolis practice. A path of black volcanic gravel wound through the plantings. It was Saman's intention to have his forest function as a park as well as a source of wood, and so they'd tried to produce a more natural setting.

He and Gulal examined the maples, pinching the young leaves, smelling the crushed scent. They talked about the acid content of the soil and possible maladaptations to lunar gravity, the concentrations of nitrogen-fixing bacteria and nematodes in the latest soil batches. It was a relief for Erno to let himself fall deeply into a purely scientific problem.

They walked back to the nursery. "You can stay here," Erno told Gulal. "I want to do some work."

He changed into coveralls and drove a cart carrying several dozen of the latest seedlings away from the already planted sections, two hundred meters down the tube to the pond they had constructed. He wanted to work alone, with his hands.

For the next two hours he amended the soil, hauled the pots from the cart, shook the seedlings from the loamy earth and planted them. His shoulders loosened. Sunlight streaming down from the cavern roof cast his shadow on the dark soil. He breathed deep the smell of geosmin and 2-methylisoborneol. The leaves of the seedlings were pale green on their tops, silvery beneath.

He used Alois's artificial hand as unconsciously as his own. Through it he read the temperature of the soil. Could he trust it? If Amestris had indeed lied about meeting Sima, where was she spending the afternoon? He had never been much affected by jealously. As for lies—well, their entire relationship had started with his lies.

He kept his head down and worked. His problem wasn't knowing whether Amestris had lied. His problem was how to create a forest. If he was sure of anything, he was sure that these seedlings he was planting would be dead in three months.

He needed Lemmy's help. He would have a better chance to persuade Lemmy if he could meet him in person. That would mean getting Lemmy out of the Society, or, despite Erno's exile, getting himself back into it. If he could not persuade Lemmy to help, he would have to steal the samples.

Erno was on his knees patting the earth around the base of one of the seedlings when a shadow fell over him. He looked up to find Amestris. As if she had caught him committing a crime, his heart was instantly in his throat. He brushed his hands on his coveralls and got up. "Hello," he said.

Amestris said, "I've just come from seeing Saman."

Erno took another seedling from the cart. "How is he?"

"He's very happy about his forest." She paused. When Erno faced her, she was gazing at the dozen trees he'd planted. "Should he be?"

Erno stood holding the pot in two hands. "What do you mean?"

"I mean, is there going to be a forest? Your trees are dying."

"Those were the first varieties. These new ones—"

"I've been reading your mail. I saw your correspondence."

Erno set the seedling down. "Excuse me," he said. "I need that shovel."

When he bent over to pick it up, she put her foot on the blade. She forced him to look her in the eyes.

Since Mayer, she was the only person who had trusted him. She had pulled him up from Dorud just when it seemed he had finally hit the absolute bottom. But she was rich and he was not, and all she really wanted from him was the chance to get back at her father. He was in the vulnerable position, just as much as in every relationship he'd had with women from the time he had been a boy.

"Are you sleeping with Saman?" he asked.

She looked astonished, and then she laughed. "You care about sexual fidelity? A Cousin?"

"I'm not 'a Cousin.' I'm your husband." He held his grimy hand up under her nose. "See? I'm right here, right now."

She pushed him away. "Get your hand out of my face."

He stepped back. Trembling, he grabbed the last tree he'd planted and yanked it out of the ground; with the same motion he whirled, swinging it at the end of his arm, and let it go. It arced away into the air, hit twenty meters down the gravel path, bounced, tumbled, and came to rest. His heart beat fast. One of the group of workers in the distance stood up and looked their way.

"You lied to me," Amestris said. "You lied to Saman. You can't do it."

He kept his back to her, to the cold determination in her voice. His anger scared him. "I need help, like any human being. Did you think I was some miracle worker?"

She didn't answer right away. "No," she finally said. "I don't think you are a miracle worker."

• • • • •

Two hours earlier, Amestris had found Sam in the Kazedi Concert Hall at the conservatory of music. He was on the stage tuning the grand piano. One of his eccentricities was that, since he sponsored the concert series, he got to tune the pianos himself; he was as good at it as anyone on the moon. He leaned over the harp, a wrench on the pin block, a tuning fork in his left hand, completely unaware of her entrance. She watched him strike the fork, then turn the wrench slightly. He tilted his head to the side, his eyes closed, lips compressed so that the lines at the corners of his mouth stood in relief.

There were bags under his eyes. She had not noticed this before. She was surprised—he had always been so scrupulous about his cosmetic rejuvenation, trying not to look his age. She stepped up and touched him on his shoulder.

His eyes opened, he saw her, and he smiled. He put down the tuning fork. "How good to see you."

"It's good to see you."

He kissed her on the cheek. She let him. What was a kiss between old lovers? He had first asked her to marry him when she was twenty. She had turned him down. Her parents were very angry with her. When she was thirty he still wanted to marry her. When she was forty. For more than twenty years he had wanted to marry her. He wanted to marry her still.

If Sam was jealous of Erno, he did not show it. He was of her father's generation, one of those men who had made the great secular business empires, who cared about propriety and appearances. He had watched her career with sadness and a critical eye. Another woman as wild as Amestris would have felt the condemnation of everyone in her social class, but Sam had never said a word to her, nor had she ever heard of him saying anything about her to anyone else. She supposed that meant he did love her. But he still gave obeisance to those social strictures, even if he, out of love, never applied them to her. She was not sure she could forgive him for that.

"Thanks for coming," Saman said. "I was just tuning up for the Chen Wen Ho concert."

"Where is she?"

"She's in her hotel throwing up. She claims it's gravity sickness, but she throws up before every concert on Earth, too."

Amestris sat on the piano bench and leaned back against the keyboard. "You'll get her put together. She'll think she can conquer the solar system. You're good at that."

He sat beside her, facing the piano, played a G chord. "Do you ever play?"

"You know I don't. I don't have the skills anymore."

"Perhaps. You have more heart, though."

Sam seemed to be putting off something. "What did you want to see me about?" Amestris asked.

He didn't look at her. "I want to know how the project is going."

"Erno is enthusiastic. You spoke with him yesterday."

"I want your opinion."

"I'm going out there after this. We've got a start on the maples, and are beginning with the hornbeam plantings."

"Yes, I know. I've been to the nursery. I've seen the crew on the day shift putting in the new seedlings. And, on the off-shifts, I've seen the night crew pulling out the old seedlings. The dying ones."

"Not all of them are going to be robust. Erno wants a successful growth, so he's culling the weak ones."

"Is that what he told you?"

It was what Erno had told her. She sat up, and her elbow struck some keys. The tones wavered in the air.

Saman closed the fall board and looked directly at her.

"What?" Amestris asked. "Do you know something I don't?"

"I don't know how much you know, my dear. I would hate to think that you would take advantage of me, after all these years."

"I would never take—"

"Yes," he said.

She thought of how, in her youth, she had played him along while she slept with any handsome man who fell under her gaze.

He had no right to make her feel bad. "Why don't you just say what you want to say?"

"I've been monitoring Erno's communications. His modified species are dying, and he doesn't know how to fix them. He's begging for help from his mentor back in the Society of Cousins, and not getting it."

Amestris felt herself color. "Why are you spying on him?"

"This is a large investment. It's my life's work. And he has drawn you into it—you've alienated your family in order to marry him. If your firm fails, you will be ruined financially. You're at risk, too."

"What do you know about genobotany? What do I know? He's an expert."

"So he says."

"So far he's done exactly what he said he could do."

"So far." Sam touched her hand. "He doesn't have to have bad intentions. He may simply be out of his depth."

She pulled her hand away. She could see it perhaps—how

everything Erno had done might have been conjured out of the air, fueled by desperation. But the entire enterprise had been conjured out of the air.

What was love but something conjured out of the air?

"You have no right to question our marriage," she said. "*You*, especially, don't."

"I only want to protect you," Sam said.

"By spying on my husband. Did you think I would approve?"

"I was hoping that you would respect the truth."

"You don't know the truth. You only know what you want, what you've wanted for twenty-five years. Haven't you tired of this?"

Saman's face darkened, and he would not look at her. He picked up the tuning fork, slid his index finger along the gap between the tines. "No," he said quietly, "I haven't. I never will."

"Then I'm sorry for you."

"Amestris, you have to understand the position you are in."

"What? Are you canceling the project?"

"No. But I have my limit. I don't know where it is yet; still, I am not going to throw good money after bad."

"I wouldn't expect anything else from a purely business relationship," she said.

He pushed himself off the piano bench, slowly, turned his big shoulders toward the open soundboard, and picked up the wrench. He ran his hand through his disheveled hair. "You had better go and talk to your husband, then." His voice was husky.

"Yes. I had better."

Amestris stepped down from the stage and out of the concert hall.

She rode the tram out to the forest project. Sam didn't want to throw good money after bad, but for decades he had thrown good love after bad. She felt the pressure of his desire and, as many times before, it made her angry. He had said repeatedly he had no claim over her, but here he was still trying to manage her life.

She shouldn't have approached him about this project. She had known all along that, with Sam, it could never be just business, yet she had not hesitated. And as the tram moved through the dark tunnel between districts, the reality that she had given herself to a stranger, a man little more than half her age, grew within her. Whatever Sam's faults, he had never lied to her. And over the years he had been right about many things that she had ignored.

It was near the end of the work day when she reached the cavern, and the sunlight had been turned down. In the project office she found Gulal and two workers looking over a manifest. Amestris exchanged the briefest of hellos and went out to find Erno. She passed a crew among the already established plantings, and went on for a hundred meters until she saw him, on his knees beside a cart, patting the earth around the base of a seedling. He didn't notice her until she was standing over him. Startled, he looked up

"Hello," he said.

There was no point in maintaining the pretense that she had been at lunch with Sima. "I've just come from seeing Saman," Amestris said.

Erno turned away, avoiding her eyes, and pulled another seedling from the cart. "How is he?"

"He's very happy about his forest." She surveyed the dozen trees he'd planted. "Should he be?"

"What do you mean?"

"I mean, is there going to be a forest? Your trees are dying."

"Those were the first varieties. These new ones—"

"I've been reading your mail. I saw your correspondence."

Erno set down the seedling. "Excuse me," he said. "I need that shovel."

When he stooped to pick it up, she put her foot on the blade. The image Amestris had first had of him, on the street after being thrown out of the tavern in Dorud, flashed in her mind.

He finally looked at her. "Are you sleeping with Saman?"

She couldn't help herself: She laughed. "You care about sexual fidelity? A Cousin?"

"I'm not 'a Cousin.' I'm your husband." He held his grimy hand up under her nose. "See? I'm right here, right now."

Yes, he was her husband, and looking into his guilty eyes the fact of it washed over her: She'd tied herself to a miserable fake. "Get your hand out of my face."

For a second she thought he might strike her; instead he yanked up the last tree he'd planted, whirled around, swinging it at the end of his arm, and let it go. It flew away into the twilight, hit twenty meters down the gravel path, bounced, tumbled, and came to rest. Erno's face was stone. Amestris had never seen him so angry. Another frustrated man, one of the endless series she had slept with over the last three decades.

"You lied to me," Amestris said. "You lied to Saman. You can't do it."

He turned his back on her. "I need help, like any human being. Did you think I was some miracle worker?"

Oh, she was a fool, a fool at twenty, a fool at forty-five. "No," she said. "I don't think you are a miracle worker."

"What does that mean?"

"Nothing. It means nothing." She was being cruel. Out of his depth, Saman had said. It would do no good to tear everything apart. "It means we have to figure out what to do."

He picked up the shovel and slid it sullenly onto the bed of the truck. "I need a drink," he said. "You need one, too. Get in."

She got into the cab and he drove back to the shed. The place had cleared out. She watched him clean his hands, strip off his coveralls, and put on his street clothes. The long muscles in his arms, his muscular legs. His narrow shoulders, big hands that she had enjoyed on her body. He'd told her he loved her hundreds of times, but how much could she trust him to know himself? To him she was a way up, a way out.

Forty-five. If she was lucky she would live another eighty years. She had told herself that she wanted as many of those years as possible to be with him. She still wanted that. But she could not imagine where either of them would be in eighty years.

Rather than go back to the apartment, they rode the tram into the city and went to a tea shop. "Dream of a Blue Age," the sign above the door said, the words floating over a three-dimensional image of a twilit sea, mountains in the distance. Some years back it had been one of her haunts.

> *Oh, Lord of Divine Loveliness, we have been*
> *Burned to a crisp. Come now, ask of us*
> *What is it a destitute and beggarly person needs?*

The quiet young brewmaster was new. He offered them a menu. There was a long list of religious teas, but the Peace that Passeth All Understanding was not a spur to action. There were erotic teas, teas to wash away depression. Teas to spark hilarity. Melancholy teas. Ironic teas.

She selected Sharp Dealing. Erno had The Flame that Consumes. They sat on cushions at a low table.

"I'm sorry I lied," Erno said. "My desire for you isn't a lie."

"Desire is easy. I need a partner," she said. "I won't be used."

Erno lowered his voice. "Nor will I. You say you like me because I'm not like the men here. You want some cross between what you think a Cousins man is and your father. I can't be that—I'll only disappoint you."

He reached out to touch her hand. "Haven't I done what I said? In ten months I haven't lied to you as much as your father lies in a week."

Amestris wanted to believe him, but the fact that he had fooled her stung. Still, there was no point in recriminations. There was definitely no point in telling him that Saman knew the project was in trouble.

"This information blackout from the Society has made it hard," Erno said. "If I could only get some gene samples. I know for a fact that Lemmy's already got a species of ash adapted for accelerated maturity, and was working on birches."

"He won't send you samples?"

"He won't even talk with me. If I could get back there, I could persuade him. Or if I failed at that, I'd steal them. I know the lab, I know the procedures. But I can't go back. They wouldn't want to see me, any more than they'd want to see Marysson."

She took another sip of tea, her eyes narrowed. She couldn't help herself: She still loved him, her beautiful young liar. Her thoughts felt as sharp as broken glass. Erno had many qualities to recommend him, and she could use them.

"It doesn't matter what they want," she said. "It only matters what is politically expedient."

· · · · ·

Tehran Beach was at the end of the Blue Line. Erno followed the crowd from the train to the beach's vestibule, where he waited among dozens of people in the security queue. He examined the elaborate turquoise and gold tile work of the walls. The floor here was springy moss. Ahead, past the sign warning of the dangers of agoraphobia, the vestibule ended in an arch, through which he could see bright sun, black sand, blue sky. The sound of surf and the squeals and shouts of bathers floated in on a salt breeze.

In front of him three adolescent boys with curly dark hair and smooth faces fidgeted and joked. Ahead of them stood a family—the father chiding the children for their impatience, the mother carrying a beach bag stuffed with towels. A businessman in a suit, likely on his way to one of the hotels, muttered to his Aide. An old man and woman, a group of four girls and their chaperone. A young couple, shyly touching hands. It was a cross section of patriarchal gender roles.

Considering how fully Erno had assimilated, he could hardly criticize. He watched the couple subtly twining their fingers, smiling, silent, in love. He told himself that if it came to a break, he could survive the loss of Amestris; he had lived alone for a decade. They could still be business partners. But he knew that to be bravado. He had felt the grace of her affection, and if he couldn't win that back, he didn't see how they could stay together.

The line advanced. Security checked his ID and passed him through into the cavern. He ignored those heading down the steps onto the sand and instead surveyed the esplanade.

Tehran Beach was one of the wonders of the moon. The artificial cavern stretched over five hundred meters long, two hundred wide. Above soared a state-of-the-art false sky, hard blue with dazzling sun and wisps of cloud. Built into one long side of the cavern were a luxury hotel, shops, cafés, and restaurants with tables under green umbrellas. Groups of palms bordered closely cropped lawns; banks of flowers drew butterflies of yellow, orange, and black. Below the stone railing of the esplanade a broad swath of black sand, dotted with umbrellas and beach chairs, stretched down to the edge of the water.

The faux ocean, forty-five thousand cubic meters of water kept at a constant twenty-eight degrees Celsius, crashed in ponderous, slow surf upon this strand, huge dollops of spray flying through the air. The waves ran in, foam dark with suspended sand, a third of the way up toward the wall of the esplanade before retreating. On the cavern wall opposite the beach the real water merged with a projected image of the sea reaching out to a mathematically flat horizon. The impression was of a vast, breathtaking ocean, the closest thing on the moon to the Earth, the surface of a world so broad and open it could hardly be understood. It was a dream of the Caspian on a beautiful day. All this constructed, free to citizens of Persepolis, through the largess of Cyrus Eskander.

Below the false sun the surface of the false sea glittered and danced. Erno stopped to watch the blue waves run in, rising in rollers until they crested and broke into foam. The break would spread in a white line to either side as each wave tumbled onto the retreating waters of the previous wave. Men and women surfed on their float boards, and children laughed in the shallows.

A matron in a modest bathing suit coaxed a chubby infant into the water; the child lifted its foot high, then lost its balance and sat down in the wet sand. More daring young women wore suits that showed a considerable amount of skin. A team of students were constructing a sand sculpture of a griffin.

After a few minutes of leaning on the stone railing, Erno turned to the public baths. Beyond the men's entrance he was greeted by a courteous young man and directed to the disrobing room, divided into stalls so the patrons of different rank could have some degree of privacy. All men might be brothers, but until they were unclothed the forms of class still held sway. He wrapped himself in a plush white towel, slipped on the sterilized slippers given him, and moved into the baths to meet Cyrus Eskander.

Persepolis had no monarch, but every politician drew on the culture's affinity for sacred kingship. The *Shahnameh* was taught in every school. Though its kings were subject to grave errors of judgment, hubris, or even incompetence, every generation might still throw forth a supernatural hero, a Rostam, relentless in war, magnanimous in victory, compassionate toward the suffering.

The just and righteous king. Cyrus Eskander saw himself as one.

His charities were legion, a testimony to the grandeur of his family name. In addition to Tehran Beach, he had constructed within the city twelve elaborate *hammâms*, bath houses male and female. Such was his *noblesse oblige* that he was known on occasion to bathe in these places himself.

Still, even though Amestris had told him to expect it, and named the time and place, Erno was surprised to find Cyrus waiting in the steam room. Cyrus, towel around his taut belly, his shoulders well but not ostentatiously muscled, reclined on a bench reading a tablet. Erno tried to seem at home as he sat beside him on the warm tile.

"Good day, Mr. Pamson," Cyrus said, putting aside his reading.

"Good day, Mr. Eskander. May I be your sacrifice?"

Cyrus smiled. "Perhaps we shall be one another's."

The three other men in the steam room ignored them. Cyrus's glance swept casually over Erno. "Have you taken the waters yet?"

"No."

"You must. We will go in a few minutes." Cyrus leaned back on his elbows and closed his eyes. Erno did not know what to say. He let the heat soak into his body, inhaled the scented steam.

Eventually Cyrus asked, "Did you participate in your Society's athletic competitions? Were you perhaps a gymnast? You look as if you might have been one."

"No more than any boy. We have competitions. Mostly individual, except for hockey and football."

"As one would expect, your women's teams are formidable. Yet I was most impressed by the Society's *Ruǎn tā* squad in the last Olympics. It's a paradox to us—I know you will not take offense if I say it—how Cousins men, lacking in so many of the qualities that make a man, show such excellence and sportsmanship."

"Mothers, wives, sisters, aunts—they all support male athletes. We're proud of our teams."

"It's interesting to me, Mr. Pamson, that despite your years of exile, you still use 'we' when speaking of the Society."

"Old habits, I guess."

Cyrus gestured toward his tablet. "I was just reading a book by one of your athletes. It's called *Lune et l'autre*. Clever title—you understand the pun?"

"I don't know French."

"*The Moon and the Other*. But if you add an apostrophe to *lune* you get *l'une*, 'the one,' so the title becomes *The One and the Other*. But who is the One, and who the Other, eh? Male or female?"

Erno shook his head. "I doubt you'll learn anything worthwhile about us from that book. He's not a serious person."

"I understand that he—this Mr. Evasson—is challenging the Society's rules of fatherhood."

"I wouldn't know about that."

Cyrus inhaled deeply. After a moment, he said, "My beloved daughter has told me that you need to gain access to the Society in order to grow this wood for our friend Mr. Kazedi."

"That's true. If you—"

Cyrus held up his hand. "I think we should try the bath now," he said, rising.

Despite Cyrus's status games, there was nothing for Erno to do but follow.

The floor of the domed central bath was decorated in a complex abstract pattern of blue and white. Sunlight drifted down from a circular opening at the apex of the dome. Decorating the walls were bright images of figures from the *Shahnameh*, including one of Rostam grappling with the white demon Div-e Sefid. Rostam had severed the demon's legs, which seemed to be floating in the air. The demon looked rather unperturbed by this development, though Rostam was plunging a dagger into its heart.

Cyrus and Erno dropped their towels and joined the other men in the heated octagonal pool. The water smelled of roses. Faint music played in the background. Two men sat conversing in a corner, and on the other side a young man was washing the face of a much older man—perhaps his father—with a blue cloth.

Erno considered it quite likely that the ice that had produced this water had been mined from the gap where he had lost his hand. He held his replacement just below the surface, fingers spread. It looked completely natural. So many false appearances. He ran over the arguments he was prepared to use to get Cyrus's help, and waited.

After some ten minutes Cyrus gave the slightest of nods to the other men, and as one they rose from the waters, gathered up their towels and robes, and left the room.

When they were gone, Cyrus said, "Here is the situation. Though the decision has not been made public yet, Organization of Lunar States Resolution 1146, establishing an investigative committee into the condition of men in the Society of Cousins, has gained the grudging acquiescence of the Board of Matrons. They have agreed to allow a visit from representatives of the committee. There will be four lead investigators: two physical scientists, one social scientist, and one designated observer. The OLS has agreed that the observer must be acceptable to the Cousins.

"I have been involved, in a quiet way, in these deliberations. I have argued that this observer must be someone who has intimate knowledge of the Society, and that suggests it should be someone raised there. This narrows the field of candidates drastically. My current proposal to serve in this capacity is your friend Mr. Thomas Marysson, who calls himself by this *nom de guerre* Tyler Durden."

"They'll never agree to that."

"They are not in a strong bargaining position."

"What have they said?"

"They protested in the strongest terms possible. They say they will not accept a delegation if it contains Mr. Marysson."

"I'm not surprised. If you want my opinion—"

"Your opinion will be very useful to me, in its proper time."

Erno sank deeper into the pool, letting the steaming water rise to his neck. He had no status. The exile. The guest worker.

"My beloved daughter tells me that the materials you need are under tight security."

"Yes."

"I therefore am prepared to propose that the fourth member of the investigative team be you."

Erno gave a single, brief laugh. "They won't accept me, either."

"They will if their only alternative is Mr. Marysson."

Though Amestris had told Erno that Cyrus might be able to get him back into the Society, he had not thought there was any real chance. "Does Amestris know about this?"

"It was her idea."

She had not said a word about it. Did she think he would refuse? He thought about that for a moment. On the wall across from him, the greatest hero of the culture's founding epic fought with a half-human monster.

"You'll have to use considerable influence to make this happen," Erno said. "Unless you're acting solely out of the goodness of your heart, you must want something in return."

"My heart, Mr. Pamson, is indeed good. I love my daughter."

"She'll be very grateful. So will I."

"Have you ever heard of something called an IQSA?"

"No. What is it?"

"It is a device rumored to exist in the Society of Cousins," Cyrus said, "something that interests me a great deal. I would like you to help me learn more about it."

Cyrus rested his arms along the ledge of the pool. "Do you know the story of the Sasanid King Bahrâm Gur and the disrespectful village?"

"No. I've not heard it."

"You will indulge me, then. King Bahrâm Gur was a good and beneficent king, and under his reign all was in order in his kingdom. But one day he visited a village, and instead of being greeted by the leading men, offered bread and salt, and refreshed from his journey, for an hour after he entered the center of the town he was left to wait. Bahrâm Gur did not give any sign of his displeasure, but he vowed to destroy this village. He let a month pass, and then sent his priest to grant the people of the village a great boon: The social hierarchy was to be abolished.

Instead of having a headman, there would be complete equality among men, women, and children.

"The people were overjoyed. They celebrated into the night, ate and drank and made love. They reveled in their new freedoms, where no man was above any other, where no wife was involuntarily subject to her husband, where no son need without protest obey the command of his father.

"Soon, having no one to hold them to a standard, they began neglecting their work. Having no respect for the law, they fell to fighting. Dogs ran in the streets. Within a year the village lay in ruins. The remaining citizens petitioned Bahrâm Gur for help, and he graciously interceded. He had the insolent whipped, the fornicators killed, and the children bound to their work. He appointed a new and strict headman, answerable only to himself. Only then did the village recover and prosper.

"You, Mr. Pamson, come from that village. You will help me see it brought within the embrace of beneficent authority."

"Why would I help you do that?"

"Erno," Cyrus said, his brown eyes on his son-in-law, "you know that I was not happy to see my daughter marry you. I wondered what she saw in you. At first I assumed it was because she could make you obey her, which she could not do to a man of Persepolis. But I don't think that's true. I see you are a person of some puissance. The fact that you were involved in this rebellion against the Matrons confirms that you are not an ordinary Cousin. You have the makings of a man."

"A person of merit," Erno said.

"Yes. That is well put."

Ten years in exile. If he failed, he could be busted back to the mines, or the freezers. "I'm not going to undermine the Society," Erno said. "Your commission will find little to warrant any interference, and if you count on me for that, you'll be disappointed. And I won't abandon Amestris to you."

"You see, I was right. You are not weak at all."

"I'll go, but it will be for my own purposes."

"I would not expect otherwise. We have an agreement, then—between two men whose word is their bond."

Erno extended his left hand.

Cyrus looked at Erno's hand as if it were made of offal. He extended his right.

Erno switched to his right, and they grasped hands. A man's word was his bond. This was what men did—they said words and then died living up to them. The kind of thing that Erno's teachers had mocked as a veneer over centuries of treachery. And here he was, playing that game with a man who had little but contempt for him.

Cyrus explained that Erno would have to meet representatives of the OLS. He would become a public figure, and would draw attention that, Cyrus said, could only be beneficial to his and Amestris's business.

Erno said little. When Cyrus left, he retreated to the dressing room, wondering what must have been going through Amestris's mind as she approached her father for help.

Erno needed to get to the Society of Cousins to see Lemmy. He needed to see Lemmy to complete the project. He needed to complete the project in order to prove to Amestris that he was what he said he was. He needed to prove he was what he said he was so that he would be worthy of her love.

So in order to stay with Amestris, he was going to have to leave her. And she had helped arrange this outcome.

When he emerged from the building, he found Cyrus lingering on the esplanade. A small crowd had gathered around him and on the sand below, looking up with worshipful faces.

Erno had taken a few steps past them when Cyrus called to him. "Mr. Pamson! One moment, please."

Erno returned. As the people parted to let him close, he saw, seated on its haunches beside Cyrus, a dog. A sleekly handsome Doberman wearing a dark pinstriped suit. The dog looked up at Erno, ears forward, with appraising eyes. It was the video reporter Sirius. The people were giddy at this brush with celebrity.

"I'd like you to meet an associate of mine," Cyrus said. "This is Carrollton's Sirius Alpha-Ultra vom Adler. Sirius, this is Erno Pamson."

"An honor," the dog said, holding out his handpaw.

CHAPTER
EIGHT

November 8: Organization of Lunar States Resolution 1146

establishes a Special Commission on the Condition of Men

(SCOCOM). SCOCOM is charged with investigating reports

of human rights violations in the Society of Cousins, the

embargo imposed by the SoC on scientific information, the

cyber attack by the SoC on data systems throughout the solar

system, and potential violations by the SoC of OLS resolutions

regarding the production of weapons on the moon.

The Society of Cousins is requested to give

"immediate, unconditional, and unrestricted access" to

populations, individuals, social organizations, gendered

associations, and political groups within the SoC, as well as to facilities, buildings, equipment, records, and any means of transport that SCOCOM may wish to inspect. The OLS offers the Society of Cousins a "final opportunity to comply with its obligations to human rights as set out in the OLS Charter" and warns that the SoC will face "serious consequences" if it fails to do so.

December 16: The Society of Cousins announces that it will allow SCOCOM to visit the Society "without conditions."

December 23: SoC and OLS officials meet to discuss the logistics for the visit of inspectors and the composition of the investigating team. The OLS and the SoC announce that final arrangements will be made public at a meeting scheduled for the end of the month.

December 31: The mutually agreed-upon members of the SCOCOM investigating team are announced. They are:

- Myra Göttsch, Ubitech MicroFabrik GmbH, Stuttgart. Physics, Head of the team
- Li Chenglei, University of Science and Technology, New Guangzhou. Biotech
- Martin Beason, McGill University, Montreal. Social Science

- Erno Pamelasson, Eskander Environmental Design, Persepolis. Observer
- Staff and assistants

Imbedded in the SCOCOM team will be Carrollton's Sirius Alpha-Ultra vom Adler, Consortium of Lunar Media pool reporter, and his assistants.

• • • • •

By the time Mira and Cleo reached the cable station, five hundred people filled the road in front of the entrance, all the way to the edge of the park. Some carried banners reading "No Patriarchs Required!" and "OLS = Oppression Loathing Shame." But another read "Welcome Home!" People held up bright blue paper books, fabricated by one of Hypatia's students, copies of *Stories for Men*.

Mira moved ahead of Cleo through the fringes of the crowd. She was supposed to have joined the welcoming delegation earlier, but she had missed her connection and hoped to join the party at the station itself.

Reform supporters, wearing red, made up a good portion of the crowd. A dozen trans women wore identical red dresses. Men in work clothes—from the helium mines, the water and air recycling, a crew of hydroponic harvesters from Agriculture—were shadowed by constables expecting Spartans to create an incident.

Mira tried to see over the people around her. "Wait for me," Cleo said.

"There's no point in your fighting through this mess," said Mira. "Once we get to the front, I'll have to go on alone anyway. Climb onto that planter and you'll see everything."

Cleo looked doubtful. "Okay. See you later, then." She kissed Mira on the cheek.

"Later." Mira pushed forward, relieved to be rid of her.

Cleo had been lobbying for them to start a family. Forget the Greens, Cleo said—if Mira could get Carey and Val to join, they would have the start of their own power network. It was a ludicrous idea. For one thing, Mira had not seen Carey much in recent weeks. He acted as if it were his new job and his responsibility for Val that kept them apart, but that wasn't it. Since election night he'd kept his distance from politics, while Mira was in as deep as ever. They hadn't slept together in weeks. At least Carey wasn't sleeping with Hypatia, either.

Guards stationed at the doors to the terminal checked credentials. Krista Kayasdaughter and several other Board members, along with scientists in the areas represented by the SCOCOM team, would greet the delegation. Daquani Jeffersdaughter represented the Reform Party.

"Daquani makes our point for us better than I could," Hypatia had told Mira. "The fact that the only male who could get elected to the Board had to become a woman to do so will not be lost on the OLS. And the OLS is our best chance to force a change."

Even though Looker had posted nothing since the election, Hypatia still sought Mira's opinions. Hypatia's attention was now focused on the SCOCOM investigation and how it could be played to the Reform Party's advantage. She saw Erno Pamelasson as the wedge to pry open the workings of the committee.

"Can we trust the OLS?" Mira asked.

"I trust you, Mira, to work your way into that reception group," Hypatia had told her. "The fact that you testified at Pamelasson's trial gives you credibility, if you'll use it."

At the station entrance a constable stopped her.

"I'm in the reception party," Mira said.

"No, you're not. You're out here."

"I work for Eva Maggiesdaughter. She's right inside there—just ask her."

Reluctantly, the constable sent one of the others to get Eva. Eva looked toward the entrance, nodded, and the constable came back and let Mira in.

The hall was full of people she did not know, but Eva and the reception committee had gathered beyond the customs station, just past a low railing on the platform. Daquani nodded to Mira. Among the others was Krista Kayasdaughter, current Chair of the Board of Matrons.

"I wondered what happened to you," Eva said. "Let me introduce you."

Kayasdaughter offered Mira a perfunctory hug. "Pleased to meet you," she said. "You knew Pamelasson back before his exile, right?"

"Yes."

"We're glad to have you here today."

Kayasdaughter spoke with Eva for a moment, then returned to the other Board members.

Mira ended up on the back of the platform, in the second rank. She glanced across the hall through the glass walls of the lobby to the crowds outside. Unheard, they chanted, raised their arms, waved signs, as good an image as you could want of a bunch of people working at cross purposes.

In the aftermath of the election, the Society was in ferment. In refectories and classrooms, young men and women argued until late into the night. Protests sprang up in the park and public spaces. Music, most of it having more to do with dancing than politics, blasted from clubs. Fowler teemed with more life than it had at any time in Mira's memory.

In the back of every public meeting stood a constable. At every club a curfew. On the tram any woman who wore a Reform Party armband could count on being questioned by some Matron. On the other side, fatherhood proponents grew tiresome in their one-note use of Carey's custody battle as a cover for generalized resentment, and a handful of Spartans drove every online discussion into chaos.

Erno had been all over the news: images taken from his and Marysson's trial a decade earlier, recent vids from the patriarchal nets. There he was at age seventeen, standing on the stage in the amphitheater while some Matron described how his mother had been asphyxiated in a dark tunnel trying to save him from himself; here he was a month ago—older, quieter, a certain watchfulness in his eyes—interviewed with his wife, Amestris Eskander Pamelasson, the daughter of one of the most powerful capitalists on the moon, poised and beautiful in the *soigné* Persepolis fashion. About as different from a Cousins woman as you could get.

All over the moon people speculated whether Erno was working for Cyrus Eskander. A year ago he had been invisible, a man without a home, and now he was at the heart of the biggest political conflict in decades. The majority of Cousins saw him as at best a troublemaker and at worst a terrorist; a minority claimed he was a champion of human rights driven to radicalism by the repressions he had fought.

To Mira, the trouble Erno brought was the memories he awakened. One of those trial videos showed Mira testifying how, at a party, he had slapped his girlfriend, helping to guarantee his exile. Back then, she had thought of him as a loner not so very different from herself, if perhaps a bit more self-involved. He seemed more interested in writing bad poetry than in politics. His being drawn into the group of young men following Tyler Durden surprised her, and his getting involved in the prank that panicked the entire colony, a fake explosion of the crater dome, made her wonder how he had moved from the kind of complaints that all Cousins boys made to threats of violence. His unhappiness with the Society turned in a way that hers—or Carey's, in *Lune et l'autre*—had not.

What might he think of her now? If the reports were accurate, until his alliance with Eskander, Erno had spent more than a decade living at the bottom of a dozen lunar colonies. He had to know some things, to see things differently. Even if he resented Mira, and more than for the reasons Hypatia had entrusted to her, she was determined to speak with him.

Vibrations beneath her feet indicated that the cable train had entered the tunnel. From a distance came the sound of pressure doors closing and a whoosh of incoming air. Ten minutes later the forward trainlock doors slid open and the train drew up to the platform. Three cars, one cargo and two passenger. The windows were opaqued. A bridge extended itself from the platform to the doors of the passenger car.

The doors of the car slid open and from it emerged not one of the SCOCOM team, but an uplifted capuchin monkey. She wore a jumpsuit with "Consortium of Lunar Media" across the breast and carried a small satchel slung over her shoulder. The monkey paused before the platform, reached into her pack, and flung a handful of camera midges into the air. The midges formed a cloud hovering over the platform.

Kayasdaughter and the others in the welcoming party stepped back. Ubiquitous video recording was a violation of Cousins notions of privacy. As the monkey paused at the end of the ramp, a large Doberman trotted out of the train: Sirius, the media reporter, wearing a tight black vest, black trousers, and black gloves. His forehead was high, the hair over his skull sleek, and ears alertly turned forward. "No cause for alarm," he said to the constables in his curious mutter. He approached Kayasdaughter, sat on his haunches, unfolded his canine handpaw, and held it out. "Board Chairperson Kayasdaughter," he said. "Good day."

Kayasdaughter quickly gathered herself. She shook the dog's handpaw. "Welcome to the Society of Cousins. But where is the delegation?"

"Sorry for the confusion. Did our staff fail to alert you? We wish to get the arrival on vid, so that all of our viewers on the moon—and on Earth, Board Chairperson Kayasdaughter, all the way back on Earth!— shall see this historic moment. If you will?"

"Certainly."

"Gracie," Sirius said to the monkey, which came to his side. The dog mumbled something to his Aide, and out of the car came the SCOCOM team.

First was a woman, red hair pulled back, wearing a gray suit. Smiling, she approached Kayasdaughter, who stepped forward to greet her.

"Ms. Kayasdaughter," she said, extending her hand. In the wake of the dog's handshake, it was all Mira could do to keep from laughing. "I am Myra Göttsch."

Kayasdaughter shook her hand, then embraced Göttsch and kissed her cheek in the Cousins manner. Göttsch did not look comfortable in Kayasdaughter's hug. When they separated, Göttsch turned to Eva. "Professor Maggiesdaughter!" she said. "I am honored that you would come to greet us. So pleased to meet you at last."

Three others, all men, got off the train. Martin Beason, tall with an impressive black beard, broad-shouldered like the cliché of an Earth-bred human; then a lunar man, Li Chenglei from New Guangzhou. The last—slender, fair—was Erno Pamelasson.

He looked older, of course, his hair longer, his face gaunter than years before. Göttsch brought them forward. "Let me introduce Martin Beason"—the tall man bowed to Kayasdaughter—"Li Chenglei—and you perhaps know Erno Pamelasson."

Beason and Li shook hands and were embraced; Erno ignored the handshaking and embraced Kayasdaughter directly.

"Good afternoon, Kayasdaughter," he said, as any Cousin would, without honorific. His eyes passed over Mira, in the back of the platform, but showed no reaction.

When Kayasdaughter suggested that they move to the hall, Mira sidled over to him. "Hello, Erno," she said quietly.

"Hello," he said as they walked side by side. "I didn't expect to see you here."

"Funny—I expected you."

Erno smiled tightly. "I guess Alicia couldn't make it."

Alicia was the woman Erno had slapped.

"No," Mira replied. "I think she's unhappy with you."

"I can't imagine why."

He did not seem very contrite. Before Mira could decide which of the witty, ironic, or cutting rejoinders she had rehearsed to put into play, they emerged from the platform to the arrival hall and Beason pulled Erno away to join Göttsch and Li. The crowd outside saw them and chanted louder. A van drew up in front of the doors. When they opened, the cloud of cameras floated outside, some of the midges hovering and the rest scattering out under the dome. Sirius stood up on his hind legs and scanned the crowd, muttering aloud, probably commentary to his Aide. Gracie stood at the dog's shoulder. The nearest protesters fell back in surprise.

A third of them held up their books, calling Erno's name. They surged forward against those falling back, and the people in front were forced, stumbling, toward the delegates. Mira glimpsed Cleo's face among them. A chant of mostly male voices broke out: "Er-no, Er-no, Er-no . . ." The people in front pushed back; others took offense at this cheering.

The constables worked to clear an aisle from the station entrance to the van. The chanting grew louder. "Er-NO! Er-NO!"

The SCOCOM delegation, surrounded by a phalanx of constables, looked about in curiosity, taking in the crater. Sirius fell into stride beside Göttsch. Jeffersdaughter waved her arm to the Reform Party supporters, who shouted back. The constables struggled to keep the crowd back.

They reached the van. Kayasdaughter said something to Erno. Erno moved up onto the first step of the van, turned to the people, and raised his arms. "Cousins! Please!"

Cheers and catcalls. Shouts. "Go away! Traitor!"

"Let him speak!"

"Er-no! Er-no!"

Erno raised his hands higher. "There's no need for this, if you'll just—"

His voice was drowned out by a huge, hollow, echoing boom.

Mira felt the concussion in her chest. The sound came from above. The crowd hushed. Mira looked up.

A jet of black smoke billowed against the blue sky. People pointed; some cried out. A breach in the dome! The people, already pressed together, surged against one another. A woman tried to leap out of the crush, hit her head on the roof over the station portico, and fell back on the ones below. Panicked people sprang in several directions—toward the station entrance, toward the nearest pressure shelter, toward the van—anything to get into a sealed space, behind pressure doors. Mira saw a man, bounding down the slope toward the crater floor, bowl over another man. Screams and shouts.

Kayasdaughter and the constables hustled Göttsch, Beason, and the others back toward the station, but the doorways were already blocked by people trying to force their way in. Mira turned and took an elbow to her temple. She stumbled, was knocked sideways, and fell to one knee. Something struck her back and she was about to go down when someone grabbed her arm and pulled her up. It was Erno. He drew her toward the van. "This way!"

As they moved, Mira realized that none of the colonywide alarms had sounded. Her Aide was silent. And she felt no pop of her ears that she might have expected in a real pressure breach.

"Stop!" Erno cried out. "It's all right! Look!"

Up above, the jet of smoke had stretched itself out, moving purposefully. There was something wrong with it—it had no three-dimensionality; it was flat, an image. The black fluid—not smoke—ordered itself into huge letters, arranging themselves into words on the inside of the dome:

Bang!

You're dead!

By now others had realized that the explosion wasn't real. It was a copy of the prank that Marysson had orchestrated a decade earlier, with Erno's help.

Someone had reproduced it, as either a mammoth video graffito fastened to the inside of the dome, or smartpaint, or some other simulation.

"Into the van!" a constable shouted, pushing Mira and Erno forward.

For a second Mira resisted, continuing to watch the words develop on the sky. Something new was added. A signature appeared below the threat: "Looker."

• • • • •

Carey was calf-deep in waste water from the tilapia tanks when Marty Annesson rushed in.

"There's been a breach in the dome!"

Jamal Emsson looked up from the dismantled aerator he had on the workbench. Carey waded to the edge of the pool and climbed out.

Winston Alyssasson, bound for the trout tanks, set down the sack of fish food he carried.

"What are you talking about?" Carey asked.

"What happened?" Winston asked.

"Someone set off a bomb. It was timed to happen with the arrival of the outsiders."

Jamal turned on the pixwall. On the screen was a video of a chanting crowd gathered around the entrance to the train station. Constables were trying to clear an aisle among the protesters from the doors to a van. The station opened and out came Krista Kayasdaughter and other Matrons, including Eva, plus an uplifted dog and a monkey. There was a sharp crack, an echoing boom. The image jerked. The crowd rushed toward the station doors. Carey caught a glimpse of Mira. The video abruptly went blank.

Winston stripped off his gloves. "Taari was going there to see them."

Carey said, "If there was a breach, our Aides would all be screaming."

"The system must be down," said Marty.

"Or hacked," said Jamal.

Carey's Aide had no information. He tried calling Eva, but got no answer and told his Aide to keep trying. The video on the wall had begun to repeat. A commentator's anxious voice intruded: "This is all we have at present. We're trying to link to security at the scene, but . . ."

"Tell Sara that I had to go," Winston said, leaving by way of the greenhouse.

"We need to get to a pressure shelter," Marty insisted.

Jamal got up from the bench. "I'm going with Winston."

"If there's really a breach, all of Agriculture will already be sealed," Carey said. "We won't even be able to enter the crater." Carey thought about Val and his smartpaint bomb. "Something's not right about this."

"Of course it's not right!" Marty said. "Somebody blew a hole in the dome!"

The pix switched to a face: a middle-aged constable. "We have a confirmation of the situation in Fowler crater," she said. "Reports of a breach in the dome are false. Repeat: There is no breach in the crater dome. All pressurized areas of the Society are intact. There is no cause for alarm. Cousins are urged to resume their normal activities."

Sara Radhasdaughter came in from the office. "It's okay. I've heard from my sister in the Matrons office—just some sort of prank. There's no blowout."

Carey began to pull off his boots. "Maybe not, but my mother was at the station."

"There's nothing you can do there," Sara said.

Carey didn't bother to put on his street clothes, just discarded his gloves and tugged on shoes. Smelling of fish waste, he hurried from Agriculture toward the nearest concourse. He tried calling Val and Mira, got nothing, and added them to his Aide's call list. The academy registrar did not show Val having logged onto school, and he was nowhere on the LPS maps.

At a refectory people were watching another video. In this one, when the explosion happened the camera swung up to show a jet of black smoke against the blue sky, forming itself into words: *Bang! You're dead!*

"Marysson," one of the bystanders said.

"The minute Pamelasson comes back," said another, "it happens again."

A warm female voice came over Carey's Aide: *Colony pressurization has not been compromised. We repeat: Colony pressurization has not been compromised. Please return to your homes and places of work.*

Around him other people went quiet, listening to the same announcement. Carey left.

None of the pressure doors along the concourse were closed. Where the tunnel opened to the crater people stood looking up at the words written on the sky. *Looker.*

It took Carey twenty minutes to get to the station by foot. The plaza had been cleared except for some stragglers and an influx of the curious. An ambulance stood by and an EMT was wrapping the ankle of a young woman. The nervous constables would not let Carey anywhere near the station.

"I'm Carey—" he began.

"Yes, you're Carey Evasson," the officer told him. "You need to go home."

"My mother was in the reception group. Do you know what happened to her?"

She had her baton out, held at her side. "I don't have any information. Go home."

He backed off to a little knot of people who were standing at one end of the plaza. Little blue books—actual physical books, with pages—lay on the ground.

I've got your mother, his Aide reported.

"Carey?" Eva said.

"Mother," he said, "are you all right? Is Roz all right?"

"We're fine. I'm with some people at the colony offices. Roz went to check on security in Materials. Some people were injured in the panic, but as far as I know there were no fatalities."

"That's good, at least."

"Is Val okay? He's not showing up on the LPS." Her voice was worried. A discarded sign lay at Carey's feet. "OLS = Oppression Loathing Shame" it flashed, with a footprint on it.

"Val is fine," Carey said. "He was at the Glass Institute."

"You should stay in your apartment. Everyone should for a while."

"Do you have any idea who was behind this?"

"Looker—whoever Looker is. A forensic team is on it, and maybe this time they can find some evidence that will lead us to them. I'm very busy now, Carey. I'll say good-bye."

"Good-bye, Mother."

A van pulled up in front of the station. Some workers rolled out a carrier piled with luggage and shipping crates and, under the watchful eyes of the constables, loaded them into the van. Others moved bystanders away. The officer who had spoken with him before approached.

"Look," she told him, "if you won't go home, go back and do your job. This area is interdicted."

Carey moved into the park and found a bench under a plane tree. On the bench lay one of the blue books. *Stories for Men*. He leafed through it. A collection of stories from the twentieth century, testament to a certain kind of lethal masculinity. Even the titles were sodden with testosterone: "The Undefeated." "Fortitude." "The Most Dangerous Game." Another gift from Thomas Marysson. Carey had contempt for Marysson and his borderline personality, yet thanks to the custody battle some people were comparing Carey to him.

His Aide had not gotten Val. Carey left another message.

A sparrow landed on the pavement to beg for crumbs. It danced toward and away from him, opening its sharp beak, turning its head to pin him with its alert black eye.

Should I go to the constabulary, bird? Another missing boy, another panicked colonywide search? That would certainly prove my reliability as a father.

He looked up at the dome again. *Bang! You're dead!*

He called Hypatia.

"Carey, are you all right?" she asked.

"I'm fine. Look, do you know if Mira was behind this?"

"If she was, she set it up well in advance. She was at the station when it happened."

"I know."

"She was trying to make contact with Erno Pamelasson. Daquani says she was on the van from the station to the hotel, but I don't know where she is now. Daquani is fine, though."

"Did *you* have anything to do with it?"

"Don't be absurd. This isn't going to do the Reform movement any good. I'm already having to answer questions. Listen, don't worry about Mira. Right now you should be with Val. You need to maintain your credibility."

"Thanks," Carey said, and hung up.

He hurried to the nearest metro stop. The first train that arrived was crowded; Carey wedged himself in and grabbed a stanchion. On the screen at the end of the car ran another replay of the events at the station, this time a more professional vid. People stared at it while talking to their Aides, voices low, a continuous background mumble beneath the conversations other passengers were having with one another.

He eavesdropped. The water supply was poisoned. There had been an explosion at the fusion plant. "Tyler Durden," "Pamelasson," and "Looker." The prevailing tone was worry, but some of the voices held excitement. Carey tried to sort the responses out by gender and age.

A woman standing next to him, holding on to the same pole, met his eyes. "You're Carey Evasson."

"I am," he said.

She wrinkled her nose, looking over his clothes. "Working the *mita*, are you now?"

"Yes."

"They'd be crazy to let you keep that boy." The woman's eyes were steady.

"Thank you for your opinion, Cousin," Carey said, and turned his back on her.

"You're the cause of all this," the woman said, louder now, and several passengers stopped talking. Two nine-year-old boys sitting on a corner bench seat, watching him, smirked. Carey felt the woman's eyes on his back, breathed slowly, and said nothing.

Carey got off at the university and headed for the Glass Institute. The day was declining and the colony buzzed. People still gathered in streets and plazas, looking up at the words as the sky behind them went purple. Others stood around glued to various screens, talking. Lunanet access was up now, giving the outsiders' view. Endless repetitive videos of the explosion, from half a dozen angles, of different quality. Talk about the OLS investigation being sabotaged.

The Glass Institute was deserted, no sign of Val. As Carey left, Roz's name blinked in the corner of his eye. He let his Aide take it. There was no way he wanted to talk to her now.

By the time he stepped out of the Institute onto the university grounds, the dome had turned prematurely to night—probably to mask the writing. Carey stopped in a refectory, and over beans and rice listened to students at the next table debating. Maybe Val was just hanging out with friends, caught up in the excitement.

He called Val again and left another message.

He tried Juliette. "Carey, are you all right?" she asked.

"I'm fucking fine. Listen, do you know where Dora Aikosdaughter lives?"

"She's got a flat with a couple of other students at Sanger Place."

"Send me the address."

"What's going on?"

"Just send it. Please."

"All right."

In a second it showed in the corner of his visual field. He called up a map with a purple dot for the location. "Thanks," he told Juliette.

"Come see me. I need to talk to you about Hypatia. After twenty years I've finally reached my limit with her. I can't—"

"Later, maybe." He hung up.

Carey let his Aide guide him. Sanger was a rundown neighborhood a couple of levels beneath the university. In its shabby corridors more young people than you could find anywhere else in the colony sat out trading rumors. Shaven-headed couples sat in a noisy café sipping tea. Carey, fifteen years older, drew some glances.

Aikosdaughter's apartment was one of a wall of identical cells in a cylindrical plaza. The window was opaqued. He tried the chime. No answer. He put his ear to the door—were there voices? Two young women walked by and looked at him sideways. When they were far enough away, Carey pounded his fist on the door, ringing the chime simultaneously. No answer. He turned around and kicked the panel with his heel.

At last the window beside the door lit, and the door opened a crack. The face of a young woman. "Who do you think—" She recognized him and stopped. "What do you want?"

"Is Val here?"

"No. Go away."

"Let me in. I need to see him."

"He's not here."

She started to close the door; Carey put his palm against it and pushed it open. Aikosdaughter, half his size, a decade his junior, moved to block him. Her hair was tousled, she wore a loose shirt, and was bare-legged and barefoot. She met his gaze. "What exactly do you think you are doing, Cousin?"

With difficulty, Carey restrained himself.

"I'm looking for my son."

"And I told you he isn't here."

He couldn't guess what she was hiding. "I caught your boyfriend putting a paint bomb on the tower. If I'd reported him, maybe nobody would have gotten hurt today."

"I don't know what you are talking about," she said. They stared at each other. She stepped back and opened the door wide. "Come in, then. Look around. Val's not here."

By this time two others had come into the room, another woman, maybe twenty-five years old, and the young man Carey had caught on the tower with Val.

"Where is he?" Carey asked him.

"I don't know." Shirtless, he stood sullenly, hands in the back pockets of his pants.

Carey pushed past him. The apartment was tiny, and it didn't take him any time to discover Val wasn't there.

"Satisfied?" Aikosdaughter asked, arms crossed.

"Where is Val?"

"I have no idea."

He could quiz her further, but he wasn't going to get anywhere. Without a word, he left.

He was tired, and he smelled worse than he had when he'd rushed out of the aquaculture plant. Maybe Val had not been involved in the fake explosion. He wanted to believe it.

He had one more thing to check before he gave up and called Roz. Ten years earlier, when Marysson and Pamelasson had played the original prank that someone had copied today, they'd done it by going outside the colony and climbing the dome, entering through its apex, and attaching their smartpaint bomb to the interior.

Carey took the metro to the North Airlock. The sign above the complex's doors announced, "Operations Suspended." Carey went to the lockers and checked the bank that held the personal surface suits of the Green family. Val's bright purple skinsuit hung next to Carey's tiger-striped one. Its life support was fully charged.

Carey sat and stared at the suits. He might as well head home now, tell Roz and Eva that Val was missing, and face the consequences.

Instead, he stripped off his clothes and took down his suit. He rolled the skintight up his legs, the seams sealing themselves as he drew them together. When he powered up, the web of thermoregulators squirmed over his skin, adjusting itself to his body. He tugged on his boots, took down his helmet, and tucked it under his arm.

The night attendant was an old schoolmate, Ugo Urasson. Ugo was a member of the Leafs, a small family of no distinction. He was one of those guys who thought he was witty but never accomplished anything. He sat in his glass-walled booth, a glorified doorman. As Carey approached, Ugo looked up from a tablet in his lap. "Airlock's closed, Cousin."

Then he recognized Carey. He put aside the tablet. Carey saw it was playing, not colony news or status reports, but an erotic vid.

"Ugo," Carey said, "I need to take a walk."

"We're locked down, Carey."

"You know me. I'm no terrorist."

"It's not a good time for recreational hiking."

"You know the grief I've been putting up with lately. I need to get away from this insanity."

Ugo smiled. "Bro, that could just be the lamest excuse I've ever heard."

"It's the best I can come up with under the circumstances. Look, I'll lock my suit's LPS into your board. You can follow where I am every minute. Hell, come with me if you want, if you can tear yourself away from your work." Carey gestured toward the tablet.

"Don't mock me, Carey."

"Don't be a dick, Ugo. How many parties have I taken you to over the years? Remember Founders' Week? Stella and Raisa?"

"We're in a lockdown. You know that message you're getting in your ear every five minutes telling you to go home? That includes members of the Green family, too."

"I'm just a Cousin, like you. Are you going to let me out?"

Ugo sighed. "I don't need any trouble."

"No trouble. I'll be back in an hour. Less."

"Let me access your suit."

Carey gave him the code.

Ugo said, "Will you wear a bracelet?"

"For you, Ugo, anything."

Ugo retreated into his office and came back with a wristband. Carey held out his arm and Ugo locked the band around it. "One hour."

"Thanks. Our little secret."

Ugo stepped into the office and touched some controls on his panel. "Use number three," he said.

Carey put on his helmet and walked down to the personnel airlocks. The inside lit up, the door slid open, and he stepped inside.

While he waited for the air to cycle out, Carey considered what privilege could and couldn't do. Being Carey Evasson still worked on people like Ugo. Combine that with the lax security of a society that had no real experience of physical conflict, and it wasn't hard for a man like Carey to pass through this particular locked door.

But at Aikosdaughter's apartment, until she had relented Carey had been helpless. Roz could have shoved her out of the way: Roz was Val's mother. But if Carey had forced his way into a woman's apartment, he could kiss any chance of ever getting custody of Val good-bye.

Assuming he had a chance anyway.

He'd had a good run, a celebrity from a powerful family, over the last twenty years, but after he'd spent a few years in the fish farms working a job no more glamorous than Ugo Urasson's—what then?

When the pressure indicator showed a vacuum, the exterior door slid open. Ugo's voice sounded in Carey's ear, "Don't go getting lost—again."

Sarcasm was the weapon men like Ugo used against men like Carey. Carey stepped out into the tunnel to the surface.

Beyond the radiation maze a plateau looked out over the interior of the real Fowler, the hundred-forty-kilometer-wide crater containing the craterlet that housed the Society. Big Fowler was old, layered with smaller impacts. It was lunar day out here. To the north the terrain was level; from this height the big crater's north wall was so far away, it lay below the horizon. "Augment," he told his Aide. Over the landscape it imposed the names of the selenographical details.

He descended to the floor and moved toward an ejecta field from Von Zeipel, bouncing along as fast as he could. It was good to feel his muscles working. The thermosystem kept him cool in the direct sun. The map in the lower right of his visual field told him where he was.

This was the place, back in his youth, the First Imprints club had chosen for their adventures. The game was simple. One: Find a place where nobody had ever been. Two: Empty your urine reservoir in the lunar dust, leaving a trail that would last for up to two million years.

Carey took long, low, loping skips, eight or nine meters per stride, kicking up powder, leaving a trail of scuff marks among the thousands of bootprints that had been laid down here over the last eighty years. Fewer the farther he moved from the colony. His suit adjusted its albedo to reflect the sunlight slanting in from the southeast, and did its best to repel the fines that clung to his legs. His breath sounded in his ears.

He came to the ejecta field and wove his way between boulders, maneuvering through impenetrable shadows until he located the big boulder he was looking for, three times as high as a man, shaped like a clenched fist. Using his fingertips and toes, he climbed up the trail of niches in its side that he'd used twenty years before.

On top lay a depression, between two of the fingers, filled with regolith. There, in dust pitted by a billion years of micrometeorite impacts, lay the mark he had pissed when he was thirteen, as distinct as if it had happened yesterday. A tiny canyon, shadowed side dark as the sky, sunlit side a white line. He knelt down and inspected it. He felt the air flowing in and out of his lungs, his heartbeat spooling away the seconds of his life. He sat, trusting his suit's insulation to keep him from frying, turned off augmentation so he saw the landscape with no overlay, and looked back in the direction of the colony where he had lived his entire life.

Eva had told him that on the day he disappeared he had set out to join his friends in another of these games. He had no memory of it. He only remembered, afterward, holing up in the construction shelter for weeks while Eva and Roz figured out how they'd explain when he showed up again after disappearing for three months. While waiting, he had written his little book. He told the secrets of growing up male in the Society, aiming it at his mother, at all the mothers and aunts and sisters. Showing off. But no outright rebellion—no bombs on the dome, no threats to destroy or kill. He was just pissing in the dust, making marks on a screen.

Whenever he struck some opponent during a *Ruǎn tā* match, Carey thrilled at the impact of his body hitting another's. There was a pure joy to be had in smashing things, even if you broke yourself doing it. Even if you got cut or bruised or fractured a bone that would take time to heal—you'd made a mark.

Then there was getting Roz pregnant. Val was another mark Carey had made on the world, and it had taken him time to realize his son was not some achievement, but a person. A gift. And now Carey was losing him more with every day that passed.

The surface was dead. Gray powder, black sky, thousands of unblinking stars, the dust of the Milky Way. He wondered what had happened to him twenty years ago on that day of which he had no memory. He'd owned a ring, titanium with two inlaid vines circling around it. He would never see it again—or if he did, the outcome would not be happy, because his nightmare would have come true. He felt a hint of dread. He supposed that might even be the reason he was here, to test that dread by revisiting one of the places he might have gone on that day.

If they took Val away, what then? How to fill his next eighty years? It didn't matter much. Truly, the most likely thing to survive his existence was this mark in the dust he sat beside.

He stood up and, quite deliberately, scuffed his foot through the little trough, obliterating it. He stepped off the edge of the boulder and floated down to the surface, his shadow racing up to meet his feet.

The one person he ought to have called long before now, the one he ought to have tried to locate, the one convinced there was more to him than anyone suspected, was Mira. Mira, always exasperated, his toughest critic, his most generous friend, whom he'd been avoiding since she asked about the scanner. He called her.

She answered immediately. "Hello, Carey."

It was somehow surprising, in this bleak landscape, to hear her voice so intimate in his ear, as if they were lying in bed, her head on the pillow beside his.

"Mira. You're all right?"

"I'm fine."

"That's good. I saw you on the vids from the station."

The silence stretched. He squinted into the low sun. He breathed steadily. "Mira, I need your help. I can't find Val. I'm afraid he might have been mixed up in this thing today. I thought you might know something."

"It wasn't me."

"I know that. But even if Val doesn't get himself in trouble before we get to the hearing, they're going to take him away from me. If you've got any advice . . ." His voice trailed off.

A pause. The open airwaves hissed. Finally she said, "I did think of something."

"What?"

"We could get married."

"You're kidding."

He heard her indrawn breath. Her voice, defensive now. "With Cleo and me. It wouldn't be anything other than what it seems. Pick a new family name. With three of us, we'd have a better chance in the custody fight."

Right. Give them a woman parent, give them two women parents, no matter who, and they wouldn't have to worry about Carey. He could go back to being everybody's boyfriend. He could come out here once a week and piss in the dust.

"I don't think so," he said.

"I wasn't too successful with Marco, was I?"

Could she be so blind to her own motives? "That's not it."

"Forget I said anything. You shouldn't take it on yourself, what Val does, Carey. By this point in his life, is there really much you can do to change what he's going to be?"

"What I do *has* to make some difference. Why even be a parent—"

Val's signal appeared, flashing, in the corner of his eye.

He turned away from the sun's glare. "I've got to go."

"Carey—"

He closed her call and took Val's. "Yes?"

"Carey?"

Carey closed his eyes. "Where are you?"

"I'm home. Where are you?"

Wearing a space helmet, there was no way to wipe away tears. "I'll be home in an hour," he told Val. "Anyone asks you, we've been together all day."

CHAPTER

NINE

In the speeding van to the hotel, Beason and Göttsch tried to contact the OLS Secretariat but could not get a link. A constable, hand over her ear, spoke with her headquarters, while another leaned over the driver.

Li mumbled to himself in rapid Chinese, submitting notes to his Aide. Sirius, handpaws perched on the ledge of a window, had donned spex to shoot video of everything they passed. Gracie plucked at his suit, trying to get him to wear a seatbelt.

Erno stood holding a seatback, swaying with each lurch of the van, torn between wonder at his first sight of the Society in a decade and dismay at the fact that in his first minutes home someone had chosen to reproduce one of the acts that had gotten him exiled.

The van swerved along the base of the crater's interior slope toward a tunnel to the hotel. Citizens clustered around buildings designed as pressure shelters. A woman, infant clutched to her breast, gave up on the nearby shelter and loped along the path toward the tower a couple of kilometers away. Others pointed upward at the writing on the dome, blocked by the roof of the van from Erno's line of sight.

In the back Mira Hannasdaughter sat looking out, lips pressed together. Erno fell into the seat next to her.

"The driver needs to slow down," she said. "There's no pressure breach."

Before his exile they'd been in a few classes together. She had spent more time with her brother than she did with her cohort of women, and was disliked by many. Mira's testimony at Erno's hearing had not done him any good, but it was a minor factor compared to the real charges, and she hadn't lied.

"Who's Looker?" Erno asked her.

Mira turned toward the window. "Whoever it is, he's in trouble."

"At the station I thought there was going to be a pitched battle between my fans and the ones who wanted to put me out an airlock."

"Well, at least Looker defused that, didn't he?"

Erno smiled, despite himself. "How in the world did you get put on the reception committee?

"I work in Materials, for Eva Maggiesdaughter." Mira finally looked him in the eyes. "The Matrons think because I knew you I can figure out what kind of report you'll write."

"I'm not running this show," Erno said. "All I can do is to try to make them tell the truth."

"When you figure out the truth, let us all in on it."

Her cynicism had not lessened over the years. Like most people, he'd never wanted to brave her sharp tongue enough to get close.

The van driver braked and they were thrown forward. Up ahead, the tunnel entrance was blocked by people crowding into it.

"These people are out of control," Beason said.

"Quite irrational," Göttsch said. "The amount of air contained within this dome is enormous. Even in a real breach, it would take a long time to drop to a partial pressure that would cause death."

"This isn't real," the van driver said. "Just a copy of the fake Erno and Tyler did ten years ago."

Sirius was still shooting video. "If at first you don't succeed, blow it up again."

"We'll be visiting your lab," Erno told Mira. "How well do you know Maggiesdaughter?"

"Not well."

The van began to inch forward. Göttsch called back, "Erno, I need you up here."

Mira's connection to Materials was a stroke of luck; she might be his access to the information Cyrus wanted. He needed to put her at ease, show her he held no grudge, and assert a connection. What was her brother's name?

"We'll speak later," he told Mira. "Give my regards to Marco."

Erno moved to the front. The panic had subsided, the road was clear, and the van cruised into the tunnel and down the vehicleway to the hotel without further incident. As they prepared to debark, Göttsch admonished the SCOCOM team to present a calm and professional demeanor.

Erno tried to have another word with Mira, but the instant they stepped off the van she took off down the concourse.

Four constables hustled the investigators inside. In twenty minutes the hotel staff had settled them into several adjoining suites. Göttsch retreated to a private room to contact the OLS. Sirius and his assistant claimed another room and started unpacking equipment.

Erno turned on the pixwall and got the colony information feed showing video of the fake explosion and its aftermath. The administration repeated to distraction that there had been no breach of atmospheric containment anywhere in the colony.

Erno tried calling Amestris, but got no access. He told his Aide to keep at it until it could get through.

"I don't understand who this is aimed at," Li said, pacing the suite's living room. "Is it a threat to the OLS member states? To us? Or to the ruling elite of the Society?"

"It's not a warning to anyone," Beason said. "It's likely staged by the Matrons themselves to discredit their opposition."

That wasn't Erno's take. The déjà vu of the jet of smoke coalescing into words felt like a reminder to anyone who might have sought Erno as an ally that he was a criminal, an exile, a terrorist. *Bang! You're dead!*

He had not expected that his return would hit him so hard. A flood of memories washed over him: bike races on the rim road, sex with girls in the park, the night Tyler had given him that old copy of *Stories for Men*. He thought of his family, who had disowned him without regret after his mother's death. He had tried to contact them in advance of his arrival, with no reply.

"It could have been staged by agents of one of the other colonies," Erno said, "to convince the lunar public that the Society is on the brink of a civil war—justifying intervention."

Sirius, who had been back in his room with Gracie, arrived in time to reply. "It might have been a diversion, to distract attention while a second, more deadly attack was set up. That's the way I would do it."

As usual, the dog's expression was unreadable. Erno could not tell if this was one of Sirius's sardonic jokes or some legitimate insane speculation.

No one offered an answer. Beason gazed around the suite and sniffed at the most luxurious accommodations the Society had to offer. "This place smells. I think I'm going to be sick."

Erno had to admit that the apartment he and Amestris shared was twice as well appointed as the Fowler visitors' hotel. Certainly the Society was no tourist destination. Yet for some reason Beason's casual dismissal offended Erno.

"I'm going to make some tea," he said.

He retreated to the small kitchen and began brewing some anti-nausea tea, trying to get a grip on his emotions. Göttsch and Beason, though they had been on the moon for two months now, were still adjusting to lunar gravity. Göttsch was more bureaucrat than scientist. Beason, the cultural anthropologist, seemed already to know as much about the Society as he was willing to learn, with an arrogance out of place in someone who came from the political morass that was Earth.

Lunar-bred Li, from New Guangzhou, might be expected to be prejudiced, but he seemed more willing to take the Society as he found it. He was a structural geneticist whose work Erno had studied when he was an apprentice. In their month of preparation at OLS headquarters he had already asked Erno many questions about Cousins' biotech. When Erno insisted there were no bioweapons in the Society, Li told him, "Of course, you would never be trusted to know."

None of the others were particularly happy with the undue attention Erno had drawn prior to their arrival. At first Erno had bristled at the media reports about him and Amestris and Cyrus, with their distortions and outright fabrications. Then he realized that this celebrity gave him power, if he was willing to exploit it. That was why the others on the team were so uncomfortable with his notoriety, and why Beason and Erno had so quickly come to dislike each other. Still, the degree to which Erno would be able to affect the final report was an open question.

The tea was almost done when Sirius came into the kitchen. "Our Earthling friend is suffering from nausea?" the dog asked.

"Maybe I should just poison him."

"That would be rash," Sirius said. The dog's pose—was it all pose?—of continual denigration of human beings made it hard for Erno to tell what Sirius actually thought. Cyrus had made it clear that Sirius spoke for him. It was also clear, however, that the dog had his own opinions and did not trust any of the other members of the SCOCOM team.

"Who was that woman on the van?" Sirius asked.

"Her name is Miranda Hannasdaughter. She works in Materials. Her testimony helped get me exiled ten years ago."

Sirius sat on the floor, spread his legs, and nosed his groin. He was wearing casual trousers. Out of the side of his mouth he muttered, "Have you had sex with her?"

"What?"

"I'm just curious."

"No. No, I haven't."

Erno attached a bulb to the brewer and began to fill it. He found a package of biscuits in the cupboard and set them on a plate.

"She was at the station, specifically, I think, to see me," Erno said. "I think she feels guilty. If I can talk to her outside of SCOCOM's presence, she might be able to tell us about Maggiesdaughter's research."

Sirius got up on his hind legs, raised his handpaws to the counter of polished lunar basalt, and grabbed a biscuit. He fumbled it; it tumbled and he snatched it out of the air with his mouth. He crunched on it for a moment, then licked his black lips. He looked irritated.

"Göttsch intends to start with Biotech," Sirius said, "so you'll have a little time. If you can turn her, you can acquire the information Mr. Eskander needs before they inspect Materials."

"She may not know anything." And if Erno could get the tree genomes before then, maybe he wouldn't have to find out anything for Cyrus.

"Do you want some of this?" Erno asked, sealing the warm bulb.

The dog dropped to all fours. "I don't know how humans can drink that swill."

• • • • •

Kneeling on the mat in her office, eyes closed, hands crossed over her breasts, Amestris bowed her head until her forehead touched the turbah. She inhaled deeply and let her breath out slowly, a long steady exhalation of the tension in her shoulders and spine. To a stranger she might seem to be praying, and what she did made a prayer of a sort. It was not precisely Allah she sought, but some sense of herself in the larger universe. That steadiness existed. A self complete and independent, not liable to distortion by her father, by Saman, by Erno—why, always, some list of men?—or by her mother, by her work, by any considerations of Persepolis religion or politics. She listened for the vibration of space-time, the hum of the quantum foam that underlay reality, the dark energy, the missing matter of existence.

She heard it sometimes. It ran through her, as it did through everything, and when she felt it, all was right. No thing remained undone, no thing needed to be done.

But not today.

She lifted her head and opened her eyes. On the wall opposite her desk hung an eighteenth-century Morbier clock her father had given to her when she turned twenty. "Time is a gift," he had told her. "Once gone, never reclaimed."

The mechanism had been altered to account for lunar gravity, yet it still kept execrable time. The face told her it was eleven in the morning; it was after twelve. Amestris was due at the hospital where Leila was lying in for the birth of her son.

She rolled up her mat and put it into the cabinet, covered her hair, and left the office. While Erno was away at the OLS being run through the bureaucratic machine in preparation for the SCOCOM assignment, she had been able to keep EED operating in a superficial way, managing already existing contracts, forwarding any technical questions to Erno and passing his replies on to the clients. Publicity had brought them the opportunity for new business, but without Erno available they could not take it.

The hospital was within walking distance of their offices, on the other side of the market. She passed a row of carpet shops. In the windows: lunar blue, the stellar pattern, Carpathian crimson and gray.

Amestris had considered getting Erno onto the SCOCOM team a necessary risk, even if it put him into the hands of her father. She'd had time already to question her wisdom, and Erno's.

"I'll get this over with and come back," Erno had told her. "I'll put us in a place where your father can never dictate to us."

By all means. Let's go to that place where the richest man on the moon can't interfere with the lives of his daughter and the man who married her.

A line of uniformed schoolgirls, two by two, followed their teacher toward the Majlis. Surrounded by the scent of cooking kebabs and spices, by the dueling pop music from dozens of tiny speakers in rival shops, by the gabble of voices and the haze of piped-in sunlight, Amestris hurried through the market toward the Sudafi Hospital.

Cyrus had wanted the birth to take place at home. But if Cyrus would not countenance an artificial womb—if no Eskander child would be gestated by other than the flesh of the family—then Afroza insisted that Leila bring forth Cyrus's new heir in a place with the most advanced medical interventions at hand.

At the entrance to the clinic, Amestris identified herself and was admitted to the cool, quiet lobby. A discreet human attendant accompanied her to the birth suite. She was surprised to find her mother, not by Leila's side, but sitting in the lounge outside the birthing room.

"You let enough time pass, I see," Afroza said. "I wondered if you would remember."

"Please, mother. How is Leila?"

"She is as always. She has bitterly complained about the effects of this pregnancy on her body, spent months planning the cosmetic treatments she will receive afterward, and howled through the first hour of labor. She's now decided she wants the child delivered by cesarean. They have chased me from the room."

Afroza played both the sarcasm and martyrdom cards at once. There were few others a woman of her class and generation could acceptably use to get what she wanted. Her insisting Amestris be at the hospital for the delivery was another stratagem. Since Erno's departure it had been hard for Amestris to avoid being drawn back into the family.

Fatima and Kayvon were vacationing on Earth. They'd spent the last three months preparing—workouts and metabolic adjustments, antivirals and nanocleansers—so they could tolerate the mother planet's disease and brutal gravity. The only reports they'd sent back from Hudson's Bay were complaints about the barbarity of existence in a world subject to weather. Apparently the novelty of water falling out of the sky wore off quickly.

"Where is Dariush?" Amestris asked.

"He is with his cronies at the athletic club."

"Father?"

"He'll come by at the end of the day after his grandson has arrived." Afroza picked at a thread in the embroidery of her skirt. "Has Erno spoken with you?"

"We spoke yesterday before the cable train left Tsander." Amestris turned on the pixwall and tried to find a report concerning the arrival of the team at Fowler. The public affairs feeds were running nothing but boilerplate. The text news offered countless variations on the same dull statements about the organization of the SCOCOM team, and long features with sidebars about the Society of Cousins. A search of Erno's name turned up three familiar articles and two video interviews from a week earlier, one of them with Amestris.

She lowered the volume but left the wall on. "Can you tell me what it was that made Father send Erno on this mission?"

"I believe it was because you asked him to."

"I don't."

Afroza ran a finger along the abstract pattern over her knee. "I don't know how your father makes his business decisions."

"Is he testing Erno? Is there any chance he may be warming to him?"

"You give me more credit for having his confidence than I deserve, my dear."

"Mother, half of his decisions are your decisions first. Don't play the naive wife."

Afroza looked up. "You would do well to play the wise one. You put your husband into your father's hands yet expect him not to be used for your father's purposes? You use him for yours."

"I'm worried about him."

"I'm sure he's safe."

"You know that's not what I mean. Will Father help Erno get the information we need?"

"Your father is a man of his word. If he promised Erno the chance to retrieve what he needs, then he will keep his word."

"What does he expect Erno to do for him, then?"

"Perhaps you should ask Erno that. He knows more than you."

"I doubt he knows more than you."

Afroza looked up at the wall, then back at Amestris. "Besides the political advantage in having Erno on the investigating team instead of Thomas Marysson, your father expects Erno will more reliably do his bidding."

Amestris laughed. "Why would Erno be more reliable than one of Father's agents?"

"Because your father knows that Erno loves you and doesn't want to lose you."

Hearing those words from her mother made Amestris uncomfortable. "What is Father after?"

"Your father often enters these situations without having every detail planned. Of course he would like to see a regime change in the Society of Cousins. What role Erno would play in that is not something that even your father is likely to have worked out completely."

Amestris leaned on the arm of her chair. Afroza turned to the pix, some archival clip about the founding of the Society of Cousins, footage from a century earlier of their community being burned down back in California.

"How can you stay married?" Amestris said. "His secrets, his calculation. You're no fool. What's kept you so faithful to him?" she gestured at the screen. "Do you really not care that, if Father gets what he wants, all those women will lose control of their lives? What have they ever done to us?"

"What have they ever done *for* us?"

"Don't you sometimes wish we lived there?"

Afroza sighed. "Amestris, you spend too much time with men. Women are no more able to make a just society. They simply fail differently."

Did Afroza really believe that? "Even if that's so, women should have the chance to fail in their own way. Can it be worse than the countless ways men have failed?"

"Women have been there at every moment to help them fail."

"Every day here we ignore equal or worse injustices—against men as well as women—than the Cousins have. Still, everyone's afraid of them."

"Of course we're afraid. That's why the inspectors were sent."

A doctor entered the room. She glided past Amestris to her mother. She bowed her head. "Madam Eskander, you have a fine new grandson."

Afroza bowed her own head. "*Al-hamdu Lillāh*," she said.

The doctor allowed them to enter the room. Leila had somehow managed to arrange her hair and makeup to maintain her appearance of cool beauty. Her son, who would be named Cyrus, was wrapped tightly in a blanket, eyes closed, his tiny hands up beneath his chin. He had a full head of spiky black hair and a sweet, round face. Amestris congratulated her sister and, when Dariush arrived, made ready to leave.

Afroza asked, "Will you come to dinner this evening?"

"I am afraid that I have work."

Afroza didn't press Amestris. She turned back to the ebullient Dariush and his beautiful family.

Back in the waiting room Amestris found people gathered before the pixwall: the doctor who had delivered Leila's baby, several nurses. One of the nurses, brow furrowed, held his hand to his mouth. On the screen was some commotion. "What is it?" Amestris asked.

"There's been an attack at the Society of Cousins," the nurse said. "When the OLS investigators arrived there was an explosion."

On the screen a crowd gathered around the entrance to the Fowler train station. People chanted slogans and held up video banners. Police were trying to clear an aisle among the protesters from the doors to a van. The station doors opened and a number of people came out, among them Erno and the other SCOCOM investigators.

Some of the crowd began chanting Erno's name. Amestris caught a glimpse of Sirius, and then there was a sharp crack, an echoing boom. The image jerked. Many in the crowd flinched, and then began to rush toward the station doors. Some shouted, others pointed upward. The camera tilted up to show the roof of the Fowler crater—a blue sky— and a jet of black smoke uncurling against it. The video abruptly went blank.

"They've been showing this same clip over and over," one of the nurses said.

Amestris tried to call Erno, but got no response—not even a shift to his Aide. She sat down.

A newscaster came on and repeated that the video they had received was from the Society of Cousins internal public affairs feed. No further video was available, and no explanation was forthcoming from the Cousins.

The newscaster speculated about the nature of the assault and who might have been behind it. A representative from the OLS gave a brief, contentless statement. Commentators came on and conjectured wildly: The dome had been blown open and thousands killed. The SCOCOM team had been kidnapped. OLS troops should be sent.

Afroza and Dariush came out and sat with her. Afroza sent some messages. Dariush said, "They would never allow the inspections to proceed unhindered."

"I've contacted your father," Afroza said. She touched Amestris's shoulder. "He'll be here soon."

After a while Cyrus arrived. He embraced his wife and she and Dariush took him in to see Leila and the baby. Amestris stared at the screen and waited. Some of the hospital staff left and others drifted in to watch. Finally Cyrus came back out.

"What do you know?" Amestris asked.

"It appears to have been a hoax of some sort. There was a panic. Dr. Göttsch has been in communication with the OLS Secretary. The SCOCOM investigators are uninjured, and have been taken to their hotel."

"Erno is unhurt?"

"As far as I know, he's fine."

"Is there some way to contact him?"

"Regular channels should be back in order soon."

Amestris thanked Cyrus, congratulated both him and her mother, and left. Down in the lobby she told her Aide to keep trying to reach Erno.

She was at home when his call came. She threw it onto the wall.

Erno's hair was mussed, but otherwise he looked fine. A bit more drawn, perhaps, than he had a month ago. Behind him on the wall was a framed, ancient black-and-white photograph of some hard-faced woman, in profile.

"I'm sorry I couldn't reach you until now," he said. "You must have worried."

"Father told me you were all right," she said. "Are you?"

"I'm fine."

"I thought Cousins were not prone to violence."

"What are they reporting?"

"The video is everywhere. Within the last hour they've started to say that it wasn't a real explosion."

"It wasn't. We're in the hotel and tomorrow we're going to move into the offices they've set up for us. There was some panic but nothing serious. Did you see the crowds at the station?"

"Yes," said Amestris. There was an excitement to his voice that intrigued Amestris. What was he feeling, to be back there after so long?

"A lot of them waved copies of that book *Stories for Men* at me as if I were some prophet and it was the Qu'ran. I need to get the tree genomes and leave."

"Father won't let that happen until you satisfy him."

"He's so easy to satisfy."

"He'll be in a good mood when you talk to him. Leila delivered a grandson this afternoon."

"Leila is well?"

"Leila will be practicing new dance routines in a month. She's named him Cyrus. It will probably take up more news time tomorrow than anything that happens to you there. You'll have to do something spectacular to get back your media attention."

Erno's eyes softened. He smiled. "I'm happy to see you are as serious as ever."

"Is there any chance you could come to harm?"

"I can't imagine it."

"Your imagination is faulty."

He ducked his chin a little, the smile widened, and he was ten years younger.

"I miss you," she said.

"Good. I was afraid you might be relieved."

"I'm not relieved."

"How is the business?"

"We received a report from Apollo on the selenium in their water."

"And that new variety of spruce?"

Half of the seedlings had developed some strange canker on their bark. "Not good."

"You've seen Sam?"

"As little as possible."

He looked her in the eyes and she looked back at him.

Finally Erno spoke. "Send me the selenium query and I'll reply as soon as I can."

She didn't want him to go yet. "If things there get out of hand, Erno, don't get too involved. You can't control the SCOCOM report. They've probably already written the conclusions."

"Don't worry, I'll come back," Erno said, "if only because this place makes me feel strange."

"How very flattering," Amestris said, and smiled.

• • • • •

Mock Shock Blocks OLS Probe!

Tonight on *Here's the Point!* Sirius asks the question, "Who is Looker and what does he want?"

Our Mothers Warned Us!

. . . the repetition of Thomas Marysson's deadly provocation is evidence of the Reform movement's escalating radicalism, which now threatens the lives of every Cousin, female and male . . .

Matrons' Repression Sparks SoC Terror Threat!

. . . opposition leader Camillesdaughter claims the fake bomb is the work of *agents provocateurs* seeking to discredit the Reform Party.

Fake Bomb Aimed at Pamson!

. . . Kayasdaughter hints the incident may be the work of
agents provocateurs seeking to discredit the Society of
Cousins.

• • • • •

SCOCOM set up headquarters in offices on the forty-second floor
of the Diana Tower. Real, not virtual, windows commanded a spectacular view of the crater's interior. On some days humidity in the air
condensed into a haze that clouded the glass with moisture. Below
stretched farms and a portion of Sobieski Park. Flyers would occasionally swoop past their windows.

In addition to Göttsch, Beason, Li, and Erno were a staff of five
from the OLS and two assistants assigned by the Society. Beason was
sure these Cousins were spies for the Matrons. Erno would have been
surprised if they weren't.

There were two prongs to SCOCOM's investigation: first, an
inquiry into the treatment of male Cousins. This involved interviews
and examination of colony records on education, birth rates, social
mobility, living standards, incarceration, customs, and the legal system.

The second was the degree to which the Society of Cousins was
engaged in weapons research prohibited under the Organization of
Lunar States' Universal Disarmament Regime.

Though the first goal was the one that most concerned the average Cousin, the second was what SCOCOM really cared about. The

interviews carried on by Beason and his staff were secondary to the probes of the science programs that Göttsch and Li were to pursue.

A week after their arrival the team interviewed the staff of Biotech, determined to get to the bottom of exactly what sort of gene hacking was being conducted by the Society.

The first interview was with Lemmy Odillesson. Erno had not pressed for this, but Cyrus had somehow arranged it. It was up to Erno to make the most of the opportunity.

Lemmy was a small, spry man of middle years, maybe sixty-five or seventy. No standard of beauty existed by which he might be judged attractive. Lemmy, nervous, kept looking at Erno as if he expected some cue to get out of this.

The outside of the wedge-shaped conference room was a curved wall of glass. Along another stretched a mural that visual augmentation identified as Shiva watching Vishnu transform himself into the enchantress Mohini. A third was a pixwall. Sirius was at the interview, his handpaws crossed on the edge of the conference table, his long, domed head resting upon them. Lemmy seemed more unnerved by the dog's presence than by the OLS investigators.

"Do you object to our recording this interview?" Sirius muttered.

"Excuse me?"

"He said, do you object to being recorded," Beason said.

"No. I have no objection."

"Very well," Göttsch said, "let's get right to business. First, tell us your name and the nature of your work."

"My name is Lemmy Blau Odillesson. By training I'm a geno-botanist. I spent the first twenty-five years of my career studying closed microecosystems. Some time on design, but more seeking to under-stand and develop methods for regulating and repairing systems that fall out of balance. That led me into thinking about forest ecosystems and adapting varieties of Earth trees to lunar environments. I have spent the last twenty years modifying old species and inventing new ones as sources of food and materials."

"Have any of your gene hacks been for other purposes?"

"'Gene hack' is a crude term for what I do."

"What do you do?"

"Well, once you understand the programming processes within the genes, you can do any number of things. Most are impractical. For instance, I produced what I call a 'lunchbox tree,' which produces, as fruit, cellulose boxes containing one apple, a breadlike 'sandwich,' and a tuber of juice. But that was, I'm afraid, more of a stunt than a practical species."

"Back in Persepolis we have one growing in our office lobby," Erno said, attempting to put Lemmy at ease. "I used your 2130 paper as a guide."

Lemmy looked surprised. "I'm flattered you would spend the time on it."

"Do you feel, Professor Odillesson, that your work is being exploited here?" Beason asked.

Lemmy took a moment to collect himself. "Not as much as I would like. I'm not always good at practical applications: It's my goal for everything I do to be useful, given the resources I am allowed."

"So resources are withheld from you?" Göttsch asked.

"As Dr. Li can confirm, that's more a matter of the Earth multi-nationals' proprietary restrictions. For instance, our gene surgery vectors are not state-of-the-art; when querying biological function, we must use in silico tools to complement the in vivo. But ingenuity can go a long way to compensate for lack of resources."

"Do you ever wish that you might be working in, say, an Earth facility? A government-industry alliance could provide you with support that would allow you to explore the limits of your creativity."

Odillesson shook his head. "I don't want to go to Earth."

"You needn't go to Earth," Li said. "There are the OLS labs at Huygens. And at New Guangzhou we have extensive resources."

"Yes. But I would have to leave my family. I couldn't do that."

"You could bring them with you," Göttsch said.

"There are sixteen people in my family."

"You could run your own lab, with unlimited resources."

Odillesson's face set. "I don't feel any limitations."

Göttsch sat back. Sirius had not lifted his head, and his brown gaze was unreadable.

Beason leaned forward. "Are you engaged in weapons research?"

"Of course not. I'm a genobotanist."

"Are you aware of any research in the colony that could be applied to bioweapons?"

"No."

"But there are lines of research that you may not be aware of."

"We don't do weapons research."

"You just told us that there are limitations on your resources. I could imagine that someone here might, out of frustration with the system, take up such research."

Erno spoke up. "I worked with Dr. Odillesson, as you know. Research is closely monitored, and no one could get very far without the lab administrators knowing."

"Not if the lab administrators were a party to the project," Beason said.

Odillesson looked at Erno in appeal. When Erno did not help him, he said, "Dr. Beason, let me explain. I am a Cousin. I have a good life. My skills were recognized when I was a boy. All my life I have been encouraged to pursue my interests. My wishes have been taken into consideration at every step of my career. My mother and sisters and teachers have given me every opportunity. My lover took me into her bed when I was fifteen, and I have fathered one of her daughters. Aside from my work, my greatest pleasure is spending time with her, her wife, and their children and my three grandchildren. I don't know a lot about the other lunar colonies, but I can't imagine that I would be better off in any of them."

"What about your political powerlessness? You are not allowed to vote. You can't own property. Those grandchildren are not your own. You have no say in the fundamental decisions that control your life."

"I can't recall ever being made to do anything that harmed myself or anyone else," Lemmy said. "Erno knows all these things."

"Mr. Pamelasson did not feel the way that you do. Many others don't. Are their objections to be ignored?"

"I don't know. I—I don't know much about these things. I have nothing to complain about that can be solely attributed to the Society, and not to the"—he struggled for words—"the human condition."

Sirius's ears turned forward; his eyes remained lidded.

"Ah, the human condition," Göttsch said. She steepled her fingers and leaned back in her chair. "Our experience is that the condition of humans is subject to change."

Li said, "For all your privilege, few men elsewhere on the moon would accept your situation. You are a pet, given freedoms that most of your fellow Cousins never see."

"Pardon me," Odillesson said. "My impression is that such disparities of privilege are common in the—in the other lunar states."

"Your point?" Li said.

"Simply that the inequalities that men live with here are certainly no worse than those men live with elsewhere. Rather less, I would think."

"Perhaps," Göttsch said. "That is what we are here to find out."

"Those who sacrifice freedom for security deserve neither," Beason said. "It wouldn't surprise me that you are willing to lie for the Matrons."

"Lie about what?"

"About your secret weapons program."

Lemmy opened his hands before him. "How many times will you make me say it: There is—there is no weapons program."

"So you say."

The interview—interrogation, it seemed to Erno, went on for another thirty minutes. Throughout it all, Lemmy, increasingly flustered, denied knowledge of any bioweapons. Erno was surprised by Odillesson's strength in the face of the barrage. It was hard to watch. At the risk of putting himself at odds with the others, Erno occasionally posed a sympathetic question. Lemmy's eyes—grateful—shifted to him.

Finally Erno insisted, "I think this ground has been well enough tilled. If my colleagues don't object, I think we should let you go."

They relented, and Lemmy was allowed to leave. As the others began to discuss his interview, Erno said, "I'm going out to him."

Göttsch waved a hand, and Erno walked out to find Lemmy leaning against one of the chairs in the anteroom. Through a doorway, Erno saw one of the SCOCOM staff watching from his desk. Lemmy's wounded expression was an accusation. The staff person lowered his head. Lemmy ran the back of his hand over his forehead and sighed. "That was awful."

Erno placed a hand on his shoulder. "I'm sorry."

"Oh, I don't blame you."

Erno wondered why not. "Can I walk you to the elevators?"

"All right."

They passed through the offices to the hall, and Erno closed the door behind them. Waiting for the elevator, Erno said, "I need to ask you again if you might give me gene samples of your tree varieties. I can get by with spruce and maple, but if you could supply even some indications of how I might work on ash, it would be a life saver."

Lemmy gave him a tight smile. "Is your life in danger?"

"Well, not literally—"

"Because *ours* are, if these people get control of the Society."

"It won't come to that. If you help me, I'll make sure they know that the rest of the moon is under no threat from the Society."

"If I help you?" Lemmy said. "The fact that it's the truth isn't enough?"

A SCOCOM staff member came out of the office and approached them. "Mr. Pamelasson?"

"I need to go back," Erno told Lemmy. "Please think about it."

When he returned to the rest of the team, they were still in discussion. Sirius was no longer there.

"Odillesson is useless," Beason said. "They could be producing disease vectors in the next room and he wouldn't care. The Matrons must be very happy with the likes of him."

Erno took a seat. "This is not the way for us to begin. Browbeating is not going to help us. Our job should be to listen more than talk. Otherwise we'll just reinforce the Matrons' assertion that our presence here is the prelude to an attack."

"I don't think Dr. Odillesson is as ignorant as you say, Martin," Göttsch said. "He knows more than he's letting on."

Erno could not let that go. "I worked with him for two years. I was his apprentice, and I saw every sort of gene hack that was being pursued and had access to everything that had been done in the previous fifteen years. Food stocks, environmental cleansers, symbiotic microbes. Unless there's been some change, Odillesson is telling the truth. There is no bioweapons research, and never has been."

Beason looked at Erno with a trace of a smile. "Now we know he's lying—because you're lying."

"I'm not lying."

"Is that right? So tell us about GROSS."

"What is this about?" Göttsch said.

They were all looking at Erno now. "How do you know about that?" Erno said.

"So you admit it existed," Beason said.

"No. It never existed."

"Yet you seem to know what I'm talking about."

Erno squirmed. "Yes."

"Martin," Göttsch said, "please explain what you are talking about."

Beason, as if he had been waiting for this moment, was calmer than he had been at any time in the session. "I've received information from a source friendly to SCOCOM about a deadly virus, acronym GROSS, that Erno was directly involved in producing when he worked in Odillesson's lab."

"Look," Erno said, "you can't trust anything that Thomas

Marysson says. He's the person who put me onto it in the first place! Yes, someone, I don't know who, had designed it, at least in theory."

"What is GROSS?" Li asked.

Erno sighed. "It was two things, really. A pair of engineered viruses that, in combination, would induce an X-linked disease that would express itself only in female embryos. It was a genetic time bomb against female children."

"That certainly sounds like a weapon," Göttsch said.

"It worked only on children?" Li said. "That's monstrous."

"It would have no effect on adults, only embryos. But it was never made," Erno insisted. "It produces female babies with genetic diseases. The sick idea of some disgruntled male who came up with a plan to hurt the women of the Society without hurting the men. I don't even know that it was a Cousin who thought it up. Does that sound like something the Matrons would sponsor? It harms only women. It was a misogynist's fantasy."

"Not a fantasy," Beason said. "You were prepared to produce the virus."

"No, I was not. I refused. That's what led to the break between me and Marysson. He asked me to produce it, and instead I turned it over to the Matrons."

"Who kept this a secret when you were tried and exiled."

"I imagine they did not want even the concept to be made public, for fear somebody else would use it. They had enough evidence to exile me without it."

"Still," Beason said, "you can't maintain that no bioweapons were being researched here."

"Look, this doesn't make any sense. More likely it came from one of the other colonies."

Li interrupted, "That's pure slander."

Erno gripped the edge of the table. "Why would a female-dominated society engineer a weapon that would hurt women and leave men completely unaffected?"

"You left the room with Odillesson," Göttsch said. "You wanted to talk with him alone, where you weren't being recorded. What did you talk about?"

"I used to work for him. I wanted to reassure him after that third degree you subjected him to."

"You don't work for him anymore," Beason said. "You work for the OLS."

The session descended into argument. After twenty minutes Erno had persuaded Li that this did not indicate some secret Cousins weapons program, and he thought Göttsch was leaning his way. But Beason did not relent.

When the room had settled into an uneasy silence, and Erno sat there trying to master his anger, Beason got up and found himself a bulb of juice in the suite's refrigerator. He came back and sat at the table. "So, who's next?"

• • • • •

Erno studied the OLS soldier who accompanied them in the van back to their hotel, a big man in matte black flex armor, helmet, sidearm. After the station incident the OLS had sent a half dozen of these menacing pros to protect the investigators. The man turned his head toward Erno, then turned away. His eyes were invisible behind the visor.

As they pulled away from the tower, Li claimed the seat next to Erno. "Don't take what Martin says so seriously," he said.

"How should I take it? He accused me of terrorism."

"You shouldn't have lied to us."

"The GROSS virus has nothing to do with weapons. If this is the level of reasoning we're bringing to this investigation, our report will be nothing more than propaganda."

"Martin could have gone public with this story. He didn't. That should count for something."

Erno was in no mood to salve Li's conscience. "Please go away."

Li jerked himself out of his seat and moved up to sit with Beason. Erno watched the eyes of the van driver in the rearview mirror. His name was Ravi Meerasson—they must have attended school at the same time, yet Erno had never known him. Li said something to Göttsch; for a second Ravi's eyes flicked up and made contact with Erno's.

At the hotel Erno paced his room. He should have realized that GROSS would not remain hidden in his past, yet its resurfacing infuriated him. Restless, he visited the colony public affairs streams and the heated debate about Looker and what they were now calling the Bang You're Dead Incident, BYD for short. He ran across some reports on the upcoming hearing to decide custody of Valentin Rozsson. On one of the Huygens newsnets a sociologist discussed the likely strategies the two sides would take.

He thought of calling Amestris. He would like her opinion on what to do; she was astute about political infighting. He would not mind seeing her dark eyes and the cast of her lips, feeling the warmth of her breath on his cheek. If only she were here! He was in the Society of Cousins, where sex was common coin and frustration the easiest thing in the world to avoid. No complications, that was the theory. What a joke. He didn't belong here anymore. He lived in Persepolis, in a Persepolis marriage, not one where you could walk in and out so effortlessly.

Nothing was effortless anywhere. His attempts to renew some connections had not borne fruit. When he'd received no answer to his first day's message to Alicia, he'd tried his sister Celeste again. She did not return his calls. Celeste would have long since become an adult; she was probably on her own with her own family. She would not be living at the apartment where they had grown up.

He changed to a blue shirt of the type typically worn by Cousins working the *mita*, took the lift down to the basement, and left the hotel through its kitchen. He followed the concourse to the nearest station, climbed up to the platform, and took the first tram.

Through the windows Erno watched people come and go, leaned his head against the window, and let the home he had not seen in ten years pass by. He tapped the fingers of his artificial hand against the glass and cracked the window open so he could feel the breeze on his face.

In the last days a dozen things Erno had been oblivious to when he lived here had come back to surprise him. The birds, for one thing. Birds had trouble adapting to lunar gravity, and had to be genetically altered to suit underground environments. A few of the other lunar colonies had birds, but did a poor job integrating them into a balanced ecology. In the Society, birds were everywhere. Because there were not enough insects to maintain a population, feeders were located all around the colony, usually among trees. Beneath every feeder was a collector for droppings, invaluable sources of phosphates. Citizens working the *mita* came every third day to scoop the guano into bins and drive it to the fertilizer plant. This might have been done by machines, but doing the work by hand taught people how everything was connected. Erno had done this himself. It was a very Matronly solution. Every job important, all work dignified—and besides, it gave men who sought the franchise something to do. So nine times out of ten, the person you saw scooping up birdshit from below a tree was a man.

When he was seventeen he'd considered this grounds for revolution. Now that Erno had spent ten years doing such work and worse in the patriarchies—not because he was male, but simply because he was poor—he was not so sure. What surprised him the most was that he had forgotten all about it. The fact that what had been invisible to him as a Cousin was so visible to him now told him what "home" was: Home was the place you were estranged from.

The tram emerged from the tunnel into the dome and for a moment—maybe ten seconds or so—passed a school playground with a football field. Fading afternoon sun cast golden light over the natural grass playing fields. A crowd of noisy children gathered at the far end, but at this end, all alone, a five- or six-year-old boy marched down the center of the field. He had a tight cap of curly black hair, brown cheeks. The boy swung his arms, his hands gripped into little fists, chest puffed out, lifting his knees high, oblivious to the world as he sang some song to himself.

In seconds Erno was past him. The tram twisted slowly through Yousafzai district, where his family lived. He watched people, some he perhaps had passed on his way to school every day, Cousins old and young on their own way to work, or home, or to meet men or women friends, lovers, spouses, children, co-workers, counselors, mothers. A man in blue drove a cart full of produce toward the refectory. A gardener at the end of her day stood in one of the flower beds that climbed up the terraces of flats and massaged the small of her back. Beside her rose a retaining wall draped with pelts of ivy. Tile mosaics decorated the sides of buildings. Everywhere balance and proportion. Mutual support. The perfect, renewable biosphere. All things in their place. Tended, all tended, nothing left to grow wild, to fall into a feedback loop, to run off a cliff.

The tram stopped at the Yousafzai station. He walked around the square facing the apartment complex where he had grown up. Somatic evening descended; the sky turned down to deep twilight, stars came out on the dome. The words up there had already been effaced. He sat on the wall looking at the twisted stairs that ran up the slope between apartments. Everything looked the same, down to the composting bins on the terrace where he had played with the other kids.

Warm lights were coming on inside the apartments. A few meters in front of him stood the door to the one where he had lived with his mother, his aunt, his sisters. As he watched, it opened and Erno's mother, dead for a decade, stepped out, followed by her partner, Nick Farahsson. Erno was so startled he felt dizzy.

Then he saw it wasn't his mother, it was his Aunt Sophie. They walked over to him.

"Hello," he said.

"Hello, Erno," Aunt Sophie said.

"I'm surprised you're still here," Erno said to Nick. "Is he with you now?" he asked Sophie.

"Nick's a member of this family," Sophie said. "You aren't anymore. We'd really rather not see you here."

Erno had never realized how much Sophie's face was like his mother's. How could he have missed that?

"Where's Celeste?" he asked.

"Celeste married into the Indigos," Nick said. "Leave her alone."

They exchanged a few words, and Sophie's voice, also terribly reminiscent of his mother's, gained an edge. Erno got angrier. When some neighbors started to gather—there was Thersasdaughter and her niece Carmen—he got off the wall and left.

Instead of going back to the tram station, he decided to climb up to the top of the crater wall, to the rim that supported the dome. It was a long climb, all winding stairs through neighborhoods and gardens. Nightjars murmured in the branches of dryland trees. Juniper scented the dry air. The night sky grew distorted the closer he came to its edge. He and Tyler had climbed up there, behind the dome's surface, to set the smartpaint charge that created their original "Bang! You're Dead!" message. Who had created the twice-false repeat: a phony copy of a phony explosion? First that, and then GROSS—it was as if somebody, resurrecting his past, was determined to poison any chance Erno had to make a difference.

The people still out were mostly young. He ignored them and they ignored him. He thought once that he heard light steps behind him, but when he turned around he saw no one. By the time he reached the rim road, out of breath, his anger had blown itself out. He looked down over the colony: the Diana Tower like some old Earth skyscraper, the dark fields of the crater floor, the distant oaks of the park underlit by fountain lights.

Something nudged his hand. He flinched. Nothing showed there but some slight shimmering in the darkness.

A muttered voice—Sirius—said, "It's not your home anymore."

Erno stepped back. The thing beside him was still invisible, but when it moved he could detect a slight warping of the pavement, as if he were viewing it through almost still water.

"Turn off the cloak," Erno said.

The distorted air became opaque, and there was Sirius sitting on his haunches, looking up. He wore a gray camouflage suit. The mask entirely covered his face, but Erno could make out his intelligent, inhuman eyes through deflecting gauze.

"You followed me?" Erno asked.

"We need to talk."

"What do we need to talk about?"

"I've made some inquiries about Miranda Hannasdaughter. She's uniquely well placed for our purposes. Besides working for Eva Maggiesdaughter, she associates with Hypatia Camillesdaughter. Carey Evasson is her lover. Tomorrow she's going to testify on his behalf in the custody hearing regarding Maggiesdaughter's grandson. Set up a meeting with her. Don't let Beason, Göttsch, or Li know."

"After what happened today? Beason is out to get me."

"Beason is pathetic. Classic Earth arrogance. It was a crude misstep, and we will turn it to our advantage."

"I snuck out of the hotel. He'll wonder where I was tonight."

"Tell them exactly where you were. You tried to contact your family. Beason won't believe it, but it will humanize you with Li and even Göttsch."

"And you—sneaking around invisible. What's this about?"

"Being a celebrity makes it hard to pursue quiet inquiries; being a dog makes it impossible. So I resort to subterfuge." If emotions were detectable in a canine voice, there was bitterness in Sirius's. "Remember, at the very least we need schematics for the scanner. Test results, anything that will help us build a prototype."

"If it exists."

"We can be sure it exists."

"I want something in return."

"I know what you want."

"If I can't get Odillesson's genome samples through SCOCOM, you need to find me a way in."

Sirius nodded, and within seconds he was invisible again. His guttural voice remained. "I will ponder that. You should return to the hotel."

"Are you coming with me?" Erno asked.

There was no answer. When Erno reached out, all his hand met was air.

CHAPTER

TEN

YOU'RE KIDDING, CAREY HAD TOLD HER. *I DON'T think so,* he'd said. And then he'd broken off the conversation.

Mira stood the tiny glass horse Val had made on her fingertips. No more than two centimeters tall, smooth as liquid. The white blaze on the black horse's face had a trace of gold in it.

"We need to get going," Cleo called from the other room. "It's almost oh-nine-thirty."

Mira slipped the horse into the breast pocket of the formal tunic she'd chosen for the hearing. High collar, subdued green. "You go on ahead. I'll be there."

Cleo came into the room. "I want to make sure we're on time."

Mira stared at her. "I want to make sure you get out of my face."

Cleo's expression was bruised. "I'll wait outside."

Mira yanked on her black slippers and tugged a brush through her hair. Cleo's obsession with Reform Party politics wore Mira out. By undergoing genetic reassignment from male to female, Cleo had gained every right men were seeking through the movement, but that had made her only more committed to gaining those rights for everyone. "I'll never forget where I came from," she said. "I was a woman long before I got that second X."

Her earnestness was tedious. Still, what Mira had said was cruel. She was about to go out to apologize when her Aide spoke: *You have a call. Address blocked.*

She threw it onto the wall. It was Erno. "Mira?"

"Hello," she said.

"Do you have a moment?"

"Not really."

"I'm sorry to bother you, but I'd consider it a great favor if I could meet with you sometime soon. Alone. We'd need to keep it secret."

Since the OLS had sent their own security to the hotel, Mira's desire to talk to him did not warrant facing the scrutiny of armed strangers. "What about?"

He brushed the hair out of his pale blue eyes. "I guess you could call it personal. I need a favor."

"That's as may be. I need to know what I'm getting myself into."

Erno frowned. "Have you ever heard of a device called the Integrated Quantum Scanner Array?"

Cleo appeared at the bedroom door. She saw the image on the wall and raised an eyebrow. Mira froze the call.

"We really need to go," Cleo said.

"I'll be right there."

Cleo left. Mira unfroze the call and told Erno, "I can't talk to you now."

"Is there a time we can meet—privately?"

"The lab will be shut down on third shift this Thursday. Come at oh-three-hundred. There shouldn't be anyone there."

"Please don't let anyone know—"

Mira turned off the pixwall and left.

• • • • •

IN TODAY'S LUNANET HOTSPOT:V
ALENTIN ROZSSON CUSTODY SHOWDOWN

Throwing a spotlight on the notorious **Society of Cousins's** childrearing practices, peculiar family structures, and limitations on the rights of men, is the ongoing battle for custody of a fifteen-year-old boy named **Valentin Rozsson**. In a world where men have no parental rights, one man, former Olympic athlete **Carey Green Evasson**, has challenged the law by taking custody of his son. Today *If It Bleeds It Leads* brings you the hearing that will decide the case.

Background

Custody hearings in the Society of Cousins are rare, and when they do take place, they are between women. A custody battle between a child's mother and father is unprecedented.

Valentin Rozsson's mother, **Roz Green Baldwin,** has not insisted that her son be returned to her pending a decision. Traditionalists among the Cousins are impatient with her and blame the fact that until she was a teenager, Baldwin lived on Earth. At age fourteen, Baldwin emigrated to the Society in the company of her father, **Jack Baldwin** (2090–2128), a genobotanist and developer of the **Baldwin juniper**, adopted by the SoC and other colonies establishing a low-moisture environment. Rather than follow the Society's **matronymic system**, Baldwin has kept her father's name, and may harbor an attachment to the practice of custodial fatherhood arising from her upbringing. **Polls** show that a majority of Cousins believe such sentimentality should not be indulged when the fate of a boy is at stake.

Today's Coverage

The colony's open meetings practices mandate that the hearing be broadcast live on all SoC **video links**, in private and **public headspaces**. In the case of meetings that have attracted public interest, as this one has to an unprecedented degree, there is typically a lively byplay on chat fora even as it takes place.

LUNANET will bring the hearing to subscribers everywhere on the moon. The fact that this hearing is of interest to outsiders has placed more pressure on the Cousins **Board of Matrons**. After last week's arrival of the **SCOCOM** investigators and the **BYD Incident**, debate has become intense. Our remote coverage will put you right in the hearing room.

Plus, we've got the solar system's leading newshound on the story! **Carrollton's Sirius Alpha-Ultra vom Adler**, representing the Consortium of Lunar Media, will be available to **LUNANET PRIME** subscribers for **real-time commentary**. Following the hearing, Sirius will have exclusive interviews with the principals in the dispute.

• • • • •

Mira endured Cleo's chilly silence as they rode the metro to the Diana Tower. Mira's apology had not mollified her. Cleo had never impressed Hypatia or drawn Carey's attention and so was deeply envious of Mira. She might feel differently if she knew how Carey had reacted to Mira's marriage proposal.

Mira left her in the tower lobby. She showed her ID to security at the elevators and was whisked sixty floors up to the meeting room where Carey, Hypatia, and Carey's advocate, Charlene Wandasdaughter, waited. Val was not there. His opinions on the situation and how he might wish it resolved had been taken separately.

Carey wore a somber black shirt, sealed to the collar, black pants, black slippers. His hair was pulled back; it shone in the ceiling lights. He enveloped Mira in his hug and whispered into her ear, "It means a lot to me that you're willing to speak on my behalf."

Then he turned to rest his hand casually on Hypatia's hip. It didn't mean anything to him, any more than hugging Mira did. All those passionate conversations, the pillow talk—he was so good at pillow talk, so sincere, so funny, so sexy—all available to any and everyone. Mira, Roz, Juliette, Hypatia. *I don't think so.*

Mira had to stop. Carey was simply acting the way men did, gaining status by hooking up with the most powerful woman available. By rights, Hypatia shouldn't even have been there. She had no stake in the case, but since she and Juliette had fallen out, she was making sure Carey knew how important it was to have her as an ally.

"They're going to be focused on every nuance of your behavior," Hypatia told him. "You say nothing against Roz."

"I've *got* nothing against her," Carey said.

"Your big problem will be Juliette. She'll criticize your parenting. But we'll have Mira to rebut her."

Mira hated herself for the way her heart leapt at Hypatia's slightest praise; sometimes she felt herself no better than Cleo.

A young man with his hair in cornrows entered the room. "It's time," he said.

The hearing was held around a big table in a conference room. The lighting was warm and indirect. The only possible disturbance was the presence of camera midges silently floating at the edges of everyone's vision.

The other principals were already there—Roz, Eva, Roz's advocate, Carlo Ameliasson, a child welfare agent, and the three-person panel of arbiters. The panel comprised Hans Friedasson, impressively bearded, Giselle Annasdaughter, and Debra Debrasdaughter as chair. Debrasdaughter was over one hundred years old. She was perhaps the most respected woman in the Society, and few Cousins would question her impartiality.

But the fact that two of the three arbiters were women caused grumbling. Plus, Annasdaughter was an Ebony, a rival family almost as old and influential as the Greens. Commentators from the patriarchies enjoyed all this almost beyond their capacity for glee. The outside scrutiny made the Board circumspect, but also raised its defiance, and the Matrons were determined not to change the proceedings to accommodate the opinions of strangers.

Juliette and Eva, Hypatia and Mira, though they were not the principals, were all given seats at the table. The meeting began with a round of embraces, queries about whether everyone was comfortable, and the serving of tea. Debrasdaughter passed around a plate of cookies she had made herself. They were going to have a nice little conversation, with lawyers, and a judgment at the end.

The child welfare agent began by reciting facts that were undisputed:

paternity, dates, the general sequence of events. She described the unusual circumstance that Roz and Carey had been reared as siblings but were also lovers and parents. On occasion, a panel member would ask a question.

Carlo Ameliasson made Roz's case. He was a homely man with jug-handle ears and a weak chin. The most prominent male lawyer in the colony, his soft voice and fetish of never interrupting anyone did not cloak his aggression. The story he told was that Carey's request was a whim, that Carey had evinced no interest in parenting until recently, that he'd had every opportunity to share in Val's parenting with Roz, that his desire to have Val reside with him was not supported by his circumstances or character. It was not a principle that was at stake, Ameliasson said, but the welfare of a particular young man.

Eva described the difficulties they'd all gone through twenty years earlier, when Carey had disappeared and Roz's father had killed himself. When, some years after Val's birth, Roz moved out of Eva's home, Carey chose to stay with Eva. This was not unusual—sixty percent of Cousins males still lived with their mothers—but it did not argue for Carey's abiding interest in his son.

Roz told how, although Carey had spent time with Val from infancy on, he had never been consistent in his attentions.

Wandasdaughter pointed out that Roz had taken no wife nor brought anyone new into the Green family. Unlike most Cousins women, she lived alone with her one child. Wandasdaughter did not mention Roz's immigration, but the implication that Roz had never assimilated into the Society did not have to be spoken.

"Eva can tell you how loyal I am to Val," Roz said. "Val won't find a more supportive home than I've given him. I don't deny Carey's interest— we're all Greens—and I welcome his involvement. Val can have as much of Carey as Carey is willing to give him, without leaving our home. Yet in the months since Val has been with Carey, I've hardly seen him."

At this point Ameliasson brought Juliette into the conversation. For some time it had seemed to Mira that Hypatia must have gotten the psychological jump on Juliette when they first met as colleagues at the university fifteen years earlier. Juliette had played second fiddle to Hypatia throughout their academic careers, and in the wake of the election disaster, she was determined to show the world that she was not Hypatia's shadow.

"You've been seeing Carey for some time?" he asked.

"Not so much now. I was, for some months after he got his new apartment and Val moved in with him."

"So you've had the chance to observe. How would you describe Carey's parenting?"

"Well, certainly Carey spends time with Val, and I have no doubt Val is enjoying himself. Hypatia got them both heavily involved in Reform Party politics. I have been involved in that as well. It's no doubt educational for Val"—she glanced coolly at Hypatia—"but it's distracting, being the focus of so much attention. I don't think Val is getting enough sleep."

Hypatia said quietly, "I hope we're not about to abrogate Carey's parental rights because Juliette thinks Val isn't getting enough sleep."

Juliette smiled at Hypatia. "I've no question that Carey wants to be a good parent. But I believe Val's been staying out past his curfew now and then."

"What would you say to this?" Ameliasson asked Carey.

"I've kept good track of Val. Yes, we were involved in the Reform Party events leading up to the election, but that's over now. He's doing fine in school, and meeting his responsibilities."

"Are there any other people engaged in Val's care?" Ameliasson asked Juliette.

"Well, Carey has been seeing Hypatia," Juliette said. "And Mira."

Carey laughed. "So? Are we judging my sex life?"

"Of course not," Ameliasson said. "But maturity means making choices. Women make such choices all the time."

"And I've put Val first," said Carey, "as Juliette knows."

Wandasdaughter said, "This really is not relevant. There is no conflict between being a good parent and having relationships with others."

"Is that true?" Ameliasson asked.

Roz spoke up. "I don't care about these things, if Val is getting the guidance he needs. I don't mind him being interested in politics. But the men's rights movement is using Val as a political object. I want to put his best interests first."

"And I don't?" Carey said.

"We all want what's best for Val," Ameliasson said. "If he's safer with his mother, then he should be with his mother."

"Safe from what?" Carey said.

No one spoke.

"Let me make your argument for you," Carey said. "When I take Val to political rallies, I am putting him too much in the public eye. When we're home, I'm letting him run wild. You look at my history and you think that I can't possibly have the judgment to know what's good for him."

Carey faced Roz. "Roz, I admit everything you say about my haphazard interest—though ask yourself honestly, how many men are truly welcomed to take an interest in their children? You worry about my women friends, but if I married one of them, the questions would evaporate and we wouldn't be here today." His eyes briefly met Mira's.

Mira felt her face flush. She heard again the incredulity in his voice, so intimate in her ear: *You're kidding.*

He turned back to the table. "I'm asking: Why should the intervention of an unrelated woman matter more than my connection to Val? After Roz, who is his next of kin? If he gets sick and a decision has to be made on his treatment, who's consulted? If he's hurt, who gets notified? If he does something wrong, who gets held responsible? If he's raised poorly, who gets blamed? I assert that, as much as Roz, I should be that person."

"Don't worry," Roz said, "if something happens to Val, I'll blame you."

"I welcome the chance to be blamed. I'd consider that a privilege. More than the informal acknowledgment of my relationship to him and your kind indulgence of my interest, I want a legal obligation, a right, a duty."

"You want to possess Val," Annasdaughter said.

"To the degree that any parent possesses a child, yes—yes, I do."

Hans Friedasson said, "If you want to be a father, you already are one. If you want to be a patriarch, forget it."

"I don't have the beard to be a patriarch."

The densely bearded Friedasson glowered. A couple of midges floated in toward him. "Personal remarks won't help your cause."

Carey sighed. "Cousin Friedasson, I apologize. I was out of line. I hope you'll forgive my desire to make my point."

Ameliasson jumped in, "This sounds like it's all about you, Carey. What about Val?"

Carey resumed, his voice in control. "I hope it's not necessary to assume that because something makes me happy, it must be bad for Val. This is about my being considered *optional*. The default statement is: Val has a mother, a grandmother, aunts, sisters—and oh, yes, he has a father, too.

"What is a man? Is a man just a woman who can't bear children? I think our answers to these questions have been impoverished. Val will learn things by living with me—valuable things—to go with all the things he learns from Roz, our family, the schools, and his friends. Together we might create a new emotional space—not some return to patriarchy, but something the Founders wanted for men, and women, too.

"Maybe I haven't earned your trust. If so, I hope it's because of my failings as a person, not simply because I'm male. I respectfully ask you to treat me, and Val, as individuals."

Annasdaughter said, "Too much individualism has come close to destroying the Earth."

Carey held his hands up in surrender. "You've got me there. I don't think I can save the Earth."

Debrasdaughter laughed. Eva smiled.

That line would be main menu fodder in the patriarchies. Carey had never looked more handsome, or sounded more sincere.

It was quite a performance. Mira should have known that Carey, having grown up sharing the dinner table with the most important Matrons, would not be flustered to be put on this stage. With his natural charisma it was a good bet he would win over at least two of the three arbiters. Even Friedasson might, upon consideration, decide the beard joke was a harmless jape rather than a lack of respect.

Mira ought to be gratified. She had pushed Carey to use these abilities when no other woman in his life—not Roz, not Eva, not Hypatia, not any of his girlfriends—had done so. She'd seen it in him. She expected that the only person who could really understand her nudging him not as undermining his autonomy, but as a gift, was Carey himself. His glance, as he had casually stuck the knife into her heart, had told her that.

"Do you have any more to say?" Debrasdaughter asked Carey.

Carey shook his head. "Not just now."

She turned to Roz and Ameliasson. "Any questions?"

Roz said, "I never denied that Carey has a legitimate claim. But does that mean Val has to live with him?"

"That's what we are trying to figure out," Debrasdaughter said.

Hypatia whispered something to Wandasdaughter, who then said, "We have one more thing. In response to Cousin Mariesdaughter's comments, Mira Hannasdaughter would like to speak to the issue of Carey's fitness to be a father. Carey and Val first lived with her after Val left Roz, and she has direct experience of how Carey has been handling his child rearing."

"Very well," Debrasdaughter said. "Mira?"

Wandasdaughter asked her, "Do you dispute what Juliette said about Carey not keeping a careful watch on Val?"

"I don't dispute anything Juliette said. I just don't think it's relevant. Half the adolescent boys in the Society spend their waking lives figuring out new ways to test the limits of our tolerance. Carey is no less responsible than my mother was, for instance. That's not enough reason to deprive him of custody."

Mira took a breath. Now was her moment. "That said, I think Val, living with Carey, is more at risk than he would be with Roz."

Hypatia looked at her sharply. Wandasdaughter was flustered into silence.

Annasdaughter broke it. "Why do you say that?"

"I don't want to say it—" said Mira.

But she did, actually. She wanted to say it very badly.

"—but I'm afraid I need to. Let me start by telling you, first off, that I am Looker."

Consternation crossed the faces of the tribunal. Carey watched her. Mira was acutely aware of the camera midges floating at the edges of her vision.

"If this is true," said Debrasdaughter, "you open yourself to community sanctions."

"It's true."

Wandasdaughter struggled to get things back on the rails. "What does this have to do with Val's custody?"

"If you'll let me show you, you'll see. May I use the pixwall?"

"Go ahead," said Debrasdaughter.

Mira opened a link on the tabletop and accessed her private files. She typed in her password and called one of her Looker videos onto the wall, the one intermixing images from the Oxygen Warehouse and the history of Western art. "You may have seen this video. It was posted in a dozen places around the colony last May."

"You could easily have downloaded this," Annasdaughter said. "There's no proof that you made it."

Mira called up a second file, split the screen and ran it side by side with the graffito. "Here is the raw footage I shot of the deserted nightclub where Thomas Marysson did his last public performance. You can see where I cut and edited portions of this footage into the final video."

Silently they watched as she showed them three examples of raw video and the final use of that footage in her graffito. "The fact that I own this footage demonstrates at least that I had something to do with the creation of Looker's video. Now, here is an unused portion of the footage I shot that night."

On the screen stood Carey, half naked in the dim light. "I'm going to have to take care of that," he said in the video. Mira let them watch enough to know it was definitely him.

"Carey helped me shoot this video," Mira said.

"These images could be synthesized," said Friedasson.

"You can have whoever you wish examine this. It's genuine."

Debrasdaughter spoke. "Perhaps we can find out more directly. Carey, is she telling the truth?"

Carey watched Mira levelly. It was hard for her not to squirm under his gaze. "Yes," he said. "That's me."

"This doesn't prove that Carey was part of your subversive postings," Friedasson said. "Maybe he didn't know what you were going to use this video for."

"Two people were almost caught posting it, in the Gilman neighborhood," Mira said. "Some images of them were captured. You can't tell much from them, but you can see that they were a man and a woman. The woman was me. The man was Carey."

Annasdaughter turned to Carey. "Is this true?"

Carey looked Mira in the eyes for a long moment. His breathing was audible. Finally, he said, "Yes. Yes, it was me."

Carey sat heavily in his chair. Roz almost looked sorry for him. Wandasdaughter was nonplussed. Hypatia finally spoke, "These are misdemeanors at worst."

"We should ignore misdemeanors?" Debrasdaughter asked.

"It's hardly surprising that a male Cousin might be involved in protest," Hypatia said. "It would be surprising if a man as intelligent as Carey, with the capacity he has to accomplish worthwhile things, confined himself to playing games."

Mira said, "Carey helped me create the BYD video."

As she dropped this bombshell, Mira watched Carey. It was hard to do. He did not take his eyes off her.

"That's not true," Carey said, his voice steady. "I never did that."

"Can you prove that you had nothing to do with it?" Annasdaughter said.

"Why are you lying, Mira?" Carey asked.

"Carey, please don't talk to Mira right now," Debrasdaughter said. "Can you prove that you had nothing to do with this?"

"I shouldn't have to. She should have to prove I did it."

"You admitted that you worked with her on these other vids."

Carey looked trapped. "Yes. But I had nothing to do with the fake explosion. I was at work when it happened."

"Mira," Debrasdaughter said, "can you prove that Carey was involved?"

"No. But he was."

"You must ignore all of this," Wandasdaughter said. "This is hearsay, without a shred of proof."

Annasdaughter said, "Regardless, both of you are guilty of serious offenses."

"Mira," Debrasdaughter said, her old woman's voice puzzled, "you were called to speak on Carey's behalf. Why are you testifying against him?"

Mira said, "I think Carey has every right to get involved in protests and fight for his rights. I appreciated his help in doing the work I did, and I'm not ashamed of it. But I don't want to see Val hurt."

"Not ashamed of the panic and the injuries you caused?" Ameliasson asked.

"Carey can make his own choices. Even if admitting I am Looker gets me exiled, I don't want Val's generosity twisted by people seeking power. Despite my sympathy for his motives, Carey should not be given custody."

By the time Mira had finished speaking it was case closed, Hypatia thwarted, Carey sunk, Mira on the edge of exile. All of them defeated, and Mira had done it in minutes, entirely by herself. Hypatia sat back, a speculative expression on her face, watching Mira. Mira would bet her left arm that she had surprised Hypatia in a way she thought Mira incapable of.

Carey just looked at her, unreadable.

You're kidding. Mira met his eyes for as long as she could stand it, then turned her face to the cameras. *I don't think so.*

CHAPTER

ELEVEN

AFTER THE DECISION WENT AGAINST HIM, AFTER THE
tense voices in the hearing room, after Mira avoided his gaze and Roz
sought it, after Wandasdaughter requested a review, and after Hypatia
made him promise to meet her later that evening, Carey left. A constable
and a social worker accompanied him to his apartment to surrender
Val. Carey felt a little outside himself as they descended the elevator.
Rather than the outcome, or even how Val would react, he was thinking
of how angry Mira must be at him to make her lie like that.

To avoid any people who might be gathered outside the tower,
they went down to the metro station and took the train to his apartment. All the way, camera midges followed them, into the train, out of

the train, getting it all down, until the annoyed constable hauled out her aerosol, sprayed them, and the devices fell dead to the pavement.

In his neighborhood people in the concourses shouted encouragement, catcalled, or simply watched them pass by. At his apartment the constable, aided by her senior who was already there, parted the people who had gathered before his door. Carey stopped at the threshold.

The senior constable looked familiar. He had slept with her at some point. What was her name? Abidemi—Abidemi Bethsdaughter.

"I'd like to have a few minutes alone with Val," Carey said. "I promise we won't be long."

The social worker didn't want to let him go, but Bethsdaughter said, "All right."

Carey found Val sitting on the bed in his room.

"Did you watch?" Carey asked.

"It's not fair," Val said. "They don't care what *I* want."

Carey sat down next to him. "The court officer is outside."

"You didn't have anything to do with BYD."

"It doesn't matter. I can't prove a negative."

Val got up and paced. Carey should have confronted him long before about where he had been on that afternoon. He should have done a lot of things.

"Calm down, Val. It's not going to be any different than the way you've lived your whole life so far. You can't change this."

"But I can! Mira didn't do it. It was me and Dora and Mike Kristasson."

Carey shook his head. "You know how wrong that was, don't you?"

Val eyed him sullenly. "I don't need to be protected."

"If you keep doing things like that, no one can—or should—protect you. But telling them you were involved won't keep you with me—they'll say it proves that I don't have you under control."

"I don't want to be under control! That's all we are here—you, too! Any real masculinity scares them to death."

Where had he picked up such tripe? "Look, I know you're angry; you want to prove you're not anyone's child. But what you're doing *is* childish. Just stop it."

"We could run away."

"Please sit down."

Val sat. Carey felt an unfamiliar tightness in his chest. He hugged his son. Val stiffened at first in Carey's arms, then relaxed. After a moment, Carey ended the embrace and held Val by the shoulders. "I'll always be your father. Nothing can break that, unless we break it ourselves. I need you to help me. I need you to go."

Val pushed away. "All right, I'll go." He looked at his hands for a moment. "Can I pack?"

"A couple of things. Be quick." Carey stretched, rubbing the small of his back. "Don't say a word about BYD, not even to Roz."

"Mira must really hate us, to lie like that."

"Just promise me you won't ever do such a thing again."

Val kept shoving clothes into a bag, all sullen distance.

"All right, no promises, not yet," Carey said. "But no talking either. If Mira wants people to think she did it, let her deal with the consequences."

A knock on the door.

Val shifted the bag onto his shoulder. "Will you at least come with me to Roz's?"

"I don't think that's a good idea. Besides, I have to work today." Carey steered him out of the bedroom. "We'll talk."

He opened the door just as the social worker was about to knock again.

"I'm coming," Val said to her. He stepped out, and some of the bystanders shouted. The camera midges were back in force, hovering just below the corridor lights. The social worker, a middle-aged woman with a kindly face, laid her hand on Val's shoulder, and he allowed it. She and Val and the constables moved off through the people.

Carey stepped back into his apartment, closed the door, and slumped against it. He rubbed his fingers across his forehead. After a minute he went into the kitchen, dialed up some tea, and walked around the apartment while it brewed. He couldn't help but feel some relief, and shame for feeling relief. All the time he had complained about his mother hovering over him, made light of her warnings, teased the Matrons in his book—all that time he'd had no idea what it meant to be responsible for someone else.

He looked around the apartment. The brewer, green light telling him that the tea to lighten his mood was ready, had been given to him.

The furniture had been given to him. The room itself had been given to him, by Hypatia. By rights he should be living in a men's dorm, not in a private apartment with three and a half rooms.

Nobody he worked with in aquaculture had anything like it. The things he had done to earn it did not count for much. How freely they indulged him, how much he deserved their condescension. He was useless.

Sipping the tea, he returned to Val's room. On the wall stood an action shot of Carey at age fifteen in the bright red hockey sweater of the Cousins team, slashing down the ice, the puck centimeters off the blade of his stick.

He opened a pix window and called Thabo.

"Carey, I'm sorry," Thabo said.

"Listen, can you meet me at the gym tonight? I need to work out. Maybe we could spar a few rounds. Go to the Men's House afterward?"

Thabo looked uncomfortable. "Listen, Carey, you know I'd like nothing better. I don't believe a word Mira said. But the whole family was watching and they've been all over me. Can we try in a couple of days?"

Carey watched Thabo squirm. Some seconds passed.

"Sure," Carey said. "In a couple of days." He closed the window.

He drained the last of his tea. He could go to the sauna, find a partner, and fuck all night. After returning Val to Roz, Abidemi Bethsdaughter would be off shift. Carey could give her a call.

He turned the pixwall to mirror and examined himself. A

handsome, full-grown man. High cheekbones. Blue eyes. If he were to die tonight, what would he leave behind?

Of course, his mother would not let that happen. Val could die, and Mira could die, and pretty much anyone in the Society could die, but not Carey.

He bashed his fist into the pix, pulled it back, punched it again. The image distorted, recovered. He kicked it, he punched it again. He kept hitting, the pain jolting his knuckles, his wrist, all the way up his arm, until finally the wall broke and his image fragmented into a half dozen copies, each complete, each a different size.

He let himself slip to the floor slowly, insubstantial as mist, and cradled his hand in his arms. That was stupid, busting his hand. It was the kind of stupid thing that women of the Society expected even the most civilized of men to do from time to time. It was consistent with somebody who would terrorize the colony. The sort of thing that frustrated men, given the wrong circumstances, did.

He hadn't ever felt this much alone. It was an interesting place to be, a frightening one. Perhaps liberating as well. If they believed Mira's story, which he had corroborated to a degree, then he was in great trouble. Investigation might prove him innocent, but if not, he would face serious sanctions, up to and including exile. He had no doubt that, at least for a short time, his celebrity would find him a place in one of the patriarchal colonies. He could get a lot of mileage out of playing the part of the persecuted male Cousin.

But then he'd have to live in one of those colonies, and he didn't want to. Val was here. Eva was here. Roz was here. Thabo, his friends. His story wasn't over yet. He wasn't done with the Society of Cousins.

He sat for some time. He flexed his fingers, testing them, then got up, cleaned his battered knuckles, sprayed on some false skin, and took a painkiller. He'd told Val that he needed to work; he might as well make that true. He pulled on coveralls, went to the aquaculture plant, and put in four hours focused on pH levels and microbial densities.

Jamal and Winston seemed no more happy to see him than Thabo had been to get his call. While Carey worked, his Aide shortstopped half a dozen messages from Hypatia and a query from Sirius, the uplifted canine.

After the shift ended he decided to give in and go to Hypatia's. At the very least she could suggest ways to negotiate the legal system if it should come to formal charges. He arrived to find her living room full of people. The place felt like one of the parties the martial arts team held after they'd lost a close match. A mosaic of non-Cousins video feeds ran on the wall; in one window a panel of opinionators debated the custody decision.

Carey's appearance roused everyone's attention. "At last," Hypatia said. She embraced him. Others did the same. "Where have you been?"

"I went to work."

Hypatia kissed his cheek. "I understand."

"The patriarchs are all on your side," someone said. "They're talking about sanctions."

On the wall were images of Carey in the hearing room, of Val leaving their apartment with the authorities. Endless babble about Mira and her claim that she was Looker, her revelation about Carey and BYD. Speculation about arrests, punishments. Sirius interviewed a series of female Cousins, all of whom expressed satisfaction with the result. Carey could only imagine how a patriarchal audience would eat that up and come back for more.

Half the people in Eva's living room were lifted, and the air was thick with smoke, hypotheses, and accusations. Cleo said, "Mira was acting strange all yesterday. Who could have gotten to her? How could she do this?"

"Nobody got to her," said another woman. "She's always been a loose cannon."

"Nobody was more anti-Matron than Looker, and now she does their bidding?"

"They'll make her Invisible," Daquani said. "They may even exile her."

"They won't do a thing," said Amelie Anitasdaughter. "The Matrons love this story. The prodigal daughter."

Carey remembered the look on Mira's face as she'd wrapped up her testimony. She'd managed not to flinch under his betrayed stare for some time before looking away. Her expression he could only describe as one of aggrieved satisfaction. Her tone of voice asserted she was doing what was right, and she was enjoying doing it, but her eyes revealed a well of hurt and something like panic.

Mira might tell herself it was a matter of principle, but Carey knew it was all about the two of them. Her offer of marriage, even if it dismayed him with its condescension and ignorance of what he felt, had been sincere, and he had blown it off. Plus there was something between her and Hypatia. Mira was primed to betray him, and he'd been an idiot not to see it coming.

"The OLS will love this story, too," said Jon Faruzahsson. "Giving Carey custody would have defused their attacks. Instead they have an object lesson in Matronly arrogance."

"Nothing will defuse the attacks," Cleo said. "It's just a convenient hook to hang their arguments on."

"The patriarchs paid Mira to be Looker," said Amelie. "Everyone's talking about *agents provocateurs*. She's perfect."

"What does Mira know about patriarchs?" Cleo said. "I don't think she had anything to do with BYD. She couldn't pull that off by herself."

"But Carey helped her." Daquani looked at Carey, waiting for a response.

Carey let them talk. He could see how Mira had worked herself into saying what she believed to be the simple truth: He wasn't capable of fathering. Then in the same moment she'd used the fact that he would put Val's welfare ahead of his own to take Val from him. Fuck Mira. Even if she was right—and, flexing his damaged knuckles, he knew she was—fuck her three times over.

Mira's testimony confirmed what the Matrons already believed: Men could not be trusted to respect limits. Even if Carey had proved over and over that he was a good man, according to their definition. A rebel only in the accepted way. Not a warrior—thank god, they thought, he wasn't that kind of trouble. Just, in the end, one boy among others.

"She couldn't have done this to you if you hadn't helped her," Jon said to Carey. "If you didn't let her get you on vid. What a fool!"

The talk stopped. All eyes on him, waiting for his reaction. Jon looked momentarily uncertain.

"She was my friend," Carey said.

Hypatia, who had sat silent while the others ranted, said quietly, "Politics trumps friendship."

Everyone turned to Hypatia. In the background the voices of the competing broadcasts babbled.

"We'll use it," Hypatia said. "Carey becomes a martyr, betrayed by a woman who with the same act betrayed the cause she claimed to believe in. She was one of us, manipulated by Eva Maggiesdaughter in order to regain control of her son. An object lesson in why the status quo must change. Why we need to appeal to the OLS."

How easily Hypatia accepted the result. How easily she assumed Carey would go along with whatever her next move was.

"No," Carey said.

On the screen now, Sirius was doing an analysis of the political reaction across the moon. Carey lifted his chin toward the video. "They want to crush the Society. We want to reform it."

Hypatia touched him on the arm. "Sirius is dying to interview you. People are eager to know your reaction. They may not care about the politics, but they care about the story. Feed that. You've been betrayed. Mira told you she was on your side, she shared your bed, and when the chance came, she knifed you in the back. You are hurt, angry."

Carey shook his head. "I don't want to complain about Mira."

"Your restraint shows a true generosity of spirit." Hypatia's voice was understanding. This was the flipside of her sarcasm; on occasion she had to be sincere or she would just be the glory hound her enemies accused her of being. Dedication to the ideal justified her immense egotism.

"I can tell how angry you are," she said. "Use that righteous anger in the service of our cause."

Carey looked around the room. They were surprised. Some were embarrassed for him, others annoyed. "I don't believe in righteous anger."

"We can't change the Society without a fight," Hypatia said.

"If there is a fight, the Society will be destroyed."

"So we do nothing?" Jon said. "Everything stays the same? The Matrons win?"

Most of the room seemed completely flummoxed by Carey's reaction. Hypatia drew back and watched him.

"What do you *want* to do, Carey?" Cleo said.

"I want to work. I want to do something useful with my time."

Hypatia said, slowly, "This is the most useful work you can do. It's work that only you can do. You have to give this interview."

"Oh, I'll do the interview. Believe me, I want to talk to them."

"Then let me help you prepare," she said. "We'll strategize. We can run some scenarios, test the semiotics."

Carey laughed. "Hypatia, you are an inspiration, but I don't think I want your help."

"You need it," Hypatia said.

"I don't think so," Carey said.

"Look," someone said.

On the pixwall was an image of Erno Pamelasson over a banner headline: "Terrorist on OLS Team?"

• • • • •

Interview with Adil Sparrow Abekesson, conducted by Bushnagi Misra of the SCOCOM staff, 13 February 2149. Abekesson, ninety-six, worked for forty years as a constable, rising to chief of watch. He ran unsuccessfully three times for the Board of Matrons. At the age of seventy-two he resigned from the constabulary, declared male privilege, forsaking the franchise, and pursued a career as a vacuum sculptor. His works have been on display in galleries on Mars and Europa as well as the moon.

I am a direct descendant of Adil Al-Hafez, one of the seldom-acknowledged founders of the Society of Cousins. He and Nora Sobieski were lovers. They came here, with a hundred others, and lived in a hole in the ground for twenty years, working to build the Society. He died at the age of fifty-three from exposure to radiation from an unpredicted solar flare. She gets a park named after her; he gets some obscure ridge on the lunar surface.

Before the crater was pressurized we lived in what is now part of the dorms in East Three. Very primitive. I was no athlete, even less of a scholar, and I guess I gave my mother a hard time, but I was popular with the girls. I wasn't the best student—I hated to be stuck in one place, doing one thing. I wanted physical activity, interacting with people. I decided to become a career constable.

The constabulary is a volunteer organization, but it's hard to get in. You have to demonstrate the right temperament. I liked to compete with others, but I scored high on social compatibility and so they let me in. They'd already figured out that although you don't want too much aggression in your average citizen, you need a degree of it in a police force. Plus, it provides an outlet for people like me.

Q: *People like you?*

Men.

Q: *Cousins women aren't competitive? No desire to dominate? No violence?*

Oh, sure. There's some vicious competition between women in the Society. They attack each other over ideology, they're jealous of their prerogatives, they jockey their sons into status positions, they gang up against each another, they fight with their sisters and daughters—lots of daughters carry on vendettas against their mothers once they start their own families.

If you are able to become a Sienna or Green or Ebony you have an edge, but if your family was founded last week you are nobody. The Greens have been living in some of their places so long they act as if they own them.

But not so much violence, no. If you cross one of the unwritten rules, to say nothing of the written ones, you get shamed. What's the biggest punishment we have? Exile—to be cut off from your family, friends, society. Short of that, it's Invisibility, which is maybe even worse because you are still here, having some minimal contact with other Cousins, but except for those interactions necessary to your survival they ignore you. The highest suicide rate is among the Invisible.

Q: *Why don't people ignore the declaration of Invisibility? It can't be enforced if the average Cousin doesn't enforce it.*

Some people do ignore it, but only in the smallest of ways. The constabulary will write you up, and you will come before a Council of Peers. But it seldom comes to that. How are any social rules enforced? Not just here— anywhere you go, it's the pressure of conformity. A society

will not function when people do as much as the law
allows and no more than it requires.

That's why the constabulary is volunteer; it comes out
of the community.

Q: *So you volunteered to be a constable out of desire
to serve?*

No. I wanted the power to tell people what to do.
Maybe it was mixed with wanting to see people do the
right thing, but I'm old now, there's no point in me hiding
my motives from myself or anyone else.

About forty percent of the constabulary are men, same
as the general population. More men apply than women,
but still they're in the minority. They'll tell you it's not by
design, it's just because men drop out. And they do—once
they realize that chances for advancement are limited.

I started out partnered with Kristine Umber
Kristinsdaughter. You may know about her; she was
eventually Chair of the Board of Matrons. But back then she
was just a constable, albeit she had five years on me. They
always paired the new men with experienced women.

In normal times, there's not a lot for a constable to
do. You've got the legal right to use force, but not the
occasion. A constable here is as much a social worker as
a police officer. We're often dealing with juveniles who
get themselves into trouble. Their mothers are watching.

Domestic disturbances are rare. Lost children, industrial accidents, crowd control at civic events and celebrations. That's most of the job. Acts of physical violence—we see maybe a couple of dozen per year, usually between adolescent boys. Murders—there hasn't been a murder here in thirty years.

The constabulary is small, about seventy members for a population of sixty thousand. In Persepolis the ratio is two hundred fifty per hundred thousand; in New Guangzhou it's three hundred fifty; in Mayer, that libertarian utopia, it's five hundred. Tell me about the freedoms in the outer world.

Most of the constabulary are part-timers, with a core, one-third of the total, who are career. I was career. I wanted to be a watch captain; eventually I wanted to be the chief of the watch. I got to be chief of the watch, only the second man ever to hold that job. I was watch chief for eighteen years, longer than anyone ever.

I was well liked. At least two women married into the Sparrows just to be with me. I was a father and an uncle to a flock of kids. Kids liked me. Men liked me. Women liked me. I ran for the Board of Matrons three times. You know about that?

Q: *You lost all three times.*

I came close the first time. I was the first man to

run for the Board in more than a decade. I got a lot of support from people in the Tower; the social workers liked me, I was popular with the constabulary and the colony bureaucrats.

But I'm a Sparrow, and my mother started the family only one generation back. Look at the list of Board members over the last thirty years and you'll see the same family names over and over: Crimson, Sapphire, Amarillo. Like they say, all the colors of the rainbow. Except we don't get rainbows here.

Q: *Don't you feel that this system is oppressive to men? You're scrutinized every minute of your life.*

Privacy is overrated. At least we don't have the everyday violence that goes on everywhere else. You make sure you write that down. Yes, Cousins men don't have as many legal rights, but they're free from the exploitation that goes on in patriarchal societies.

In a hierarchy, whether it's founded on money or power—and the ones who have money get power, and the ones with power get money—there's one man at the top and everything flows down from him. At most maybe there's a few at the top, but there aren't many, and they're usually men. At each level a person can step on the neck of anyone on the next level down, until you reach the bottom and there's nobody to step on, except maybe your children.

You can step on people on your own level, too, and maybe establish a little pyramid down there with you at the top, but you're still down there.

Here, that happens some, but it doesn't rule. The Matrons won't let it.

Q: *Aren't the Matrons at the top of the pyramid?*

After one generation, the levels get mixed around. Some women get wide influence for years, even decades, but to get there they have to have lots of friends. They have to earn the respect of most other women. The families take care that nobody gets the invested personal power that a prime minister or a caudillo or a dictator has.

Still, for a man it's impossible. That's my story, I guess.

I complain about the powerful families, how if you choose a political career they put a lid on your ambitions, but what is man in the patriarchies? A strong back and a pair of hands.

And you look at human history. Men are very creative when it comes to wielding force. They are crazy with the desire to hurt. It's not culture, it's biology. All that twenty-first century cant about behavior being culturally determined was blasted away eighty years ago.

So what's your option? Either change men by messing with the human genome, or create a social structure that limits their autonomy. The Society chose the latter.

Tough on the ones like me. But if you pile up the total injustice I have faced in ninety-six years, does it exceed the amount I would have faced if I lived in Tycho, say, or New Guangzhou?

• • • • •

As evening settled in, Erno sat under an olive tree in a café and watched the girls and boys flirt in every possible combination. Soon some of them would retire for a session in a university practice room. Ten years earlier he had been one of them, trying so hard to seem deep, his every other sentence a lie. Declaiming his lousy poetry, imagining some soul connection while he admired women's breasts.

> *Her hair was still tangled, her mouth still drunk*
> *And laughing, her shoulders sweaty, the blouse*
> *Torn open, singing love songs, her hand holding a wine cup.*
>
> *Her eyes were looking for a drunken brawl,*
> *Her mouth full of jibes. She sat down*
> *Last night at midnight on my bed.*

In Persepolis, Amestris would be preparing for dinner with Sima or Hala. Or maybe she was still in the office, trying to appease their lingering clients. Or in the apartment, listening to music, swimming in a mist of mood tea.

On the café wall ran a *Here's the Point!* segment about the Val Rozsson custody decision. Mira claimed she and Carey Evasson were behind the BYD hoax. He remembered the flicker of her eyes when, in the van fleeing the cable station, he'd asked her who Looker was. Under the circumstances, could he rely on her to meet him at Materials later?

As he pondered this, he was startled to see his own face on the screen, over the banner, "Terrorist on OLS Team?"

A bright young female correspondent said, "Sources in the OLS Secretariat's office confirm reports that Erno Pamelasson, member of the team investigating the treatment of males in the Society of Cousins, was, before his banishment from the rogue colony, involved in bioweapons production. Details have been smokescreened by government PR operatives, but in the last twenty minutes exponential pressure has been put on the OLS Secretariat by numerous expert investigation subroutines. OLS Secretary General Raine Devra has agreed to open her receptivity to a thirty-minute press opportunity. We plug you now into the Unfiltered Lunar Forum."

Erno drew back a little into the shadows beneath the tree. Around the tables some of the students turned their attention to the pix.

The Secretary General appeared on the screen. In polished tones she made a statement about the GROSS virus and Erno's involvement in the plan, stressing how the virus was never instantiated. She then took questions.

"Madam Secretary, how is it possible that you appointed this man to the SCOCOM team without knowing about his terrorist history?'"

"What makes you assume that I did not know?'"

"Why would you appoint him if you did?'"

"Because he is not a terrorist. He was a rebel against the Society of Cousins, not in service to it.'"

"Yet you kept it a secret. You trust a banished gene hacker from a renegade colony to represent the rest of the moon?'"

"Who better to give us an insight into the secret researches of the Cousins than a person who has worked in the very labs where such weapons would have been created?'"

While the Secretary General did her dance for the reporters, Erno slipped away from his table. Given that he might be thrown off the SCOCOM team by the time he returned to the hotel, now could be his only chance to find out anything about the IQSA. It was barely the end of the second shift, but rather than risk getting stopped, he should go now. He sent a text to Mira: *coming early*.

Better not to use public transit, so he had a long walk ahead of him. He left the campus, crossed to the inner slope of the crater, and descended a pathway through the woods. The path was scattered with needles from the taller pines, and the juniper scent was heavy. A kilometer and a half later he struck off on a quiet road across the crater's farmland.

At the entrance to the Northwest Lava Tube more people were out. Erno walked purposefully down the concourse. Periodically a tram glided by overhead. He passed what had been the old Oxygen Warehouse, but where the club door had been there was a blank stucco wall.

Beason might be the one who had leaked Erno's secret, but one way or another it had to trace back to Marysson. Marysson would figure he could lie his way out of any uncomfortable questions about GROSS. Lying was easy to do in the OLS, where spreading misinformation seemed to be the purpose of popular newsnets.

Past the free enterprise zone, Erno took the tram down a side tunnel to Materials. When the avatar at the complex's gate asked him for his ID, he gave his SCOCOM security clearance. He had a bad moment, but then the doors slid open.

Mira waited on the other side. She looked surprisingly calm for somebody who had just admitted to crimes, blown Carey Evasson's parenthood rights to flinders, outraged the Reform Party, crossed Hypatia Camillesdaughter, and put herself on news feeds across the moon.

"Thanks for meeting me," Erno said. He looked around. "This place is deserted."

"Once a month they schedule a skeleton shift," she said. "That's why I said come tonight."

She took him to an office containing two desks, one of them almost bare, the other with a tablet, stylus, and some personal memorabilia. Mira sat in one of the chairs and nodded toward the other.

He took it. "I expected, after what happened today at the hearing, you wouldn't be able to meet me," Erno said.

"My roommate is moving out and right now everyone's confused.

Tomorrow I may be kicked out of the Society. But it's tonight."

Erno leaned back in the chair, watching her. He had no good idea what relation this woman bore to the girl he had known a decade earlier. "I can give you some pointers on being exiled."

Mira opened a drawer in the desk and took out a ring. She played with it, idly slipping it on and off, not looking at him. She said, "They won't exile me. You'll probably be gone before I will."

"You saw the report about me?"

Mira stood the ring on the desktop and spun it. She studied the spinning silver sphere. "I did. This is probably our only chance to renew our acquaintance. Still writing poetry? You were crazy about words. It was your only attractive trait."

He smiled. It had always seemed to him that Mira was as much performing a parody of insensitivity as being insensitive. "My poetry stank."

The slowing ring wobbled and drifted toward a photo of Mira and her brother, her maybe nine, him six. Mira stopped the ring. She looked him in the eye.

"So who are you working for, what do you want, and why do you expect me to give it to you?"

There was no point in attempting to keep anything secret. "I work for myself, but I'm doing this one thing, sub rosa, for Cyrus Eskander."

"Your father-in-law."

"If I had any other option, I wouldn't do it. He hates the Society."

"And you don't?"

"Ten years away have changed my viewpoint. I use whatever influence Cyrus lends me to work against him."

"Yet you run around in secret doing his dirty work while SCOCOM whets the ax for us. What does he want?"

"He thinks this information embargo is all about covering up tech that Eva's developed. A scanner. According to physicists, Eva's papers from thirty years ago say it's possible to scan any object down to the subatomic level. But building such a scanner is difficult. Nobody on Earth has ever been able to do it."

"Physics is full of dead theories," Mira said. "The luminiferous ether. String theory. If Eva's theory doesn't work in practice, then it's wrong."

"I'm told that in cases of exotic physics like this, constructing such devices is as much art as engineering. One lab may succeed where another fails."

"In the time I've worked here, nobody here has ever said a word about a scanner."

"That's an equivocation," Erno said.

"Oh, my—alert the constabulary." Mira kept her eyes on the photograph. "If Earth physicists couldn't build one, maybe Eva couldn't either."

"Cyrus's sources say it was constructed, and used."

"How would they know?"

Erno didn't know. "This would be a large project. There'd be an assembler along with the scanner to instantiate objects after they were scanned. It would require a huge amount of energy. Is there anywhere in this complex that could house such a lab?"

"And keep it secret? No."

"What facilities do you have?"

Mira spun the ring again. "You never answered my other question: Why should I help you?"

Erno put his finger on the ring, pinning it to the desktop. He slid it toward her. "Cyrus suggested I take advantage of the fact that you testified against me at my trial. He says if I play that right, I can get you to help me."

"You must not have been paying attention this morning. Selling people out is my specialty."

"You didn't sell me out. I deserved what I got."

"So now I give you cred for honesty, and you reverse psych me into betraying Eva."

"Read it any way you like. You don't need to try so hard to say no. Just say no, and I'll go away."

"You assume a more intimate connection between Eva and me than exists. Anyway, Cyrus should just wait. I don't think the embargo will hide any secrets much longer."

"Then it doesn't matter if you help me."

A fleeting, sardonic smile passed over Mira's face. "No, it doesn't." She slipped the ring into her pocket and stood. "Come with me."

Mira led him through a maze of hallways, past the large double doors of the Materials warehouse, and down an elevator. The elevator opened onto another hall, at the end of which was another double door. The sign beside it read "Fusion Lab." Mira typed in a security code and the door locks snapped open.

"This is our biggest dormant facility—a stacked-pinch test reactor. The last time they used it was to evaluate a method to increase the efficiency of the ^{3}He-^{3}He reaction."

Mira turned on half the interior lights. The cavernous room was ten meters high, maybe forty across, with a windowed control room on the opposite side. The air tasted stale.

The reactor was set into a circular pit, three meters deep and twenty in diameter, in the center of the room. Magnetic field generators surrounded a vacuum torus hedged in by proton detectors and shielding. Overhead, between heavy electricity cables, grapples dangled from a moving crane. At one end of the room stood a flatbed cargo truck with a closed cab. Along the wall ran a series of metal cabinets.

They circled the reactor pit.

"Do they use this to power the lab?"

"The lab is on the colony grid. It doesn't need supplementary power."

Erno was no physicist; he would have to take Mira's word that there was nothing here of any special interest, but it seemed like a lot of lab space to leave unused. They entered the control room and looked around. Nothing.

Erno circled the reactor. Lights glinted off the milled steel fittings.

"This device I'm talking about would need a large energy source like this," he said. "Are any facilities connected to it?"

"Nothing I've ever seen. Wait. I have a copy of a colony architectural survey from twenty years ago in my Aide. I'll call it up on augmentation." She held her head still for a moment, then turned to survey the room. "Everything looks the same—" She began walking around the reactor to get a view of the far side. She stopped and pointed to a bank of cabinets. "There," she said.

"What?"

Mira walked over. "In the blueprint, instead of these cabinets, there's a door."

The cabinet she indicated was massive: four meters tall, six wide, two deep. Erno opened the doors to reveal shelves of equipment. He tugged out a box, set it on the floor, and leaned in to lay his hand against the back wall. He closed his eyes. His hand felt uncomfortable, nervous, as if he were suffering from restless muscle syndrome. After a second he left the cabinet, moved down a few steps, and placed his hand on the wall beside it.

He had the feeling there was a large, deep space lying beyond the wall.

"What are you doing?" Mira asked.

"My hand is artificial. I can tell—"

From the corridor came the sound of voices. Mira took three quick steps, turned off the lights, and closed the lab doors.

She started for the control room but Erno grabbed her sleeve and pulled her toward the truck. They climbed in and crouched on the floor of the cramped cab.

"Who is it?" he asked

"I don't know."

They were almost on top of each other. In the faint light of the lab's emergency lights he saw Mira frown. Knees drawn up, she took up very little space. Square shoulders, small hands. He thought he could make out a mole on her throat. He had never been this close to her.

They kept an uncomfortable silence, listening. All Erno could hear was their own breathing.

"The constables wouldn't normally come down here, would they?" Erno said. "Is there extra security?"

"No," Mira said. "Nobody."

"Somebody must have seen me."

"They could just as easily be looking for me."

There was no way they could hear anyone in the corridor from in here. Minutes passed.

Mira said, "Is it any better out there? The other colonies? I mean, if I do get exiled, what are my options?"

"It's not easy if you're not a citizen. I thought, since I was a man, I'd have an advantage. And in a lot of places that's true, but until I got to Persepolis I was struggling. I was struggling even after I got there."

She didn't say anything. Erno was very aware of her beside him.

"But you won't be exiled," he said. "I don't believe you had anything to do with BYD."

"You can't possibly know that."

He shifted, trying to find an easier position, his leg up against hers. "I know what a lie is." He remembered her at his trial, responding in monosyllables to the questions of the tribunal. He hadn't really known her; she'd been Alicia's friend, and even then, despite his own obsessions, he could tell she was trouble.

Maybe trouble was spun in your DNA, a product of brain chemistry, neurology, parental programming—whatever. In the end you struggled against yourself as much as against circumstances. It weighed on Erno. Your desires and those of others inevitably clashed. You might find moments of connection, places where you ran in parallel, but in the end was any peace, justice, or equanimity to be found in the human world?

Another memory came to him, of Mira running across a soccer field with her brother. "If they make you leave, you're going to have a hard time without Marco."

"Please shut up," she said. "Marco—"

Outside the cab the lab doors opened and the lights came on. Erno put his hand over Mira's mouth. Her body went rigid.

The precise temperature of Mira's lips came to him: thirty-seven degrees.

A woman's voice called, "Check the control room."

Mira took Erno's wrist and moved his hand from her face. They huddled against each other. Erno listened to Mira's shallow breathing, smelled the slightly sour but not unpleasant scent of her skin. Her dark eyes, very close, looked tired.

A metallic clang sounded just outside the truck.

The woman's voice again: "Why don't you just announce that we're here?"

"Shut up, I just dropped it." A man.

"Was she sure she saw Pamelasson?"

"That's what she said."

"What would he be doing here? This is a waste of time."

"*Check the warehouse,* she said. Well, we've checked the warehouse. Now we've checked the lab. Nobody ever comes down here. Let's go."

"All right."

Steps, retreating.

Erno realized how close he was to Mira; his hand lay on her shoulder. He slowly let it fall. Her body was warm, and she didn't draw back. Her face was very close.

• • • • •

Carey's interview on *Here's the Point!* was shot three days after the hearing, in a little public garden with a backdrop of woods running down to the Fowler farmland, the gleaming Diana Tower in the distance. Carey sat on a bench and Sirius, wearing a blinding white suit with a midnight blue tie, reclined in his own special chair. The cameras and the lights were managed remotely. Some Cousins who'd gathered at the garden cheered when Carey showed up, but they were kept back so viewers would get only the picturesque backdrop and the conversation.

The accusations against Erno had taken some of the attention off Carey. He ignored calls from the Reform Party. He avoided the gym and concentrated on work. He'd applied to be moved to a citizen's co-op, explaining that since Val was gone he had no justification for an apartment. "Just me, now," he told them.

Sirius's assistant, the capuchin monkey Gracie, fussed with the dog's jacket, making sure his collar lay flat. She took two capsules from her belt pouch and held them up for Sirius to swallow. Carey had never had much contact with uplifted animals, and the uncanny difference between them and, say, his mother's cat, Hector, was unnerving. For the first time in his life he wondered how the minds of the uplifted differed from those of humans. But what did he know about the mind of anyone?

Gracie whispered something into Sirius's ear, the dog nodded, and she scampered away.

Ten seconds, Carey's Aide told him.

"Here we go," said Sirius.

Sirius began with the obligatory review of Carey's athletic career, shifting into a brief recap for viewers of the issues involved in and the result of the custody hearing. He commiserated with Carey.

"I've read your memoir, *Lune et l'autre,*" Sirius said. "As someone who has been 'othered' all of my life, your account of a boyhood spent in a place where, though you might be petted—and I can relate to that— you are seldom taken seriously, aroused my deepest sympathies. Yet you wrote, at age sixteen, with a *joie de vivre* that bespeaks a spirit open to the almost infinite possibilities of life in our expanding solar community. Have your experiences in the twenty years since dampened that enthusiasm, Carey?"

The sarcastic dog was noted for the number of techniques he used to get under the skin of his guests. "I'm twenty years older now," Carey said. "Some of the things that were funny to me then carry more weight than I thought at the time. Injustices still exist."

"How could injustice not exist in a place that considers biology to be destiny?"

"Isn't biology destiny? Your biology, I would imagine, has determined much of your life."

"My biology has been altered extensively by human intervention. Shouldn't Cousins culture be at least as flexible?"

"When I wrote *Lune et l'autre* we boys and girls used to stay up late and talk about such things. And I do think that the Society could not exist if we were simple biological determinists. The Society was supposed to offer as much opportunity to escape biology as any in history. Men, for instance, were supposed to be freed from the necessity to be soldiers and workers. Still, assumptions are made about human nature, male and female, about gender and sex, that shape what we're allowed to be."

Sirius perked up, his tongue visible between his lips.

"Nonetheless, aren't Cousins men allowed the utmost privilege? And you are a prince among them. Many of our viewers remember you from your silver medal in the last Lunar Olympics."

"That career is over," Carey said. "I don't wish to be defined solely by sport."

"The leaders of the Society point out that you could pursue any one of a number of careers, and be supported in your choice as you have been in your athletic career. But I understand that you have renounced this male privilege and are working in colony agriculture. You are a voter now. Do you contemplate a political career?"

"No. Assuming I don't get exiled, I contemplate a career raising fish."

"That seems like a waste of your talents."

"I'm trying to figure out what my talents are."

"You're one of the most celebrated of Cousins. How can you give that up?"

"I don't want to be a celebrity. I've been as much a celebrity as the Society has."

"What do you do at the aquaculture facility?"

"I manage the growth of ragworm to feed salmon in tanks, I see to the transformation of fish waste into fertilizer, and several other jobs essential to the welfare of the Society."

"That seems a bit of a comedown."

"It depends on your point of view."

Sirius grinned into the camera. "Yes. And now you'll get the view from the bottom instead of the top. But *here's the point* . . . you might have gained the vote without having to muck about in fish waste, if, in your recent election, the proposition to extend the franchise to all males

380 • JOHN KESSEL

had gained a majority. It failed. Among our OLS viewers, and I think among Cousins as well, many believe that not all votes were counted."

"I think it was a fair election," Carey said.

"Your ally and lover, Dr. Camillesdaughter of the Society's university, is planning a rally. She will petition the Board of Matrons to extend the vote by executive order."

"I wish that effort well."

"But you won't take part in it?"

"I don't plan to at present."

"I don't wonder, when it seems that your political activities were one of the reasons you were denied custody of your son Valentin. Let's talk about the hearing, then. What about Val? How do you feel about having him taken from you?"

"His mother and I are on good terms. I will still see him. He's still my son, and always will be."

"You seem remarkably sanguine about the result. There's no need for you to hide your emotions, Carey. All of us in the lunar community sympathize. And we have reports that in the aftermath of the judgment, your immediate reaction was rage—some would say a quite justifiable rage. Isn't it true that on the evening of the hearing, in a meeting of the Reform Party, you got into a shouting fight with Dr. Camillesdaughter?"

"There was no shouting."

"So we were misinformed? You and Dr. Camillesdaughter are still allies?"

"I'll say this: Dr. Camillesdaughter is a serious advocate for positions I agree with, but sometimes she represents an exhausting damage control problem. I lost my temper with her. Anger won't get us anywhere. Cousins culture has to accept the idea of a man as a custodial father, and that won't happen overnight. It'll take a redefinition of Cousins manhood. That's what I'm interested in now."

"That sounds like Tyler Durden's project—to redefine manhood for the Society of Cousins."

"Marysson's program was just another version of the toxic masculinity the Society was founded to escape. Plus proving his dick was bigger than anybody else's."

"I hope our viewers will pardon your blunt speech." Sirius grinned, showing his very pink tongue. "For a man who has legitimate grievances, Carey, you are surprisingly at home with the status quo."

"Far from it. But I won't be used anymore, not by the Matrons, and not by Professor Camillesdaughter. And I won't be used by the patriarchal power brokers who sent you here."

Sirius grinned wider still. "I'll pass that along to our producers," he said. "To our viewers, too, seventy percent of whom are women—those supporters of the tyrannical patriarchy." He winked at the camera. Carey had never seen a dog wink. Something about it seemed very wrong.

"Let's talk about how you are going to manage this retreat from the public eye, Carey. You are a beloved person in the Society. Your mother is a former Chair of the Board of Matrons. You have had many lovers. I have visited the homes of ordinary Cousins, and I cannot tell you how many times I saw a young woman with an image of you as a wallpaper. You face is known, thanks to this custody dispute, by most of the people on the moon. People like you."

"Yes, Sirius, people like me. I'm the completely unthreatening version of the alpha male. I'm available for any purpose. I have a dazzling smile."

"And, it seems, a talent for mockery. But completely unthreatening? I think that reputation is at this point decidedly in the past tense, Carey—though it must have stood you in good stead when you were manufacturing these subversive videos with your lover Mira Hannasdaughter. And helping her hack the dome video system to produce the BYD hoax that resulted in injuries to dozens of people. By most definitions this was a act of terrorism."

"You'll have to speak with Mira about that. I was not involved in BYD."

"So, you didn't help her in her career as Looker?"

This was the one question that Carey had most expected to be asked. "Yes, I helped her."

"And she repaid you by betraying you at the hearing. How do you feel about that?"

He'd spent much of the last three days trying to figure out the answer to that one. Why had she chosen to betray him by revealing she was Looker, when she could simply have, for instance, told about how he didn't know where Val was on the afternoon of BYD? He often thought of her offer to marry him. He felt ashamed of how easily he'd rejected her; at the same time the offer itself still made him mad.

"I was dismayed," Carey said. "But Mira is not the problem."

"So her destroying your chance to be with your son, setting back the cause of reform for all men, is just an unfortunate happenstance. Your own role in setting back reform is something other Cousins should simply accept, now that you've abandoned the struggle and prefer to spend your time with ragworms."

Carey drew a deep breath. "You're good at what you do, Sirius."

"Thank you. I am highly evolved. Though I think I have yet to attain the ability to ignore contradiction that comes so easily to the human mind."

"I don't know—you have a good grasp of sarcasm. I can't answer these questions, but here's what I can tell you: I want to do ordinary work to support the people I live among. I'm not interested in destroying the Society; I want to reform it.

"I don't wish Mira any ill. I don't wish Hypatia or the Board of Matrons any ill. I don't wish Roz Baldwin any ill. I just want to be left to do what I need to do. I'm not going away. I am a citizen of the Society. But despite those images on young girls' walls, I am not any kind of leader. I suspect you exaggerate the degree to which others care about any of this. I'm just a person doing, at last, some useful work. There are a lot of us here."

"Nicely said. The Aristarchus Olympic team might have wished you'd pursued your talent for political rhetoric instead of *Ruăn tā*. But

I joke. I, and my viewers all over the moon, thank you for your time, Carey." Sirius held out his handpaw.

Carey leaned forward and took it. "It's been my pleasure."

The lights went down.

"That was perfect," Sirius said. "Enough surprises to suck in the fans, but enough of the old themes to reassure the ones who aren't paying much attention. You reject victimization without forsaking the sympathy of the ones who see you as a victim. You present as an autonomous man and a tool at the same time."

Carey stood up and stretched. He towered over the dog. "You make it sound calculated."

"It wasn't? Then you have a natural gift for bullshit. You undercut Hypatia—'an exhausting damage control problem,' that was brilliant—without leaving yourself open to accusations you're undercutting her. She's the egomaniac, you're the natural voice of the opposition."

"I'm not the voice of anybody."

"That's it! Exactly the image you need to project."

Why was Sirius trying to antagonize him? Were the cameras still running, hoping to pick up some show of anger, or catch him in some contradiction? Sirius had risen in the lunar media by courting controversy, yet never truly challenged the assumptions of his audience or producers.

"If you'll excuse me, then, I'll go," Carey said.

Sirius looked about the bower. No one was near. "Not yet. I need to speak to you about a proposition."

"Are you still recording?

Sirius lifted a handpaw and waved the cameras away. They floated off among the trees. "Done. We're in complete isolation here."

Carey sat back down. "So?"

Sirius stretched his handpaws, flexing the rudimentary beringed thumb that showed through his white half-gloves. "This situation is no less combustible than it was before the election. The SCOCOM report is going to be negative—it will inflame suspicions against the Society. Eventually, the OLS is going to intervene."

"An intervention would be a disaster—for everyone concerned."

"Nevertheless, it will come. You are in a position to do something for yourself and the Society you profess to care about. There will be a regime change. There will be a new government. It will be imposed from without, but at the top it will have to be led by a citizen of the Society. If anything of your social structure is going to be preserved, the person leading the new government will have to be someone who cares for the ideas on which the Society was founded."

"That's a lot of speculation."

"The persons who employ me—we'll let them remain nameless— are prepared to see that you are offered this job. You would be the governor of the Cousins Protectorate."

"It won't happen."

"Then perhaps your army will repulse the OLS troops when they arrive. Oh, that's right—you have no army. When the takeover happens, the only way the things you have established here will have any chance of persisting will be if someone like you is in a position to stand between the OLS and the Society. To advocate on its behalf, with some chance to be heard. Why not let that person be you?"

"I won't do it. And I won't be quiet about it. I'll tell people you've made this offer."

"Speak to whomever you please," Sirius said, and even the barrier of his canine accent could not hide his disgust. "I expect they will see the simple truth of what I say."

Gracie came back and once again spoke into the dog's ear. Sirius flexed his handpaws, then hopped off his chair. "Oh, and while you are telling your friends about this offer, why don't you tell them about your mother's invention? Shouldn't people have all the information essential to make informed political decisions?"

CHAPTER

TWELVE

Mira pulled back from their kiss. She felt Erno's fingertips tangled in the hair at the back of her head. It was the hand he'd said was artificial.

But he avoided her eyes. "They're gone," he said.

"Let's wait." She studied his face. She'd been thinking about kissing him from the moment he showed up in the lab. Maybe it was that he had no place here, and nothing would come of it. Maybe it was because he was from far enough back in her past that he had not seen her fail at every relationship in her life. "How did you get that hand?"

"My hand?" He held it between them, looked at it warily. "I stole it."

She listened to his steady breathing. His watchfulness was not the aggrieved adolescence he'd stewed in before his exile. The kiss hung between them, unacknowledged.

"Who did you steal it from?"

"A man in trouble." Erno peeked through the cab window into the reactor room, then settled back down. He seemed uncomfortable in a way he had not been even when the constables had been searching a couple of meters away. His eyes met hers. "In the patriarchies it's not like here, where you can't fall through the bottom of society without somebody stepping in. Out there, if you don't have a family, you're finished."

"As often as not, family's the problem," Mira said. She turned her cheek, thinking he might lean closer. He didn't.

"Sure, I used to hate my mother hovering. I never really understood how much I missed this place until I got off that cable train. You don't know what being kept down is until you've been a guest worker."

"Still complaining," she said. "You used to rant against the Matrons; now it's the patriarchies. You're a rich man, married into a powerful family, named to a government commission. You should do something with that power instead of complaining."

Erno shook his head. "I must be a lousy kisser."

"Pretty much the same as everyone," Mira said.

"From a kiss to a takedown, just like that." He didn't sound hurt. "The classic Mira playbook."

"You don't know me that well."

"I've been wanting to kiss you since I was fourteen."

"You wanted to kiss everyone. You had sex with any woman who would have sex with you. Never even tried with me."

"You were the one person I knew who was as angry as I was. I can't tell you how much I wanted to draw your number in some sex practicum."

"You could have just asked."

"As if you would have said yes."

"You asked every female in sight. Why not me?"

Erno said nothing. "Why did you turn on Carey Evasson?"

"He hurt me. He really wasn't taking care of Val. Hypatia thought she had me in her pocket. A half dozen other reasons. Human behavior is overdetermined."

"I was never impressed with him," Erno said. "His snide little book."

She would not let him evade the implications of their kiss. "So, why not me?"

"If you want to know—your brother. You and Marco were a closed system. You trusted him more than any of us. You might tease him but heaven help any other person who did."

"We were siblings. More than that—Marco was my Y-clone."

"You don't miss that connection until it's gone," Erno said. "My sister and aunts won't even talk to me now. At least you've got him."

"Marco's dead," she said.

She opened the cab door and got out of the truck. Erno climbed out and came around to her side. He stood there stupidly, hands at his sides. "I didn't know."

Mira turned her back on him.

"What happened?"

"A year after you left my mother emigrated. She was lousy at networking, worse at marriage. She had no real allies. Marco was one of her bad ideas—she imagined having a son in addition to a daughter would make us a family, when she didn't want either of us."

Mira looked at the exit light over the lab doors, blinked until the red became a blur. "She left Marco with me," she told Erno, "then she disappeared. I wasn't old enough. Nobody falls through the bottom here? Well, no one seemed to care about Marco and me."

As she spoke, the emotion welled up in her. "I let him take too many risks. Marco was killed in a flying accident. I should have stopped him. No one else could stop him but I could. But I didn't—and he died."

Mira held back her tears. She felt Erno's hand on her shoulder. When she turned to face him he said, "I'm sorry."

"It happened because of the way we live. So I became Looker, and started making my videos."

Erno didn't say anything for a moment. "I remember Marco would always be waiting for you at the end of the school day. You used to get annoyed. He didn't like it when you started hanging out with Alicia and the other women."

"He always wanted to be with me."

"My mother complained about you. When you got that maintenance worker in trouble, she was one of the constables who arrested him."

"Teddy Dorasson." The thought of him made her feel guilty. "I didn't mean to get him in trouble. I just needed to get away from the girls' retreat, and he was my way out." Mira pushed the truck door closed until the latch clicked. "It must be an hour since we came in here," she said. "The constables are gone."

Erno didn't move. "Did the Matrons really ignore you after your mother left? They hardly leave anyone alone, let alone boys without mothers."

Mira looked up at him. "Do you think I'm lying?"

"I'm not denying what you feel." His voice was low.

"I already blame myself for it," she said. "I never stop blaming myself. What's your point?"

"I'm sorry. The Matrons should have offered you more help."

"They offered plenty of help. We didn't want their help."

"You don't have to persuade me," he said, an edge coming to his voice. "When Sirius asks your take on the custody hearing, tell him your story. It will be a big hit in Persepolis, and really boost the image of the Society in the OLS."

"Fuck you," Mira said. She pushed past him to circle the reactor.

Instead of following, Erno flicked on the lab's lights and returned to the wall he'd been examining. Still fuming, she stopped pacing and stared at him.

His back was to her. He said, "I'm sorry I said anything."

Mira crossed her arms, trying to quiet her racing heart. Erno's shoulders were hunched and he had his left hand splayed flat against the wall.

"Are we done?" she asked.

"Not yet—bear with me."

"Hurry up."

Erno spent the next ten minutes placing his left hand carefully against the lab wall in various spots, moving steadily along, as if measuring it for drapes. She watched, mind whirling with anger and shame.

Erno had always been arrogant even though he had no accomplishments that justified arrogance. His poems, his politics, his lies. He called Carey self-involved, but he paid attention only to what mattered to him.

Except—except how could what he'd said hurt her so much if it was wrong? It was like he'd zeroed in on a bad tooth. Even if every detail of the story she told about Marco's death and her place in it and her feelings about it were true—even if there was not one syllable of self-justification in the story—the fact was that she had somehow fallen into telling it over and over. She had *turned it* into a story. And then she had made that story into the core of her identity.

How had a man as self-absorbed as Erno managed to see this when so many who knew her better had not? He looked a fool, half crouched against the wall as if he expected it to whisper in his ear.

"What are you doing?" Mira asked.

He still wouldn't face her. "I can feel things. This hand has a kind of neurological sonar. There's a room beyond this wall, a big one."

He stood straight, and finally managed the nerve to turn to her. His expression was grim. "We can go now."

She closed and locked the fusion lab. When they reached the exit to the Materials complex he broke the uncomfortable silence. "I'm sorry for what I said. I had no right." His long blond hair fell over his forehead, and she remembered it brushing her face as she kissed him.

"It's all right," she said.

"Please don't tell any one else I was here."

There it was again—his self-interest.

But she told him yes, and in silence he left.

Instead of going home, Mira went back to her desk and sat brooding. She thought about the hearing. After it was over everyone in the room—not just Carey and Hypatia, but Eva and Roz and the three judges—had looked at her sideways, as if she were an explosive device whose trigger they did not know. She took the ring from her pocket and played with it. Two vines wrapped around each other, circling to meet themselves, intertwined but never connected.

Eventually a pair of constables entered the office.

"What are you doing here?" the older one asked.

"Thinking."

"Has anyone else been here?" The woman looked around the dimly lit room, the cubicles, the dark offices. "That SCOCOM rep—Erno Pamelasson?"

"No."

The other, who had been watching Mira, spoke up. "You're Mira Hannasdaughter," she said. "You're Looker."

"Guilty as charged," Mira said.

"Not yet," said the older woman, "but soon."

• • • • •

Uplifting a canine to human intelligence and preparing it to function in society is a complex and, even in the best of circumstances, brutal process, fraught with difficulties. It is by definition unnatural.

Among the interventions necessary to produce an uplifted dog are:

- Engineering of germ plasm
- Gestation in a surrogate mother; the increased skull size of the modified canine requires birth by cesarean
- Extensive biometric modification surgery
- Implanted AI and memory
- Endocrine alterations
- Laryngeal grafts
- Comprehensive behavior training
- Antisenescence and life extension drug therapy

To offer only one example of the difficulties uplifting presents: Despite continual improvements in techniques, the canine paw is ill suited for modification. By no extreme of surgery or augmentation have biotechnicians been able to produce anything resembling a simian hand on a canine. Uplifted dogs are thus dependent on mechanical devices, humans, or other simians to accomplish the simplest physical tasks.

The psychological effects of uplifting on the canine are less obvious but far reaching.

Normal puppies share everything, even the womb, with their siblings. In a litter, puppies pull ears, bite each other's necks, tumble on top of each other, paw, push, lick. But an uplifted dog is, from gestation on, of necessity a singleton. Nothing the designer, breeder, developer, or teacher can do makes up for a lack of peer socialization. A puppy on the road to uplift may have contact with other dogs and uplifted animals, but she spends the bulk of her time in the presence of humans.

Socializing the uplifted dog is a difficult process, and solipsism an ever-present danger. Given the immense amount of attention she receives at every stage of her development, the puppy perceives herself the center of the universe. She is not eager to share the stage with another creature.

Living in a world of yes, the uplifted puppy can lack bite inhibition and develop an exaggerated sensitivity to touch. At maturity such dogs exhibit boundless enthusiasm but no governor. They are unable to handle frustration or get out of trouble graciously. They may struggle with impulse control or be prone to violent reactions.

On the other hand, lacking littermates, the uplifted dog typically bonds unbreakably with his human parents and mentors. Behavioral training regimes modify and regulate the dog's undesirable impulses and profitless habits. Countless stories attest to the uplifted canine as devoted companion and committed friend.

History celebrates the dog for its loyalty, obedience, and desire to please its master. But the uplifted canine mind, as various as the human mind, does not work as the human mind does. Given the vast range of its functions and malfunctions, the mind of the uplifted dog remains fundamentally mysterious.

• • • • •

The hotel suite's dining table had become a second workspace for the SCOCOM team when they weren't in the Diana Tower offices. Beason paged through another of the interviews the staff had taken, then pushed away his notebook. "This is useless. Let's simply conclude the SoC is rotten top to bottom and let the Secretary General take it from there." He stood up from the table. "She hasn't got the backbone to ignore a negative report if her political future is at stake."

"If you file such a report, I'll go public," Erno said. "You're hunting for a *casus belli*."

"Nobody will take you seriously," Beason said. "You're lucky we haven't sent you home."

I am home, Erno thought. But no: He had no home. For three days Göttsch had not let Erno out of the hotel. Erno occupied himself viewing interviews and drafting an analysis of the employment situation of male Cousins, waiting for Sirius to get him access to the tree genome stocks.

Mira's accusation of fecklessness wore at him. It was none of his business what happened to the Society, but he could not help but feel he was betraying it by doing nothing. Yet he didn't want to do anything. He just wanted to leave.

He remembered Mira's kiss and tried to figure out what, if anything, it meant. Having sex in the cab of the truck would have been the Cousins thing to do. He found Mira as attractive as he had when they were fourteen, and Mira had initiated the kiss. But he was married to Amestris—true, in a marriage of convenience, if you included great sex as a convenience. So why not? Was he falling into patriarchal notions of marriage? But a true patriarch would have enjoyed sex with Mira and gone home to his wife.

"A report now would be premature," Göttsch announced.

"You're the sociologist," Erno said to Beason. "You should be interested in this upcoming rally, the circumstances that led to it, the people behind it, the potential it shows or doesn't show for change. You've drawn your conclusions before you've even investigated."

Beason waved his hand at Erno. "The rally is a Potemkin protest. I've seen the statistics, and we have a growing mass of interviews, every one of which shows the prejudice against men in the Society."

"There hasn't been anything like this rally in Cousins history," Erno said. "Twenty percent of the populace may be at it. Camillesdaughter has drawn together a coalition behind extending the franchise that could transform the Society."

"The Board of Matrons may not allow the rally," Göttsch said. "We should wait to see what happens."

"We're here to investigate and file a report," Erno said. "We're not supposed to advocate action."

"Don't be a fool," Beason said. "Of course we're here to advocate action."

"We're not filing any report yet," Göttsch said. "I have not spoken with Dr. Maggiesdaughter. Her paper modifying indeterminacy theory is one of the most brilliant of the last thirty years."

"What has that got to do with our charge?" insisted Beason. "You just want to satisfy your own curiosity."

"You'd be well served to be more curious yourself, Martin," Göttsch said.

Li spoke up. "The GROSS viruses were an inelegant plan and, if it had been tried, unlikely to have worked. This public furor is wrongheaded. Erno should be reinstated. There are real biotech threats we should be investigating."

Göttsch shook her head. "That's as may be, but the publicity puts us in a delicate situation. Whether we can put Erno's name on the final report will depend on how this plays out."

Erno got up from the table. "You'll need my input to give the report credibility. And I'm not going to stay confined to the hotel forever."

When Göttsch, Beason, and Li left for the SCOCOM offices, Erno texted Sirius: *I need to speak with you.*

Not now.

The more Erno had gotten to know the dog, the less he understood him. Sirius had an encyclopedic knowledge of human cultures. He held a PhD in history, but he had forsaken academic work to pursue his career in the media. He claimed that species prejudice put a lid on any advances he might make in the academy, and besides, he was already sixteen years old. But this was so superficial a motive that Erno suspected it reflected little of his real self.

Erno knocked on the door of Sirius's suite. No answer. He knocked again.

From behind the door the dog growled, "If you must, come in."

Erno entered. The room was appointed with a round gel mattress, a communications center, a pixwall, a special desk, and a dog chair Sirius had brought with him. A pad and stylus lay on the desk. The pixwall showed an Alpine meadow surrounded by dark green trees, beneath a stunning blue sky.

Sirius was seated on the mattress, unclothed, being groomed by Gracie. He had his eyes closed, ears relaxed, as Gracie pulled a small brush the length of his back. The room smelled of forest.

Sirius opened his eyes and looked at Erno.

"That's enough, Gracie," he said.

The monkey, still holding the brush, whispered in Sirius's ear.

"Not now," Sirius said. "Mr. Pamson demands my time, and how might I, a mere dog, deny Mr. Pamson?"

Sirius, the champion of animal rights, did not seem to mind owning Gracie, whose intelligence did not pass the threshold granting her the right to self-possession. Gracie returned the brush to a grooming kit, folded it up, put the case on a side table, and left. Beside the kit lay a drug caddy with multiple compartments full of pills.

Ignoring Erno, Sirius hopped onto his chair and picked up the stylus in his right handpaw, dropped it, then picked it up again. With agonizing care he tapped it against the pad. Erno studied a window within the wall pix, a chart listing the major lunar colonies and the voting status of men, women, and animals in each.

Erno waited for Sirius to finish what he was doing. Sirius had a video on the pad, his sleek head hovering over it. He began to whimper. Erno stepped closer to look over his shoulder. On the screen a Doberman puppy romped with a couple of dark-haired children in a brightly colored playroom. The children teased him with a rope toy. Plump, floppy-eared, with bright brown spots above its eyes, the puppy bounced and growled and nipped at its human playmates. The delighted children squealed. They fell together in a heap. The little boy put his arms around the puppy's neck and it licked his face.

Sirius hung his head just above the pad, breathing irregularly.

The puppy had the high domed forehead of the genetically augmented canine, but was otherwise unlifted.

"Is that you?" Erno asked.

Sirius sighed, a very odd sound. "Archive," he told the pad, and the screen went blank. He shoved the tablet away with force and swiveled his chair around. His fathomless black eyes rested on Erno for some seconds.

"All right. What do you want?"

The SCOCOM team treated Erno like an interloper, and Sirius made him wait for no reason. "I want access to the tree genomes. I'm not needed here."

"You're needed to acquire the information that Cyrus Eskander asked you to get."

Erno took the only human chair in the room. "I told you already: The machine exists."

"I promised you would get those genomes—if you got the IQSA. You haven't done that yet. If the first effort yields only partial results, you close the deal with the second."

"If you want more from me, you'll have to spike this talk about me as a terrorist."

"A report will hit later today. The OLS has examined the virus plan and determined that it was first, a plot against Cousins women, second, never created, and third, brought to the attention of the Matrons by you."

"That won't mollify the fanatics in the other colonies."

"Nothing will ever mollify them."

"Exactly. So how can I get the genomes? I can't show my face anywhere near a biotech facility."

"You don't need to show your face," Sirius said. The dog trotted to his closet and dragged out a backpack. Using both of his handpaws he unseamed the pack and pulled out a jumpsuit.

"This is a camouflage suit," Sirius said. "Use it to get your precious genomes. If you're caught, I will deny any involvement. It's a better chance than you've earned."

Sirius held the suit out, fumbled, and dropped it.

"Damn it!" he muttered.

Sirius seized the suit in his jaws and tossed his head, flinging it across the room at Erno. The sleeves flopped and tumbled in slow motion, and Erno snatched it out of the air.

This seemed to enrage Sirius even more. He shook his head and whined.

"What's the matter?" Erno asked.

"I depend on monkeys to accomplish anything. And half the time you botch it, as you have the simple task of getting this information."

"I'm sorry."

"Yet you'll live another hundred years, while I'll be dead in ten. I'm an abomination. A monstrous violation of nature."

Erno had never seen Sirius in this mood. "It must be hard to be an animal."

"I'm an animal? And what are you? Your theories, your art, your music, your science, all just a veneer! The best of you—you on your very best day—are bemused. The worst—your prime ministers, generals, popes, CEOs, bankers—are nothing more nor less than demons. You rape, exploit, destroy, and call it principle."

"Bad cultures, bad behavior," Erno said.

"*CULL*-ture," the dog's whine dripped with sarcasm. "If it's just *culture*, point to some time in human history that was different."

"Here. Violence in the Society is controlled."

"With the world of men ready to take over at the point of a gun. These women would be better served to make those bioweapons that half the moon, projecting their own homicidal impulses, believes they have."

The fur along the ridge of Sirius's back stood erect. He retreated to the closet and took down shorts and a brilliant blue shirt. He struggled to put on the shorts.

"I'll call Gracie," Erno said.

"You will not call Gracie."

Sirius managed to don the shorts, but he fumbled with the shirt cuffs. He looked up at Erno in silent accusation.

"Help me," Sirius said.

Erno got down on his knees and sealed the cuffs. Sirius trembled.

"I go quietly and see things. Not one of you knows what I see," Sirius said slowly, in a whisper. His limpid black eyes, irises invisible, watched Erno's hands. "Yet you call me your creation."

"Cyrus's creation."

"Yes, Cyrus made me." Sirius pulled away from Erno. "'I am His Highness's dog at Kew,' he recited mockingly, 'Pray tell me, sir, whose dog are you?'"

Erno was stung. "I'm Cyrus's dog, too."

"Well, you make a poor dog. I send you out to fetch an answer, and you come back with guesswork."

"The IQSA is there. I'd bet on it."

"You have nothing to bet, you purblind twit! Take the suit and steal your genomes. Go back to Persepolis and tell yourself you've proven your manhood—as you will have most gloriously, in time-honored tradition, over the bodies of your fellows, done."

"Fuck you," Erno said, "and your nihilistic bullshit."

"Oh, dear—nihilism!" The dog sounded like he was choking, but he was laughing. "Don't take me so seriously, Fido—I believe in lots of things. Scent. I believe in scent. You, for instance, reek of cowardice. I can smell your egotism, your rage, your fear, your sentimentality, your self-delusion. You should all be put down before you do more damage to a pristine universe and the poor creatures who must share it with you."

Erno took the camo suit and left.

• • • • •

Two days after the constables found her in the lab, the Board of Matrons ordered that Mira be suspended from Materials. She didn't know whether Eva had any say in the matter, or what Eva might have said if she did.

She was cleaning out her desk, putting the few items that were hers into a box, when Roz came over to speak with her. Since the hearing, Mira's feelings about Roz had become complicated.

"I'm sorry they're doing this," Roz said.

"Right," Mira said. "You're broken up."

Roz sighed. She sat down on the corner of the desk. "You tell yourself that we're completely different, Mira, but we're not. Neither of us fits into the world of forced sisterhood. We both lost the most important person from our childhood—your brother, my father." She paused, looked down at the desktop. "Your sarcasm is a defensive posture that I know all too well. It took me a long time to let it go."

At another time Roz's presumption might have sparked Mira's hostility. But she was tired, and she was in trouble, and maybe Roz had a point. She tried to think of something to say. The best she could do was "I liked working here."

"Don't assume you won't be back. I've been trying to find a way to tell you how grateful I am for what you said in the hearing. I know you love Val—and Carey. That must not have been easy."

Mira put the picture of herself and Marco into the box.

"When I worked at this desk," Roz said, "I felt I'd always be an immigrant. They called me 'High-G' because I was from Earth. It took me years to realize that I didn't need to be alone."

Mira really didn't want to hear this. "How's Val?"

"He's fine," Roz said, but her brow was furrowed.

"Look," Mira said, "you do know that while he was with Carey he was hanging around with the most radical of Hypatia's crew, right?"

"You were part of Hypatia's crew."

"Not really." Mira closed the box. "Even if she's right about some things."

"Being right isn't everything." Roz eased off of the desk. "Did you ever by any chance find a ring lying around this workstation?"

Mira had it in her pocket. Whenever she was nervous she worried it with her fingers.

"No," she said. She picked up her box. "Look, I know you are trying to help me, and it's pretty clear I need help sometimes. Just keep an eye on Val, okay?"

Roz looked as tired as Mira felt. "I will."

"Good-bye, then." Mira carried her box out of the lab.

Others besides Roz had felt free to confront Mira lately. In the wake of the hearing, more than one person had accosted her. Somebody plastered one of Mira's own videos over her apartment door. She got hundreds of personal messages with every extreme of reaction. But then at the refectory a neighborhood woman who had never once paid her any attention came to sit and reassure her that her troubles would pass.

She ran into Cleo on the tram one night. Cleo came to stand facing Mira where she sat.

"I don't understand you," Cleo told her. She towered over Mira. Her voice was husky with emotion.

"I don't understand myself, Cleo."

"Self-flagellation doesn't make you a good person."

"Then you'll just have to flagellate me instead."

"Oh, yes, your conscience is so much better tuned than mine."

Cleo got off at the next stop. Mira remembered the look of her departing back, shoulders squared, and the long strides she took.

Mira followed the preparations for the rally from a distance. They said this would be the largest protest in Cousins history. The administration had given permission, had even sent a staffer to work with the

Reform Party on the logistics. The Board made a show of reaffirming the Society's commitment to openness and democracy.

Hypatia had a wonderful time being interviewed on patriarchal public affairs shows. She was at her absolute best, deploying the buzzwords of the Founders while undercutting everything they stood for. Searing wit, academic theory, *double entendres*, playing up the Society's reputation for sexual license with every gesture, every well chosen outfit. Masculine by the terms of the patriarchal world but hot hot hot, with just enough queer markers to broaden her appeal.

It looked like a third or more of the colony support staff, overwhelmingly male, would forsake their jobs for the day. Bureaucrats scrambled to arrange for backups in essential services. The constabulary signed on a score of trained volunteers.

Meanwhile, Erno had disappeared from public view. There was talk that he was being sent back to Persepolis, but no confirmation. He'd made no attempt to get in touch with Mira since their meeting. She didn't know whether she should follow through on her promise to keep quiet or tell somebody about his spying for Cyrus.

Their kiss lingered in her mind.

The more she thought about it, the more Mira realized that she needed to speak with Eva. Among women of influence, Eva was the only one whose opinion Mira might find valuable. Plus, if there was a room behind the wall of the stacked-pinch reactor lab, Eva would know all about it.

A week into her enforced idleness Mira messaged Eva asking to meet. Eva's reply gave Mira no hint of her attitude: She simply set a time for Mira to come to her home.

Mira arrived at twilight. Above, evening flyers were black silhouettes against the lambent sky, red and green running lights at the tips of their wings.

Eva greeted Mira at the door. "Come in." A brief embrace.

What they said about the Greens and privilege was right: Mira had never seen a home of such size and luxury. For a moment she had second thoughts. She and Eva were too different: Eva cool and rational and steeped in the status quo, Mira scattered and wary and sometimes purple with rage against the moon itself, let alone other people. Whatever her failings, Hypatia understood that. What could Eva know about being Mira?

The living room opened onto a terrace that looked over the interior of the colony. The flyers were coming in now. Mira watched one of them glide down to the aerofield in Sobieski Park. The semen smell of a blooming callery pear wafted in from outside.

"Some tea?" Eva asked. "Nothing special, just caffeine."

"That would be good."

Eva went to the sideboard and adjusted the settings of a brewer.

"Thank you for agreeing to see me," Mira said as she walked around the room. She slipped her hand into her pocket and played with her ring.

On the wall hung a painting that must have come from Earth. It showed a woman in an elaborate yellow gown drying off a naked boy after bathing him. The boy was placid and inexpressive, as if half asleep. The mother had her hand on a towel that covered the boy's groin.

What struck Mira was not the subject, but the physical reality of the painting. Canvas—fabric made from plant fibers—stretched over a wooden frame, the image created by layers of oil-based pigments laid on with a brush made from animal hairs. The painting even smelled organic. So primitive an artifact as to be a window into another time. Literally irreplaceable. Its value could not be measured in economic terms, yet it hung on the wall as if there were nothing unusual about such a thing ending up in an apartment in the Society of Cousins on the far side of the moon.

Mira sat on a chair by a low table. A black-and-white cat trotted out, paused, and stared at her. She extended her arm at floor level, the back of her hand toward him. He came over and sniffed her knuckles, then bumped his head against her hand. She scratched him behind the ears. "Isn't there anyone else here?"

Eva looked over her shoulder. "No. It's just you, me, and Hector." She brought two glasses of hot tea—actual hand-blown glasses, not bulbs—on a tray, set it on the table, then sat on the sofa opposite Mira. Hector jumped up and settled down beside her. Mira tried the tea. Eva waited, not offering Mira much guidance.

Mira drove straight ahead. "I don't know what you think about my testimony, or what part you took in my getting suspended. But you let me come here, so you must be at least willing to listen. I have some things that I have to tell you, and some advice."

"Advice? For me, personally?"

"Yes."

Eva sipped her tea. "I have mixed emotions about your testimony. Did you lie about Carey?"

"I am Looker. He did help me with some of my videos. The footage I showed was genuine. All that was true."

"And BYD?"

"I didn't have anything to do with that. Neither did Carey."

"You didn't need to lie. The vids you showed would have done it. They were going to take Val back anyway."

"Somebody had to keep better watch on Val. Carey wasn't doing that."

"You know there's more to it than that." Eva watched Mira for a moment. "But there's no point arguing about it. We'll do what we can to take care of Val. You can help with that, if you ever hear anything about him that we might need to know. But this can't be why you asked to see me."

"It was, in part. I could use"—Mira searched for the words—"some help. I don't want to be exiled. I was hoping that, if you do something for Carey, you might help me."

"I think Carey is in more trouble than you are."

"Carey's more famous than ever. It would be suicidal for the Matrons to banish him. I'm the one at risk."

"I can put in a word for you with some people," Eva said coolly. "It might do you some good." She put down her glass. "I'm still waiting for this advice."

Mira put down her own glass. "Erno Pamelasson came to see me, the same night that this news came out about the GROSS virus. I don't know why the Board never revealed that about him at his trial. Half of the Reform Party sees him as a martyr. Nobody would have felt that way if they'd known he was a bioterrorist."

"We didn't want to publicize the virus. He was involved in an incident that got his mother killed. That was more than enough to get him exiled."

"Well, Erno came to see me at the lab. He wasn't acting for SCOCOM. He's working for Cyrus Eskander. He wants the IQSA."

Mira watched Eva, looking for some sign of recognition.

"What is the IQSA?"

"A machine in a walled-off lab behind the stacked-pinch reactor. He called it the Integrated Quantum Scanner Array. He thinks it's in there. I don't know what, if anything, he's said to anyone else."

"He *thinks* it's there?"

"I took him down there. He was the one who figured out that there is a room behind the wall."

"So he never saw any device."

"He's convinced it exists. He says keeping it a secret was the reason we're under this information embargo."

Eva gazed at her unhappily. Mira took the ring out of her pocket and slid it onto her finger.

"I asked you not to pursue this," Eva said.

"I told you the embargo was suspicious. Erno said if he got the details of its construction, schematics, data on operation, he'd keep it quiet. But it will go to Eskander, and then, I guess, it's out."

"It won't be out—Eskander will want to keep it a secret as much as I do. I want to suppress it. He wants to own it. You should have come to me as soon as Erno asked after it."

"If you'd trusted me enough to tell me what was going on when we talked after the lab meeting, I'd have had a reason to. Instead you tried to placate me. That invitation to your picnic. All that talk about my joining the Green family."

"That was genuine."

"So you say." Mira had the ring on her little finger, turning it with her thumb as she spoke. "Here's my advice, then: Reveal it all. It's going to come out anyway. Use it as a bargaining chip with the OLS."

"The OLS will have to know regardless," Eva said. "If it's going to be out there—I always knew it would be, eventually—the OLS could at least try to control it."

"Is it a weapon?"

"No," Eva said. "It's not a weapon."

"Erno said there was a scanner and some sort of instantiator, like an object printer."

"That rather underestimates the matter." Eva bit her thumbnail, then sighed. "The IQSA can duplicate any material object."

Mira thought about that. "Anything?"

"Anything."

"It works?"

"It most certainly works."

Mira considered the possibilities. Clearly the thing, if it really worked, might have widespread industrial applications.

"But why did you suppress it?" Mira leaned forward, forearms on her knees, hands clasped in front of her. "You'd be famous throughout the solar system. A patent would earn the colony a huge amount of foreign exchange."

"I have thought—" Eva stopped. She stared at Mira's hand. "Where did you get that ring?"

Mira pulled it off. "It's nothing. I found it."

"You found it." Eva's voice had gone flat. "May I see it?"

Reluctantly, Mira handed it to Eva. Eva held it between her thumb and forefinger; she turned it, examining the twined vines inlaid into its surface.

After a moment, Eva released her breath, placed the ring on the low table beside the tea tray, and slid it toward Mira. "This ring has been missing for twenty years. How did you get it?"

"I—I found it behind a desk."

Eva's eyes darkened. "Don't treat me like a fool." She stood up and paced to the terrace, then back. "Did you find his body? Somewhere on the surface?"

"What are you talking about?"

"You come here asking about the IQSA, and you've got Carey's ring, and you don't know what I'm talking about?"

"It's Carey's ring?"

"As you well know."

"No, I don't. I told you, I found it in the lab."

"Are you working for the OLS?"

This was absurd. "All right, I lied. I didn't find it. Carey gave it to me."

"Stop lying! Carey—the Carey who wore this ring, is dead! He was wearing it when he disappeared. Only somebody who found his body would have it."

"What are you talking about? Carey isn't dead."

Eva sat down, leaned forward over the table, studying her. She picked up the ring again, got some control over her voice. "Carey's alive, yes," she said hoarsely. "But it's not the Carey that got lost when he was fifteen. The IQSA can duplicate any material object, organic or inorganic, down to the atomic level. When Carey disappeared, I used it to recreate him."

Mira stared at Eva. Eva just looked back. "What?" Mira said. "Carey was hiding out, writing—"

"Carey disappeared because he was lying dead somewhere on the surface. You know that or you wouldn't have this ring. You or someone else must have found his body, after all these years."

"No. I found it behind the desk, like I said. It was Roz's desk. Maybe Carey gave the ring to her."

Eva was nonplussed. "If Carey gave it to her, why would Roz hide it?"

"I don't know."

Eva watched her. She looked tired. When she spoke again her voice was distant.

"Carey disappeared on the night of Founders' Day. He and some friends planned to meet out on the lunar surface, but he never showed up. You know about the unsuccessful searches, how he was assumed lost. Well, that was the truth.

"What nobody knew was that, in testing the IQSA a month earlier, I had scanned Carey. After he was gone, I still had an exact description of his quantum state at the moment the scan was taken. In the months after, I redoubled the team's efforts to produce an assembler capable of using a scan to create a duplicate. We succeeded. And so, without anyone knowing it, I reconstituted Carey from the earlier scan."

"Carey isn't real? He's a copy?"

"He's as real as anyone. He came back the exact person he was, with memories, abilities, expectations, experiences—exactly as he was the microsecond that he was scanned."

"Does he know he's not—that he's a copy?"

"Yes—remember, the scan was made a month before he disappeared. His last memory was of being sealed into the scanner. We had to explain to him what had happened since then to get him to go along with the cover story. He hadn't experienced any of the events that occurred between the moment he was scanned and the time he died. He had to pretend he'd forgotten, or depend on his charm to gloss it over. It shook him, the knowledge that he had died."

"Did anyone else find out?"

"A few. Roz knew from the start—she helped me. A couple of people on the research team; some on the Board. The implications of such a power were enormous. We decided to keep the IQSA a secret.

"For twenty years I've been waiting for somebody to invent it again. But apparently they couldn't reproduce my work. So now they want to steal it."

"Has anyone else ever been duplicated?"

"No one."

"Wait a minute—has anyone else ever been scanned?"

Eva looked uneasy. "Yes—a few people. A handful. But nobody but Carey has ever been recreated."

Mira felt her mind ticking over the idea. Carey had died, and come back? The implications were huge.

"You have to realize, Mira, what a mother goes through. From the moment her child is born she has a hostage to fortune. I couldn't help myself. Given the kind of risk taker Carey was, I had to scan him. I thank the Goddess that I did."

A hostage to fortune.

"Do you know about my brother, Marco?"

Eva stopped. She closed her eyes. She opened them again. "Yes."

"You selfish bitch," Mira said softly.

"Mira, you don't understand—"

"How could you keep something like this a secret?"

"It wasn't my decision."

"So, are all the children of the Board of Matrons scanned? Their families, their lovers?"

"We *had* to suppress it. An invention like this offers untold opportunities for abuse. In the hands of the patriarchies, it—"

Mira picked up the ring and flipped it at Eva's face. Eva flinched. It struck her on the cheek and bounced over her shoulder, tumbling end over end. Even at this distance Mira could see it, glinting in the ceiling lights, every detail visible as it landed and rolled on the tiles of the terrace, beneath the table there, coming to rest against the planter that marked the balcony's edge. It made very little sound, but in the silence it was very loud.

CHAPTER

THIRTEEN

COUSINS!

Seize the Future!

Save the Society!

Extend the Franchise!

1200

1 May

Sobieski Park Amphitheater

We urge men and women from every quarter of the Society
to stop work on 1 May and attend the Rally for Justice and
Equality. Show the Board that it cannot run roughshod

over the rights of individuals! Demonstrate to the rest
of the solar system that there is a vital and widespread
opposition movement in the Society of Cousins!

• • • • •

Unpowered, the light-bending suit was designed to look like coveralls, with form-fitting ankle-high soft shoes. Erno could leave the hotel and pass through the colony without attracting attention.

But to reduce the risk of contamination with biological agents, Biotech was located in a satellite complex three kilometers from the crater, accessible only through the vacuum. One had to suit up, leave by airlock, traverse the lunar surface, and pass through the facility's own airlock. For the period that he was in the pressure suit he would be visible.

When he reached the entrance to the North Airlock, Erno stepped behind a building opposite, unrolled the hood from his collar, pulled it over his head and down over his neck. It fit snugly and the bottom sealed with the collar. Built-in goggles covered his eyes. He turned on the suit and it instantly began bending any light that fell on him around his body, leaving him effectively invisible. The eyes were the only weak spot: The goggles needed to admit enough light for him to be able to see, but they had to transmit enough of what was visible behind him so that they could not be seen. In practice, they were visible only to someone looking at him face on, and then only as two ovals of dimness floating in the air.

He crossed the plaza to the airlock complex and waited until someone exited, then slipped in before the sliding doors closed. Light-footed, he headed for the locker room. The display in the lobby indicated that out on the surface it was three days into night. On the screen, beyond the lights of the arrival pad, lay a moonscape lit by starlight.

In the locker room Erno sat invisibly and watched a woman and man suit up, recalling as they changed into their skintights how aware, as a teenager, he had been of women's bodies. When they were gone he stripped off the camo suit. From the emergency rack he chose a suit that approximated his size. He powered up the skintight and pulled it on, its thermoregulators adjusted themselves, and he found a pair of boots and a helmet.

With the camo suit in the surface suit's beltpack, he snuck to the utility airlock he had used back in the days when he was late for his apprenticeship and wanted to avoid being seen. As he was opening the lock's interior door, the night attendant appeared in the corridor. "Just a moment," he called.

Erno stepped into the airlock and hit "close."

"Stop!" the man said, but the door slid shut before he could reach Erno.

Erno saw the man's face through the port in the airlock door, shouting. He turned his back. For a while he could still hear the man, but as the air cycled out it faded. This airlock was a lot cleaner than the maintenance airlock of Persepolis Water where he and Taher had walked out into darkness near absolute zero. He wondered what Taher and Devi were doing at that moment. He wondered what Amestris was doing.

When the air, and with it the man's voice, was gone, he opened the outer door.

It would be an hour and a half before the next shift change, so the radiation maze, vehicle pad, and rover stop were deserted. The attendant was sure to sound an alert. Since Erno had come out of North instead of West, he would have a five-kilometer walk around the perimeter of the crater to reach Biotech; anyone looking might not expect him to be headed there. He loped along the surface of the graded road, five meters at a time, kicking up dust.

After he had the genomes, he'd resign from SCOCOM—there was no chance at this point he could affect their final report—and return to Persepolis. There would be a reckoning with Cyrus. He and Amestris needed to get out, relocate to some other colony out of the shadow of her family.

Exactly what Sirius predicted he would do.

He still had some affection for the Society, but the Cousins experiment had failed under the weight of prejudice, egotism, self-indulgence, power games, and individual character flaws. Humans here were the apes that Sirius excoriated. The Society was doomed. It was not Erno's problem.

Occasionally he checked to see whether anyone was following. He used image augmentation to raise the visibility of the surface. To his left, the exterior crater wall rose at first gently, then steeply, softened by a billion years of dust that coated the slopes, except where disturbed by crews that had constructed the dome eighty years ago. He passed a gargantuan set of stairs—the risers were a meter or more—used for inspections. To his right lay the lunar surface and in the distance the southern ejecta field of Esnault-Pelterie, ghostly in the starlight.

When the road from the West Airlock came into view—a string of lights like a necklace—he struck off toward it through a field of dormant solar collectors. His visual augmentation lined the road with green borders. It was hard to judge distances, but a readout in the corner of his eye showed him how far he was from Fowler and how much farther he had to go.

Above him the Pleiades shone fiercely in Taurus. The Milky Way, a billion stars unfurled like a flag from one end of the sky to the other, shrank his troubles to insignificance. He remembered fleeing across this dead black-and-white world with Tyler when their little revolution had come to its clumsy end. He'd realized that his mother was right to warn him that if he followed Tyler he would get somebody killed: At the moment he'd grasped this truth, unknown to him, she was already dead.

Half an hour later, winded, he came to the Biotech bunker. In the shadows beside the entrance he found a spot that would be safely out of sight of the rover when it arrived with the next shift. He waited. It was cold, and his suit worked hard to compensate.

Forty minutes later the bus from the West Airlock arrived. As a score or more workers got off and headed into the radiation maze,

Erno, his faceplate opaqued, slipped into the rear and lagged behind until they reached the personnel airlock. The doors opened and the departing shift workers came out. Inside the big airlock he stood off to one side, facing the port in the door, while air flooded the chamber and the inner doors opened.

In the locker room he was the last to strip off his surface suit. Once alone he shoved his gear into a locker, put on the camo suit, and turned it on. He headed for the complex's main corridor.

So as not to disturb anyone passing, he kept close to the wall. He turned a corner and had to dodge a woman coming the other way wheeling a rack of sealed mini-ecologies. She missed the sound of his step, the displacement of air.

He went to a cubicle off the break room where as an apprentice he used to hang out. The workstation there was always vacant. His old login no longer worked. He tried a scalpel Sirius had obtained from some spooks in OLS Information Security. It was hard to type when he could not see his hands, but after a little fumbling he got into the archives.

It didn't take long to track down the records of tree manipulations. Erno was astonished at the volume of work Lemmy's team had done. There were varieties of spruce, maple, ash. He didn't take the time to figure out which would be most useful; he downloaded their codes, closed the station, and left.

The freezer containing the genomes was attached to the big lab, down one level. Through the window in the lab's door he counted three people he would have to pass to get to the freezer. He waited. When a worker came out of the room, he slipped in before the door closed. He stood, back to the wall, just inside.

The people at the other end of the room were not a problem. One of the two nearby techs sat before a tabletop studying a three-dimensional electron micrograph of what looked like some cellulose molecules, intent on the image in front of her. The other tech was Cluny—a man Erno had detested back when he worked here—ten years older and thicker. Erno waited until Cluny went to the far end of the room, then moved as smoothly as he could to the door to the samples freezer. When no one was looking, he opened the door and in no more than a second was inside.

On the freezer's terminal he called up the samples he wanted: hornbeam, spruce, ash. He threw in three varieties of oak for good measure. From a cabinet he took a cryocase, about as wide as his palm, twenty centimeters long and a couple thick, that would fit into the sealed pocket of his suit. In a minute or so the system had drawn the samples out of the liquid nitrogen slush and deposited them in the retrieval bin. Six cylindrical vials, each a centimeter long, kept at seventy degrees Kelvin.

He was about to use tongs to transfer the vials to the case when he heard the door opening. He shoved the cryocase into the suit's pocket, grabbed the vials in his left hand, and took two quick steps to the wall.

Cluny backed into the room carrying a tray of samples. Erno held his breath. A meter from him Cluny set the tray down on a counter, noticed the freezer screen was lit, and went to examine it. The vials in Erno's hand burned with fierce intensity. He ground his teeth and tried not to move. Gradually the pain subsided; in fifteen or twenty seconds, it was completely gone.

Cluny scanned several pages on the touchscreen, then turned, a scowl on his face. Flat against the wall, Erno prayed Cluny would not notice the vials floating, unsupported, a meter above the floor.

Cluny left the room. Erno caught the door before it closed and slipped out.

While Cluny spoke with the woman at the design table, Erno crossed the lab. He opened the door and stepped out. Behind him Cluny's voice stopped. Erno ran down the hall.

He came to one of the cavern greenhouses. The permeable barrier that separated the greenhouse from the corridor was opaqued. Erno felt a slight change of pressure as he passed through. Safely out of the corridor, he finally opened his hand.

The frozen vials had stuck to the fabric of his camo gloves and damaged the light-bending cells—though his arm was still invisible, he could see the palm and fingers of his hand. When he tried to roll the vials onto his fingers to put them in the case, he found they were stuck to his palm. He couldn't grab them with his natural hand for fear of the intense cold, but he had to stash them quickly—he was amazed they hadn't yet fractured from the heat of his hand, and then he realized that the artificial hand had gone cold to match them. His wrist ached.

He crouched, shook the hand, and the vials fell to the floor. They took some of his skin with them, but it didn't hurt. He picked up each vial and placed it in the cryocase, closed the case, slipped it into the camo suit's pocket, and sealed it.

He was sweating. The hard freeze had not done the suit any good—the fabric over his palm had torn away, and most of his left hand was visible. He examined the palm, floating before him unattached to anything. A little blood clung to the rags of the glove, and the flesh where the skin was torn away was bleached white. Still no pain. As he watched, the torn palm reknit itself, a skin formed, and within moments it looked completely healed.

But it was still visible. Erno pulled the wrist of the sleeve down as far as he could over the hand and held the end closed with his curled fingers. The rags of the glove were slightly visible, and where his forearm was, the air seemed to shimmer a bit, as if he were seeing through rippled glass.

He looked around. This was the biggest of the greenhouses, but even so it had been expanded since he had last worked here. The high roof's solar lights were barely visible through the canopy of trees.

The trees. They crowded close. Foliage-laden boughs turned the pathway into a green tunnel. Erno was sweating. It was not just hot: The air was thick with moisture—no place he had ever been on the moon was this humid, this dense with life.

Instead of leaving, he walked down one of the paths through the forest. That's what it was: a forest. Trees from seedlings to full grown surrounded him, more varieties than he could identify, so dense that he could not see more than five meters in any direction. Light filtering through the leaves fell on the path in patches. The walls of the cavern were lost. From around him came bird sound. He identified the call of a cardinal—*bright bright bright, cheer cheer cheer*—and then farther away an answering call, then the first again.

Organic smells flavored every breath. Rotting leaves blanketed the ground beneath the trees. He brushed aside the leaf litter and scooped soil into his naked left hand. The hand was back to normal, telling him the dirt was twenty-three degrees Centigrade. He held it, rich and dark, to his face and inhaled, rolled his fingers through its warmth, and a small worm pushed its blind head from the dirt. He watched the worm move, then gently tipped the soil back onto the ground. He brushed the dirt from his fingers, drew his hand up into the broken sleeve, and continued down the path, breathing slowly, listening, astonished and intimidated. Something moved in the underbrush. There were animals here, a complex and functioning ecology.

Compared to Lemmy, Erno was a stumbling amateur. Erno's planned wood farm was a monoculture, no more an ecology than the potted plants in Cyrus's home. This was orders of magnitude more difficult.

He heard voices and stepped between the trees. Around a bend in the path came two young women, graduate students talking about going to some theater performance that evening. They passed him, and Erno went on.

As he moved deeper into the cavern, the trees became larger, until the path opened into a clearing. Sunlight poured down on a huge tree at its center. The trunk, perhaps five meters in diameter, rose from a mass of buttress roots that spread like low walls. In proportion to its huge bole it was relatively squat, its canopy perhaps ten meters above the floor. Foliage grew from a mass of tangled, thick branches. Every branch was laden with clusters of what looked like walnuts.

In the base of the tree, set into the trunk, was a door, and at intervals around its circumference were oval windows fitted with glass. As Erno stood there, the door in the tree opened and out stepped Lemmy Odillesson.

Lemmy carried an instrument caddy and had microscope goggles pushed up onto his forehead. He wore shabby pants and broken boots that Erno remembered from ten years before. He clambered over one of the roots, crouched at the foot of the tree, slipped the goggles over his eyes, and selected a syringe from the tray.

Lemmy had been talking about developing these "home trees," as he called them, for twenty-five years, pursuing an eccentric vision of people living in underground forests, the trees recycling their wastes, producing oxygen, bearing fruit, conforming themselves to human needs in complete symbiosis. It had seemed crazy to Erno, back before his exile—who wanted to live in a tree, like a character in some fairy tale?—but now that he saw Lemmy with his creation he could imagine at least some people reveling in the prospect.

Whatever its practicality, the Society had backed this research, without expectation of payoff, for decades. Lemmy had taught biotech apprentices like Erno the fundamentals of gene manipulation while behind his back they mocked him. How ludicrously unserious they judged Lemmy, when there were major issues of fucking and freedom to be addressed. He was not much of a man by the standards of Thomas Marysson or Cyrus Eskander. Beason and Göttsch had intimidated him. If and when the OLS took over, Lemmy would be swept aside without a second thought.

And yet, intent on his work, Lemmy moved with what could only be called grace. Erno stepped closer, let his false hand free from his sleeve, and laid it against the tree. The fine-knit gray bark was cool.

Lemmy turned and looked up, still wearing the goggles. Erno drew his hand into the sleeve again. The little man stared at him. With his weak chin, shock of unruly brown hair, and absurd goggles, he looked like a mole.

"I can see you," Lemmy said. "I can see the optical microfibers of the suit you're wearing."

Erno let his hand slide out of the sleeve. "It's me, Lemmy. Erno Pamelasson."

"Ah," said Lemmy. He pushed the goggles back onto his forehead, exposing his dark brown eyes. He stood out of the crouch and rubbed his fist against the small of his back. "Persistent young man. Did you get what you needed?"

"Yes."

"Then perhaps you should leave before somebody who gives a damn about you shows up."

Erno wanted to make Lemmy understand that he was not responsible for how the world worked. Before he could figure out what to say, the two women students came hurrying out of the woods. "Dr. Odillesson!" one of them said. "Someone broke into the samples freezer."

Face burning, Erno stepped aside to let them pass. As they spoke with Lemmy, he abandoned any hope of justification and hurried out of the greenhouse.

It was evening in the dome by the time Erno made his way to the hotel, retracing his steps, but he managed it without further incident. Bone tired, hungry, he turned off the camo suit in the public rest room off the lobby and rode up to the suite.

Göttsch, Beason, and Li were back from the SCOCOM office, in a state of high excitement. "Where have you been?" Li asked. "Did you leave the hotel?"

Göttsch said, "Dr. Maggiesdaughter has called a press conference for tomorrow at the Materials lab. She promises to reveal the reason for the information embargo."

Erno sat in one of the armchairs. "You'll have to go without me."

"What? You're a member of this team."

"I'm discredited by my association with terrorism. You'll do better not to have me there."

Göttsch seemed prepared to argue, but Beason pulled her aside. While they discussed it Erno retreated to his room. He put the cryocase with the samples in a desk drawer, slumped in the chair, and called up a poem he had been working on.

Lemmy's scornful words weighed on him. Erno had come here interested only in getting the genomes, and now he had them. He wanted out. He imagined himself walking back to Amestris, alone, under the black sky and indifferent stars.

He asked his Aide, "How far is it from here to Persepolis?"

• • • • •

Eva hadn't told Carey why she needed him to meet her. Maybe she would ask him to reconsider leaving the family. He wasn't going to change his mind, but it would not hurt to talk, so before he was due at Aquaculture that morning he found himself at her door.

When it opened, instead of Eva it was Roz.

"Where's Eva?" Carey asked.

"She had to work at the lab overnight—getting ready for a press conference. She'll be here. But first I need to speak with you." Roz led him into the uncommonly quiet living room. Dawn light filtered in from the terrace.

"What's this about?" Carey asked.

She looked at him, looked away again. Her shoulders were stiff with tension, and she fussed about the room while he stood waiting. He'd seen her like this: She had something that she needed to tell him but didn't want to. The same look she'd had twenty years ago, at the moment he had fallen in love with her.

Jack Baldwin was Eva's lover, and he and Roz had been living with the Green family. The sexual tension was thick between Carey and

Roz, but Jack seemed oblivious to it. Roz was an Earth girl, raised by a man, miserably awkward, uncomfortable among Cousins and clearly, Carey could tell, in love with him. That hadn't kept Carey from sleeping with her, but he hadn't taken her too seriously.

Until the afternoon he'd come to consciousness, hauled out of the assembler coughing and blinking, moments, he thought, after his mother scanned him with her new invention. The lab was empty except for Eva and Roz. They rinsed the nanodevices off his naked body, gave him a robe to wear, sat him down, and made him drink something warm. Slowly, quietly, Eva explained that he had not just been scanned; that had happened months ago. Some time between then and this moment, she told him, he had died. They had just reassembled him from the scan.

Carey made them explain it again. Then, when he did get it, the world tilted and he felt as if he might never regain his balance.

"It's okay," Roz had said, holding his hand. "You're fine."

He felt befuddled, a beat slow. He looked into her face. Her eyes glistened.

"Where's Jack?" he asked.

He vividly remembered how stricken Roz had looked when he'd said that. It anchored him. He stopped thinking about himself. Roz was suffering. He wondered how the world seemed through her eyes; he wondered what went on behind them.

Later they told him that Jack had killed himself. In the face of that, how could Roz be worrying about Carey? Some people had bigger problems than he did. He had seen Roz and himself, for the first time, from the outside. That was when he'd fallen in love.

There was no corresponding moment when his love for Roz had worn itself out. Years later. Some time after the birth of Val, for sure. Val meant everything to Roz. She pointed out to Carey that Val was the one person she knew who was genetically related to her. At the time he thought that Val had little to do with him; he'd been wrong about that.

Now he saw that Roz was as troubled as she had been that day they'd resurrected him from the dead.

"Are you all right?" he asked. "Is it about Val?"

Roz held out her hand. In her palm rested a man's ring. He picked it up: titanium with inlaid green vines twining around it. It was his ring. He hadn't seen it in more than twenty years. "Where did you find this?"

"I got it from Eva, who got it from Mira."

His nightmare had come true. "Mira found my body?"

"She found this ring behind my old desk at the Materials lab. Where I lost it."

"*You* had it?" He was genuinely mystified. They'd told him he had died out on the lunar surface, lost someplace no one had ever discovered. Roz couldn't have the ring unless she had found his body. Or unless he—that earlier Carey, his predecessor—had given it to her before he got lost. "If you had it, why did you keep it a secret? Did I give it to you?"

Tears filled her eyes. "You didn't give it to me. I had it because I know what really happened to you—I mean to that Carey, the one who died. He wasn't lost on the surface. That's why none of the searches found him: He was never out there. He was killed by my father."

"What?"

Roz sat on the sofa, leaned forward, arms crossed over her stomach. "Dad was working at the Biotech lab on his soil project. It was Founders' Week and the place was deserted; everybody was celebrating. Carey came out there to talk to him—about me, about us." Her voice was choked. "They got into an argument. Dad pushed Carey and he hit his head. It was an accident."

"You were there?"

"I got there just after it happened," Roz said.

"How do you know it was an accident?"

"He told me it was. He wouldn't lie to me. You never understood him. I—I couldn't turn him in. I was a stranger here, I didn't know what would happen to me, with no parent; it would ruin everything. I was sick, scared."

"You didn't care that he killed me?"

"I was destroyed by it! Still, I helped him dispose of the body. I buried Carey's clothes and surface suit out in the Esnault rubble field. But I forgot to bury the ring, and when I got back I still had it in my pocket. I kept it. But then I lost it."

"What did you do with the body?"

"Father burned it, and added the ashes to his soil cultivation batch. He used that soil when he planted his new junipers on the crater slope." Roz pointed out the terrace. "Out there."

Carey walked out onto the terrace. The dome was brighter now; it was full day. He leaned on the balcony rail and looked over the woods. The pear trees were white with blossoms.

"I thought when we were able to bring you back, everything would be all right," Roz said. "But Dad never got over it. Eva and I kept her plan to use the scan to recreate you a secret from him; there was no guarantee it would work. Before we succeeded, he killed himself."

He turned to face her. "You should have told me."

"I was fifteen. I didn't know how you'd react," she pleaded. "My father was dead, and telling you wasn't going to bring him back. You'd only hate him for it—and hate me, I thought. I'm sorry I never told you."

Carey looked at the ring again. It was as if it belonged to a different person. He almost laughed: It *had* belonged to a different person, a person who just happened to be him. He slipped it onto his finger. A little tight. His fingers were thicker than they'd been when he was a boy. He was the age now that Jack had been when he killed himself.

"Why did he do it? Kill me."

"It was an accident! He lost his temper. You had a temper, too, you know. He couldn't deal with us being a couple."

Carey tried to grasp it. All his nightmares, his worry that his body might be found—pointless, and Roz had known it, and kept silent.

"No wonder," Carey said. "The way you looked at me in bed sometimes. So desperate. So clinging. You saw me dead."

"You saved my life, you and Eva, after he was gone." Roz blinked away tears. "And then, after Val was born, you discarded me. You discarded me as if I were nothing."

This was the tone that made him crazy. This was the Roz he'd known for the last decade, the protector of her great grievance, the story of his abandoning her. "I couldn't throw you away," Carey said. "I never owned you. But you were lying to me."

Roz's lips pressed together. "It wasn't just me you left," she said, voice rising. "You left Val, too. Then after years of ignoring us you seduced him away, and in a few months you've filled his head full of this Spartan crap. You're a 'father' now. So manly, so special. You're an idiot."

Carey laughed. "You spent twenty years protecting your father and his weird sexual possessiveness. *He* was the man who owned you."

"You want to own Val! That's all you talked about in the hearing. You've never put his interests ahead of your own."

"Maybe I understand Val more than you do."

"He used to be the kindest boy. Now he blames me—and Mira, and just about every other woman—for taking him from you. He's the victim, and you're the hero."

The door to the apartment opened. Eva came into the room to find them standing opposite each other, rigid as statues.

"Well, this doesn't look good," she said. She looked at Roz. "You told him?"

"Yes," said Roz.

Carey said, "I'm going now."

"Not yet," Eva said. She tried to embrace him; he wouldn't let her. There were dark circles under her eyes. "Whatever is going on between you two right now," Eva said, "I need your help—both of you."

• • • • •

The banquet room of the Hotel Manuchehr glittered with the assembled guests.

"Amestris! You look lovely! I'm so glad to see you," said Maryam Mokri, an assistant to the Finance Minister.

"We so seldom see you since your marriage." This was Parissa Firdaus, who did genetic surgery in New Tabriz.

"How are you?" asked Donya Rasdani, married to the Prime Minister's press secretary. "They are wise to keep your husband out of the public eye after that terrorism accusation. Have you heard from him?"

Amestris said, "Erno keeps me informed."

"It must be hard to maintain your business with him unable to do his part."

"Do you think," Parissa said, letting the words roll from her tongue as if she did not care about the answer, "his sympathies lie with the Cousins, or is he capable of being an objective observer?"

"There's such a thing as an objective observer?" Amestris said.

The annual fundraising banquet for OLSESCO was well attended by the politically connected and the wealthy. OLSESCO ran a number of charities aiding people with issues of gender: gynandromorphs, hermaphrodites, ambisexuals, bisexuals, intersexuals, perisexuals, neuters, androgyns, gender queers, gays, lesbians, and the varieties of transsexuals. In Persepolis this work received considerable public criticism, but the committee had its share of strong supporters.

Amestris attended every year, as did most of her women business friends and government officials. This year's guest list counted almost two hundred women, transgendered, noögendered, cyborged. In addition to the OLS Associate Secretary General were leaders from sixteen colonies. Amestris had known some of these people for twenty years. But she had not replied to the invitation until late and was thus unable to share a table with Sima Mozaffari, which might have made the evening tolerable.

"We don't let those with personality disorders or mystical delusions onto SCOCOM," Barbara Sydney, OLS representative from Rupes Cauchy, told Amestris. "We know what the investigators believe and have charted their cortexes. The report they produce will be as true as anything ever is."

"Since Amestris won't say anything," Donya said, "maybe you can tell us, Dr. Sydney, what is going on in the Society of Cousins?"

"The committee expects the preliminary report in the next day or so," Sydney said. "A draft is already circulating, but it's under embargo."

"They're waiting until after this protest being held there," Maryam said. "The Reform Party is calling for a Public Determination by the Board of Matrons."

"What's that?"

Maryam was very interested in Cousins politics. She never hesitated to pass on her insights, if a person who got all of her information third hand could be said to have insights. "Despite the failure of the men's voting initiative, the Matrons have the power, by unanimous vote, to extend the franchise to all men in the colony. The reformers claim that such an action is the only way the Society will survive OLS scrutiny."

"Does the OLS really care about the condition of men?" asked Parissa. "This is all about fear of biological weapons—right, Dr. Sydney?"

Sydney lowered her voice. "It hasn't made the news yet. Eva Maggiesdaughter, former Chair of the Board of Matrons, has called a press conference for tomorrow. They're holding the conference in one of the laboratories. The media will feast on this. It will be everywhere tomorrow."

"Her son, Carey Evasson!" Maryam said. "What a compelling person! He would be so much better off if he left the Society."

The conversation skated off into speculations about hidden Cousins weapons programs. They glanced at Amestris as they avoided discussing Erno's involvement in bioweapons.

She excused herself and went to the ladies room, but was accosted there by other friends. This time it was all about her family: "So Dariush is resuming his career? Is that a mistake? He retired at the top of his form. What will happen if he finishes fifth, or twentieth?"

"He has a son now," Amestris said. "He wishes to prove himself again."

She could not escape the webs in which she was tangled: her father, her mother, her sister, her family, Erno, the politics of SCOCOM, the rumors of difficulties at EED. If only she had a different name. Every present moment was colored by the years that had come before.

Sima entered the women's lounge. She embraced Amestris and whispered in her ear, "Saman is here tonight. Have you spoken with him?"

"Not yet."

"We should talk. Call me tomorrow. Don't forget."

Amestris was grateful for Sima's nonjudgmental acceptance. "I won't."

When she returned to the banquet room, she spotted Saman at a table with several prospective wives. If anyone might burden her with the past, it was Saman. She did not want to talk about dead trees or classical music—but he also knew her in a way that these other people did not. He understood her father and her mother and the matrix of obligations they represented. He had a kind heart. If only he did not love her.

He saw her coming toward him and smiled. The woman to his right fussed with her purse. Saman stood and bowed slightly.

She leaned toward him. "Saman, can we get out of here?"

"Of course," he said softly.

He made his excuses to the others at the table and escorted Amestris to the hotel's lounge. They sat at a tiny table and ordered coffee.

"I'll let you go back in a minute," she said. "I need to ask your opinion."

"About what?"

"Erno's lies."

Saman raised an eyebrow. "You come to me for this?"

"I expect you'll be honest with me—no matter what you feel."

He frowned. "Erno can't be the first man who's lied to you."

"I fooled myself. I thought, as a Cousin, he might be different."

"So he claimed to be able to do something that he can't do? That sounds like every man I ever knew, and most of the women. If I were in his position and wanted to keep you, I would lie."

Amestris smiled. "But I fooled him, too."

"What lie did you tell?"

"I told him not to say he loved me, and I wouldn't say it to him."

"I believe I have heard you tell someone that before."

She looked into his eyes, expecting to see the sadness that he burdened her with, but found only amusement.

"Yes, I guess you have," she said.

"But in the case of Erno it turned out to be a lie?"

"I fell in love."

"So you married him."

"That wasn't how it started. We had a business to found, and he wasn't a citizen. It was a marriage with a purpose."

"As are most marriages. Your parents', for instance. Such marriages sometimes lead to the deepest kind of love."

"I don't know what kind of marriage it is now. I don't think he knows either. That hasn't kept him from feeling he has some right to me."

"Doesn't he have some right?"

"No more than I am willing to give. I do give him things—at some times, in some places, when I want to." Amestris studied the grounds in the bottom of her cup. "He thinks because I listen to him, I understand, and because I understand, I care. How can I love him and at the same time not care?"

"You're not the same person he is. It's a banality, but it's true."

She looked Sam in the eyes again. "Come with me."

Some people must have noticed them leaving together, but Amestris did not care. She took Saman to their apartment. She felt Saman's hand lightly on her back as they entered the building. As soon as they closed the apartment door she pushed him up against the wall. She took his hands and pinned them at his sides, kissed him on the lips. They kissed for a long time, his mouth seeking hers, hers on his, sometimes rough, often delicate, the barest brush of lips, the tips of their tongues flirting with each other. She closed her eyes and pressed her body against him.

They moved to the bedroom, and it was some question whether he was pushing her onto the bed or she was dragging him down onto it. They had not made love for more than twenty years. He was older now. Still an attentive lover, taking his cue from her, and when her cue was that she did not want control, he took that too and made her do what she wanted him to make her do.

She laughed. She had not laughed for some time.

After their lovemaking, she got them iced sharbat. They lay in bed and sipped. The lovely smell of sex. He could not stop looking at her, as if she were some miracle. She remembered that look.

She tried not to think about Erno.

"So, are you happy?" she asked him.

"I am very happy." He lay on his side, stretched out, and rested his hand on her thigh.

"Don't think that this means anything."

"It clearly means something. I won't presume I know what."

"Erno is coming back, no matter what SCOCOM reports. I want him back, though I don't know how it will be when he's here. He may have what we need to grow your forest. The business may be even more successful. Keeping separate from my family is going to be difficult, if not impossible."

Amestris didn't add that, after tonight, it was going to be hard for her to be around Sam, too.

Sam raised himself on one elbow and looked down at her. "Leave Persepolis."

"That's not what you want."

"Let's set aside what I want. Mazra moved to New Mumbai, and she says that it's wonderful there, under the tent, open to the sky. She says she will never live in an underground city again."

"Yes, and her children will be sterile from the cosmic rays."

He raised an eyebrow. "You plan to have children?"

Amestris had to smile again. "Of course not."

She kissed him and got out of bed. When she returned from the bathroom Saman was dressing. He said, "I'm not as convinced as you are that Erno will fail to create my forest. Desperate men accomplish remarkable things."

"I don't think that will solve my problem."

Saman kissed her. "We'll see." He put on his jacket and left.

Amestris lay in bed for an hour afterward. It was early in the morning, and she was very tired, but she could not sleep. She remembered the first time Erno and she had been together, the roughness of it, the heat. Strangers, their bodies raging for each other, a little fear adding a delicious edge.

A desperate man, Saman had said. She'd seen that in Erno from the start. At some level had she known he was lying about his abilities all along? Accepted it because she could feel that he wanted something more than sex? She needed him, too, needed to believe what he told her with his body and his voice.

It would be easier if she didn't love him. He was as much younger than she as she was younger than Saman.

She considered Saman's advice. Moving to New Mumbai, Aristarchus, any of the nearside colonies would be no escape. But Fowler—that was another matter. For one thing, if they moved EED there, they could draw directly on Cousins environmental experts. The question was whether the Society would allow such an outpost of foreign capitalism. They never had before. But perhaps, if the SCOCOM report forced an opening, it could be done.

For another thing, Erno would be in a place he knew, not so dependent on her. If it ever came to divorce, Amestris told herself, he would be better off there than here.

And in the Society she'd have, perhaps, the opportunity to learn a different way to be female.

As if, from across the moon, Erno had heard her thoughts, her Aide announced a message from him. She opened it.

Ghazal for Amestris

Four thousand one hundred kilometers
to Persepolis. Who would not make
that hegira, for love of Amestris?

To get there walk due south,
follow Canopus, keel of the ship
which sails the skies above Amestris.

Over the dead landscape,
the seven sisters blaze; not so bright,
nor distant, as the love of Amestris.

I pass through corridors unseen,
conscience fraught, our salvation held
within my tattered glove, Amestris.

While Cousins men and women
swim the erotic sea—the consummation
we are deprived of, Amestris.

This place is my home, some say,
where I belong. No home
exists without your love, Amestris.

Does my rival lie beside you
as I write these lines? Figures in my mind
my torment prove, Amestris.

Abashed, Erno vows to surrender
his foolish doubts: abandon himself
rather than lose your love, Amestris.

And below this:

I have the genomes.

• • • • •

Video Archive

Press Conference, Materials Laboratory, Society of Cousins

30 April 2149

The conference is held in a laboratory of the Materials

complex in the Fowler colony. Behind a window, two technicians work in a control booth. One end of the room is dominated by a large sphere that looks like nothing so much as a huge blue marble, five meters in diameter. The sphere is divided along its equator, its top half connected to hydraulics in the ceiling. Several banks of instruments arc around the sphere, including a transparent chamber about a meter square and two tall. In front of the device a podium has been set up, beside which is a metal table holding two gel pads and a small animal carrier.

At the room's other end, almost as large as the marble, is a nanoassembler of somewhat arcane design. Beside it medical equipment, including a gurney and a bank of physiological monitors.

Through closed double doors comes the hum of the fusion reactor in the next lab.

Along one wall, a bank of seats holds the dozens assembled for the press conference. Sirius is there with his crew and assistant, Gracie. The SCOCOM investigating team, Göttsch and Beason and Li, minus Erno Pamelasson.

Board of Matrons Chair Krista Kayasdaughter is there, along with several other Board members, a couple of directors from the lab, and some scientists. At one end of the front row is Carey Evasson.

Rosalind Baldwin speaks with the techs. At one point she crawls under the big blue sphere, then comes out again. Finally she sits down among the lab personnel, at the opposite end of the row from Evasson.

Dr. Eva Maggiesdaughter, who has stepped out into the reactor room, returns and speaks with Carey. He listens, then nods. She speaks with Baldwin, has a word with Kayasdaughter, then steps to the podium.

Eva Maggiesdaughter: Thank you for coming today. Let me get right to it: I'm here to demonstrate our Integrated Quantum Scanner Array and associated technologies. Keeping this device a secret was the reason for the embargo on scientific information the Society of Cousins instituted last year.

I believe that some of you are familiar—Dr. Göttsch, certainly—with my papers of thirty years ago that elaborate some implications of Redling Theory. They suggest it is possible to scan material objects at a degree of resolution below the Planck-Wheeler length, or, to put it in simple terms, to make an end run around the uncertainty principle. The IQSA has been engineered to take advantage of this possibility. We are able do this with any matter, living or inert. To demonstrate the IQSA's scanning ability, I am going to give you today an extreme example.

Maggiesdaughter signals the booth, and with a thunk the hydraulics start and lift the top half of the sphere toward the ceiling. The interior is lined with thousands of silver hexagonal cells. Suspended parallel to the floor, at the equator of the sphere, is a mesh platform. When the top hemisphere is clear, the platform rotates out of the lower half toward Maggiesdaughter.

Maggiesdaughter moves to the animal carrier and takes out a large black-and-white cat. Either the cat is exceptionally trusting or he has been sedated. Maggiesdaughter flips him onto his back and rubs his belly. The camera floats in for a close-up. The cat's purr is picked up by the mikes; his front paws curl up as he stares sleepily into the lens, bonelessly limp.

Maggiesdaughter: This is Hector, my cat.

Maggiesdaughter puts the cat into the transparent chamber beside the sphere and seals it. The cat curls up on the floor, tail in front of his nose, and closes his eyes.

Maggiesdaughter: I'm going to spray a mist of nanolenses into this chamber. It will be necessary for Hector to inhale them, and for them to pass through his lungs into his blood.

She presses a control that floods the chamber with gray mist. Hector's fur twitches. He sneezes.

Maggiesdaughter: The lenses will allow the scanners to gather a complete, instantaneous description of the cat's quantum state.

When the mist in the chamber clears, Maggiesdaughter, wearing gloves, transfers the cat to the mesh scanner table and touches a sparker to the cat's foot. Hector goes rigid. The table draws back into the center of the scanner. The upper hemisphere lowers and seals. Maggiesdaughter motions to the techs at the controls.

The hum in the room grows louder, but for a machine of its size and complexity it makes little sound.

It is over almost as soon as it began. They open the sphere and Maggiesdaughter takes up Hector, sprayed silver and stiff as uncooked pasta. She deactivates the immobilizer and brushes the dust from his fur. Hector takes a convulsive breath, shudders, opens his eyes part way, and sneezes again. Maggiesdaughter scratches him behind his ears, then places him onto one of the gel pads on the table. He settles his head on his paws.

Maggiesdaughter: We now have a complete scan of Hector down to the subatomic level. Once the sedative has worn off, he will be a little traumatized by the fact that we had to immobilize him. The inhaled nano will be metabolized out of his body within a day. Otherwise, he is unharmed.

She walks over to the machine at the other side of the room, a second chamber, not as big as the scanner, this one lozenge-shaped.

Maggiesdaughter: This is the assembler. Michael?

A new sound as the assembler comes to life. This machine produces a keening whine, and Maggiesdaughter has to raise her voice slightly to be heard. She touches a screen.

Maggiesdaughter: I am calling up the scan of Hector that we just made. This device, using an immense amount of energy and a stock of undifferentiated matter, which it breaks down into fundamental particles, will assemble a copy of the cat out of those particles.

She goes on to speak at some length about stable quantum states and zero eigenvalues for momentum, singularities and the free field vacuum state.

Maggiesdaughter: But this is all addressed in my second paper of 2118. The practical solution—

The whine of the assembler fades. Maggiesdaughter looks over to the booth, touches a control, and the front of the lozenge swings upward, revealing a red-lit interior. She puts on gloves and reaches into the chamber.

Maggiesdaughter: And so we have—a new version of Hector.

Maggiesdaughter holds another cat, similarly rigid and silver with nano. She unsparks the nano. Like Hector, the cat sneezes. She brushes the dust off his black-and-white fur. The cat struggles feebly, then relaxes as she holds him in her arms, carries him back to the table, and places him on the second gel pad. The cat sniffs at the original Hector, shies away. Groggy, he crouches, haunches trembling, and watches the observers.

Maggiesdaughter: This new Hector is identical to the original Hector as he existed thirty minutes ago, at the microsecond that he was scanned. He has all the abilities and memories that the original had at that moment. He is unaware that he is a copy. The only difference between the two is that the original Hector has lived some minutes longer, and the new one has no awareness of what occurred to the original during those minutes. If we were to run the scan through the assembler a year from now, to the new Hector we would so create it would seem that he had just been in the scanner a minute before.

Some of the observers are talking to each other now in low murmurs. In the front row, Carey Evasson watches the two cats on the table.

Maggiesdaughter: Let me demonstrate another capability of the assembler. I have loaded another scan.

She touches the screen. The assembler's door closes. Again the high-pitched whine. When the machine quiets, Maggiesdaughter opens the chamber, reaches in, and removes an apple. She steps to the front row of the observers.

Maggiesdaughter: The original of this apple—here, take it—

She hands the apple to Myra Göttsch.

Maggiesdaughter: —was scanned over twenty years ago. Yet what you hold is the apple exactly as it was at the moment of the scan. Go ahead, take a bite.

Göttsch hesitates, then bites the apple.

Maggiesdaughter: How is it?

Göttsch: It tastes fine.

Maggiesdaughter: And I could produce a hundred or a thousand copies of the same apple. One might use the IQSA to copy any object. However, the amount of energy required and the cost of constructing and maintaining such complex technology make it economically untenable to duplicate ordinary objects. To make an apple this way is a criminal waste of resources. This is not the costless duplicator of people's fantasies.

I think if you give it a little thought, you will realize that use of the IQSA has the gravest moral, ethical, and practical implications.

Consider one obvious implication: I have created an exact duplicate of Hector. I must now take care of him for the rest of his life.

Perhaps with a cat we can put aside any

squeamishness: Not everyone believes that owning an animal entails any moral obligations. But we could, for instance, make an exact copy of any one of us in this room. I think you will see the difficulties this raises.

What is the practical use of a duplicate human being? It would not be possible to tell the original from the copy. Each would have exactly the same memories and abilities, the same loves and hates, ambitions, expectations, and flaws. Which of the two—or three, or four, or one hundred— would possess a legal identity? There would be no place for them—the history that created the original, the place that she had earned in the human world, would not be available to the copy.

The one situation, I think, where the IQSA might have great value, however, would be in preserving things that, should they be lost or destroyed, would be irreplaceable. A great work of art, perhaps. Or something that has no monetary value, but great emotional importance. For instance, a child.

When I and my colleagues created the IQSA and had assured ourselves that scanning would not damage the original, one of the first things I did, in secret, unknown to anyone else in the lab, was to bring my son, Carey, here and scan him. He was fifteen years old.

To my dismay, within three months I had the chance

to test my machine—and my character—when Carey went missing, presumed dead. With the assistance of Rosalind Baldwin, I used that scan to create a duplicate. Carey came out of the assembler with no idea that he had died. He thought he had been in the scanner just a second before. He did not know what his original had done in the months between the scan and his death. But he was my son, and I loved him. I don't regret doing what I did.

Around the room attention turns toward Evasson. A camera homes in on him. He looks somber, but does not flinch. Li and Göttsch put their heads together.

Maggiesdaughter: My colleagues were appalled. I myself found it hard to justify my actions.

I knew that the secret of the IQSA would not last indefinitely. We do not, except in the most severe cases, abandon disruptive technologies. We regulate them. I proposed that we should release the news of our invention and set up a system to tightly control its future use. But my sisters and brothers pointed out to me that not everyone treats technology in this rational way. So for twenty years, we've kept the IQSA a secret.

I have a few more things to say, but I can see that

you are eager to ask questions. I want to thank my son for being willing to come here today and, with me, take some of them.

Carey joins her at the podium.

Martin Beason: If this little magic act turns out to be genuine—which I sincerely doubt—how can you have suppressed something with such power to transform the world?

Maggiesdaughter: The fact that it has that power is reason to take the greatest care with it.

Beason: Information wants to be free.

Maggiesdaughter: Information, as I understand it, does not have volition. Most of the Earth has pursued this freedom, and the results have not been happy. The Society was set up, among other reasons, in flight from that sort of thinking.

Göttsch: I look forward to the opportunity to speak with you at length about the physics of this. But that's for another venue. Why are you revealing this now?

Maggiesdaughter: I believe one of the reasons the OLS sent you here is that knowledge of the IQSA's existence reached certain powerful people outside the Society. I've been expecting it for twenty years. The principles of quantum scanning have been established for thirty. I don't know why no one elsewhere in the solar system has been able to build such a scanner. But I offer it freely now to the entire human race. There are great benefits and equal risks inherent in this technology.

A series of questions follows about the Cousins' information embargo and how this relates to the IQSA. Maggiesdaughter admits that the entire reason for the embargo was the futile hope that the Society might be able to keep the IQSA secret longer.

Maggiesdaughter: I am proud that we in the Society of Cousins got there first. It gives the lie to those who say that we are incapable of innovative scientific research. It gives the lie, too, to the idea that any technology that humans invent must be used in any way it is possible to use it, without regard for the consequences. I am a scientist but I am also a Cousin. I am proud to be both, and thus to have my research fall under the control of wiser people than I.

Nevertheless, as we speak I am sending you complete specifications for the IQSA and assembler, along with data from extensive trials and video of previous test runs. Rather than see this discovery fall into the hands of those who might use it for their personal gain, we are committed to complete openness of scientific inquiry, and willingly share this information with the rest of the human race, to do with as they see fit.

The rest of the solar system now has one less justification for intervening in our affairs. I hope this helps people understand that the Society offers no threat to the rest of the moon.

Sirius: Dr. Maggiesdaughter, this is fascinating! But I'd like to ask Carey a question. Carey, can you tell us, what's it been like to live your life believing you are a copy of a dead human being?

Carey Evasson: I am not a copy of anyone. I'm Carey Green Evasson, as human as anyone here.

Sirius: Sadly, I myself am not human, you may have noticed. You'll have to excuse those who will not believe this demonstration. Pulling apples out of the air is the oldest of conjuring tricks. If, as Dr. Maggiesdaughter professes, it can be verified, you'll then have to excuse us for being wary of a person who was assembled out of fundamental particles in that chamber.

Evasson: I expect that the first person who saw an uplifted dog was reluctant to treat him as a fellow cognizant being, worthy of the same rights and privileges as a human. The history of the human race has been one of extending recognition of full humanity to those who were once excluded—other races, women, children, the differently abled, the multigendered, cyborgs, clones, the augmented, the genetically modified. Even to uplifted animals.

The dog moves forward, teeth bared now.

Sirius: Yes, we all know of the liberal-mindedness of Cousins, even if they don't allow the uplifted to enter their sealed society. But what, tell us, is to keep you from making an army of duplicates and overwhelming the rest of the moon?

Maggiesdaughter: The fact that to do so would be a monstrous atrocity, just the sort of misuse of this technology that we hoped to prevent by keeping it secret.

Evasson: Such a plan is more likely to be put into effect by the people who employ you, Sirius, than by anyone here.

Sirius: I am employed by a media conglomerate. We don't need clone armies.

Maggiesdaughter: Carey is not a clone.

Evasson: Deny that you told me, Sirius, not two weeks ago, that the OLS would take over the Society of Cousins. You offered me the position of governor if I would go along with you.

Sirius: Deny it? Of course I deny it. This is the most desperate sort of lie. I have no position in any government, no influence over SCOCOM. You can see by the astonishment on the faces of the OLS investigators that this is the first they have ever heard of such imaginings. Don't try to distract us.

Evasson: You're not working for SCOCOM.

Sirius: As I just told you. You should get your paranoid theories straight. Are we here to steal this magic duplicator, or are we here to subjugate your utopia?

If your mother and her scientific team can create this device and keep it secret for twenty years, then what other dangerous technologies can she unleash on the world? If she's willing to use it, against the will of her own government, to violate every code of scientific research and human ethics, how might she use it against societies her government considers hostile?

Maggiesdaughter places her hand on Carey's shoulder, but he shrugs it off.

Evasson: Less outrage and a little more honesty might be appropriate.

Sirius: I'm a mere dog, not a citizen of your or any other lunar society. But I would advise the human race to think twice before accepting this poison pill, cooked up by people who reject the mores of and deliberately separate themselves from the rest of the civilized world.

Evasson: I can't do this.

Evasson whispers something into Maggiesdaughter's ear, and leaves the lab. Two camera midges follow him.

Maggiesdaughter: If we might have a question from someone else?

• • • • •

Erno watched the broadcast of the press conference he had insisted he would not attend, but he turned it off when it broke down into charges and countercharges. Erno's notoriety as a possible terrorist was about to be eclipsed thirty times over by Carey Evasson's. The revelation that Carey had been brought back from the dead twenty years ago, added to his fame from the custody battle, was already main menu all over Lunanet. Add the upcoming protest rally, and the Society would become the hottest site for junk news in the solar system.

The SCOCOM team would return to the hotel soon, ready for an all-night session of political calculations. Sirius would want to talk to Erno: Eva's dumping her secret had thrown a monkey wrench into Cyrus's plans. None of this mattered to Erno; he was well out of it now, and did not look forward to being drawn into any hysterical debates.

He showered quickly, dressed in formal clothes, and set off for the Men's House. Before his exile Erno had spent a lot of time hanging out there with other disaffected young men Tyler recruited for his dissident movement. The place was crowded. The tea room was as it had been a decade ago: tables, sofas, lounge chairs. Pixwall, low lighting. Games were in another room; elsewhere were a meeting room and a chapel. Upstairs were rooms for any men who might want to pair up.

The brewmaster behind the bar was no one Erno had ever met, but he did the subtlest of double takes when he saw Erno. He straightened his neat white coat and came over.

"What can I get for you?"

Erno looked over the list. "Something for emotional awareness."

"Raise or lower?"

"Raise."

The man turned to his synthesizer and adjusted its settings. Erno looked around the room. Some boys in the corner, lifted out of their minds, laughed and mocked one another. They made a lot of noise. A couple of men, one old and one young, played chess. Two men in the corner stared into each other's eyes.

From another group, a man stood and came over to the bar. "I was wondering when you would show up here," the man said to Erno.

It was Sid, one of Erno's old friends. A big, handsome guy who had spent hours in the gym working out in the heavy-G trainers.

"You're still here?" Erno said. "I thought you were moving to Earth."

Sid smiled. "Yes, well, you were going to be running Biotech by now."

The brewmaster came over. "Here you go," he said to Erno, setting a steaming glass on the bar. "Let it breathe for a minute or two. What'll it be, Sid?"

"Something that will make me forget how fucked we are."

"Does that 'we' include everybody, or just you?" the brewmaster said. "I want to know how much to brew."

"Shut the fuck up, Paolo. Go on strike."

Sid had joined Tyler's masculinist movement, but when things fell

apart and Erno went on trial, like most of Erno's friends Sid disappeared. He had slimmed down, no longer sporting a ripped physique.
He still wore his hair long, dipping over one eye.

Erno sipped his tea. It had a biting sweetness. "What are you doing
now? Still spend half your days in the sauna?"

"I'm working now, a helium miner. I'm back home again; I was
with Doris and Doreen Soniasdaughter for a while. Both of them have
daughters by me."

Paolo brought Sid's tea. "Come sit with us," Sid said. "We can talk."

Sid introduced him to his cronies: Tommo, another miner, and
Pierre, a video artist. Tommo asked Erno what it was like in the patriarchal world. Erno told them about the labor market in Mayer. Pierre
asked about the mosaics in the roof of the bazaar of New Tabriz.

But Sid wanted to talk politics. The tea was starting to take effect
and Erno sensed this was Sid's attempt to sound important. He imagined
Paolo's psychotropic chemicals buzzing through his cingulate cortex.

"I don't know what Maggiesdaughter expected to accomplish,"
Sid said. "It just confirms the Matrons' paranoid secrecy."

"What about Evasson?" said Pierre. "The OLS will invade? Sirius
offered him the job of governor?"

"Is the OLS going to intervene?" Tommo asked Erno.

"I don't know anything about an intervention," he said.

"Why bother to rally for the vote, then, if intervention is a done
deal?" Pierre asked. "Why did SCOCOM even bother with all their
interviews and their show of impartiality?"

The fact that Erno essentially agreed with Pierre made him want to argue against him. He could tell them about Cyrus's interest in the IQSA, but letting strangers know Cyrus's business was not smart. "Göttsch and Li want to do a fair report," he said. "But their prejudices make it hard for them to see clearly. Beason would be happy to see an OLS takeover."

"Then it's up to you to persuade Göttsch and Li," Sid said. "You always wanted to change things. Now's your chance."

Erno slid his left hand toward his glass and touched Sid lightly on the wrist, and it was as if a window opened into Sid's mind. The hand's sensitivity must be boosted by the effects of the tea. Sid was as invested in being the alpha of his group of friends as he had been when they were seventeen. Nothing had altered his condescension toward Erno. Underneath Sid's arrogance was a pit of self-loathing. This torrent of understanding staggered Erno; he jerked back his hand as if it had been scalded.

Sid raised an eyebrow. "Nothing to say?"

Erno fought to control his reaction. "I can't do anything. They've used the GROSS story to neutralize me."

Tommo said, "The way they've flipped it around is classic. You *refused* to be a terrorist. It must drive you crazy to hear that stuff."

Erno could tell, from the way Tommo sat and moved, how emotionally needy he was. "From the outside it looks that way, maybe," Erno said. "It's not that simple."

"We have to work together," Tommo said. "That's why, no matter what you think about Camillesdaughter, the rally is central. If we divide into little factions, the whole movement collapses."

Pierre watched Erno with half-lidded eyes. "We need you to keep the OLS off our backs."

"I've done what I can," Erno said.

"If the OLS brings reforms," Tommo said, "it can't be any worse than what we've got."

Sid drained the last of his tea. "The SCOCOM staff came to the fusion plant and interviewed anybody who wanted to be interviewed. They didn't seem to have a position on any of this."

"You're a fool," Erno said. He turned on Tommo. "The first reform our friends from SCOCOM will bring is to build a freezer." His voice rose. "Pierre—forget your videos, unless you want to starve. Sid, you'll be mining helium-3 until you're a hundred and forty years old. Who knows what Doris and Doreen Soniasdaughter—and your daughters—will do. Nothing very ennobling, I'll tell you that."

"So why are you here?" Pierre said quietly.

"You'll just let SCOCOM call for a war?" Tommo said.

"You're on an OLS committee," Sid said. "Your father-in-law is the wealthiest man on the moon. And you're just helpless?"

They looked at Erno, waiting. He glanced away and saw, across the room, Carey Evasson leaning against the bar, watching them. Carey's eyes met Erno's, and he lifted his glass slightly.

Erno turned to Sid. "Find somebody else to feel superior to. I'm off that duty. And have another tea, because like you say, you are fucked and there's not a thing anyone can do about it."

Feeling their eyes on his back, he left the Men's House.

His thoughts chased themselves in a circle. Their talk resembled nothing so much as his futile political posturing with Fabrizio and Zdeno. How certain he'd been back then that he knew the way things should be. Yet Sid was right: Erno wasn't a penniless ice miner anymore. He had some influence.

He stood alone at the tram stop, waiting. Few people were out this late. No reply so far to the poem he'd sent to Amestris. She should have been overjoyed at his getting the genomes. In the distance he saw lights in Sobieski Park where a crew was working late to prepare the stage for tomorrow's rally.

The tram arrived, and he got on. He was careful not to let his left hand brush up against anyone in the car. Two women sat side by side across from him, voices low. They looked at him and smiled. Did they recognize him? Were they talking about him? Sid and his condescension. Mira. Amestris.

He told his Aide. "Arrange a conversation as soon as possible with Hypatia Camillesdaughter. I need to speak with her tonight."

As he was getting off the tram at the hotel, he got a call. It was Camillesdaughter.

"Can we talk?" he asked her.

• • • • •

Carey's Aide kept reminding him that he had a message from Roz, until finally he told it to shut up. He didn't need more Roz right now. The Men's House was crowded when he came in, but nobody ventured to talk to him. Maybe they hadn't seen the press conference. Maybe they just wanted to let him be. If so, he was grateful.

"What will it be?" Paolo asked.

"Has my son been in here at any time today?"

"No, he hasn't. I would have noticed. So, no tea for you?"

"You tell me, Paolo. What should I be drinking tonight?"

"You look like a man who needs some cognitive enhancers. Maybe something to calm you down."

"I think I'm pretty calm, given the circumstances," Carey said.

"You look calm. Still, I expect you have some thinking to do."

"Set it up, then."

While Paolo was busy with the synthesis, Carey eavesdropped on some conversations. Most of the talk seemed to be about tomorrow's rally. A lot of men were going to skip work to be there.

Once he'd left the press conference, the anger he'd felt at Sirius drained away. It was out at last, and he no longer had to worry about it. People's eyes watching him: That might be difficult for a while, but the relief was worth it. If he was famous—the athlete, the wronged father, the privileged son of a powerful woman, the prince of Cousins—it mattered not one bit.

Paolo came back with the tea. As he sipped, Carey heard some voices raised behind him. He looked over to see Erno Pamelasson arguing with a table of other men. Carey smiled, and Erno locked eyes with him. *There* was his only rival for the title of most famous male Cousin. They had that, if nothing else, in common. Carey lifted his glass to Erno. Erno turned back to the others at the table, said something, stood, and left the Men's House.

"Good riddance," said a man next to Carey at the bar, to no one in particular. "He should take the rest of those pussies with him."

"I guess he's not worked out the way a lot of people hoped," Carey said.

"You think? He's no better than Camillesdaughter's ball-less pet boys. I can't believe Tyler ever trusted him."

Carey examined the man. Deep-set eyes, very short hair. "It does seem that somebody has neutralized him with the virus story," Carey said.

"He was neutralized before he got off the cable train," the man said. "If he hadn't shoved the knife into Tyler's back ten years ago this fight would've been over long ago. He's just what the Matrons want men to waste their time on—rallies, reports, petitions—a joke. Accomodationist eunuchs diverting rage into useless half-measures. Non-measures." He stared at Carey. "Just like you."

"Do you really want to do this?" Carey said. "Let's not."

The Spartan puffed up like a rooster. "Afraid of me? Aren't you the big *Ruǎn tā* master?"

"Come to the gym sometime, we'll see how it goes."

The man was about to reply when there was some commotion near the door and Mira walked into the room. She came toward Carey. The Spartan followed Carey's eyes to her and blocked her way. "This is the Men's House."

"I know where I am," Mira said. She pointed at Carey. "I need to speak with him."

The rest of the men in the room had stopped talking.

"He doesn't have to speak with you if he doesn't want to," the Spartan said.

"I know that, too."

Paolo said, "Cousins, you need to calm down." He looked at Carey, appeal in his eyes.

"We'll go outside," Carey said. "Work on your rhetoric," he told the Spartan.

He followed Mira out of the building.

Outside it was full night. Across the path they found a bench under the trees. It was where they had planned to meet for one of Mira's Looker exploits. That was the night Val had gone with her to post videos instead of Carey—the beginning of all this trouble.

Mira looked tired. "Before you say anything," Carey started, "maybe you can tell me why you lied at the hearing. If it was because I turned down your marriage proposal, you should know how condescending that was. It might seem to you that I've had the upper hand in this relationship, but that's not the way it's felt to me. I've been played by women my whole life, and I won't be played anymore. If you're going to tell me about my failures as a father or a friend or a lover, please keep them to yourself."

As he spoke, Carey felt the heat rising in him, and he heard the bitterness in his own voice. He waited for her comeback. He was sure it would be good.

Instead, Mira reached out and touched his chest, her fingers testing him as if he might be a mirage. It stopped him cold. He stepped back, away from her.

"I'm real," he said. "I've been real all along."

"You're a bunch of atoms thrown together."

"So are you. So is everybody."

"Why didn't you tell me?"

The smell of the junipers around them reminded Carey of what Roz said had become of his body. He was already on his second life. The fact that he was here with this woman he had loved, about to tell him off for something he probably deserved to be told off for, was a gift. Every second was a gift.

"Let me guess," he said. "We're going to talk about Marco."

Mira seemed to swell with anger. "He could have been saved! You knew all along!"

"When all this happened to me, I didn't even know him, or you. He would have been, what—four years old?"

"That's the point! If you hadn't kept it a secret, then the IQSA would have been out there for years before he got killed. He could have been scanned. When he died, he could have been brought back, just like you."

"I was fifteen, Mira. I could hardly grasp what they were telling me, that I was a copy."

"Instead you let people think it was all a prank. You got famous for a lie."

"A lie I've been carrying around for most of my life." He ran his hands through his hair. "My mother should have destroyed that machine the day after she brought me back."

"Not the day before?"

He looked her in the eyes. "Marco's been dead eight years. Are you going to spend the next hundred replaying that?

Mira sniffed. "Yes." She sank to the bench.

"Bad idea."

He stood watching her for a moment, then sat down beside her.

"Look," he said, "I haven't always done the right thing. Every time I saw those toy horses of yours, all I could think about was how he was dead and I was alive. I know my feeling bad doesn't matter. And I have no right to tell you how you should feel."

"He's dead, and you're alive. It's not fair."

"Nobody said it was fair."

She looked at her feet.

"That ring you found was like throwing a bomb into the Green family," he said.

Carey told her the story of Jack Baldwin killing him, and Roz's part in the cover-up. "Apparently my remains are fertilizing the junipers below my mother's apartment." He sighed. "An awful lot of melodrama in our family, huh?"

Mira sat silent. Finally she said, "I guess, between me and Roz, you've picked some lousy girlfriends."

"You don't understand Roz. She seems rigid, but she's trying desperately to keep everything together. You—you have your good points, too."

She looked up. "I'm sorry I lied about you."

"It doesn't matter."

She touched his forearm. "I've missed you."

And then they were in each other's arms. He had forgotten just how small she was in his embrace. Her breath was warm on his neck. He swallowed. He had not felt this way in a long time, perhaps ever. Something rose in his chest, something quite extraordinary. They did not talk for a while.

"What a mess we've made of things," Mira said into his shoulder.

He let her go, looked into her face. Intelligence, a strong heart. "It's a group effort."

Carey didn't know what to say about the two of them. "Listen, there is something you can do for me, if you're willing—before you get banished or I get dissected or the OLS turns this place into a theme park. We need to help find Val."

"Find him?"

"While Roz was at the press conference he disappeared. He's probably just acting out. He didn't like being forced to go back to her, and he's charged up about the rally. I don't think he'd do anything foolish, but for a while there he was hanging around with some Spartans."

"Do you know who?"

"I have an idea. He's likely to be at the rally. If I go to Hypatia, she might help us find him."

"She's going to want you on the stage with her."

"I doubt that."

Mira looked at him. "You don't know, do you?"

"What?"

"Over the last three hours, you've probably drawn more media hits than any other person on the moon."

CHAPTER

FOURTEEN

!!!NEWSMELT NOW!!!

Your *inside* source for thinktropic datablasts

<u>**Super Science Shocker!**</u>

. . . that scientists at the Society of Cousins, in secret, have

developed, in the so-called Integrated Quantum Scanner

Array, a means of duplicating people. Not the cloning

we are familiar with, but a radical new technology that

presents frightening possibilities.

The Matrons pride themselves on having no standing

army. It turns out they don't need one. All they need is one lethally trained soldier, and the weapons to equip him, and they can instantly create an army of copies, all of them identically committed to the radical state and with identical ability to inflict their ideology on . . .

Copy That, Carey!

. . . OLS Olympic champion martial artist, feverthrob symbol of shackled manhood in the Society of Cousins, recently the center of a dispute over the custody of his son, turns out to have *died* at the age of fifteen! Brought back to life by his brilliant scientist mother, what must it be like to know that you are not an original, but a copy? How has this affected his psyche? How real a human being is he?

And if you like this Carey, maybe you can buy one for yourself?

Fuse Lit on Cousins Powder Keg!

. . . attempt to force the Board of Matrons to use its executive power to extend the franchise to all men in the colony. That proposition was voted down in the last, disputed, election. Camillesdaughter, leader of the Reform Party, is going ahead with the planned strike and protest rally.

Meanwhile, this Friday, OLS investigators from the Special Committee on the Condition of Men are due to present their report on the renegade colony to the OLS

Secretariat. Sources close to SCOCOM . . .

• • • • •

A third of colony support workers were on strike, but somebody had to keep everything running. The sad history of the last centuries showed that even planetary environments needed to be tended; how much more vital on the moon, where the biosphere was not a natural phenomenon.

Edouard complained to his mother and to Ellen about the way other men chased the latest delusion. He put on his mocking voice: "I *demand* the right to vote," and, "Oh, yes, I am a father! Look, I have six children by four different women." Ellen would laugh, and Edouard would kiss the nape of her neck and dance her around the room.

At dome maintenance, where the desire to join the demonstration was almost universal, Supervisor Roxannesdaughter did not see how they could function for a shift without any inspectors, despite the sensors located throughout the structure.

Edouard volunteered to put in an extra shift. So here he was, the skeleton in the skeleton crew, inspecting the interdome alone while his Aide played the speeches for him, a thumbnail of the Sobieski Park stage in the corner of his visual field. Edouard: the man who scorned co-workers abandoning their jobs but volunteered to serve in their place so they could, the man who thought the masculinist movement absurd but who still had to know what was going on.

Dome maintenance occupied the top floor of the Diana Tower,

a level below the airlock at its summit. In the inspectors' locker room Edouard put on a white jumpsuit and hard hat, strapped microscope/ X-ray goggles to his forehead, and took up a multi-spectrum lamp that could be set from infrared through ultraviolet.

He unsealed the code-locked doors, entered the interdome, and turned on the lights. Ahead of him a forest of struts ran between the inner dome, his floor, and the upper, his ceiling. In the course of his shift he would work his way from the center to the outer edge of the dome, crossing left to right and back again between the supporting ribs in the wedge that was his day's responsibility, clocking in at stations along the way.

The Fowler dome was eighty years old, and though over the decades its monitoring and safety systems had been upgraded, it was nonetheless a piece of mid-twenty-first-century lunar architecture, remarkable for the time it had been constructed and the resources of the Cousins who had constructed it. It was fundamentally two domes, one inside the other, with an air space between containing support and safety systems. Eight umbrella-like ribs rose from the rim of the crater to join at the central spire. The titanium outer skin was covered with four meters of regolith. The regolith layer, inelegant as it was, ensured that Cousins received no more than four millisieverts of radiation per year, a load no higher than an average sea level inhabitant of Earth. The inside dome was faced with the screen that produced the artificial sky. Over the course of the last eighty years, forty percent of the structural members had been replaced, but still the supports between the inside and outside were under continuous inspection.

The dome breathed. Within a single month the exterior temperature of the surface varied from one hundred twenty degrees Celsius at noon of the two-week day to minus one hundred fifty degrees Celsius at lunar midnight. The regolith, besides protecting the interior from ionizing radiation, moderated these temperature changes, but the dome still expanded and contracted over the course of the lunar day, stressing the joints between the metal layers and the girders, beams, and stanchions where they were bolted to the skin. Where the supports met the great cermet ribs Edouard inspected the bearings for wear and deformation. He scanned the layer of composite that covered the inside of the exterior dome looking for cracks or spalling.

Edouard's time in this cold, silent place was the closest he had ever come to religion. Since he was a boy he'd been fascinated by Corentine Macysdaughter, its designer. He read of Macysdaughter's training in engineering, her career on Earth before joining the Society in the early days of its resettlement. He had seen her, once, a year before her death, when she spoke to his vocational class—a tall, thin, very old woman with a deep voice who spoke with great precision and a Cameroon lilt. Edouard's greatest wish had been to be an architect, but he did not have the gift. It was enough to be an inspector, to touch every day the physical instantiation of Macysdaughter's mind.

Save for being partnerless, today was like any other. The curve of the surface he walked created a horizon that receded before him as he advanced. The voices of the rally in his ears drowned the echo of his steps. Somebody was talking about gender essentialism. He moved on, not hurrying, not dawdling, alert and patient in this place where he had spent most of his adult life.

The speaker made reference to Carey Evasson and his petition for legal custody of his son. Ellen and Edouard had spoken about Evasson that very morning. The revelation that he was a duplicate of the boy who had gone missing twenty years ago made him, by any measure, the most famous person ever born in the Society. The patriarchal media blasted images of him all over the moon. The rally speaker called this only the most egregious example of how the bodies of Cousins boys were the possession of the social system.

Edouard was distracted from this cant by some motion he caught out of the corner of his eye. A wavering in the air like a heat mirage. When he looked he saw nothing but the forest of struts receding into the distance. Still, he turned off the audio and listened for any stray sound. He pointed his lamp and circled through the area. Nothing.

Annoyed again at his absent co-workers, he resumed his rounds.

An hour into his shift, Edouard arrived at this sector's dome integrity emergency system. The tanks of sealant, painted bright red, filled the space between inner and outer domes. In the event of a serious breach, within thirty seconds the system would release up to one thousand cubic meters of nanocontrolled exotic material. Liquid at first, the intelligent carbon would flow to the breach and, solidifying from the edges inward, form a skin over any hole to prevent the escape of air. In the history of the Society the system had only been activated once—when a meteor had punched a ten-meter hole through the dome in 2096—and it had performed flawlessly.

Although the tank was under continuous sensor monitoring, Edouard spent the next half hour checking the integrity of its stress points and the primary and backup distribution systems. Satisfied that everything was in order, he moved on. He felt secure enough to turn the audio feed of the rally back on.

Coming up, they said, was an appearance by Erno Pamelasson. Edouard had been a young man, only thirty, when the business with Thomas Marysson had happened. Pamelasson and Marysson had managed to break into the dome not far from here, open one of the access portals and attach a smartpaint bomb to the dome interior. That was the original BYD incident. Edouard did not care for the fact that Pamelasson was back, now working for the OLS. Yet many hailed him as some sort of hero. They waved around that bigoted, politically insane collection of archaic stories. What did that accomplish?

Pamelasson had just begun speaking when Edouard spotted something lying at the foot of one of the struts. At first he thought it might be a slab of concrete fallen from the ceiling, but when he shone his light up at the roof, instead of some hole from spalling, he saw a second object affixed there.

He got down on his knees to examine the one on the floor. It was roughly rectangular, maybe fifty by forty centimeters, fifteen thick. A matte gray surface. It did not belong here. Edouard's throat constricted.

He touched the surface of the thing. It was cool but not cold. He slipped his fingers beneath the edge and tried to lift it, but it was glued to the floor and would not budge. He pulled his microscope goggles down over his eyes to examine its surface.

In his ear, Erno Pamelasson warned about intervention by the OLS. ". . . change is necessary. Most of you think that, too; that's why you are here today. But the changes they hope to bring in the aftermath of their report . . ."

• • • • •

Hypatia Camillesdaughter leapt at Erno's offer to speak at the rally. He didn't have a lot he wanted to say, except to repeat in more rational terms what he had told Sid and his friends in the Men's House. That would be something, at least, to salve his conscience, and then he could go.

People began gathering at the university three hours before the rally. Excited students and citizens, eighty percent of them men, crowded the ballroom that functioned as the green room. Speakers played loud music. The Student Men's Association had a booth where they handed out red T-shirts with the phrase *One, or the Other?* printed on the breast. The committee preparing the petition to the Board distributed signs for people to carry down to the park where the events would take place.

A man in a red pullover, a centenarian with wild graying hair and a nasal voice, gave instructions on how to behave. "We'll be going out live to all the patriarchal colonies. Citizens of every OLS member state will be watching. Cameras everywhere. You can never be sure what you say or do won't be seen by millions of people. Be respectful to the constables. We need to convince these people, Cousins and non-Cousins, that we are worthy of their respect."

Erno found Hypatia and the protest organizers in a seminar room crammed with signs and posters and boxes of the red shirts. On the wall was a big flowchart of rally logistics. Here the mix was an equal number of women and men.

Erno spotted Hypatia speaking with Carey Evasson while Mira stood by. Hypatia wore a tightly fitted black military-style jacket with white gold buttons and a high collar; her hair was short and showed her cheekbones to good advantage. Though the three stood equally close to one another, Erno had the impression Carey and Mira were together and Hypatia was the odd one out. Apparently the melodrama between Mira and Carey at the hearing had not ended their relationship. He supposed it was none of his business. Who could understand all the currents in this pond?

Hypatia's eyes flicked over Erno and back to Carey. Mira watched as Erno approached.

"They aren't part of the movement," Hypatia was telling Carey. "You shouldn't worry about them; they're a minor distraction."

"And Val?" Carey asked.

"I haven't the faintest idea where he might be. I was under the impression his mother had him on a short leash." Hypatia's expression was wary. "You're sure you won't speak?"

"No, thank you," Carey said. Mira touched Carey's shoulder and he turned. He saw Erno, but said nothing. They left.

Hypatia greeted Erno with the brusqueness of someone who had just dealt with some unpleasant business and was eager to move on. "Thanks for agreeing to participate," she said. "Your voice is one that people want to hear. Just a word or two will mean a lot to all the men and boys looking to you for leadership."

She introduced him to the other organizers. A few he had met already through SCOCOM. It was likely that some of them didn't think Erno's participation was a good idea, but nobody said anything.

Erno assured Hypatia that he would not relitigate his exile; he only wanted to give the perspective of a Cousin who had found his place outside Fowler yet had concern for the Society's welfare. He was given ten minutes between the coach of the hockey team and Daquani Jeffersdaughter from the Board.

By the time they decamped for Sobieski Park, the crowd in the plaza was in the hundreds. As the van descended from the rim road, Erno saw the thousands of people gathered in the amphitheater. People crowded the lawn around it so densely that he could not see the turf. On the theater stage a live band was playing, below a video banner that at present carried the slogan "No person's freedom demands the sacrifice of another's." Flyers in bright wings circled overhead.

The van drew up behind the stage. Erno descended with the others to the sound of amplified traditional jazz. "Race music." Erno loved that archaic music and had studied its history. Cousins men had been trying to appropriate the rhetoric of racial discrimination for their own purposes, with mixed results. Erno had used that language himself as a young man, before he'd seen real racial discrimination during his exile.

As soon as they got out, Hypatia was beset by a dozen people with questions. A young woman behind the backstage barrier stood on her toes, her arm raised, calling, "Hypatia! Hypatia!" Hypatia exchanged a few words with each of the speakers, posed for photographs, held her hand over her ear and spoke with her Aide. Camera midges swarmed above; she seemed to glow in their attention.

Erno climbed to the edge of the stage and looked out at the crowd.

The amphitheater had a capacity of three thousand, but there had to be four times that many here, a fifth of the population, and more arriving every minute. Two-thirds of them were somatically male, but females were well represented, and many had brought children. Large numbers wore their work clothes. Five men who should have been out on the surface maintaining solar collectors were there in dayglow pressure suits, helmets thrown back. A line of old men and women sat in the front row, red shawls over their shaven heads. Sanitation workers in yellow hazmat suits held up a banner, "Say Yes!" Agricultural workers in blue coveralls, red scarves around their necks. A woman with a boy on her shoulders, his hands encircling her forehead. Some aquaculture workers in hip waders. Scientists and technicians in lab coats. Athletes in shorts. A flock of girls and boys waving blue-and-white school flags. A few members of the hockey team, sans skates but wearing uniform sweaters. Posters held up high with pictures of Nora Sobieski, Adil Al-Hafez. Teachers, food workers, maintenance.

The band stopped playing; there was some applause, and they downed their instruments, waved, and left the stage. A murmur swept the crowd. After a long few minutes, Hypatia came forward from behind the banner. The crowd erupted in cheers—though Erno heard some booing.

Hypatia held up her arms until the crowd quieted. She smiled out at them. She leaned on the podium and appraised them, as if it was their job to live up to her expectations. "Hello," she said.

Laughter, and a chorus of "Hello!" back at her.

"The fact that so many are here today," she said, the mikes picking up her voice and sending out it over the massed people, "means that the number of those who want change is growing. It may not happen today, or tomorrow, or next week, but I want you to take away from this afternoon the certainty that, if you hold it in your hearts and express it in your actions every day, change will happen. That no person's freedom demands the sacrifice of another's."

The crowd cheered.

And so it began. Erno listened to Hypatia and the speakers that followed with a mixture of hope and cynicism. Hypatia was not a selfless broker of the reformers' dreams. The OLS was not a neutral organization of statesmen. Cyrus was not interested in seeing this unruly village continue as it had. Yet the faces of the people, the flyers above, the trees of the park, the expanse of the artificial sky so blue above them, brought back the idealism that had moved him when he was a boy. Instead of the sense of grievance that had poisoned his every judgment, he felt the possibility of change—even if no one could be free of self-interest, and so many beautiful bright dreams came eventually to grief.

An hour into it they told Erno he was next, and before he knew it he was on the stage. The aroma of bread wafted up from one of the food stands. He took a breath, and began.

"You know who I am. I used to live here. I committed crimes and I was given a fair hearing and I was exiled. I say those words without irony: I was treated fairly by the Society and its leaders.

"For more than ten years I've lived in places where the Society, when it is mentioned at all, is spoken of with distrust and incomprehension. You've seen plenty of that on the nets. Yet I want to tell you that there are people out there for whom the Society is not a threat, or a reproach, but a source of hope.

"Just as we got here today, I heard the band playing a very old song. I was surprised to hear it, frankly; it dates back to a couple of hundred years ago. This song, it has words that go, 'What did I do, to be so black and blue?'

"I used to dwell on that question entirely too much in my youth.

"In gender class, you learned all the roles that men traditionally fall into: the Alpha, the Lieutenant, the Enforcer, the Clown, the Good Citizen, the Outsider, the Loser, the Hero. Well, this is the theme song of the Outsider, or the Loser. What did he do to be so black and blue? The answer is, all too often, nothing. Other men needed him to be black and blue, so they did not have to be.

"If you had to classify me back when I lived here, I was probably the Clown. The mocker, the would-be satirist. In the years of my exile, I tried hard to fit into any of the other roles that seemed available. Few of us are stuck in one of these roles forever; sometimes an Alpha can be a Loser and sometimes the Hero is the Outsider. But most of us tend to orbit around one or another.

"The goal of the Society, as far as men were concerned, was to make it unnecessary for any male human being to force himself into one and only one of these roles. To end up black and blue. The Founders said there was no need to organize a society around this and only this set of options. They wanted other possibilities for men and women—and transsexuals, and bisexuals, and nonsexuals, and all the other somatic and psychological flavors of human being. But they failed to accomplish this, and I wonder sometimes if it is possible. It's not as if we Cousins are some different species, free of the flaws that come with being human.

"The thing I have to say today is simple: If the Society of Cousins has failed to eliminate the need for those boxes, let me remind you that, outside of the Society, it's worse. And if we Cousins have created some new boxes that have left some of us feeling frustrated or stunted, it's nothing compared to the degree to which our efforts have mystified, outraged, and frightened people, both men and women, out there."

Here there came a ragged cheer from the crowd, people holding their banners higher and shouting things Erno could not make out.

"The SCOCOM team I serve on has come here, ostensibly, to

490 • JOHN KESSEL

listen to us in the effort to understand. Beneath that listening, I think all of us know—which is why the Matrons resisted their coming—is the expectation that the Society would be asked, even forced, to change. I believe, despite my chastening experiences in that patriarchal world, that change is necessary. I guess most of you think that, too, or you wouldn't be here today.

"But the changes they hope to bring in the aftermath of their report—"

From above the amphitheater there came a flash of light, followed seconds later by an explosion. Erno felt the shock of it in his eardrums, in his chest. He looked up.

• • • • •

Before she even strapped on a feather, Sarah spent twenty minutes inspecting her gear. Satisfied that everything was in order, she fastened the tail foils onto her calves. Jihan, today's takeoff facilitator, helped her don her right wing, then her left, and tighten the chest harness. Sarah synced all of the inputs with her Aide, put on her helmet, and powered up. The readouts came up on her visual field and her wings fluttered as the servos activated. Testing the controls with each of her fingers in the gloves, she rotated the thousands of feathers in her right wing, then her left, getting a feel for the cyborg bird she had become. She felt alert, mentally prepared, completely present. She inhaled deeply and slowly exhaled, relaxing the muscles of her shoulders and back. She felt strong.

The wind whistled across the jump stage. A kilometer below, the floor of Fowler spread out green and brown, blue where the pond snaked through Sobieski Park. Two teenaged flyers, one in red and the other in striped yellow-and-black, zipped past the tower stage, dangerously close, and a flight patroller swooped in, sounding her whistle to get them to move off.

Sarah had been flying since she was nine. She had logged more than five thousand hours in the air and was rated Expert. Her high-performance wings had a hair-trigger response, unsafe for novices. Iridescent blue and white, she imagined herself the largest blue jay ever to take wing.

Jihan nodded to indicate Sarah's turn. Heart racing, Sarah jogged to the edge of the platform and launched herself off into space. Her leg foils, buoyed by the wind, lifted her parallel to the ground.

It was all so slow at first, weightless, before gravity began to draw her down. She let herself fall at a slight angle, picking up speed, wings half furled, then spread them wide and caught the air. The stress hit her arms and shoulders, but it was nothing but invigorating. Leveling off, she slowly climbed upward, feeling as good as she had ever felt in her life.

Sarah avoided other flyers. She liked to fly alone, to feel her body work, the wind buffeting her face, senses completely awake and taking it all in. She did her best thinking while aloft. She drew in the cool air, scented her own sweat, heard the faint whistle of the wind over the carbon-fiber feathers, the chuff of her wings when she lazily beat the air.

She followed a radius out from the tower for a couple of kilometers, and when the slopes of the crater rose up she banked right, keeping a good margin above the buildings and trees, toward the park.

In the distance, flyers circled above the amphitheater. Thousands already covered the lawns and filled the black stone benches of the theater. Live music from one of the bands—she could hardly see them—drifted up from the stage. Beyond this, on the aerofield, a flyer in green wings—Sarah recognized the wing tattoo as her friend Alma's—glided two meters above the turf, pulled into a stall and landed daintily on her feet, trotting forward without a wobble.

Sarah glided, circling the park. The crowd was the largest she had ever seen; they were saying it might be the largest in the history of the colony. Men and women in red shirts and workers' coveralls, carrying signs and banners, singing songs and chanting. Some looked up at her and waved. She might have been down there herself. In Sarah's opinion there had been enough trouble already: The Board ought to listen to the reformers and relent. Extend the franchise to men. It was a little like jumping off the flight platform, a risk, but life was risk and what was the Society but a big risk their ancestors had taken? Most men didn't vote any differently from women anyway, if they took the trouble to vote at all.

A dozen flyers circled the park now, too many for her comfort, but she was not ready to land. Maybe in an hour or so, once she had gotten a workout. So Sarah twisted her tail foils and steered herself away, beating her wings, climbing. Her shoulders worked; she drew deep, strong breaths and felt the sweat cool on her skin where the breeze evaporated it. Her visual display told her that her blood was highly oxygenated, but she knew that already by the feeling of strength that coursed through her.

Higher and higher Sarah climbed, headed for the other side of the crater, then banked and followed the perimeter road, spiraling gradually upward toward the roof of the world. The music and noise faded in the distance. She passed over the university; below her people in the plazas and courtyards looked very small. Thermals above the pavement lifted her higher still.

The rally was in full force when Sarah soared over the park again. Maybe ten thousand people down there now. She was so high that she could not make out individuals, and even the flyers below her seemed to be almost on the ground in comparison to how high she had climbed. She glided a hundred meters below the face of the dome, where she could see the sunlit sky as an illusion of the optical surface. She felt great solitude, complete vibrant life, a fullness of being that could only be called joy.

From above and behind Sarah came a flash of light, then an immense sound, astonishingly loud. A blast of air swatted her like the hand of a giant. Something tore in her shoulder. She tumbled, pain searing, her ears deafened and ringing. Something struck her helmet. Shards of metal and fiberglass shot past her; something hit her leg. A large metal fragment tore through her left wing.

All her readouts were red; she was spinning, and she saw a fan of blood arcing away from her calf. She pulled her wings in, crying out with the shoulder pain, and folded them back, letting herself fall to get away from the explosion. Clouds of debris surrounded her, glittering and dark. Larger, tumbling fragments as big as she was fell toward the ground below, toward the crowds of people who surged, moving like a single living thing.

Sarah spread her wings, shoulder screaming, and regained her equilibrium. Only then, banking, did she get a glimpse of what had happened, at the same time that she felt the tug of a great wind.

In the dome above her yawned a vast, gaping blackness. A hole in the sky. Huge—fifty, a hundred meters wide, it had to be—and through it, creating a gale that she fought helplessly, poured the air she swam in, an irresistible force dragging her upward. She curled into a ball, wrapping her wings around her legs, willing herself to be dense, to fall, but the moon's gentle gravity was helpless against the torrent blowing her out into nothingness.

• • • • •

Mira and Carey had spent much of the night looking for Val. The Glass Institute, the university commons, the places where he hung out with friends. Nothing. They'd vowed to resume the next day and gone to bed.

Early, early in the morning Mira woke and watched Carey asleep on the pillow, his face placid. Mira stroked the hair at his temple lightly with the tips of her fingers, pushing it behind his ear. He had died—and yet here he was. Did what had happened to him even count as a death?

She remembered the way he'd smudged dirt on his face in the Oxygen Warehouse, that night when she'd shot the video she'd used to betray him. He was playing a game, trusting her to play along. Back then, Carey had offered her connection to social acceptance. At some level she'd hated that it took a man to draw her within the circle of normality, and she'd resented him for it.

What a fool she'd been. She lay against him, their hearts ten centimeters apart. She would not assume that this night implied anything going forward—but it did. It *would* go forward, not easily, but that didn't matter. Years would pass, and their hearts would be connected throughout those years, no matter whether the Society changed, whether the OLS intervened, whether they were in the same family or not. She knew it. What astonished her most of all was that he knew it, too.

Carey's eyes fluttered open.

"Hello," he said softly. He kissed her on the cheek. His eyes were very somber. "You look—happy."

"I am happy."

"Is that possible?"

Mira poked him in the ribs, and they wrestled until he pinned her to the bed and kissed her again. "I love you," he said.

Her heart rose, and she let it. "Go easy on that word."

"Wait around, you'll see."

They got up and dressed. They went directly to the university, where the rally organizers were meeting. Carey rolled his eyes at the numbers of people wearing red shirts that said *One, or the Other?* In the green room they found Hypatia at the center of a chaos of students and allies, dressed to kill and full of energy. Her face lifted when she saw Carey. If she was surprised to see Mira with him, she didn't show it.

She held a hand up to stop the young woman who was speaking with her.

"I'm so glad to see you both," she said.

Mira's distrust must have showed on her face.

"No, I mean it," Hypatia said. "Mira, I know you did what you did for what you thought were good reasons. I respect your ability to see past politics. It doesn't matter if we don't always agree."

"I thought you were all about solidarity."

"You and Carey are together despite what happened. That's solidarity. You'll see I'm right someday."

"I'll be sure to come by and apologize."

"There's still time for you to get on the list of speakers," Hypatia told Carey. "You don't have to prepare anything. You don't have to agree with me, and I won't try to steer you. Just a word or two would mean a lot to all the men looking to you for leadership."

"We're trying to find Val," Carey said. "He was in tight with Dora Aikosdaughter and some of her boyfriends."

"You shouldn't worry about them," Hypatia said. "They're a minor distraction."

"And Val?"

"I haven't the faintest idea where he might be. I was under the impression his mother had him on a short leash." For a second

Hypatia's eyes looked away from Carey, and Mira followed them. Erno Pamelasson stood at the door. Hypatia went on, "You're sure you won't speak?"

"No, thank you," Carey said. Mira touched his arm and he turned. Erno was approaching. Mira and Carey left.

"Do you think she's lying?" Carey asked.

"Can Hypatia tell when she is lying?" They were out in the crowded courtyard. A man in a red pullover, one of Mira's old professors, was instructing students on how to behave at the rally. "What now?" Mira asked.

"We should split up. You go to the park. I'll try Aikosdaughter's apartment. If we don't find him, let's meet at the fountain at fifteen hundred."

She didn't want to let him go. "All right," she said. She stood on tiptoe and kissed him. He squeezed her tightly, so much taller than she, his chin resting on her head.

"No words needed," he whispered into her ear. He let her go and moved off through the crowd.

Mira made her way down the crater slope. She was not alone: From all quarters of the colony people were gathering. Couples and families, teachers with school groups in tow, workers taking time from their jobs, people in the omnipresent red shirts. A bell tinkled behind her, and three young men rode past her on bicycles. None of them was Val. Between the buildings she glimpsed the park. Old-fashioned music floated up on the air. Flyers circled above.

Once she reached the amphitheater she moved around the perimeter, then struck out down one of the aisles, searching the faces. There were so many young people that she wondered if she would spot Val even if he were there. She looked for the characteristic hunch of his shoulders, his bright red hair.

She had her back to the stage when, to a chorus of cheers, Hypatia opened the rally. Mira turned to watch for a moment, until someone asked her to move or sit down.

Hypatia didn't say anything Mira hadn't heard before.

Mira moved around to the side of the stage. The parade of speakers began: some gender theorist from the university, a young mother who worked in colony administration, a helium-3 miner, the coach of the hockey team. Through all this she moved through the crowd without glimpsing Val, and she began to wonder if they weren't overreacting in their concern for him. She looked toward the fountain, but it was way too early for her meeting with Carey.

When Erno took the podium, Mira was on the lawn above the amphitheater. It was a long way down to the stage, but speaker midges in the air carried his voice clearly. Erno's speech wasn't very well organized; he seemed to be working up to a warning about the intentions of the OLS. He left out Cyrus Eskander's search for the IQSA and his own role in it, but at least he was willing to speak. She couldn't figure Erno out; he seemed so fatally conflicted. She supposed there were worse things to be than conflicted.

Then she spotted Val, across the amphitheater from her, moving between the people standing beyond the top row of seats. He was taller than the others, and his red hair stood out. He paid no attention to Erno's speech.

She set out toward him, but once she moved into the crowd she was too short to see him anymore.

"—I believe," Erno was saying, "despite my chastening experiences in that patriarchal world, change is necessary. I guess most of you think that, too, or you wouldn't be here today.

"But the changes they hope to bring in the aftermath of their report—"

A flash of light came from above, and three seconds later the crack of an explosion. Mira felt the sound in her chest. She looked up.

A smudge of dust and smoke marred the sky. Someone near her said, in disgust, "Not again."

But this smoke did not resolve itself into words. It wasn't smoke at all—it was a cloud of debris, pieces of the material that made up the dome, falling now, growing in size as they fell. Metal fragments, titanium struts, tonnes of regolith from the exterior, structural members, and pieces of the projection screen, tumbling and spinning as they fell toward the people gathered in the park.

Above them they left a hole in the sky. A black hole, larger than a speck, smaller than a blot, a crow's eye staring down. It didn't look very large. Mira wanted to brush it off the blue dome. She couldn't feel any breeze, but she imagined she heard a thin howl, the sound of life being sucked out of the colony.

Mira tried to push through the crowd. It would take a long time, thirty seconds or more, for anything to fall the kilometer from the dome to the surface, but people cried in panic. The sound system squealed. The debris was coming down—that was the first thing they realized, and they scattered, leaping like startled deer, knocking each other over, shouting.

Erno's voice came over the sound system: "The tower! Get to the tower. Don't panic. There's time. Go anywhere that can be pressure sealed!"

A woman near Mira cried out and pointed up. Mira looked up in time to see a struggling flyer in blue and white wings, tiny at this distance, sucked through the hole into the airless nothing on the other side.

Leaping people collided in midair and bounced off others trying to escape. Mira pushed between those around her. The debris began to hit. It was all raining down: fiberoptic sheets. Metal plates. Insulation. An avalanche of regolith. The sound was immense and horrifying: crashing, squealing, the thud of metal and rocks hitting turf, crushing stone benches, trees, bodies. Screams, cries, shouts. In horror, Mira saw a ten-meter reinforcement strut crush a woman tugging a child.

Mira dashed through momentary spaces in the roiling crowd. A boulder landed a couple of meters away, splattering the pavement as if it were water. A shard of concrete cut her cheek. People fled the rain of junk, but it spread as it fell. The density of the debris swelled. The air grew thick with dust and rocks. For a billion years it had existed in a vacuum; now it was within an atmosphere.

But not for long.

People knocked over and trampled one another. Some few tried to pull the injured from beneath the rubble. She saw a man pinned under a slab of concrete, leg pulped. Another lay with his head severed by a sheet of titanium. Some cowered under trees that might as well have been made of tissue paper.

Mira passed a broken-backed flyer lying on the ground, feathers of his orange wings still fluttering under the malfunctioning servos. Mira thought he was dead until he pulled his hand free of his control glove. Mira crouched beside him and began to unfasten the straps of his wings.

"Don't worry," she told him. Blood trickled from the corner of the man's mouth. Something struck her shoulder. Dirt rained down around her. People's legs flashed by in the corner of her vision. An insistent voice began in her ear: *There has been a dome containment breach. Please proceed immediately to the nearest designated pressure shelter.*

A man knelt down beside her and freed the flyer's other arm. The flyer groaned, eyes opened wide—they were pale blue—and stopped breathing. Mira tried to feel his throat for a pulse, but the other man grabbed her arm and tugged her to her feet.

"Come away, now!"

A falling metal strut speared through one of the wings, pinning it. Mira let the man pull her away.

They got out from under the rain of deadly junk onto the green turf several hundred meters from the amphitheater. The man who had pulled her away was in his sixties, maybe. He looked like he might once have been an athlete, but he wore the coveralls of an Ag worker. His scalp was cut and blood flowed down his temple. The rain of falling debris lessened, stopped.

The blackbird's eye still marred the sky. The self-sealing mechanisms weren't working, yet the air still felt dense enough to breathe. How long had it been since the explosion? Eight, ten minutes? How long would it take before the air escaped and the pressure doors of the tunnel entrances closed? They had to get away.

People headed for the Diana Tower, for the cable train station, or the nearest tunnels in the crater wall. Others turned back to the amphitheater where hundreds lay buried in the rubble, many still alive. Mira looked toward the tower longingly, hoping that Val, that Carey, had found shelter.

She told the bleeding Ag worker, "You're hurt. The air's going. Get to the tower." She ran back toward the people trapped in the debris.

• • • • •

From the Executive Summary, *Commission on the Society of Cousins Dome Disaster* (*aka "The Fowler Report"*)
The safety devices of the Society of Cousins dome were designed to seal a breach of up to twenty meters in diameter. The explosion that occurred during the Reform Party protest blew a hole in the dome one hundred meters across.

The volume of air contained within the crater was just over ten billion cubic meters. The Cousins pressurized their home at 0.8 atmospheres with 25 percent oxygen content, the equivalent of air pressure at an altitude of 2,100 meters on Earth, about that of Mexico City.

At 0.5 atmospheres, the partial pressure of oxygen becomes low enough that most human beings begin to experience hypoxia, lose consciousness, and die.

Given the volume of the Fowler crater and the size of the hole in the dome, the pressure within would fall from 0.8 to 0.5 atmospheres in about forty-five minutes.

• • • • •

Sixty-seven-year-old Micah Avasson lived in the singles dorms. He worked in the rack farms, as he had for twenty-five years, harvesting tomatoes, leaf lettuce, cucumbers, and kale from towering walls of hydroponic trays under grow lights. In his youth he had been a gymnast, a member of the Cirque Jacinthe, but he had long ago aged out of that. He'd never been a star anyway, just a strong back and shoulders, holding a rope, bracing a pyramid. Force, not grace, was his hallmark, and in truth he was not even that strong.

They had once toured the other lunar colonies; Micah remembered it as if it had happened to a different man. Out there they got as much attention because they were Cousins as they did for their performances, and every night men and women waited for them in the hotels, the clubs, the theaters, all interested in sleeping with the exotic strangers. These people inevitably found the experience disappointing, though Micah had been gratified by the crooked energy the patriarchal men and women brought to bed with them.

Back in Fowler he'd married into the Rust family for a few years and had fathered a son, but once the son was born his wife did not seem to have much use for Micah, and he left. His wife had been Pamela Megsdaughter. His son was Erno Pamelasson.

After the divorce Micah had fallen back into his birth family, the Snows, for a while, and had not seen much of Erno beyond the age of three. When his performing career ended Micah forsook the male privilege, took a job in Agriculture, and against the protests of his mother moved out of the family. One of those rare solitary males. He had his girlfriends, his co-workers, his circle of acquaintances, but few permanent connections. That was fine. To Micah the Society of Cousins meant the freedom to do as he pleased with the time he did not spend on his tedious job.

He was heading alone into the dark pit that waited at the end of every life. But everybody went down alone, even if children and wives and brothers crowded around the hospice bed, a lover holding one hand and a best friend the other. Sometimes the lover and the friend were even the same person. It didn't matter. You broke through into that final blackness unaccompanied. Why pretend that it could be otherwise?

But as the number of the years behind him began to exceed the number he could reasonably expect ahead, Micah began to feel vulnerable in a way he never had before. So when Erno came back to the Society, he could not help but take an interest—from a distance.

He was at the rally not because he thought the condition of men in the Society required change—thank you, madam, I'm fine just the way I am—but because he wanted to see the face and hear the voice of his son.

In videos Erno looked much older than he had before his exile, when he had come to see Micah before the events that got him kicked out of the Society. On the Reform Party stage Erno looked still older: baby fat gone, his jawline sharp as a chisel, his eyes drawn. Micah sat in the front row and studied his son's face, the way he lifted and lowered his hands as he spoke, the timbre of his voice. The sentiments of Erno's speech—well, Micah didn't pay much attention to that.

When the explosion came, Micah flinched, looked up, and ran. This was no fake. While others stood stunned, he dodged his way between people. He avoided leaping, for fear of landing in some chaotic mess. When people were too densely packed to squeeze through, he pushed them out of his way. Most stared upward dumbly. Some pushed back. Others jumped, not getting any forward momentum, wasting precious seconds floating, and coming down not far from where they'd started, usually on someone's head. Micah worked his way up the steps of the amphitheater as the debris started to fall around him. Screams and blood. When he hit the park grass at the top, he bounded toward the cable train station.

Something knocked him to his knees. He didn't know how long he knelt there, stunned—probably no more than a minute—but when he came back to himself the crowd was fleeing all around him.

He got up and headed toward the Diana Tower. The debris rained down. His Aide spoke in his ear: *There has been a dome containment breach. Please proceed immediately to the nearest designated pressure shelter.*

A flyer in broken orange wings lay on the turf. A small woman fumbled with his straps, trying to get him out of his gear. Micah looked at the tower a couple of hundred meters away through the trees, then got down beside her and worked to free the flyer's other arm. The man groaned. The woman put her cheek to his mouth. Metal and rock still fell around them. Micah grabbed the woman's arm. "Come away, now!"

A falling strut speared one of the wings. The woman came with him.

They reached relative safety, outside the shadow of wreckage. Instead of heading for the cable station or the tower, Micah looked back. The rain of debris gradually came to an end, though the air was filled with choking powder from the lunar surface. The black-haired young woman looked up at the dome. The hole was still there. The insistent voice in their ears told them to take shelter.

The woman said, "You're hurt. The air's going. Get to the tower." Then she ran back toward the amphitheater and the injured, trapped, and dead.

Micah felt something trickle down his face, and when he touched his hand to his temple it came away bloody. He felt no pain. Aside from the dust, the air was still breathable.

Nearby a man collapsed while carrying a boy in his arms. They both wore red T-shirts that asked, *One, or the Other?*

Micah bent over the man. "Can you stand?" he asked.

The man looked at him, dazed. "What?"

The boy was up, rubbing grit out of his eyes. Micah got his arm under the man's and helped him stand. "Come on," he said.

The man's legs were rubbery and Micah had to take most of his weight, but it wasn't much. The boy followed them to the tower. A couple of constables at the door helped people into the lobby. Micah passed the man and boy off and turned back toward the park.

Water still splashed in the fountain, and escaping air rustled the leaves of the trees. Back at the amphitheater Micah helped two women trying to free a third trapped under a girder. They couldn't budge it, but Micah squatted, got a grip on one end, and lifted it enough so they could pull the woman free. They carried her away.

Out of shape for this kind of work, he was breathing hard. Someone called, "Over here!" and Micah went to work with another man trying to free an unconscious person half buried in regolith. "Is she alive?"

"We have to get her out!" the man said.

The woman's arm was exposed. Micah felt for her pulse.

"She's gone," Micah said. "You need to get to shelter."

The man's face crumpled. He let Micah help him between the dead and dying toward the tower. Micah bounced back to help others. Emergency workers wearing respirators were out now. One of them shouted, voice muffled, for Micah to go back, but he stayed. He freed two women, then a teenaged boy who turned out to be dead. The boy had an erection poking up under his shorts.

The cries of the wounded got sparser. Micah's heart beat fast. He felt a headache coming on. When he got the next person out, he pointed her off in the wrong direction; he had to chase after her to send her toward the tower.

The air had grown thin and cold. He gasped.

He started climbing the amphitheater steps. Normally he could leap up three at a time, but his legs were not responding so well, and he had to detour around a pile of sheet metal, rock, and girders. He saw a man's legs sticking out from under a piece of the sky. This one had an erection, too. Bad timing, pal.

He reached the top of the bowl and made his way toward the cable station. Between the bodies and debris, fluttering birds lay on the turf. He had gone a hundred meters when he realized this was stupid—the cable station was at least half a kilometer away, while the tower was closer. He turned and started back. The tower rose up in front of him, beyond the treetops. Biggest erection of all. The sky was still blue. The black hole was still there.

He moved through the trees. Ahead of him two men, leaning on each other, stumbled toward the doors. Micah had to stop. His heart raced and he felt dizzy. He couldn't think. His pulse sounded in his ears. A voice was calling him, a thin voice in the thin air, but he could not tell where it came from. He knelt down in the grass.

• • • • •

The student neighborhood was deserted; most who lived here were at the rally. Carey leaned on the door chime, and eventually someone answered. It was the guy who had been there when Carey came the last time. He wore one of those idiot *One, or the Other?* shirts.

Carey thought again about how pretentious he had been when he was fifteen, showing off his pathetic French. "I'm looking for Val—"

"Seems you look for him a lot," the kid said.

Carey restrained himself. "Have you seen him?"

"I have not seen him, and he's not here, and no, he hasn't been here since that day you came before. I think you need a new hobby. He's not even your responsibility anymore, is he?"

"Don't be a dick about this," Carey said.

"Right. I'm a dick. And you're not even the original."

Carey grabbed the boy's shirt and yanked him close. "It would be a betrayal of everything we believe in for me to resort to physical violence. Where is Val?"

The kid looked scared. "Dora met with him last night. They were going to the rally."

In the concourse behind Carey, a flashing light came on and a klaxon sounded. Carey let go of the boy. "What's that?" the kid said.

"A pressure breach," Carey said. He moved away from the door. A couple of people out in the concourse stopped to stare.

"If you have any self-respect, you'll call me if you see Val," Carey said, and ran back toward the crater. The air pressure felt normal. At the concourse's pressure doors, yellow emergency lights flashed but the doors were still open. Nearer the tunnel's exit the people streamed in from the crater; Carey had to dodge men and women rushing toward him. He passed a teacher with a class of fearful school kids holding hands two-by-two in rehearsed emergency procedure.

He grabbed a fleeing man. "What is it?"

"The dome!" the man said, glancing back over his shoulder. "They blasted a hole in the dome!"

Where East Six joined the crater, a broad plaza looked out over a district of schools and offices that stretched halfway down the interior slope. Fleeing people ran toward the tunnel entrance. On a wall of apartments people were out on their terraces, hands on railings, peering upward.

There was a hole in the sky. Carey could see a cloud of white near the hole—moisture in the air freezing into crystals as it escaped.

And down in Sobieski Park, the amphitheater and surrounding turf was a boiling chaos, people leaping like kernels of popcorn in their eagerness to escape. Most of the seats and the stage lay buried by a mass of rubble, below clouds of dust and grit that filled the air.

A voice sounded in his ear: *There has been a dome containment breach. Please proceed immediately to the nearest designated pressure shelter.*

He tried calling Mira but the system was overloaded. Cursing, he moved toward the park against the mass of fleeing people. Vehicles careened up the roads from the crater floor. Constables waved people toward East Six. Carey fought the torrent.

A constable grabbed him. "Back into the tunnel! Air pressure's dropping. The doors will close!"

Carey tore out of his grasp. He got behind an emergency vehicle headed toward the park. When it reached the bottom and the road was blocked by fallen wreckage, three emergency workers wearing respirators jumped out. Carey followed them.

The stage was obliterated by heaps of regolith and structural materials. Grim results lay everywhere; people crushed, trapped. Val could be buried beneath this debris. Carey climbed over some twisted girders and slipped, with a sickening lurch, on a woman's arm protruding from beneath a fragment of the dome screen. It might be Mira's arm—but no, this had the words "*Si vis amari, ama*" tattooed on the forearm.

He gasped for breath. How long before the air got too thin to breathe?

"Help me, help me, help me . . . ," a voice groaned from beneath the rubble. A man in a dark suit was bent over, trying to lift a strut. Carey grabbed hold of the strut and crouched. "On three," he said.

The man turned to look at him. It was Erno Pamelasson.

"One, two, three!" They both strained, shoulders and backs working. The strut came up a few centimeters. An emergency worker crawled forward and dragged a young man out from under. Another bloody *One, or the Other?* shirt.

"Okay," she said, and Carey and Erno let the strut drop.

Carey breathed hard. The wounded kid had an erection. Carey laughed. "A hard way to go," he said.

"Priapism from hypoxia," the EMT said, voice muffled by her respirator. She looked up at them. "Take shelter. Get to the tower."

Erno tugged Carey's arm. "Over here," he said.

A few meters away some others were trying to lift a big titanium sheet, but it was covered with regolith. Erno found a broken beam and levered it under one end, and Carey shoved a block of concrete under it for a fulcrum. After minutes of fumbling, leaning on the beam with all their weight, they managed to raise it. One of the EMTs got down on her belly to reach the person trapped underneath. She backed out, sat back on her haunches.

"She's dead," the EMT said.

They let the plate fall back. Carey's heart would not slow its racing; he felt dizzy. He wanted to make sure it wasn't Mira who lay under there. Erno grabbed Carey's arm to steady himself. Erno's pants leg was plastered to his skin with blood.

Another emergency worker yelled at them through his respirator. It took a moment before Carey understood. "Into the tower! Now! We don't need two more dead!"

Erno leaning on his shoulder, they started climbing over the rubble and bodies. "Have you seen my son?" Carey gasped. "My son, Valentin?"

"I think—no," Erno said. "I think"—he gasped—"I think I know . . ."

A vicious headache throbbed in Carey's temples.

Dead and dying lay all around them, buried and half-buried among the debris. Carey thought he saw the fingers of one woman twitch as they climbed by. He stopped but could find no pulse at her throat. Erno tugged his arm and they kept climbing. He wanted to close his eyes so he wouldn't risk seeing Val, dead.

They reached the park and staggered through the trees toward the tower. The air was cold. The amount of rubble on the ground diminished. They passed a flyer lying dead on the grass, strapped into broken orange wings. The only people outside now were emergency workers with respirators. Carey was amazed that the doors of the tower were still open. They must have over-ridden the automatic pressure sensors, but soon someone would make the call to seal the building.

Fifty meters, twenty-five. Past the big fountain, still functioning, Carey felt a spray of ice crystals on his cheek. He looked up at the tower, thinking of the night he'd caught Val out here trying to affix the paint bomb.

Erno tugged on him. "Come on."

A couple of women ran out and helped them the last few meters into the tower. A wind of escaping air blew into their faces through the doorway. Inside, Carey and Erno crumpled to the floor. "Okay," someone called out. Almost immediately the doors slid shut behind them.

Carey leaned back against the glass of the lobby wall. People crowded everywhere on the polished stone floor, several hundred it had to be, crammed in there. Many were injured. Office workers with first aid kits worked on people dulled by shock. A man held his hand over his lips. A woman clutched the arm of another woman, weeping. Others gathered at the glass wall overlooking the park, the trees, the pond.

Carey's heart slowed, and he could breathe again. Erno sat crumpled beside him, his leg bleeding. Carey leaned his head against the window. The emergency workers were still out there, but even they would have to give up soon unless they donned pressure suits. By that time anyone trapped in the wreckage would already be dead.

A bird fell to the grass, fluttered a little, and lay an arm's length away on the other side of the glass, its beak opening and closing. Carey had learned the names of all the birds living in Fowler when he was a kid. This one was small, with brown and gray feathers, a rusty cap, and a white stripe above each eye: a sparrow—a chipping sparrow.

"Everything's going to die," Erno said.

Carey was desperately thirsty. The thought that Mira might be lying buried out there made him sick. He saw her face from the night before, when they had argued outside the Men's House. And that morning, watching him as he awoke. He could not stand the thought that her fierce heart might be stopped.

"Look!" someone cried, and Carey lifted his head to see something none of them had ever experienced: Outside, flakes of snow swirled in the air, moisture condensing in the rapidly cooling interior.

"It makes no sense," Carey said. "Who would do this?" Some of the Matrons hated the protesters, but they wouldn't destroy their own home. The Spartans—they'd be killing their own people. But some men had always been capable of suicidal rage. Val ranting about emasculation. His attempted prank with the paint bomb.

Erno swallowed. He moved his leg, and grimaced in pain. "The dog," he said.

"What?"

"Sirius. He has reasons, or the people behind him do." Erno surveyed the crowded atrium. Office workers had come down from the floors above. "I don't think this is over yet."

"What do you mean?"

"Sirius—when BYD happened he talked about an explosion as a diversion to distract people from a second attack. 'If at first you don't succeed, blow it up again.'"

Carey's mind seemed to clear. "Another bomb? Are you sure?"

"No, I'm not," Erno said, trying to stand, slipping back down. Blood was smeared on the floor beneath his leg.

Carey looked around the lobby, jammed with the stunned and injured. "There must be a couple of thousand people in this building. We've got to get everyone out."

"He'd plant it in the SCOCOM offices," Erno said, "on the forty-second floor." On his second try, Erno managed to find his feet. "You don't know him. I'll—"

Erno was in no shape to take on anyone. "Stay here," Carey said. He looked around. "Tell the constables. Get the people down to the metro station. Find Val—and Mira."

"It'll be planted against an exterior wall," Erno said, limping with Carey toward the elevators.

They stumbled their way between groups of people on the floor. Carey hit the elevator call button. When a constable came toward them, Erno called to her. "Officer! Thank the Goddess!" Erno limped toward her, putting himself between her and Carey.

The elevator opened. Carey stepped in and hit the button for forty-two.

"Just a minute," the constable said.

"Officer," Erno said, losing his balance so that the constable had to catch him. "We need to get—"

The doors slid closed.

Nicely done. Carey felt the weight of acceleration as the car rushed upward. Maybe Erno was wrong, deluded by shock and paranoia, and Carey would find nothing on the forty-second floor but an empty office suite. He hoped so. He hadn't been in the tower since the custody hearing. He regretted the icy hostility of his last meeting with Roz. He wondered where she was, where Eva was, where Thabo and his friends from the Salon were. Val and Mira. Any of them could be dead.

He looked at the ring on his finger. He had imagined it lost and dreaded finding it. Two vines, intertwining, never meeting. Men and women, men and men, women and women. The one and the other, the living and the dead, irrevocably woven together, never touching. Was that true? He felt different, older than he had ever felt, completely aware of the past and future yet more present in the tragic, hopeful moment than he had ever been.

The elevator slowed. Forty-two, the indicator read. The doors opened and he stepped out. On the wall a discreet sign: "Organization of Lunar States, Special Committee on the Condition of Men."

Carey opened the door to a wedge-shaped room that ran from the spine of the building out to the walls. The exterior was one huge window looking out over the crater. Most of the false sky was still functioning. The snow had diminished to just a few hard flakes. The hole in the dome was clearly visible from this side of the building; Carey could see the ragged edges of the gap, the black border of nanofluid flowing in to close the gap, futilely, fragments blown upward by escaping air the second they solidified.

He listened for sounds, heard nothing. The place was deserted. He started working his way through the suite. Empty offices, workrooms. The layout was similar to the administrative law floor that he was familiar with. He opened the door to a conference room.

A mural covered the left wall: Shiva watching Vishnu transform himself into the enchantress Mohini. The right was a pixwall. The window wall stood directly opposite Carey. And in the center of the room, on the long conference table, sat Sirius, front legs outstretched, head lowered onto them as he stared out the window. Hearing Carey, he lifted his head and turned.

His face split in a doggy grin. "Carey!" he growled. "What a pleasure to see you."

Carey stepped closer to the table. A tight gray suit covered every centimeter of the dog's body. Beside him on the table was a hood of the same material.

"What are you doing here?" Carey asked.

"Enjoying the view," Sirius said. "This will make spectacular video, if any of the cameras survive."

"People are dead."

"Oh, I trust that most of the people who were in the amphitheater have taken refuge in the tower. I saw them streaming toward us. Are there a lot of them down there?"

"Not so many."

"And I suppose they've closed the doors by now, to preserve the air pressure. To help those suffering the unfortunate effects of decompression."

"No. They want to keep the doors open as long as possible. So that any last-minute stragglers aren't caught outside. It would take a lot of time for the pressure to drop to dangerous levels in here. Especially as the tram tunnels would bring air from the underground levels."

"So the tram station is still open? People are leaving?"

"Yes," Carey said. "By now the building is almost empty."

"You know, I find that rather unlikely. Why should they leave this pressurized refuge if they don't need to? Would you lie to me?"

Carey moved toward the window wall. He scanned its base. No sign of explosives.

"No," Carey said. "There's no point in lying to you. You're too smart."

"You wouldn't want to reconsider that offer, would you? The fact that you're a copy of the original Carey Evasson, though it might be a liability in some political careers, with proper handling can be turned to your advantage."

"I don't want a career in politics."

"Pity. So why don't you take a seat and we'll watch this spectacle together?"

Carey opened the cabinets along one wall. No sign of anything that might be a bomb. He needed to check the other rooms. The dog watched him.

Carey was about to leave when he noticed a discolored patch on the window. It looked like some sort of adhesive had been spread there. He stepped over to examine it.

When he reached out to touch it, his fingers stopped short. Something came between them and the glass. He pressed his palm flat against the object, then felt around it. Warm to the touch, it was roughly rectangular, maybe fifty by forty centimeters, fifteen thick. Carey slid his fingers under the edge of it, trying to pry it loose.

"So clever! Use those fingers, Carey! Those large, useful, ape fingers! Aren't they strong enough?"

Carey got a little purchase, and the thing slowly started to come away from the glass. If he could get to the elevator and ride up to the flight stage, he could throw it from the tower.

He heard the scuffle of nails against the tabletop a second before he felt Sirius's teeth in his shoulder. Claws raked his cheek, going for his eyes. Carey seized Sirius by his neck and tore him away, ripping his own shoulder open, and hurled the dog across the room.

Sirius twisted in the air, landed, bounced, and found his feet. The short fur on the back of his neck stood up. Fiercely grinning, he launched himself at Carey again.

Carey twisted backward toward the floor. As Sirius flew over him he swung his leg up and caught the dog on the side of his head. Carey bounced off his hands and back up again.

Sirius hit the edge of the table, recoiled, fell to the floor, and rolled. Before the dog could regain himself, Carey took a step and shot his foot into the dog's neck, crosswise. Sirius recoiled, bounced, and lay still. His sides rose and fell. His eyes were open, and his tongue twitched within his slightly opened mouth.

Returning to the window, Carey used all his strength trying to tear the bomb away. His shoulder hurt, and blood ran down his cheek. He pulled harder. The bomb began to come loose, then came away completely. It was quite dense. Carey tucked it under one arm and stepped toward the door.

Sirius lay, face turned toward Carey, some light still in his eyes. Faintly he growled, "Too late."

• • • • •

**From the Executive Summary, *Commission on the Society
of Cousins Dome Disaster* (aka *"The Fowler Report"*)**
The second explosion, blowing a hole in the side of the
Diana Tower, occurred fifty-three minutes after the first had
punctured the dome. By that time approximately eighteen

hundred people who had been caught by surprise at the Reform Party rally had taken shelter in the tower. Out under the dome a handful of rescue workers, wearing respirators and in some cases surface suits, were trying to save some last survivors. At least six hundred lay dead beneath the wreckage that had fallen from the dome, and approximately two hundred more pinned among the debris would die when the atmosphere was exhausted. Eventually their bodies would freeze, but they would be long dead before the temperature dropped to that level.

The emergency doors of the tunnels to the underground concourses throughout the colony had closed automatically when the pressure dropped to 0.6 atmospheres, approximately thirty minutes after the dome was punctured. Those people trapped in the tower, even if they had been able to make their way across the floor of the crater to one of these tunnels, would find themselves closed out.

The metro tunnels would have allowed them to move from the pressurized tower to the pressurized colony sublevels, but the tramway was equipped with its own automated pressure doors, and when, after the second explosion, the pressure in the tower dropped, these activated, sealing the tunnels off from the rest of the colony.

Outside the lobby window, the dead bird lay dusted with snow. Nothing moved out there now except a couple of emergency workers in surface suits.

Erno argued with the constable, a tall woman with broad shoulders and tattoos across the backs of both hands. He gestured toward the lobby windows. "Nobody can survive outside. If the tower loses its air, we'll have no escape."

"Calm down. The tower is built to hold pressure even if the dome fails."

"Someone could blow a hole in it even easier than blowing one in the dome." As Erno's voice rose people took notice of him. "There must be a couple of thousand refugees in here. We don't want to be trapped. We should move to the underground."

"The underground is closed off at the next stations," she said with some exasperation. She pointed her baton toward the women gathered near the information desk. "We're trying to get the system up and running again. But until then no one can get out of here. Now tell me what your friend went up there to do."

Erno tried to keep his temper in check. "He's trying to save our lives. We can still go down into the station, and if the building is compromised, seal it off. We can survive there until we can be rescued." Erno leaned on his lacerated leg and lost his balance, catching himself on the woman's shoulder.

The constable pulled back. "Control yourself."

"I'm sorry," Erno said. "I know this must—"

"Listen, I worked with your mother. I have no idea what you're up to, but I'm not going to take advice from the man who got her killed."

Erno ground his teeth. "Yes, I got her killed," he said. "That's no reason to let anyone else die."

"You need to sit down and shut up. You're upsetting people." Some others had come over to listen.

"Erno?" A woman's voice from behind him.

He turned. It was Mira. Her face was smeared with dust.

"Maybe you can explain to her," Erno said. "I think somebody's going to blow a hole in the tower. We'll be trapped. We need to get everyone down into the station."

Another constable came over with a woman dressed in civilian clothes. It was Krista Kayasdaughter. "What's the problem?"

Erno explained, urgent, keeping his voice low.

"Many of these people are injured," Kayasdaughter began. "Moving them—"

Then came the thud of an explosion, distant, and the building shuddered. The lobby's glass panels rattled in their frames. Outside, a rescue worker in a bright orange surface suit jerked his head upward. Another did the same, and then they both turned and leapt away from the building.

"What is it?" someone shouted. Others got to their feet. People put their hands to their ears, listening for news from their dead Aides.

Seconds later, falling glass and masonry began to hit the ground outside. A long metal strut landed end down, then slowly pitched toward the tower. The top gained speed, and people, screaming, backed away from the windows. The beam hit the reinforced glass and cracked it, but did not break through. A whistle of escaping air began.

Those on the floor near the windows scrambled back. A woman tried to pick up a boy whose video shirt showed the image of Carey in martial arts competition, above the words "Accept No Substitutes."

At the core of the building the doors to the stairwell slammed open and people surged out. An elevator car crashed; its doors burst open releasing clouds of acrid smoke. Seconds after the smoke billowed out, it was sucked back in and up the shaft. A breeze, developing into a gale, pulled the air in the room toward the elevators and the stairwell.

"Close those stairwell doors!" a constable shouted.

"There are people up there!" another said.

"The metro!" Kayasdaughter shouted. "Get everyone down into the station!"

In panic those people on the ground floor who could move rushed toward the broad archway and switchbacked ramp that led down to the station. Against the crowd, Erno forced himself toward the stairwell. He was knocked down, stepped on, and then Mira was by his side, helping him stand. She shouted in his ear, "Where are you going?"

"Up. I need to get up there." He lurched toward the stairs. He should have gone with Carey. He knew Sirius; Carey didn't.

The constable, her gray eyes determined, put her hand on his chest. "Get back! Get down to the station."

Mira tugged Erno's sleeve. "Let's go down. Help me look for Val Rozsson. I saw him at the amphitheater. He could be here."

Erno said, "Carey's on the forty-second floor."

Mira looked as if Erno had hit her. "No."

"Get back down, or get out of the way!" the constable said, pushing them with her baton. The whistling of the escaping air grew louder. "People are going to die. Let me save at least a few."

"What was he doing—" Mira said.

"Trying to stop this."

The constable turned to help an old woman cowering against the wall by the elevator banks. People still boiled out of the stairwell.

A klaxon sounded and above the archway to the metro station a yellow light began to flash.

"We have to go," Erno said.

Mira looked at the stairwell like a starving woman, then relented. "All right," she said.

She helped him walk. People were still coming down from upstairs. Mira and Erno made it through the archway beneath the deafening klaxon and down the ramp toward the platform. The automatic doors began to close before they had hit the bottom. Screams and pushing came from behind them, and Erno pitched down the ramp.

Mira clung to him and eventually the press of bodies lessened. They found a place to sit near the bottom, and leaned against each other. The klaxon continued for a few minutes, and then suddenly stopped in mid-alarm. In the echoing stillness it left, Erno heard the voices and crying of the people in the station.

He looked out over the platform. The Diana Tower station was the largest in the system. A gleaming wall mosaic depicted the dome on a sunny day, flyers soaring overhead, green fields, trees in the park, the blue of the pond, crater slopes covered with wildflowers. The dazed and wounded crowded the platforms and the stairs over the tracks.

Mira sat and stared hollowly at her shoes. Erno never should have allowed Carey to go up alone. They should have gotten help. But no, there was no time: Erno's failed efforts to get anyone to listen confirmed that they'd had no alternative. He wondered how many people were still in the tower, and whether there was any chance they could survive.

"We should look for Val," Erno told Mira. He put his hand on her shoulder and tried not to recoil from the despair and grief that flooded into him from her.

"Come on, Mira," he said, "let's look for Val."

Mira turned her face to him as if he were speaking some unknown language.

"Carey told me he was looking for Val," Erno said. "He asked me to help him, too."

"You know what Val looks like?" Mira said, dazed.

"I've seen him on video," Erno replied.

She got to her feet and they worked their way awkwardly through the people crowded on the platform. The pain in Erno's leg was great.

The faces of the people they passed showed shock and fear. They sat, patient as wounded animals. What talk Erno heard was low. Some weeping, some quiet sobs. Occasional voices raised in anger.

They looked up as Mira and Erno passed among them. A fog still veiled Mira's eyes. After ten minutes she pulled up and said, with more direction to her voice, "Let's split up. I'll try the other side."

She crossed over the stairs; Erno continued along the platform. A blond girl with her knees drawn up under her chin. A handsome man cradling his broken arm against his chest. Aid workers bandaging and giving painkillers to the injured. A group of schoolboys in the *One, or the Other?* shirts. A constable, eyes bleary, coughing repeatedly, a woman beside her giving her a sip from a bulb of water. Some of them recognized Erno, with surprise, with wonder, with distaste.

People had climbed down the maintenance steps from the overcrowded platform to the tunnel and found places to sit. Others struck off toward the next station, though they'd be stopped before they reached it by the emergency doors that had sealed.

Erno imagined what might have happened to Carey. He had taken on the task of saving the tower without hesitation or question. Erno didn't know for sure that Sirius—or Cyrus—was involved, but he still cursed himself for not acting. The time to have done something about this was before it happened. The fact that Sirius had brought camouflage wear with him should have tipped Erno off that something was seriously wrong.

In the middle of the platform, Kayasdaughter stood up and called at the top of her voice for their attention.

"We're going to be here awhile, until we can get in touch with someone outside and make clear the situation," she said. "Avoid unnecessary exertion, so that the air in here can last until we can be rescued. Help each other."

Erno made his way over the crowded pedestrian bridge to the other platform, only to meet Mira coming up the opposite stairs. "No luck," she said.

"Me either," Erno said. "But he could still be here."

There was no room to sit on the bridge. They descended to the platform, then down into the tunnel itself. It was relatively clean, lit by bioluminescents. Twenty meters or so along they found a place to sit. Erno's leg throbbed. His eyebrow itched, and when he touched it he felt dried blood. He was thirsty beyond words. Mira rested her arms across her flexed knees and lowered her forehead against them, her thatch of black hair flowing over her wrists. The tunnel smelled of sweat and regolith.

Erno sneezed. Mira lifted her head. "You look awful," she said.

"No doubt."

"How's your leg?"

"It'll be okay."

They sat in silence for a while.

"I can't believe he's dead," Mira said.

"He may not be. There could be some airtight rooms on the higher floors."

Another silence.

"What was he doing up there?"

"I sent him up to the SCOCOM offices. That was the likely place to set a second bomb. I think this was a false flag attack. The people who want to intervene will claim that SCOCOM was a target."

"They're coming," Mira said, not a question but a statement. "They offered him the chance to be the OLS governor, but they'll be just as happy he won't be around. He would have been a thorn in the side of whoever they get to do the filthy job."

"They'll find somebody."

"Whoever agrees will be the most hated person in Fowler."

Erno couldn't argue with that.

Mira laid her head back on her arms. Erno felt helpless to comfort her in the face of all this death.

For the first time all day he thought of Amestris. She would imagine him dead. He wished he could save her that anxiety. He wished they were at home together, in their bed. When he got back they had a lot of things to take care of. The genomes would save Sam's project—astonishing how trivial that seemed now, when it had been his sole reason for coming back to the Society.

But no, that wasn't true. He'd had a dozen other reasons to come back, some he'd felt, others he'd kept secret even from himself. Not much had gone right. He tried to anticipate what would happen next. Someone had to speak openly about the machinations within SCOCOM's investigation, about Cyrus and the IQSA, about Sirius's rage. About Carey's futile trip to the forty-second floor. About the little boy Erno had seen marching down the soccer pitch in the grip of some fantasy. What someone was there, other than he?

As Erno sat there, it came to him that he was not going to leave. He had never really left the Society, emotionally—the years of anger he'd carried with him from colony to colony had kept it alive in him— and he could not abandon it even now. He'd thought he would come back, get what he needed, maybe do a little good for the Cousins with SCOCOM, accept magnanimously their gratitude, and leave without looking back. Use the Society and get away. But he needed, for his own sense of self, to be here.

Even if they didn't want him. Maybe he could be of use to whoever had to deal with the foredoomed intervention. Amestris could help, if she would make the move with him. Maybe he could persuade her.

His thoughts had spun on in this way, slowly, more exhaustion than planning, really, when he was brought back by someone moving up the tunnel. Looking down the track, Erno saw a man coming their way. Long red hair, filthy with grime, and, when he drew closer and the light caught them, blue eyes. It was Val.

CHAPTER
FIFTEEN

IF MASCULINITY IS A PERFORMANCE, WHO
WROTE THE PLAY? WHO ARE THE ACTORS AND
WHO ARE THE AUDIENCE? AND WHAT HAPPENS
WHEN THE DRAMA'S OVER AND THE CURTAIN
FALLS?

—CAREY EVASSON, *Lune et l'autre*

A WEEK AFTER THE DISASTER, MIRA WAS WORKING
at a primary school that had been turned into a clinic for the injured.
Ebullism and gas embolisms were common, hemorrhages, and other
signs of barotrauma. Of people injured by falling debris, they had the
less serious cases. When this was over there was going to be a good
market for replacement limbs.

Public buildings were converted to living space for the thousands who had lost their homes. Mira had taken three survivors into her apartment: Tess Sabrinasdaughter had lost her partner, and Sabat Olgasdaugher and her son, Ryan, had shared an apartment with two other women now living in a temporary dorm. Mira was so numb, she did not care about having to stumble over strangers on her way to the bathroom.

At times she felt he was in the next room. Any minute now he would come in with a bulb of tea. She remembered his attempt at a comedy routine in the Oxygen Warehouse, mocking the idea of the untreated sociopath. The way he had looked at her, dismayed but unsurprised, when she'd lied about him at the hearing. His self-assurance, boyishness, sometimes insufferable ego. Her sheets still smelled of him, as did the old sweater he had given her. She wore it all the time, though it was absurdly large on her.

Four hours after the dome blowout a battalion of six hundred OLS peacekeepers had arrived by rocket from Apollo. To the patriarchs that might seem a nominal force, but to the Society it was overwhelming. OLS troops, sixty percent of them men, were everywhere in their black uniforms and body armor, carrying pulse rifles. Checkpoints had been established at every major pressure door in the colony.

The Lieutenant Colonel in charge, Ah Haitao, had set up headquarters in the tourist hotel, but plans were already underway to repair the Diana Tower and establish permanent OLS offices there. The tower had not suffered irreparable structural damage, and it was estimated that it could be repressurized within six weeks. The dome, it was feared, would take as long as eight months to repair.

Everything that had been alive within the crater was dead. Images of frozen trees and grass, dead animals, empty residences, offices, and schools, well lit but devoid of atmosphere, were burned into Mira's mind. Recovery of bodies continued; currently the toll of the dead and missing-presumed-dead had reached 2,532. Of these, seventy-seven had not been found or identified, among them Carey Evasson, SCOCOM representative Martin Beason, and the investigative reporter Carrollton's Sirius Alpha-Ultra vom Adler.

OLS investigators sought evidence to establish the perpetrator of the terrorist attack. Everyone thought it significant that the second bomb had been planted in the SCOCOM offices, but whether this indicated animus toward the OLS or that the OLS was the source of the explosion was hotly contested.

Video of Erno and Carey working together in the rubble saving people's lives was played all over the moon. Witnesses had seen them together in the tower. Erno had warned in advance of the explosion and tried to move people into the underground. To many, these facts made them heroes, while others were not so sure. How could Erno know there was going to be a second explosion? They pointed out that Erno had occupied constables while Carey ascended to the forty-second floor.

As Looker, Mira had undergone three days of questioning and was released. Forensics had shown that she was not responsible for the BYD Incident, and in the aftermath of the greater disaster, nobody cared what she did anymore. She could hardly care herself what she did, moving through the dry hours like some expert simulation of Mira Hannasdaughter.

In the middle of her day Mira left the school, through halls decorated with children's art, to take a break at the nearest refectory. She was drinking a cup of hot soup when Eva Maggiesdaughter sat down across the table from her.

"Hello," Eva said.

Eva's eyes were red, sunken. She looked ten years older than on the evening Mira, in a rage, had raced away from her home.

"Hello," said Mira. She didn't feel that rage anymore. She studied the older woman.

Eva scanned the crowded cafeteria. People looked like they had slept in their clothes, if they had slept at all. Two helmeted OLS peacekeepers stood at the entrance, rifles slung over their shoulders. One of them tried to chat with a young woman, who ignored him.

"All these displaced people," Eva said.

Eva's home was in vacuum. "Where are you living?"

"I'm with my sister and her children. She's not doing well. Her son is still missing."

Mira looked down at her hands. "I'm sorry."

"We lost Hector, too." Eva smiled ruefully. "Both versions of him. But there's more where he came from."

Eva's attempt to laugh crumpled and they were quiet for a moment.

"How is Val?" Mira asked.

"He's hurting. Roz, too. I need to thank you for finding him and keeping him safe."

"But I didn't save Carey." Mira's voice caught in her throat. "You know that he had nothing to do with this. Carey was trying to stop it, not cause it."

"He was a hero," Eva said, a certain bitterness in her voice. "Another story for men." She gazed at the tables of Cousins tallying their losses, figuring their prospects. "It doesn't matter. The patriarchies were bound to force their way into the Society."

Eva sounded so rational, passing over Carey's death as if it were another item to be ticked off on a checklist of political consequences.

"The Society's over. People like me—Looker"—Mira said the name with contempt—"made it easier for them. We gave them a pretext."

"It's not over yet."

Mira warmed her hands around her cup. "Seems over to me."

"We have to do what women have had to do throughout history," Eva said. "We'll have to be subversive. We've established a system of values, myths, songs, art, stories, games, jokes. An army can't defeat a song. We have to keep these things alive, and when the time comes, they'll burst forth and blow all their power away like smoke."

"I don't know if I can believe that," Mira said.

Eva rubbed her temples with thumb and forefinger, then laid her hands limply on the table in front of her. "To tell you the truth, I don't know if I can either."

"Carey's dead," said Mira.

Eva stared at her hands.

"It's just a habit with me, Mira, to be the rational Matron." In the low buzz of conversations and the clink of silverware, her voice was hard to make out. "Sometimes I hate that woman. It's a weakness, not a strength. That's me. And Carey's dead."

Mira saw the grief in Eva's face, and it was more than she could take. "I loved him," she said. "I finally figured out how to do that."

"He loved you, too."

"And now he's gone."

It all came down on Mira then, the weight of the things she had done and not done, her mistakes, things she'd said to Carey and that he had said to her, her petty jealousies, her desires true and foolish, the fundamental unfairness of the universe. Images of her mother, Marco, Carey. The tears came, and once they started she could not hold them back.

Eva reached out to touch Mira's wrist. Through her tears Mira noticed, for the first time, that Eva's fingers were Carey's fingers, strong and blunt.

"I came here telling myself that it was to help you," Eva said. "I thought I was strong enough to bear all of this. But you could help me. I need you to help me. Will you become a Green?"

Mira avoided Eva's eyes. The soldier had given up trying to flirt with the woman. In the food line, two inappropriately rowdy teenaged girls poked at each other, bouncing on their toes, nervous with the energy of youth. Behind them, an old man scowled. Mira turned back to Eva.

"Yes," she said.

• • • • •

The light from Erno's helmet glinted on something in the frozen grass. He crouched, his leg protesting. A medallion. He held it on his gloved fingertips and let the light play over its surface. The enameled disk bore the image of a woman in Roman dress wearing a crescent moon crown, driving a chariot, bow slung over her shoulder.

"What's that?" Li's voice sounded in his ears.

Li was at his shoulder. Erno held the medallion out to him. "The Goddess."

"Oh," Li said, interest evaporated. He turned back to the OLS forensics team.

Erno slipped the medallion into his belt pouch and rejoined the others touring the destruction. Each footstep he took on the dead grass snapped off blades frozen stiff as crystal. The damaged sky was turned off, leaving the crater in profound darkness. In the airless space, the shadows thrown by their lights were stark. Places he had grown familiar with as a boy now stood lifeless, colors washed out in a deserted underground world like the ruins of some ancient civilization. Troy after the sack by the Achaeans, Machu Picchu four hundred years after the conquest.

Near the path to the tower his light swept over a set of broken orange wings, pinned to the ground by a fallen dome strut. A dead flyer, a young man, remained strapped into his harness, a frozen smear of blood across a tear in his neck. Erno hurried to catch up with the others.

One of the OLS soldiers accompanying them shone a powerful spotlight up the side of the tower to the place where the blast had blown open its side.

"From the looks of that, and the debris pattern, I'd say the charge was planted on the inside," the leader of the forensics team said.

"I agree," said another.

They entered through the lobby. A dust of frozen water vapor, already scuffed with bootprints, covered the floor; Erno was surprised that it had not sublimed away. They crossed the lobby and ascended the stairs. No one spoke. Erno listened to the sounds of their breathing over his phones, followed the jerking of light and shadow from their helmet lamps. The stairwell, encased in the building's core, was intact all the way up to the thirty-eighth floor. There they found the railing twisted and the walls of the elevator shaft blown out. The rooms of the thirty-eighth through forty-fifth floors above them were exposed like cells of a honeycomb. As their lights played over the broken walls, Erno saw a desk listing halfway into space where the floor had fallen away beneath it. Charred cabinets, a picture hanging sideways, floor tiles, tablets, drink bulbs, and debris everywhere; exposed plumbing and wiring.

Previous investigators had rigged a temporary bridge from the stairwell to the forty-second floor. One at time the party climbed up to the SCOCOM offices.

"Careful where you step here," the chief investigator said.

The interior walls on the east side had been blown to flinders. Some warped structural members still stood between the floor and ceiling. Beyond, all that remained of furniture and office equipment were fragments scattered against the remaining walls.

Neither Sirius nor Beason had been seen since the day of the disaster. It was assumed Beason had been in the SCOCOM offices when the second explosion occurred, but nobody knew for a fact. Erno maintained that Sirius and Carey had both been there.

That left Göttsch, Li, and himself to file the final report to the OLS. Though the intervention of troops had superseded their deliberations, the report was still necessary to justify any further action. Erno argued for an intervention of minimum duration. He wanted Sirius's role in this—and Cyrus's, if it could be proven—exposed.

Erno's sending Carey up alone to face Sirius was something for which he had no remedy. He told himself that with his injuries he would have been useless. Carey was the hero type and Erno was the beta male, not the confrontational leader. Erno had watched one of the videos people were making so much of, showing him and Carey working to help those buried in the amphitheater; after three minutes he decided he would never need to see it again.

When they turned their lights toward the exterior, they saw where the glass wall of the tower had been completely blown out, but the floor and ceiling were intact. Beyond the lip of the floor, their lights disappeared in the yawning blackness of the crater's interior.

The lead investigator ventured near the clifflike edge, illuminating the floor and ceiling. "Blasted outward," he said. "Would you concur?"

"Yes," Göttsch said. "This isn't probative of any particular theory of the agents involved."

"The bomb must have been planted inside the elevator shaft,

perhaps in one of the elevator cars. A lucky thing. If the blast had occurred here, the decompression in the tower would have been instantaneous."

"Perhaps whoever did it had no access to the offices."

"Sirius had complete access," Erno said. "Carey must have found the bomb and moved it away from the outside to the elevator. He saved a lot of people."

"We are familiar with your theories," Göttsch said. "We don't know that Sirius was even here. Let the team do their work."

"They'll need to do it fast," Li said. "Colonel Ah wants the building repressurized as soon as possible. They're going to start cleaning this place out tomorrow."

"That's not enough time to complete an investigation," the forensics man said.

"You'll have to speak to the Colonel about that."

Erno turned back toward the interior and poked gingerly through the fragments of material against the remaining walls. He was just thinking that they'd have to microanalyze to determine whether any human remains were mixed with this debris, when he nudged a scrap of metal and his light fell on what he thought was a sliver of bone, a centimeter long, with a bit of frozen brown flesh attached to one end.

He crouched for a moment, wincing at the pain in his knee, and listened to the voices of the others over the common circuit. He didn't touch the bone. He felt his breath draw in and out; he imagined he could hear the steady pulse of his heart in his throat. It could be

Beason. It could be Sirius. It could be Carey. A DNA test would tell them.

He brought one of the forensics people over to what he'd found. The man became quite excited and summoned his colleagues. Meticulously they took samples and recorded microvisuals with special cameras. They speculated but drew no conclusions.

Erno told them he was going back to the hotel. They sent an OLS soldier along with him. Erno and the solider, a taciturn man of about his own age from New Guangzhou, made their slow way down, then across the crater floor to the emergency airlock that had been erected near the entrance to East Seven. As he removed his helmet, Erno took care not to disturb the dressing on his forehead. The wound there would leave a scar that could be erased cosmetically, but Erno was thinking of keeping it. His knee throbbed. He had torn the meniscus; a simple nanosurgery would repair it but he had not taken the time to do anything yet.

The hotel was crowded with OLS officials. The troops had taken over a men's dorm in this sector, but the officers were all here. Emergency workers from the OLS humanitarian agencies bustled about the lobby. Erno went up to his room, hung the Diana medallion he'd found from the light stand over his desk, and set to work on his statement for the SCOCOM report. Although intervention was a *fait accompli*, Erno was determined to see that the report included his observations of Sirius's machinations.

An hour later one of the staff came to his room. "There's someone here to see you," the man said.

"I'm working," Erno said.

"I think you'll want to see her."

Erno went out to the suite's lounge. The OLS security man who usually sat watching videos in the living room was not there. Instead, standing in the center of the room was Amestris.

"Hello," she said.

Erno stood there, quite shocked. She wore a traveling suit, her hair done up under a shawl. "I couldn't wait until you returned, and so I spoke—"

"Don't explain," he said, and embraced her. He held her tightly, his eyes closed. He smelled her hair. Her warm breath brushed his neck.

At last he let her go.

She touched the bandage on his head. "You look tired. Your eyes are bloodshot."

"Why didn't you tell me you were coming?"

"Would you have wanted me to come?"

"No." He kissed her. He sighed. "Yes. Come with me."

He led her back to his room. They lay on the bed and talked, and then they didn't talk at all for some time. Erno had not realized how much he had missed her. She kissed his forehead. Erno felt more peace of mind than he had in weeks. How had she managed to get here? It was a miracle, but not a miracle. "Your father sent you."

"He didn't send me," Amestris said. "I came with him."

"He's here?"

"Yes. I needed to see you. I needed to touch you again." She paused. "I don't want us to live in Persepolis."

Erno's hand rested on her shoulder. He perceived her anxiety, and something else—hope?

"The OLS is going to open up the Society," Amestris said. "They'll allow investments, free enterprise. I think we should move EED to Fowler."

It was not what he'd expected. He'd been steeling himself to explain to her how he felt he needed to stay in the Society despite his estrangement from it. Now she was offering to give it to him without his having to appeal. It unbalanced him.

"This place is crippled," he said. "It's going to be a long time before it's a functioning society again. There will be unrest and conflict for years. Plus, you don't know how people live here, what it's like."

"I want to be a part of the Society if there's a place for me."

"There may not be a Society anymore. Plus, it's dead boring. You're going to miss the stores and theaters."

"We can visit Persepolis now and then."

"After your father gets through with Fowler, I'm not sure Eskander is a name that will be popular around here."

"We'll work to make a place for ourselves. Unless you can't stand it here and need to escape."

Erno shook his head. "No, I want to stay, too."

They talked for an hour, had something to eat, and talked still further into the night. He told her his story of the disaster. To have

Amestris here, to be able to touch her, hear her voice, see her move, was almost more than he could fathom. It made him very happy. Only gradually did it come to Erno that Amestris wanted to live here as much for her own reasons as to be with him. When he touched her he could feel her fear that he might realize it.

It was a blow, but not as much as he might have imagined. At least she wanted to be here.

The next morning her father joined them for breakfast. After they'd finished, Cyrus said, "Amestris, my dear, I would like to speak with Erno in private. Do you mind stepping out for a while?"

"Not at all." Erno watched her as she got up and walked out of the suite, cool as a shadow.

Too many people were dead for them to play games. "What do you want?"

Cyrus folded his serviette and placed it beside his plate. "I want to talk to you about the future of the Society. Specifically, I want to discuss with you the possibility of your taking on the job of OLS administrator of the interim government."

Erno almost laughed out loud. "Are you joking?"

"I do not believe so, no."

"I have no experience of government. I—"

"You have run a successful business. You have lived in a dozen different lunar colonies. You have served the OLS as a SCOCOM investigator. And most significantly, you were born and raised in the Society of Cousins."

"I'm a traitor to the Society."

"You're an agent of change," Cyrus said. "People saw you rescuing the injured, they heard you talk about how people outside the Society of Cousins looked to it for hope. They know you urged those in the tower to take refuge in the underground station before the second blast."

"I didn't get to give the warning about your intentions that I was going to give."

"That's unfortunate. It would have served you well to have gotten that on the record."

"You should know, if I have any say in the matter, you will be arrested for mass murder."

Cyrus looked as calm as gravity. "You do me a grave injustice."

"You sent Sirius here to do your work."

"I did not send him here to kill anyone."

"You must have known that he was insane."

"That is a terribly humanist thing to say. Sirius was a dog. His motives did not always translate into human terms."

Erno did not need to argue. He needed to write down what he knew, and the more he told Cyrus, the more Cyrus would be prepared to thwart him. "Why are you asking me?"

"Carey Evasson was asked to be the administrator of the protectorate the OLS will establish here. He would have been ideal for that job. Now we have to find someone else. You are my son-in-law. I know you care about the Society of Cousins. I think you might be our best choice."

"It's not your choice to make. Besides, I'm too young for this job."

"In a new beginning, youth is a good thing. The person to take on this responsibility needs to be a Cousin. But it can't be someone who has ever held public office in the Society. The OLS wants a completely new administration."

"That will make for a very inexperienced government. You're throwing away expertise, institutional memory, continuity. It will be a mess."

"Perhaps at first things will not run as efficiently as they might. That's unavoidable."

"You don't need me. You need a woman, for one thing. Appoint Hypatia Camillesdaughter. She's never held political office, and she's been vocal in opposition to the Matrons. I'm sure she would leap at the opportunity."

"For OLS—and my own—purposes, it should be a man. The man I want is you."

"No, thank you."

"If not you, then Thomas Marysson."

"Not that again. You used him to get me onto SCOCOM. Is he the only argument you've got?"

"I have the argument that you care about the Society of Cousins and do not want to see it destroyed. Make no mistake, there will be changes. Even if you take this job, you will not be able to prevent all of them.

"But you can prevent some, perhaps. You can see that the changes are made in the least disruptive way. You can integrate them into the existing social structure, as much as possible. You may seek advice from Cousins: There will be a Board of Citizens, and a Majlis. You have ideas, I know. You are a man who senses another's soul. The Society will be well served by your good intentions."

Erno thought about it. Hadn't he spent most of his youth complaining about the people who ran the world? Cyrus clearly thought he could manipulate Erno, but Erno knew the Society in a way that Cyrus never could. He could seek the opinions of the Matrons and make sure that their vision was not obliterated. He could protect the most vulnerable and ensure some semblance of justice.

It all depended on how far he could trust Cyrus.

"That story you told me about Bahrâm Gur," Erno said. "You're asking me to take the role of the new headman appointed to rule the disobedient village. As if I will act as your factotum, only in your interests. Which I will not do."

"I would not expect otherwise. The history of Persia is the history of kings in conflict with their most powerful champions."

"You're not a king, and I would never be your champion."

Cyrus inclined his head. "I stand corrected."

It would be a test of Erno's character, the most difficult test he could imagine, and he seriously doubted that he was up to it. He was not a leader. He was the one who muttered sarcastic comments in the back of the room while the leader was doing serious things up in the front.

"I'll need to have the power to appoint administrators," Erno said. "To appoint judges."

"With some consultation, yes."

"I want this in writing."

"The duties and powers of the administrator will be laid out in all specifics."

"Amestris will move here. We'll live here permanently. We will not associate with you. I will make it clearly understood, publicly, that we are not working for you—rather the opposite."

"I agree that this will be the best way to go forward," Cyrus said.

Erno held out his left hand. "Shake my hand."

Cyrus looked at it, looked Erno in the eyes, then took it in his own. Thirty-six degrees centigrade.

"You'll follow through on all of these things?" Erno said.

"I will," Cyrus said.

Nothing but sincerity. Erno let go of his hand.

"So, you will take on this difficult work?" Cyrus asked.

"Yes," Erno said.

THIRTY

YEARS

LATER

CHAPTER

SIXTEEN

THE PASSENGERS ON THE MORNING ROCKET FROM Mayer were tourists, businessmen, some OLS bureaucrats, university students on exchange programs, a group of musicians from Linne, and a few Fowler residents returning from vacations on Earth. Erno went directly to his assigned first class compartment.

He took two serentol and opened the book of poems he'd been reading.

> *What is the price of Experience? Do men buy it for a song*
> *Or wisdom for a dance in the street? No, it is bought with*
> *the price*

Of all that a man hath, his house his wife his children
Wisdom is sold in the desolate market where none come
to buy
And in the withered field where the farmer plows for
bread in vain

A family came into the compartment and took their seats: man, woman, daughter. The daughter was about twelve and sat across from Erno next to her mother, while the man settled into the acceleration chair beside Erno. The man fussed with his straps, asked his wife and daughter if they had theirs secure, then, lying back in the chair, had a good look at Erno. He did an almost comic double take.

The man twisted against the straps to hold out his hand. "Akira Forbush, sir."

Erno looked at the man's hand. He took it, gave it a firm shake. The impression flooded into him that Akira Forbush was a vain man who thought himself honest, so caught up in his own view of things that he was incapable of imagining another. "My wife, Helen, daughter Yuriko," Forbush said. "It's an honor to meet you."

"Thank you," Erno said, returning to his book. Without encouragement perhaps the man might leave him alone.

"Where are you returning from, Administrator Pamelasson?" Forbush asked.

"Please, just Pamson. I had some business to attend to in Mayer."

"Representing Fowler?"

"No, as a private citizen."

"Eskander Design," his wife said. "You did the Mayer environmental reboot. The birds! We grew up in Mayer."

"We market treehouses," Forbush said. "Sylvan Homes."

"Yes, of course," Erno said. "I've seen your work."

"You're getting back in time for the ceremony?" Forbush asked. "They're expecting protests."

"I think it's a good thing to let people air their grievances," Erno said.

Helen said, "We thought these matters were settled twenty years ago, or we would never have moved to Fowler."

They didn't want to hear a different opinion, but lately Erno had been having trouble maintaining his equanimity. "We had conflict back then, too."

"But you put them down when they got restive," Forbush said. "Like the Alisonsdaughter Rape protests."

"There was considerable debate within the administration whether that was the right course of action."

"In a situation like this, it doesn't do to equivocate," Helen said.

Forbush gave Erno a look twenty degrees cooler than he had in the beginning. "Equivocation is the politician's stock-in-trade," he said to his wife.

Erno was saved—all of them were saved—by announcement of the takeoff sequence. The screen above them switched to a view of the ship's berth. Then the rocket launched and acceleration pressed them down into their couches. After only a few minutes the engines cut out and they were in free fall. A shallow trajectory, twenty minutes of zero gravity, then deceleration.

"I feel sick," the girl said.

Her mother pulled an inhaler from her carryall and made the girl take a sniff. Erno turned off his book and closed his eyes. He let his hand, his damned stolen left hand, float above his chest and listened to the mother's low voice distracting the girl with talk of the live music they had planted in her grandmother's apartment and how much more developed it would be the next time they visited.

Erno's attempts over the years to track down Alois Reuther had been futile. He'd searched multiple colony records. He'd obtained lists of indigents consigned to the freezers in eight colonies. He'd called in favors from OLS immigration monitors. He'd leaned on business associates and clients in other colonies. In the end he'd traveled to Mayer in person, not so much because he hoped to find out anything he had not discovered otherwise, but to reconnect with the boy he'd been forty years ago.

The Hotel Gijon had been transformed into luxury condos. He could not visit the room where he had lived while there, nor Alois's suite, as walls had been torn out and completely reconstructed. He spent an uneasy half an hour in the home of a commodities broker and her family, sitting on an expensive sofa that must have been more or less where his gel mat had lain. While his gracious hosts asked him about Fowler's politics, he looked at the white wall opposite him and imagined the stuttering eagle soaring over terrestrial mountains. In the hallway outside he flashed on the feel of Alois's hand on his chest.

He went down to the Café Seville, which had managed to make itself over as quaint instead of shabby. He sat on the fresh tiles of the patio and watched the *flaneurs* saunter down the street as he drank a demitasse of strong coffee. The Mayer air was clean, thanks to the environmental redesign he and Amestris had supervised. He inhaled slowly, and let it out.

After a while he got up and inspected the alley where he had found Alois's hand. It was much as it had been forty years earlier. There was nothing to see, but when he closed his eyes the image of Alois lying on the settlement agent's cart, handless arm hanging off the side, rose before him. These images were coming to him more and more. He fantasized going back into the café and borrowing a cleaver to cut off the hand and throw it into the back of the alley, freeing himself of it and its suggestions, reminders, memories.

He'd thought the hand would be an asset in his political career. It would tell him if someone was lying. He would sense their moods, what they wanted and did not want, and be able to manipulate them. He'd leaned on that ability. It hadn't proved to be as useful as he had thought.

Eventually, every time he touched someone, a sense of that person's soul washed over him. But knowing another's soul didn't mean you could make them do what you wanted. Some opposed him simply because of that deformed character he was now so accurately reading.

The inestimable advantage became a source of anxiety. He wondered if this might just be some mental disorder that he was generating from his own need to know what others were thinking. It became a burden, a torment that made him reluctant to touch anyone.

Following the career of a politician when you had no real aptitude for it might threaten to produce tragedy, but most of what eventuated was farce.

"Passengers please prepare for deceleration," the transport announced. Erno opened his eyes. Helen Forbush gathered in the floating tablet tethered to her daughter's wrist and slid it into her carry-all. On the screen above them the rugged surface of farside passed below, harsh sun throwing solid black shadows. Deceleration began. The transport vibrated with the force of the jets and gravity returned. Twenty minutes later, an hour after they'd left Mayer, it landed in Fowler Port.

Erno retrieved his bag, cleared customs, and caught the train from the spaceport to the colony. The Forbushes were in the same car, along with a tour group. As the train swooped up the crater exterior before entering the tunnel to the colony, they had a good look back at the gleaming spaceport, constructed during Erno's second term as head of the OLS Provisional Authority. He knew every detail of the graft and corruption involved. Still, it was beautiful.

At the station Erno told his bag to follow him and walked out to the tram platform. In the pull-up outside the entrance, a private vehicle awaited the Forbushes, but Erno insisted on using public transit.

Forbush gave Erno a sideways glance as his family climbed into the car while Erno waited on the platform.

The leader of the tour group assembled his party at the scenic overlook at the back of the tram platform. Above them stretched the bright blue sky, faux sunlight broken by puffy white clouds; below lay the expanse of the crater interior. Standing on the pavement while his charges milled around taking videos, the tour leader launched into his spiel.

"Welcome to Fowler, home of the notorious Society of Cousins, site of the largest-grossing romance in the history of the solar system, Julianna Bennet's *Sunlight or Rock*. We are standing within the largest hard-domed crater on the moon. This crater, which is not properly the crater Fowler but a much smaller, symmetrical impact crater within Fowler proper, was domed in the year 2085, twenty-two years after the emigration of the Society of Cousins from California, on Earth, in 2063."

The tourists looked out over the landscape. Since the rebuild, its floor had been turned over to luxury residences and office buildings. Huge residential tree homes with human-integrated architectural additions sprawled over most of the land that had once grown food crops. But Sobieski Park was still there and the Diana Tower still rose from its center.

"Over on the western slope you'll see the ruins of the Men's House, where Dirk Taylorsson made his deadly vow in Bennet's tale of star-crossed love. To the south, on that little rise, stands the Temple of

Diana, damaged in the dome breach of 2149, scene of Naswalla West's forbidden tryst with Scarlett Sapphosdaughter. Goddess worship is still practiced among the citizens; almost fifty percent of the current population still self-designate as 'Cousins.'

"What you see looking out over this landscape today differs in some ways from the setting of the novel, in the days when the Amazon-led Board of Matrons ruled over a population of aggressive women, complaisant males, and downtrodden persons of variable gender. If you turn on your augmentation you may superimpose images of that time over your visual field. I remind you, if you do so, to watch your step. For those of you so inclined, Experience Travel can provide a VR tour of the Society as it existed before the OLS intervention, during which you may interact sexually and otherwise with Scarlett, Naswalla, Dirk, the Matron Elainesdaughter, and all the other characters we have come to know and love."

The serentol had worn off and Erno could not wait to get home. When the tram arrived the tourists piled in. Their leader chatted with them about the upcoming memorial ceremonies marking the thirtieth anniversary of the dome disaster.

Erno got off at the university stop. Across from the station a Faravahar mosaic lifted its wings above the entrance of the Zoroastrian temple. He walked down the crater slope to his neighborhood, his bag following behind him.

The home where he and Amestris had lived for the last twenty years was more luxurious than any that had existed in the Society when he was growing up. They had two bedrooms, separate studies, a fully equipped kitchen, a dining room, and a large living room with a balcony. A Kazedi grand, sleek and black as obsidian, dominated the living room.

Erno sent his bag to the bedroom to unpack itself, set some clarity tea brewing, opened the doors to the balcony to let in the air, and stood looking out over the lushly wooded neighborhood. The single-family homes here were more widely separated than any that had existed before the reformation. His and Amestris's was one of the more modest ones, but it still was well beyond where anyone had lived while the Board of Matrons ruled.

Thinking of this did not steady Erno.

When the tea was done he took it into his study. It brightened him, and his mind flitted from thought to thought. At his desk he tried to work on the speech he would give at the memorial ceremony in three days. So far he had a sentence:

> When preserving the status quo becomes the sole *raison d'être* of a society, then change becomes treason.

An hour later he still had only the one sentence. The tea didn't clarify anything. Whose status quo was he talking about? The Society before the reformation? Or the Society as it was today? He had no answers. What did he have to say about the disaster that anyone needed to hear? Could he repudiate his entire career? Would anyone believe him? Would anyone care?

He leaned way back in his chair, laced his hands behind his head, and stared up at the ceiling. He didn't think about anything for a while.

Renewalists would be holding a counter-ceremony, and protesters would be at the memorial. The colony was in a ferment it had not seen in decades. Young people everywhere were disgusted with the way things were. The Renewalists had a slate of constitutional amendments they propounded to restore some laws to their Cousins state. They called the Matrons era a utopia in comparison to the Society under the new constitution. He could not argue with them.

Every person Erno touched was restive.

Maybe if he could talk to the Renewal organizers. He changed clothes. He got out a casual jacket, nice but nothing excessive. Lemmy might be at the meeting; he was one of Renewal leaders. Erno finished his tea and took two more serentol before he left. He'd used serentol a lot back when he was in the legislature; it took the edge off his anger and let him listen more than he was able to otherwise. He used it too much.

Erno set off across the floor of the crater. Late afternoon sunshine threw green shadows of the trees onto the path, reminding him of his walk thirty years before through Lemmy's test forest that had made so much money for the people who had stolen it—that had made so much money for *Erno*—and created Kazedi Woods in Persepolis. Amestris had been in Persepolis with Sam for the last month. Erno considered calling her, but he did not want to call her: He wanted her to call him. In truth, despite the fact that they had not spoken for a week, he had nothing to say to her.

He wondered if Amestris had visited Cyrus. At the age of eighty Cyrus had begun to show symptoms of incurable neo-Alzheimer's. He'd had the foresight to have himself scanned when he first obtained the IQSA. Once he understood the inevitable decline he faced from the disease, he had a magpie implanted in his brain to record his experiences. He left instructions that when the Alzheimer's had progressed to the point where he could not function, a new Cyrus should be created from the scan and the recordings used to bring that new version of himself up to date on what had happened to him in the decade since the scan.

Unfortunately, the new Cyrus had not really experienced that decade, and the recordings were a pale shadow of the life Cyrus had lived, so his new version's ability to integrate with the ten-years-advanced world he'd been thrust into was imperfect. Worse, the new Cyrus was subject to the same decline, so after another ten years he had to repeat the process. Twice now the increasingly demented Cyrus had been hidden away in a private care facility and replaced by a younger version.

Each time he did this, he lost more of himself. Gradually, Cyrus's influence had leached away. The Eskander family and his business associates were increasingly unhappy to be ruled over by this poorly functioning simulacrum of the Shah of Ice, with his spotty memory and ignorance of the contemporary world. Eventually day-to-day control of his commercial empire was taken out of his hands.

The original Cyrus, over a hundred years old now, did not know who he was and could neither feed nor bathe himself. The first duplicate, ninety-one, was in a room next to the first. Rumor had it that the current Cyrus was failing, and Erno didn't know whether Afroza would bother to repeat the resurrection yet again.

Amestris seldom visited him. Yet there she was in Persepolis again, while Erno was here.

Erno wobbled a little as he walked along the greenway. He told himself it was not the drugs, but dizziness from that morning's episode of zero-G. The path wound its way through the woods, crowded with parents and children, young people on rollers, cyclists, couples walking.

Eventually he came to the far side of the crater and climbed the slope to the home of Eva Maggiesdaughter, where Carey Evasson had grown up, almost a shrine to the Cousins family. He hesitated at its doorstep.

With the serentol, the tea, his fatigue, the confusion weightlessness had brought to his inner ears, and his climb up the crater, he felt woozy. He stood up straight and knocked on the door.

●　●　●　●　●

After saving the final version of the vid she'd made for the counter-memorial, Mira lingered at her editor. Frozen on the screen was an image from the hours of video that camera midges had recorded on the day of the dome disaster: Carey and Erno attempting to lift a sheet of titanium while an emergency worker crouched to pull out the person trapped beneath.

Carey's long hair, dusty with gray powder, has come undone and fallen over his forehead. His lips are slightly parted, almost a grin. Shoulders tense, he is in complete control of his body, doing what he needs to do.

In making her vid she'd used no images of Carey, but it had been impossible to avoid him in the raw footage. She couldn't help studying them. How young he looked. He had been ten years older than Mira, and now Mira was nineteen years older than he was on that day he died. She'd learned not to spend much time looking back and it had served her well, but for a moment she wondered what that Carey would think if he saw her today. A pillar of the family. A responsible person, the crazy part of her no longer on public display.

The point of the counter-memorial was to look forward: The Renewalists sought to bring the Society that had existed before the takeover into the future. They treated the intervening thirty years as a series of mistakes. Mira thought the ones born since that day, who had no memory of the Society as it had been, had idealized it. But they were right to use the past as a rallying cry, and she and the Green family were doing what they could to support them.

Roz stuck her head into the editing room. "They'll be here soon. Come out and eat something."

Then Roz noticed the image on the screen. She toggled on the room lights. "Too much time in the dark."

Mira smiled at her. "More light!" she said.

She turned off the pixwall and followed Roz out to the kitchen.

They had some gazpacho and talked about the meeting. Mira and Roz had offered the Green home as the site for the Renewalists to prepare their counter-memorial. Most of the family was out or at work, but as a director of Darkside Materials & Fabrication, Roz could take the time off, and Mira worked out of their home.

By the time they'd finished eating, the organizers started showing up. First Harald Smithsson and Greta Barbarasdaughter, married to each other in the kind of two-person union that the OLS had tried to make the norm. Strozzi Palmyra, an immigrant from Tycho. Alessandra Sofiasdaughter. All of them under forty. The last to arrive was Lemmy Odillesson, at one hundred and five a generation older than Roz and Mira.

They gathered around the big table out on the terrace, afternoon sunlight throwing shadows of trees across their faces. A light breeze rustled the leaves.

Mira showed them her video, *A Brief History of Anger*, and talked about the installations she had arranged. They discussed the order of speakers, the music, the expected turnout. They reviewed their precautions to keep the event peaceful and the contingencies in case the police tried to provoke trouble.

For the most part Roz and Mira kept quiet. The younger people liked having them around—Roz was a highly placed executive and Mira well known for the Fowler Project, which had preserved much of the cultural heritage of the Society. They brought with them the cachet of having worked with Eva. Lemmy, who over the last thirty years had parlayed his knowledge of biotech into prominence as an opposition leader, received the younger organizers' deference for his legendary persistence.

The afternoon was fading and Mira was in the kitchen getting something to drink when there was a knock at the front door. She detoured to the entryway and opened it. On the doorstep stood Erno Pamelasson.

Taken aback, she said, "Well, this is a surprise."

"May I come in?" His eyes were guarded. He was dressed in an expensive jacket of natural fibers, and he shifted awkwardly from foot to foot. He'd aged pretty well considering the toll his career had taken, but he looked tired.

She opened the door wider and ushered him into the living room. Strozzi sat in one of the chairs there. The others, out on the terrace, looked up with expressions of astonishment.

"You know Harald Smithsson and Greta Barbarasdaughter?" Mira said.

"We haven't met in person," Erno said.

"This is Betty, this is Alessandra, this is Strozzi."

"Good afternoon, Administrator," Harald said.

"Hello, Erno," Lemmy said.

Erno brightened. "Hello, Lemmy," he said. "It's been a while. Good to see you. Have you seen that latest on the subtropical ecology they're planning for Rima—"

"What brings you here?" Greta asked.

Erno stood uncertainly. Mira realized that he was lifted. She gestured to an empty chair, and he sat. "I'll be brief. You may know that I'm scheduled to speak at the memorial. I would like to speak out on behalf of your movement."

"You aren't a part of our movement," Greta said. "Quite the opposite, in fact."

"What exactly do you expect to say?" Alessandra asked.

"I was thinking I might finish the speech I started to give at the Reform Party rally thirty years ago, that day everything came crashing down. I was going to speak out in defense of the Society and against intervention by the OLS. I was going to say that the injustices that existed here didn't warrant the destruction of a way of life that gave people less exploitation than I had lived through over my ten years in the other colonies."

"It's too bad you ignored all that when you took over," Harald said.

Erno took it without protest. "I made many mistakes. But I'm here to offer you any help I can give. I know that the current administration is not well disposed toward you. I don't have as much influence as you might imagine, but I do know some people in the First Minister's office and in the legislature. I offer my name."

"Your name," Greta said.

"You think your name would help us?" Strozzi asked.

"Well, I—"

"We know of your efforts," Greta said. "But we don't want you to speak."

"I was there on that day. I've never wavered in my public opinion that no Cousins were behind the disaster. It was an outside job."

Lemmy spoke up. "The people who support us know that, Erno. The people who don't know that won't support us."

"I can't help?"

"Certainly you can't speak for us," Greta said. "I'd prefer, actually, if you didn't even come out in support, Mr. Administrator. We're trying to create a new movement here, without any obligation to the past."

"But what you want is to restore the Society to what it was intended to be. From the time I was a boy, that's what I've wanted. I may not always have been able to do what I wanted, and sometimes my judgment was bad, but I've spent most of my life trying."

Betty laughed. "That's not the general perception of your career."

"You sold off the public enterprises," Strozzi said. "You built a freezer system."

"You were a functionary for repression," Alessandra said.

"That's really not fair. I prevented the abolition of Cousins marriage. I—"

Strozzi shook his head. "It doesn't matter what you did or didn't do. You can't understand us. You'll say things we don't believe."

"When you were sixteen you were a radical," Alessandra said. "How old are you now?"

Erno looked at Mira. "I'm the same age as Mira—fifty-eight."

No one said anything. The daylight beyond the lanai had gone, and Roz turned on the room lights.

Mira could tell that Erno expected her to speak up. She saw the repressed anger in his face. She'd seen that same expression when they were seventeen at his trial for exile, and later, when they were twenty-eight hiding in the cab of the truck in the stacked-pinch reactor lab. It was not an attractive expression, yet she felt for him. She said nothing.

Finally Greta spoke.

"I'm not saying your motives were bad. I think you did what you thought was best. You accomplished some good things. But in large part, you failed.

"We don't want our movement saddled with the baggage of your failures," she went on. "You have enemies, friends, allies, connections with the OLS, with Persepolis, with the economic exploiters. You're a wealthy man, and you have history. Anything you say, even if we agree with it completely, will get buried under that baggage. If it didn't crush our efforts before they began, it would at least distract everyone from the work that needs to be done."

Erno looked around at their slightly embarrassed faces. He looked at Roz. He looked at Mira. What did he expect her to say? Mira supposed she needed to say something.

Before she could speak there came a noise from the front of the apartment. The sound of the street door. Loud voices in the entryway, laughter, and Val and Carey walked into the room, gym bags over their shoulders.

"Mother," Val said to Roz, "I don't want to disappoint you, but—" He saw Erno sitting there, and stopped. "What's he doing here?"

No one spoke. Erno finally said, "I was asked to speak about your father at the memorial—"

There was a silence. "That's priceless," Val said. "Going to talk about how he died?"

"I tried to go with him; he asked me to find you instead."

"Please, don't do this," Roz told Val. "Erno's come to offer his help with the counter-memorial."

"I was there, Mother. He knew that anybody who went up the tower would never come back alive."

Carey stepped forward. "Will you ever be done with this morbid shit? It was thirty years ago. None of it matters. Come on, Val. Martina is waiting."

Val turned on him. "It matters."

"Well, you can do what your mother says," Carey said. "I don't have to listen." He stalked back toward his room.

Roz looked exasperated. Val was ready to keep at Erno, but Mira intervened. "Erno, you should go. We all appreciate your offer, but it isn't helping us."

Erno said, "You let them believe the worst about me."

"Please, go," said Mira.

"Yes, go," Val said.

Without another word, Erno left the room. They heard the front door close after him. Val dropped his bag and went into the kitchen.

"That was ugly," Alessandra said.

"I hope he didn't tell anyone he was coming here," Harald said.

He stepped back onto the terrace and picked up one of the tablets. "We have a few more things to settle, and we can all go home."

Roz said to Mira, "I'll talk to Val; you've got Carey."

"All right," Mira said. Roz headed for the kitchen while Mira went back to Carey's room.

Reviving Carey had been Cyrus's idea. As soon as he got his hands on the IQSA and its associated files, Cyrus had used the old scan of Carey to produce a new copy. Carey came out of the assembler thinking he had just entered the scanner seconds ago—a beautiful, promising, funny, irreverent, trouble-loving fifteen-year-old boy.

They told him that twenty years had passed. They told him that he himself had died, not once, but twice over. They told him that he and Roz—this couldn't be Roz, this grown woman—had a son. He met that son, who was the same age he was. Everyone Carey knew was twenty years older.

Eva fought for custody of Carey, but the legal status of a duplicated person was not established. Cyrus became Carey's legal guardian—after all, this new Carey was Cyrus's creation—but he allowed Carey to live with Eva if he wanted to. Carey tried it, but the strangeness of it drove him away within a week, and he ran back to Persepolis and Cyrus.

From day one Carey was a celebrity. The fact that his older, dead self was famous all over the moon, called by some a terrorist, by others a hero, made it impossible for him to be treated as a person in his own right.

Val had been shaken by Carey's death. Then Carey was suddenly back, not as his father but as a boy: When Val finally met him, he realized, a boy equally shaken, so similar to him that they might have been brothers. Val turned seventeen, and Cyrus offered to sponsor his career in glass art. Val had gallery shows in Persepolis and New Guangzhou and in the process got to know Carey. Cyrus made sure that both had money and were given every attention. They rented an apartment together. They became famous, on vid throughout the system, pursued by AI cameras, never a moment's privacy. They toured the moon, visited the Earth, Mars.

Eva and Roz objected to all of this, but under the new government Val and Carey were adults and the Greens had no power over them. Both women were deeply upset by this situation, amid all the other changes they were fighting. Eva had lost all formal political power, but coming after her earlier theoretical work, the revelation of the IQSA made her one of the most famous scientists in the solar system. She used that. Whenever she was invited to scientific gatherings, whenever she was asked to comment on public affairs, she brought her commitment to the Society of Cousins with her and became a roving ambassador for the preservation of the old ways.

Eva was currently on Mars at the annual meeting of the Interplanetary Union for Pure and Applied Physics and would not be involved in the counter-memorial. She left that sort of thing to Roz and Mira now.

Six years ago, Carey and Val had asked to come back into the

Green family. There was a lot of debate about it. In the end the family deferred to Roz, and Roz talked with Mira. Mira's heart pulled her in six directions. Eventually, not without trepidation, Roz told Val and Carey they could come back.

So here they were, each forty-five years old. Despite his initial fame, Val had not devoted the energy required to become a serious artist. For his part, Carey had vowed not to live the life that his older version had lived. He abandoned athletic competition. After he read *Lune et l'autre* he decided never to write anything. Carey's charm was intact, as was Val's. Sex was easy; friends were easy. They dabbled in politics, they dabbled in business, and they accomplished nothing. Until coming home they had lived on the largess of Cyrus. Now Carey worked in the aquaculture plant of Nguyen Agriculture.

Mira stopped outside of Carey's door. She knocked.

"Go away, Roz," Carey said.

Mira studied the Cassatt painting in the hall. The surface was crazed with fine cracks. Freeze-drying an oil painting was not a good idea. "It's me," she said. "We need to talk."

"Go away, Mira."

She entered the room.

He was over by the wardrobe, shirt off. He didn't look like the *Ruǎn tā* master that she remembered. His eyes met hers. "I didn't say you could come in."

"Yet here I am. Tragic miscarriage of justice."

"What do you want?"

Mira's reputation for abrasiveness had faded with the years, but that didn't mean she didn't still feel it. "I want you to fucking grow up," she said. "Life is hard enough—why do you have to make everything harder?"

He pulled a shirt on over his head, tugged it down over his belly. "I *am* grown-up," he said. "I've held up my end of every deal I have ever made with this family—even the ones I didn't choose."

"On the other end of those deals are people who didn't have a choice either. Roz doesn't deserve the contempt you radiate toward her."

Carey sat on the sill of his open window. "You're right. I shouldn't have said what I said. I'll apologize. But please don't tell me about something *he* did, or what *he* told you, or whatever about *him*."

"I don't do that. I never do that."

"You're the only one. If I never hear another word about him I'll be a happy man."

"You think so? I don't think that has much to do with why you aren't happy."

"And you're such a paragon of good spirits."

"I've been better at it than you. What do you think we can do about that?"

He didn't speak for a moment. He leaned against the frame and looked at her. "I can't tell you, Mira. I don't know. I hate being like this. I only know how hard it is to go through life being compared to another version of yourself—and found lacking."

"I never tried to make you feel that way."

"You never intended to. But sometimes when you look at me it's not me that you see."

Mira's first instinct was to argue, but she held it back. "Maybe I see you better than you see yourself," she said. "There's nothing lacking in you—no more than anyone else."

Carey smiled ruefully. "Nice equivocation."

His self-pity was hard to take. Mira sat on the bed, an arm's length away from him. Three years earlier they'd spent quite a few nights together in this bed. Faces inches apart, talking in the darkness. She'd watch the glint of his eyes, rest her hand on his chest. He had let her in on his frustrations, and she'd told him how lonely she felt sometimes.

Mira had told him a great deal—but not everything. She never talked about the Carey she had known. She'd prided herself on her maturity, how she'd done it for his sake. In retrospect, she couldn't say which of them she was protecting by not speaking. Their relationship was—ought to have been—settled long before, when she realized that she didn't love him.

She put her hand on his knee. "You've had to deal with things that nobody else has experienced, but you've been privileged in ways that most people could only imagine."

"Please don't talk down to me. I really don't have—"

It was more than she could take, his self-involvement. She drew her hand away; she stood up. "Let me tell you what I don't have, Carey.

I don't have the patience anymore to put up with this. Don't worry, I won't measure you against him, because in every way that's meaningful, you lose. Unless you start doing something to prove to me that judgment is wrong, I don't want anything more to do with you."

In the stunned silence that followed, Mira could hear her own breathing.

Carey's grip on the windowsill tightened. Mira had said the thing that he most feared, but she didn't regret it. She prepared herself for his comeback.

Instead, he said, "All right."

He sat very still. "I make the same mistakes all the time," he said. "Thirty years of the mistakes of a teenager—at forty-five."

"That's just the way some people react to a life expectancy of one hundred and twenty."

Carey snorted. "You are funny."

Mira watched him. "It still doesn't mean there's anything wrong with you."

Carey laughed. They stared at each other. She couldn't help herself: She laughed too.

"You want something to drink?" Carey asked.

"Yes."

He opened the drawer beside his bed and took out two drink bulbs. He gave her one. "Apple juice. Nothing but apple juice."

She reached out her hand, and he put it into her palm. His thumb brushed her finger.

"Thank you," she said.

He ran his hand through his hair, a gesture she'd seen Carey make—her Carey—a hundred times. It sent a chill down her spine.

"It's not easy being us, is it?" he said.

"No, it's not." She pulled the tab on the drink bulb. "Sometimes it sucks."

•••••

Erno stood on the pavement outside the Green home, junipers rising on either side of him. Night had fallen while he had wrangled with them. He drew in a deep breath. The air was so much more humid than it had been when he was a boy—another gift from Cyrus, the generous king: abundant water, a new climate.

As soon as Val and Carey had come into the room, Erno had known he was dead. He had tried to keep his temper. They were all so sure of themselves. Not one of them had ever sat across the table from Cyrus Eskander.

Night birds chirped in the trees. In his agitation and bitterness, there was no point in his going home. It would be nice if Amestris tried to call him; she had to know he would be back from Mayer by now. He imagined her in Persepolis in one of the fine restaurants, or at the theater or concert hall with Sam.

He felt his pulse thrum in his body. What he'd just gone through had burned away whatever remained of the drugs he'd taken earlier. He vibrated with anger, face flushed from the dressing down, and his effort not to shout back at them, and the burden of the truth they'd laid on him. He carried baggage? Yes, he did.

Nobody expected him anywhere tonight. Why not go all the way? Don't hold the memories at bay; no, he should immerse himself in them, let them wash over him until he drowned or was forced to swim. He could use another hit. He needed one of the melancholy teas, that was it. That would set him up just fine. He made his way to a teashop and had a cup of Melanchol, then had another. It was mid-evening by the time he stepped back into the concourse. He was hungry. He set out for the club district.

More than forty years ago he had walked down this same concourse; he imagined his footsteps printed on the pavement, down the nave of the lava tube, seventeen-year-old Erno Rust Pamelasson sneaking off to indulge his latest enthusiasm, the masculinist standup comedian Tyler Durden. That was the night he had discovered *Stories for Men*.

For all the Society's reputation for sexual license, the free enterprise zone of his youth could not compare with Dorud or Mayer's New Pigale or the Blue Lantern quarter in Sabine. You needed vast gulfs between the rich and the poor to generate a really imaginative red light district.

Since then, however, this lack at Fowler had been remedied. Hustlers in the concourses offered to sell passersby every pleasure they might want to buy. The odor of trash rolled from alleys, spices from the restaurants. One thing that had improved immensely in Fowler over the last thirty years, Erno had to admit, was the food. Persepolis had brought with it its cuisine. Among the little restaurants and clubs here you could sample Iranian, Turkish, Indian, Italian, Chinese, Japanese, Ethiopian, and classic American food. There was more music now, too. You could buy sex, something that would have been unthinkable to the Founders. There was crime. Black market tech. Illegal biomods. There were even murders.

The Evasson occupied the space that had been the Oxygen Warehouse. He could remember vividly the things he had seen and felt when he was seventeen. The synthetic silk suit he'd been so absurdly proud of—the jacket he wore now was worth ten times as much. His mother coming into his room to plead with him not to take risks. He'd thought he had been putting only himself at risk; he didn't know she would pay the price for his idiocy.

That boy was so far away now. He wished he could go back and talk to him. Here's a bitter joke, he would tell young Erno: You are going to spend thirty years trying and failing to preserve those things that, at age seventeen, you would throw away in a minute.

But what business was it of his to criticize that boy for being angry when at this very minute the anger burned as hot inside him as it had forty years ago?

The bar was modeled after the old clubs back on Earth, serving actual alcohol. Erno ordered a bourbon on the rocks. He tossed off the sweet, aromatic liquor, burning his throat on the way down, and had another. Alcohol was a depressant. Layering it over the Melanchol already in his system was not wise, but he was tired beyond endurance with feigning wisdom. He needed escape.

No escape possible. On the walls of the restaurant were myriad images of Carey Evasson. Carey at twenty-five in the Olympic *Ruǎn tā* finals. Carey at sixteen after writing *Lune et l'autre*. Carey at thirty-six at a Reform Party rally.

"You want to see a menu?" the bartender said. He had dark brown eyes and a trim beard. Erno could get drunk and the man wouldn't care, as long as he caused no trouble.

Erno looked at the menu. He ordered eggplant sautéed in tomato sauce, basil, and cheese.

If he couldn't rightfully challenge Young Erno's anger, what could he tell him? What story had he lived?

Here's a story: When he was young he reveled in his righteousness, how he was honest, not ridden by compromise like his elders who had allowed the world to become so twisted that good things went unappreciated and bad dominated everywhere. It was a sick society. Young women and men like Erno, they all saw it, even if their parents did not, and when they got old enough, with one glorious gesture they would sweep all of the rot away. If people's minds could be enlightened, the Society could be made well again in a day.

He'd followed that fantasy right into exile.

Then he'd seen the more powerful injustices of the outside world. He'd come back. Yes, the change they were fighting for was necessary, but they didn't realize how much worse the world was out there, how the things they fought for, if their cost was the destruction of the Society, were not worth that price.

He'd seen farther and better than those who had never been outside. He knew the risks, he knew Cyrus and at least had a fighting chance to deal with him. Standing up to the patriarchies and the OLS would not save the Society, only destroy it faster.

He had taken the offer from Cyrus with full knowledge that Cyrus would try to steer him, thwart him, make Erno his agent. Erno had his eyes open. The choice he had was to risk getting his hands dirty in order to preserve what was good and change what needed changing. Sitting it out was not an option.

The *Shahnameh* was preoccupied with stories where a champion struggles with his own king. The king makes an unethical decision; the warrior knows it is wrong, but how does he deal with it? Reluctantly acquiesce? Refuse to have anything to do with the matter? Try to dissuade the king? Undermine his efforts secretly? Openly oppose him?

Erno had done all of these things with Cyrus. He *had* gotten his hands dirty, and his mind and his soul, too. So here he was, drinking booze in the same room where that angry boy had toted up his bill of injustices, an angry middle-aged man who had nothing he could rightfully complain about.

The young were in the streets seeking a revolution. They didn't care what Erno or anyone else had accomplished. The Society had been betrayed, and they wanted to go back to its roots. They wanted to be Cousins the way the Founders had been Cousins. Erno saw himself in them, yet they wanted nothing to do with him.

By the time a woman came over and sat next to him, he was thoroughly drunk. "Hello," she said brightly.

He looked at her blue eyes, her brown skin. Orange hair. Even in the low light he could tell that her clothing was shabby.

"Hello," he said.

"Will you buy me a drink?"

"I can do that." Erno signaled the bartender.

"Some tea," she told the bartender. "Some Affection, a little Contact."

The bartender went off to his synthesizer.

"Affection and contact," Erno said. "We all want that."

"It's available," she said.

"If you're looking for that from me, I'm afraid you will be disappointed. Fresh out of affection; not worth the contact."

"Don't close off any avenues yet," the woman said. She put her hand on his, and despite his swimming head he saw immediately that she was on the edge of despair, and that beneath her coolly modulated voice was a repressed scream.

He snatched his hand away. Her eyes showed a moment's panic.

"You need money?" he asked. Her lips twitched. "You're headed for the freezers?"

"It's that obvious," she said. Her voice was flat.

"What's your name?"

"Carrie. Carrie Britasdaughter."

"No family?"

"No one I can count on."

The man came back with her tea. She looked at him, looked at it. She took a sip.

Erno took out his wallet. "Your wristward," he said to her. She reached out her slender arm. He touched his wallet to it and downloaded three thousand ducats.

When she saw the figure on the screen, she looked at him in astonishment.

"You have nothing to thank me for," he said.

She slid from the seat and left the club.

Five minutes later, as he drank another bourbon, a young man took her seat. "Something to brighten me up," he told the bartender. "A Joy Blast, if you've got. Make it so it will knock every fucking trouble out of my brain."

"Coming up," the bartender said.

The man sat there, forearms on the bar, staring at his hands. He noticed Erno watching him. "What are you looking at?" he said.

"Nothing," Erno said. "I'm not looking at anything."

• • • • •

He went home. His head throbbed from the alcohol and the place where he'd hit his head on a chair when the guy at the bar shoved him. The mirror showed a bruise near the old scar on his temple. He held a cold cloth to it, took three painkillers, and went to his study. He considered calling the organizers of the memorial ceremony and cancelling his appearance, but he didn't have the spirit for that right now. Time enough to decide later. Maybe he would give the same speech regardless, and let the Renewalists figure out a way to disavow him.

He called up the sentence that was all he had so far. ". . . change becomes treason." He was fifty-eight. If the actuarial tables were right, he had another sixty years. He was far from finished, and yet that was not how he felt.

He brewed up another glass of Melanchol and sat in the living room on the bench in front of the piano. The walnut case of the Kazedi grand was evidence of at least one success: He had presented Sam with the forest he needed to realize his dream of the complete lunar piano. Erno opened the fall board and touched the keys. He had not heard Amestris play in months.

After ten minutes he went back to his study and called her. She answered immediately, and her image came up on the wall. She was dressed for the evening. Elegant, desirable.

The minute she saw him her brow knit. "What happened to your forehead?"

He touched his fingers to the bruise. "It's nothing."

She looked skeptical.

"I was just thinking of you," he said.

"I'm glad you called."

He gestured at her clothes. "You've been out?"

"Sam and I were at a concert. Nadezhda Vasnetsov is here. She did a great performance of Rachmaninoff's Piano Concerto No. 2. You would have loved it."

"I'm sure I would have," Erno said.

"How was the trip to Mayer?"

"I didn't find anything I didn't already know."

"I'm sorry," she said. Her dark eyes were very different from those of the woman in the club. "I know how much it troubles you. But maybe you should let it go."

From outside the opened window came the call of a whippoorwill in the trees. "I'm working on my speech."

"That's good." Amestris looked guilty. "Erno, I—I won't be back for the memorial. In fact"—she sighed—"I'm not coming back for a while."

Erno's first feeling was betrayal. He wanted to protest, but then something in his heart flipped. It was like finding out that the team you had bet on had lost when you already suspected that they would lose. The chance of their winning had been a long shot. Maybe you hoped for the win, but the loss did not come as any real surprise.

"You don't need to explain," he said.

He didn't need any explanation. It had been good for Amestris to come to the Society; it freed her from her family. She had played the part of spouse of a prominent political figure as it might never have been played in Persepolis. She found her own voice, independent of her father, of Erno, of Sam. She made friends, served in the legislature, and managed the uneasy cultural space between Persepolis and Fowler with grace and wit. The love between her and Erno was real, but it was as much the product of their shared lives as of any passion. She didn't need Erno the way she had when he'd shown up in her office at the Persepolis Water Corporation.

Amestris's dark eyes were steady on him. "If you were here," she said, "you'd need only touch me to know what's in my heart. We'll speak again soon, right?"

At one time Erno would have asked her to come home, to lie beside him, to hold him in her arms, as she had a thousand times.

"Yes, sure," Erno said. "Whatever you do, Amestris, I don't want you to dwell on this."

"Always asking for the impossible." She smiled.

"I suppose so," he said.

He ended the call.

On the living room shelf stood the battered twenty-first-century edition of *Stories for Men* that Tyler had given Erno in the deserted tunnel behind the Oxygen Warehouse. Alicia had handed it back to him when he'd sat in the Administrator's office. Next to it on the shelf rested Erno's book of poems. A real, physical book, published in those same early days of his administration, when he was a novelty, a promise for a different future. When people had thought there was something to him, when even he thought there might be something in him worth attending. His poems. Some of them weren't bad.

He drained the last of the tea, then brewed another cup and sat out on the balcony. He would go deep into regret, indulge his sadness, let it carry him away. As he often did, he let his eyes follow up the tower to the place where Sirius had blown the hole in the building. Erno wished sometimes that it had been he and not Carey who had gone up there, so that their lives might have been reversed. Carey was the man of charisma whom everyone liked. Carey might have done a better job of it, even if he did not have a magic hand.

The door chime sounded.

Erno considered not answering, but it came again. At last he got out of the chair, passed through the living room, and opened the door.

Mira stood there.

"May I come in?" she said.

"Why are you here?" he asked. "Don't you have more important things to do?"

"That's a little dramatic, don't you think?" Mira stepped toward him, and he yielded the doorway. She swept past him into the room. She saw the tea on the table. "Do you have anything for me?"

"It's late."

"You're still up."

"You win." He went to the little kitchen. "What kind do you want?"

"What are you having?"

"You don't want what I'm having."

"I'm pretty sure you're right about that. Make it some Equanimity. You should try it yourself."

She sat and watched as he set it to brewing. Small and dark, her face

a little more lined—she had not spent much effort on anti-aging treatments. "Have you figured out what you'll say at the memorial?"

"Nothing. Nobody wants to hear what I have to say."

"Stop it."

"It's the truth."

"The Renewalists rejected your offer—with bad grace. They aren't interested in being graceful. It was still a worthy offer, and I for one thank you for it."

"You didn't have much to say this afternoon." He felt his temper rise. "You let me hang there as if I were everything they think I am. You know me better than that."

"I do. But I'm surprised you still have such a thin skin after being in politics for so many years. Actually, that was always one of your weaknesses as a politician."

"If you came here to cheer me up, you could be doing a better job."

Mira laughed. "And that was one of your strong points—a sense of humor. Maybe I should have said something, but it's not my duty to tell them what they ought to do. They're making lots of mistakes, it seems to me, but you and I have had thirty years to make mistakes. They deserve their own chance."

"Maybe they should learn from our mistakes," Erno said.

"Do you think what Greta said was wrong? If you were to join them, it would become just as huge a distraction as she said."

He poured her tea and handed it to her, then poured one for himself. "Yes, she was right," he said. "Let's sit down."

They went into the living room. Erno felt embarrassed at the luxury of the place. Though the Greens were not exactly poor.

Mira drank some of the tea and sighed. "Nice."

"My specialty."

"As for Val and Carey," she said, "they have their own problems. I'm sorry that it's come to this. They've both blamed Eva and me and Roz for everything that's ever gone wrong for them. The rest of the people who were there are suspicious of anyone who's not of their generation."

"They have no right to be suspicious of you, or Lemmy. You fought me on every issue I was wrong on. Lemmy—Lemmy's a saint."

"Yes, Lemmy's a saint. But you're not finished yet. You can't publically speak for Renewal? Well, let's figure out some other way you can help. There must be one. We have to go forward."

Forward? Erno's heart couldn't take it anymore.

"Mira, there is no forward for me. I've wasted all my future. I made too many wrong choices."

He wanted to make her look at him. To see him at last the way he saw himself, the way that he was, the secret weaknesses—hell, secret, they were written on his face—the rage, the failure to live up to his convictions, the despair, the self-indulgence. The pain he felt whenever he thought about his mother. His dead father. The trees he had stolen that had been turned into another way for rich men to get money they didn't need. The machine he'd given Cyrus. The things he had lost that would never come back. All behind him, every thing he'd felt or done frozen forever,

inscribed in his eyes whenever he studied them in the mirror. The words he spoke that didn't mean anything. The ideals he believed in that he had not lived by, the suffering people he could not save, that he didn't even want to save, like the man in the bar who had knocked him down.

"I can't do this anymore," Erno said. "You should go away."

"You've done as much as you could. You tried. Don't let what other people say determine what you think about yourself."

"It's not what they say! I know what they think!" He thrust his hand out at her. "This fucking *hand*. It's a curse. I stole it, and it will not leave me in peace. Every day it proves to me what a failure I am."

"Erno, you have to let the world be the world. You're a person of merit."

He lowered his head into his hands. The bruise on his forehead smarted. He felt his skull in the palms of both the real hand and the artificial. Such a small space—a liter and a half of neurons—to contain all that he was. All the memories crammed into that skull, how could he let them go?

He looked up at her. She stood very close. "Please, Mira, you don't have to do this. You're kind, but you don't mean it."

"I don't mean it?" She took his left hand and pressed it to her heart.

• • • • •

A person may live in a place for a long time, may see it every day in all its particularity, and still not know it. You see what you see because you are who you are, and who you are is shaped by forces genetic, environmental, and cultural that, despite a century's effort to escape them, still prevail. Long ago it was proven to most people's satisfaction that the word "know" is such a chimera that to apply it to anything is an act of hubris, or of faith.

On this particular afternoon, Mira and Erno met for their evening walk at the cable train station, the place where, thirty years ago, they had seen each other for the first time in a decade. They embraced in the Cousins way, a kiss on the cheek, the brief impress of another's body. Not inescapably sexual. Public affection was supposed to defuse alienation, distract from the isolation of the human condition. Sometimes it worked. They crossed the road and descended the slope, down flights of steps and switchback paths to the crater floor, into Sobieski Park.

On these long walks, which they had been taking regularly of late, they talked about many things: their childhoods, Mira's mother, people they had grown up with, family gossip, the prospects in the legislature for the Renewalist constitutional amendments, the many species of songbirds that filled the trees, the intricacies of balancing a closed ecology, whether Amestris and Erno should turn Eskander Environmental Design into a nonprofit, the latest play at the Black Box Theater, their favorite books, Carey and Val, Mira's *A Brief History of Anger*, what was next on the agenda of the Fowler Project. Spaces fell open in these conversations in which they walked for minutes without speaking at all.

As they threaded their way through the park, sunlight and shadows flirted with one another on the crushed regolith path. All these trees had been planted since the destruction of the original biosphere:

The park was more densely wooded than it had been in the days of the Society, a temperate broadleaf mixed forest microbiome. Beneath the trees lay pine needles, last year's leaves, old spiked sycamore pods, dried half-winged maple seeds.

But there were still clearings, and flowers, and the pond, and a landing field for flyers, and the amphitheater. The smell of cut grass filled the air. As Erno and Mira came out from among the trees, they heard voices. Across the lawn a crowd of people had gathered. There had been spontaneous protests in the wake of the memorial ceremonies, and tensions still ran high. Mira stepped off the path to see what was happening, and Erno followed.

A knot of thirty or forty men, women, and children gathered in a rough circle. From the outside Erno and Mira could not see to their center. The people were silent, but somewhere in their midst a woman was speaking in a public voice.

The men wore bright embroidered shirts or old-fashioned suits that might have come from some European city. Women wore saris with purple sashes, colorful dresses, their hair pulled back or piled high and glistening. A young ungendered person wore a video suit with shoes that changed color. A group of four in matching black shirts carried acoustic instruments: fiddle, guitar, flute, mandolin.

As they got closer Mira recognized Cleo among the standing people, and Juliette.

"It's the Amarillos," Erno said.

Some of the people at the edges noticed Erno and Mira. The

Amarillos, one of the old families, had survived the transition to the post-Matrons Society. There had always been a rivalry between them and the Greens, and although Amestris was friends with Juliette, Erno had crossed them more than once as Administrator.

They got close enough to see within the circle of those standing. Some people sat in chairs. At their center, three stood on a low platform: an old woman in a spotless white robe, and a young woman and man in matching yellow dashikis. The man and woman faced each other, holding hands, eyes shining.

It wasn't a political protest. It was a wedding.

The old woman said some things about unity and diversity and family and self, all very wise if you indulged your hubris, or faith. The couple looked into each other's eyes, positively glowing with love, at least as far as the onlookers, observing through the veil of their own selves, could tell. The words the woman spoke called forth a variety of deep emotional responses from everyone gathered—the ones who listened, anyway.

The matriarch finished. The couple spoke to each other, in unison:

> *"I am the one.*
> *You are the other."*

And then:

> *"I am the other.*
> *You are the one."*

The young woman had a warm contralto voice; the young man spoke with an accent not native to Fowler.

When they had finished, the matriarch, smiling, said, "Go ahead, then!"

The couple kissed, making a display of their passion before their families and friends. They then turned, beaming, to face the crowd, raising their joined hands.

"We are the moon!" they cried out.

"*You* are?" someone shouted. "What about the rest of us?"

The people laughed.

The matriarch waited until the laughter died, and said, "Let us welcome Federico Petraglia into our family!"

The wedding party cheered, accompanied by shouts of "Welcome, Federico!"

An aisle opened in the crowd and the musicians strode forward playing a sprightly tune. The couple began to dance, and as the music flowed, the wedding guests got out of their seats and joined them. From high above the clearing a flyer swooped out of the darkening sky trailing a banner with a slogan on it: *No Life Unblessed.*

Mira looked up at the banner, following it for a space of seconds. She turned her head to watch the flyer be eclipsed by the trees. Her wedding to the Greens, entered into at a time of almost overwhelming grief, had not been like this. Erno's wedding to Amestris had been half a matter of desperate stratagem. Who could say what mixture of emotion, need, and politics might stand behind this one?

Cleo spotted Mira and came over. "We didn't expect the Greens to send a delegation. And the government," she said, nodding to Erno.

"Hello, Cleo," Mira said.

"We don't want to intrude," Erno said.

"Stay," Cleo said. "If you like." She hugged them both, then turned back to where the matriarch, still on the platform, her white robe glowing against the green of the evening trees, was about to lead a toast to the newlyweds.

"No life unblessed," Mira said, so softly that Erno could hardly hear her, as Cleo walked away.

ACKNOWLEDGMENTS

I began thinking about the Society of Cousins in the late 1990s after reading a number of speculative books about anthropology, evolutionary psychology, and the differences between the great apes, including the provocative *Demonic Males* by Richard Wrangham and Dale Peterson. Over a period of years this led to the publication of four stories set on the moon: "The Juniper Tree," "Stories for Men," "Under the Lunchbox Tree," and "Sunlight or Rock." "Stories for Men" was so fortunate as to share the 2002 James Tiptree Jr. Literary Award with M. John Harrison's remarkable novel *Light*.

Those who have read these stories will recognize that many of the characters in *The Moon and the Other* appeared originally in them. But it's my intention that a reader need not be familiar with those stories in order to understand this novel, and I have felt free to alter some details and dates, among other things, that result in the novel being inconsistent with the stories.

A word about the title: In 2008, Éditions Gallimard editor Pascal Godbillon produced a collection of these four stories in a French translation, publishing them under the title *Lune et l'autre*. Since that book never appeared in the United States, I have chosen to use the English version of Pascal's wonderfully punning title for this novel, but my novel does not contain any of those stories, except for a retelling of some of the incidents of "Sunlight or Rock" in a chapter five flashback. I hope Pascal will forgive my repurposing his title and that bibliographers will excuse any confusion this may cause.

A book that took as long as this one did to find its final form owes its existence to more people and influences than it is possible to name, but let me take a crack at acknowledging the many who have helped me along the way.

Thanks to my colleagues and students in the English department of North Carolina State University, and to Antony Harrison, department head, who offered steady support of the creative writing program and my own work. Over the years the participants in the Sycamore Hill Writers' Conference, to whom I brought portions of the novel, gave me encouragement and cogent criticism. I am grateful for residencies at the Virginia Center for the Creative Arts and the Weymouth Center for the Arts & Humanities, where parts of the novel were written.

I must thank Gregory Frost, Janine Latus, Monica Byrne, and Jill McCorkle for moral support; Fariba Parvisi for a voice from Iran; Benjamin Rosenbaum for urging me, early on, to return to the Society of Cousins; Cat Warren for dog lore; Bruce Sterling and Olaf

Stapledon for Sirius; Geoffrey Landis for vacuum blowout equations; Heidi Klumpe for bioengineering; Robin Rogers for glassblowing; and Emma Hall Kessel for translating Niccolò for me.

A number of friends and colleagues read the manuscript and gave me invaluable suggestions: Wilton Barnhardt, Richard Butner, Karen Joy Fowler, Therese Anne Fowler, Kij Johnson, James Patrick Kelly, Joe Millar, Kim Stanley Robinson, and Lewis Shiner. In particular, the law firm of Barnhardt, Butner, and Shiner, members of the storied Salon, were with me every step of the way.

I am lucky in my agent John Silbersack, a consummate professional.

I must thank my editor Joe Monti who, although I thought I was done, gently asked a few questions that ended up making this a much better book.

And finally, I must thank Therese, for reasons practical, literary, and personal.

STARRING:
Mary Jekyll, Diana Hyde, Catherine Moreau, Beatrice Rappaccini, and Justine Frankenstein!

The daughters of literature's most famous mad scientists must come together to stop a murderer—and solve the mystery of their own creation.

WHAT IF THE UNITED STATES DEVELOPED
THE ATOMIC BOMB A YEAR EARLIER, IN 1944?

AMERICAN ATOM BOMB
ANNIHILATES NAZIS

THE
BERLIN
PROJECT

A NOVEL

GREGORY
BENFORD

A MAGICAL REVENGE THRILLER.

AN UNKINDNESS OF MAGICIANS

KAT HOWARD

KAMERON HURLEY

THE STARS ARE LEGION

IN THE TRADITION OF **THE FALL OF HYPERION** AND **DUNE** COMES AN EPIC TALE ABOUT TRAGIC LOVE, REVENGE, AND WAR, AS IMAGINED BY ONE OF THE GENRE'S MOST CELEBRATED NEW WRITERS.